mystic ANGEL

DEBBIE IHLER RASMUSSEN

M.O.M.M.
PUBLISHING
Mysteries of My Mind

For information contact:
authordebbieihlerrasmussen@gmail.com
Website: authordebbieihlerrasmussen.com

Published by:
M.O.M.M. Publishing
"Mysteries of My Mind"

Cover Design:
Dee Loupeti • www.deegraphicdesign.com

Interior Design:
Francine Platt • Eden Graphics, Inc. • www.edengraphics.net

EBook Design:
Dayna Linton • Day Agency • www.dayagency.com

978-1-7334645-2-9 Paperback
978-1-7334645-1-2   ePub
Library of Congress Number: Pending

Second Edition
Manufactured in the United States of America
11 10 9 8 7 6 5 4 3 2

For My Grandkids —

Remember, reading takes you into wonderful, imaginative
and mystical worlds you may otherwise never visit…

SPECIAL THANKS TO:

My Writers Group of four years—
past and present members and friends:

*Daron Fraley, Kaycee McCleeve, Robby McCleeve,
Dani Oldroyd, and Jeff Olsen*

Their numerous suggestions and critique have helped to
shape this work, and their regular encouragement kept me
going when frustration threatened to take over.

Verna Clay

Talented author and friend—Verna has been a source
of inspiration to me. Her countless suggestions and helpful
hints have proved valuable and without them this book
would probably still be on my computer.

My kids *Bobejo, Ben, Tawnie, Rik, Jenee and Jef*

and their families — who always believe in me and
encourage me no matter what I attempt to take on—
even if it's crazy. I love you…xoxo

Dear Readers,

This has been an exciting project! It actually began in the early 1980s when I was raising my six children between the ages of eleven and two. One winter I dreamed a portion of this story—got up in the middle of the night and scribbled the notes on a piece of scratch paper, tucked it away in a folder and forgot about it.

In 2009 when I was taking care of my mom, I found I had time in the evening to write, so I pulled out my dusty files, and this one made it to the top of the pile.

The idea has gone through a massive transformation as the "story" took on a life of its own. New characters emerged, waking me up at night, interrupting my thoughts on long drives or keeping me company on walks and bike rides—demanding that they too, have their stories told.

Mystic Angel—the first in the *Mystic Series*, begins when Jackson Allen abruptly moves his family from their secure, comfortable life in Southern California to the small Tennessee town of Sommerville.

Sixteen-year-old Aspen finds herself in the midst of a paranormal world she had glimpsed—but was never sure existed. Amid facts, myths, secrets, and legends surrounding the family home of her ancestors—the story unfolds into challenging and unexpected adventures involving the world of spirits, wealth, and murder.

I had fun writing these books, and I sincerely hope you enjoy reading them.

Debbie

Many believe there are worlds that exist
beyond the realms of our current reality—
we may glimpse other dimensions not knowing
what we have encountered—but this does not
make them any less real—just because you
don't believe something does not mean
that it doesn't exist...

PROLOGUE

Jackson Allen leaned against the window and watched his two children surf from his birds-eye view. He had everything—his career, his home, and his close-knit family. He had planned it that way.

His office, located on the west side of his beachfront home, was exactly how he'd imagined it would be—the place where he would direct his financial empire. After meeting Suzann at San Diego State and then marrying, they had set their sights on raising a family as close to the ocean as possible. From here, the Pacific stretched endlessly to the horizon and created some of the most beautiful sunsets on earth. From his wall of windows, he had watched his children grow up in the same waters that he had come to love.

Jackson laughed quietly letting his mind wander back to the days when the kids were little when he and Suzann had painstakingly taught them to stand on their boards and glide through the waves at Dana Point. Now more than ten years later, he often marveled at how expertly they caught the waves at Trestles, even dropping in with some of the best surfers on the coast.

Jackson glanced at the letter in his hand. He scanned its contents one more time as he felt the knot in his stomach cinch even tighter. A few sentences jumped out at him.

We're moving to take care of Jerry's mom. It's been over twenty years since you've been home. The estate needs to be settled. You know what you need to do.

The same disturbing feelings that had been plaguing him for a month, since the day the letter had arrived, now turned to anxiety. He had to tell his family, and it would not be easy.

He glanced once more at his children, then turned his back to the window and scanned his office—cherry wood bookcases, matching coffee table surrounded by expensive black leather sofas, and two high-backed chairs. His polished desk glistened in the late evening sun.

Finance magazines stacked in three neat piles next to a pitcher of untouched ice water.

On the right side of his desk, Jackson's gaze lingered on a large framed picture of Suzann. She was smiling with her chin resting on her palm. It was the same sweet smile he had fallen in love with nearly twenty-five years ago. Next to Suzann was a recent picture of their two teens, each with an arm wrapped around a surfboard, both covered with sand, saltwater, and sporting beaming grins on tan faces.

Everything was perfect.

He ran his hand across the shiny surface of the desk while his eyes drifted back to the picture of Suzann.

He had made it this far. Hadn't he created a new life, one that did not include his past? Why now, when everything was so right, did he have to be faced with this?

Because I ran away.

He shuddered to think what this move would mean to his peaceful little world on the west coast. The world he had so carefully guarded and protected. The world that now threatened to shatter into a million tiny pieces.

And what of the secret he had deliberately walked away from, the one buried deep in the caverns of his mind. Could he keep it there? Would he be able to slip in and out of Sommerville unnoticed? Leaving the past undisturbed?

He shook his head, and fear clutched his heart.

Taking a deep breath, he released the air in a slow, deliberate sigh. Sinking into his overstuffed chair, Jackson pressed the letter against his leg, crushing it into a tiny ball.

He leaned forward, burying his face in his hands as tears, suppressed for nearly a month, ran silently down his cheeks, and finally engulfed him in painful sobs.

I do not claim to be an authority on any subject—
let alone love, death or immortality. However many
experiences in my life have made me very familiar
with all three—and I find them fascinating...

– Debbie

Life is eternal; and love is immortal;
and death is only a horizon, and a horizon
is nothing save the limit of our sight.

– Rossiter Worthington Raymond

1

MAN IN THE ROAD

ASPEN CLOSED HER EYES against the invading brightness and then blinked several times before she could keep them open. The truck stopped, and she and her dad were alone.

"Hey, Dad. Where's Mom and Noah?"

"They went into the store to get some snacks." Dad turned to look at her in the back seat. "You've been asleep a long time."

"Where are we?"

"Memphis."

"Really? So you drove all night?"

"Mom helped."

"I slept through all of that?"

"Uh-huh."

Jackson peered across the top of his sunglasses. Except for newer gas pumps, the 7-Eleven convenience store hadn't changed much. The trees were taller, and there were more of them, and the addition of a traffic light at the intersection indicated what? More people, more cars, progress?

He turned to look out the side window. *I can't believe I am back here. I hope I don't run into anyone I know.* He shook his head. "That will be impossible," he mumbled.

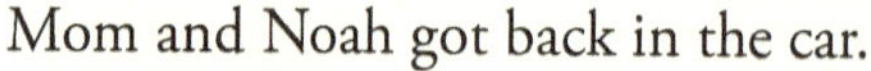

Mom and Noah got back in the car.

"What were you saying, Jackson?" Mom passed out fruit and little containers of yogurt.

She obviously startled Dad. "Nothing." He blew off her question without even so much as a glance.

Suzann Allen opened her peach yogurt and began taking tiny little bites. She did not feel hungry at all—she was just eating. She looked at Jackson from the corner of her eye. He was staring straight ahead. They were headed out of Memphis now on the way to Sommerville. The same thoughts that had caused countless sleepless nights for nearly two months once again reared their ugly heads and gripped her heart with agony. What is going on with Jackson? He had given her very little detail when he announced that the family would be moving to Tennessee. No objections considered.

One thing for certain—Jackson was different. He was no longer the loving, fun father and husband he had always been. From the day his sister's letter arrived, life had changed at the Allen house.

Suzann had tried everything she could think of to get him to open up but to no avail. Whatever was bothering him he was keeping to himself—he had become impatient and short-tempered; apathetic and unresponsive—and for a man who was typically overly affectionate with his wife, Suzann had become nearly invisible; only necessary conversation exchanged. Jackson spent most of his time on his cell phone or computer. It was as though the real Jackson Allen had vanished, replaced it seemed, by an arrogant imposter.

Suzann sighed and once again consciously willed the tears away. She glanced back at her teenage son whose angry despondent look was getting blacker with every passing mile. Suzanne didn't turn around to look at Aspen, who was taking this a little more in stride.

Although not excited about leaving California, she at least was trying—or pretending—to be happy.

A roadside sign caught her attention—Sommerville, 32 Miles, Population 5200. She suddenly felt anxious. This is a really little town, nothing like San Diego or San Clemente. She glanced again at Jackson. A part of her hated him for upsetting their otherwise happy existence—the rest of her simply wished she could figure him out.

An image suddenly flashed across her mind. She closed her eyes against the invading presence, refusing to acknowledge it as though if she didn't, it wouldn't exist.

But it did exist, and Suzann Allen had no idea what to do about it.

Aspen watched the scenery as she munched on a banana. *Nothing but trees. I can't believe we're moving to this muggy place. I'm glad the truck is air-conditioned.*

She sighed. *All these trees give me claustrophobia.*

Aspen glanced at Noah. He was slumped in his seat, staring out his window. It had been nearly two months since he had treated her like a normal person, and it made her sad. She turned to look out her window.

It seems like he blames Mom and me for this move and we had nothing to do with it.

Reaching to drop her banana peel and empty yogurt cup into a sack at her feet, she saw a man in the middle of the road.

"Dad, look out!"

Jackson stomped on the brake bringing the double-cab pickup to a screeching halt. Aspen slammed into the front seat and then flew backward, landing in a disheveled heap.

"Aspen! What is the matter with you?"

"Dad, you almost hit that man!"

"What man?!" Dad yelled.

"He was there, Dad. Right there!" Aspen leaned over the seat and pointed through the front window. "I thought you were going to hit him."

Dad stared at the empty road and then turned back around. Aspen's face was inches from his. She wasn't sure if his look was anger or fear.

He turned to his wife. "Suzann, I didn't see anyone, did you?"

Mom shook her head and turned to stare at Aspen with cloudy eyes, wrinkled brow, and thin tight lips. Aspen had seen that look a lot lately.

"Me either," said Noah, and didn't try to hide his disgust.

"I didn't ask you," Aspen snarled at her brother and sank back into her seat. She spoke softly now and pointed. "He was right there, Dad. You...you just about hit him."

Dad shook his head. "You scared me to death, Aspen." He shifted into gear and slowly rolled the truck forward. "That imagination of yours is going to get us killed."

"I didn't imagine it, Dad." Aspen glanced at her brother.

Noah rolled his eyes and said, "You are so lame. Don't you think you should buckle your seat belt now?"

Aspen glared at him and in defiance chose not to buckle her belt.

Noah had always treated her as an equal until Dad announced their move to Tennessee. He hadn't spoken a civil word to her since they'd left California. She was just a year behind him in school, and they had been on the junior lifeguard team together since she was fifteen. They spent a lot of time together, most of it with mutual friends.

Noah barked, "Close the window. The seat is getting wet!"

Aspen's heart was still pounding, and she ignored her brother's command by opening it wider so she could lean out into the rain. She closed her eyes, but behind her eyelids, she could still see the image of the old man in front of the truck.

Warm rainwater matted her dark brown hair against her cheeks. She loved the smell of rain. It was different here though, kind of woodsy; not the salt air she was used to. She took a deep breath letting the pleasant smell fill her nostrils, and then she slowly released it and opened her eyes.

She screamed and jerked back inside the truck—in the same instant she was propelled out of the window to the side of the road—she was standing inches from the same old man, his dark stare locked with hers.

Aspen struggled to get back into her seat. *Did she ever actually leave her seat? What just happened?* A strange panic gripped her, and she whirled around to look first at Noah and then her parents. They all seemed completely unaware of anything unusual—or of her.

Didn't they hear me scream?!

Aspen pushed the wet hair out of her eyes, anxiously turning back to the window. She stared at the old man until he was no longer in sight. She slumped into the seat, tucking her trembling hands under her legs. Nausea overtook her, and she leaned forward in an effort to relieve it and plopped her head in her hands.

How could they not see him? How could they not hear me scream? It's like I'm not even here!

Aspen turned her head slightly to peer at Noah who was now looking at her, but when he caught her eye, he just glared and turned away.

Sometimes I hate him. Why do I have to have a brother anyway? I wish Krista were here. At least she understands me.

Quiet tears pricked the corners of her eyes. *Tennessee is the worst place on the planet.*

2

LITTLE HOUSE

ANGER CONTINUED TO BUILD inside Noah the farther they got from the city. *Look at this stupid little two-lane Podunk country road. This is the lamest thing our family has ever done.*

Mom had attempted to convince him and Aspen that this would be a great experience, but Noah just couldn't see it. What could be great about leaving all of his friends, not to mention the ocean? And changing schools his senior year? He wouldn't even graduate with the kids he had gone to school with for the past twelve years and who knew what this move would do to his credits and getting into San Diego State.

Noah's spirits lifted with one thought. Maybe whatever Dad had to do could be done in the summer, and they could get back to California before school started.

"Fat chance," he snarled under his breath. He stared at Aspen who was leaning out the window. *She is crazy. She is always seeing people that aren't even there.*

He knew Mom and Dad were worried about her. At least Mom was. He had heard Mom trying to talk to Dad a few times about maybe getting her a shrink, but Dad did not seem too keen on the idea, and the conversations always ended up in an argument. *That has only been in the last two months—I don't ever remember them arguing much before.*

Noah had concluded over and over that Aspen probably just has a vivid imagination. But he had to admit that this time, she seemed one hundred percent sure that she had seen an old man in the road. He guessed she could be crazy, but the idea of having a sister that was a few cards short of a deck didn't sit well with him.

He was pulled out of his thoughts when Aspen, her hair dripping wet, suddenly fell back into the seat. He shook his head and turned to look out his window, but he couldn't help but notice that she look scared.

"Crazy," he muttered.

Aspen tried to engage her brother in conversation. "Can you believe all these trees, Noah?"

"Trees smheeze," Noah grumbled. "Do you see an ocean?"

His response was about what she expected, so she dismissed the idea.

Everyone was quiet as they drove past a stately white house set far back from the road. It was difficult to see it through thick trees that covered the sloping grass, but it was high enough on a hill that the second-floor windows came into view. The sheer majesty of the house surprised Aspen.

"There's a lake right behind the house," Dad was saying. He looked over his shoulder at his son. "You can walk to it."

"Can we swim in the lake?" asked Aspen.

Dad had grown up here, in the small country town of Sommerville on the outskirts of Memphis, Tennessee. He had moved to California to go to college, married Mom, and made their home in San Clemente where Aspen and Noah had enjoyed growing up by the beach.

"They can swim in the lake, can't they, Jack?" Mom touched her husband's shoulder.

Before Dad could answer, Noah snarled, "Can we *surf* in the lake?"

Aspen hurried to quash Noah's comment, "Are all the houses big like that one we just passed?"

"Not exactly," Dad mused.

"What does that mean?" Noah grumbled.

Dad didn't answer, and Mom just glanced over her shoulder at her two children and shrugged—but Aspen noticed the creases in her forehead seemed to deepen.

The closer they got to his grandparent's house—his parent's house—the more uneasy Jackson felt. He glanced back at his daughter at the same time, ignoring the side-glance his wife gave him.

This move could go wrong in so many ways.

Fear gripped his gut, and he tried to push it aside. He had not been upfront with Suzann, and he knew Noah all but hated him. He had worried about Aspen for a long time but had not addressed his concerns about her with Suzann. Instead, he made his wife feel like she was overreacting to Aspen's pretend people. But were they — pretend? He wasn't sure.

He shrugged. He had one plan—get the house sold and get out of Tennessee—back home—back to the life he had built for his family. Yes, he resolved, that is the goal. The kids will survive, and so will Suzann. Again, the familiar ache embedded itself in the pit of his stomach. *They will survive. But will I?*

The truck finally turned off the main road onto a much narrower one. On Aspen's side, the ground sloped gently, and a small stream meandered through the trees, but on Noah's side, the landscape immediately sloped up and then rose sharply. The trees were so thick, it was difficult to see anything, but high on the hill, Aspen caught a brief glimpse of another huge house.

"Is that our house up there?"

Dad sighed. "No, this is our house."

Aspen hadn't noticed they had come to the end of the road, which she would learn was their driveway. She didn't say anything. She looked at Noah, who was staring at the small house in front of them.

Mom said, "C'mon you two get your stuff out of the truck. The movers have already been here."

Aspen grabbed her backpack and climbed out of the truck. She paused for a second and glanced down the driveway. A chill ran through her as she thought of the old man and still tried to comprehend how she had been standing right next to him, which meant she had left the truck—if only for a second. *Or did I?*

She looked up the hill in the direction of what appeared to be a massive red brick house. Through the trees from where she now stood, she could see a long narrow window that appeared to be on the second story. Something moved in the window, and for a second, she squinted, trying to see it more clearly.

"Dad is anyone living up there?" she pointed toward the house on the hill.

"Nope. Not for a couple of months." And he disappeared into the house through the front door.

She had not taken her eyes from the window, but now the blind appeared to be closed. She blinked. *That's weird; I'm sure it was open.*

"C'mon, move."

Aspen didn't realize she was blocking Noah who was supporting a large box.

"Sorry," she said absently and moved out of his way. She slung her backpack over her shoulder, scooped up her worn stuffed giraffe from the seat and pushed the door closed with her foot.

"I can't believe you still hang onto that thing," Noah called over his shoulder.

She knew he was referring to the giraffe. It was a gift from her favorite aunt on her sixth birthday. Even though she was sixteen now, she couldn't bear to part with her childhood keepsake. It ended up riding in the truck with her instead of a box in the moving van because Aspen discovered it on the top of a heap intended for Good Will. When she rescued it, annoying teasing by Noah and his friends caused her to quickly stuff it in her backpack. She really didn't care what they thought. Her giraffe was a treasure, and right at *this* moment seemed to be her only friend.

She turned her attention back to their new house. It was not very big, but it was nice. Dozens of spring flowers grouped into well-manicured gardens surrounded by a thick layer of neatly trimmed grass.

Aspen leaned against the truck and sized up the one-story house. They had never lived in a home without an upstairs.

The house was made of red brick, and was sort of L-shaped. It had a long front porch with large baskets of hanging plants. The detached two-car garage off to the right was connected instead by a covered breezeway.

Like the house they had passed on the road, this one was nestled in a forest of thick trees.

Dad came out onto the porch.

Aspen asked, "Hey Dad? Is this where Grandma and Grandpa lived?"

Dad chuckled. "No. This was the servants' quarters." He motioned to where Aspen had seen the larger red brick house. "Their house is up there."

Servants' quarters? They had cleaning ladies and gardeners in California—but servants?

She followed Dad into the house to find Noah standing in the middle of the living room, the box he had been carrying lay at his feet.

"What's wrong with you?"

Noah scowled and looked at his sister. "There is only one full bathroom in the whole house. The stupid little bathroom by the kitchen doesn't even have a shower."

Now Aspen scowled too. This would be a far cry from their home in San Clemente. There they each had their own bathroom, and their parent's bathroom was almost as big as Aspen's entire bedroom.

"*Why* did we come here?" Noah challenged his mother as she passed through to the kitchen.

Mom stopped and turned around to face her children. "For the last time, Aunt Dana had to go to Oregon to take care of her mother-in-law. It is your dad's turn to help, so we are going to get the house—the big house—ready to sell." Mom was irritated and made no attempt to hide it. "This was not my idea, Noah. We will all just have to deal with it. It is not a permanent arrangement." She turned on her heel and disappeared into the kitchen.

Aspen ignored both of them as she scanned the living room. It was nice enough. A large fireplace covered one entire wall, and the oval-shaped braided rug in the center of the polished wood floor reminded her of a Christmas card, minus the tree and stockings of course.

Leaving their furniture in storage in California made more sense now because there was no way all of it would fit in this small house. Besides, it gave her hope that they would be going back.

The siblings stood motionless in the middle of the room. Aspen broke the silence. "It could be worse."

"Oh, really? How?"

"We could have to share a room."

Noah snickered at her attempted humor. "I'd sooner commit suicide." He brushed past her purposely bumping her shoulder.

"I hate you, Noah."

"Good. I like it like that." He walked down a short hall and peered into one room and then another. "At least the movers had brains enough to put my stuff in the big bedroom." He walked into the room, slamming the door behind him.

Tears stung Aspen's eyes as a wave of sadness rushed over her. Noah had never been this mean even when they had fights. She trudged past Noah's room and into her own. Her spirits rose a little when she saw her new dresser and bed, waiting for her clothes and bedding.

The furniture matched the white painted trim of the room and provided a stark contrast for the lime green valance draped above the wide bay window. In fact, the window took up almost the entire wall. This room was much different and much smaller than her room in California. However, her mother had the entire house painted before they moved in, so everything looked fresh and new.

She was amused when she saw her new, ruffled bedspread. She guessed Mom asked movers to take it out of the package and fold it at the bottom of the mattress. Even though she was a tomboy at heart, her mother liked to decorate her room in "girl" stuff, and secretly Aspen liked it.

She was glad Noah couldn't see her when she perched her giraffe on the window seat. "I'll put you here. Of course, you can't see much because of all the trees." She giggled at her childish whim, but she dearly loved her giraffe. She didn't sleep with it anymore, but she couldn't bear to put it away in a box. Sprinkle seemed like a silly name, but the day her Aunt Judy gave it to her, it had started to rain, and her aunt said, "Hurry inside, Aspen, it's starting to sprinkle." Aspen hadn't ever heard anyone describe rain like that and she liked it. So, the giraffe became Sprinkle.

Aspen sighed and turned to the boxes in the middle of the floor. She found her gray hoodie, pulled it over her head, and walked toward Noah's room. His door was now open. "Want to go look around?"

Noah just growled at her, "No."

Aspen shrugged and kept walking. Again his reaction was what she expected.

She went into the kitchen. Mom was making sandwiches from the few groceries they had purchased at the 7-Eleven, and her back was to Aspen. Normally, she would have offered to help, but Mom hadn't been herself for weeks, and Aspen did not want to have another strained conversation, so she quietly slipped out the back door.

3

"I HATE YOU!"

ASPEN STEPPED ONTO A narrow cobblestone path that wound through the yard. A soft breeze gently moved the trees and the willowy bushes along the back of the house and close by the incessant chirping of young birds.

Then suddenly—silence. The breeze and the birds stopped, and Aspen stopped too. She listened—just silence. Her eyes darted around the yard. Nothing.

The breeze picked up again just as quickly as it had stopped, but the birds were still quiet. Aspen stood still for a few seconds and then cautiously began walking again, hearing only the soft breeze and her own footsteps.

She walked past a white picket fence and bright yellow flowers surrounding a garden filled with rows of young plants. Aspen stopped again. The eerie silence was unsettling.

Looking back toward the house, she considered trying Noah one more time, but so far today, his comments had made her feel like an idiot, so she changed her mind. She couldn't help but think of the old man, but the way her family had reacted, she wondered if she had imagined him. An involuntary shiver ran through her— *how did I leave the truck? Did I?*

Past the garden and through some trees Aspen could see a small shed. She glanced around one more time and then slowly continued on the path.

The shed seemed to draw her to it, and again, she stopped to look around.

It's just a stupid shed.

Dust and cobwebs on the shed's windows made it hard to see to the inside, but the unlocked door beckoned Aspen, and she pushed it open.

An array of tools hung from evenly spaced hooks. A lawnmower, leaf rakes and other tools lined the walls, quietly waiting for summer. It was the middle of May, and the grass needed mowing, but the undisturbed dust on the mower and surrounding area told Aspen they hadn't been put to use yet.

Finding nothing particularly interesting, Aspen turned to leave. Through the open door, a shadow moved across the cobblestone path, and Aspen stepped quickly to the door. "Noah? Hey did you—"

Aspen froze. It wasn't Noah at all! She hurried back into the shed as the shadow moved closer, and the dark image of the old man filled the doorway.

A blood-curdling scream pierced the silence, and Aspen clamped her hand over her mouth when she realized that she was the one screaming.

Scrambling backward to get away from him, Aspen stumbled over the lawnmower, crashed into a metal trashcan, and sent it tumbling across the floor, and her to the cold cement. She huddled next to the lawnmower, trying to scream for her parents, but no sound came out of her dry throat.

The old man loomed above her, his eyes locked on hers. Afraid to look away, Aspen scooted closer to the wall. A soft squeaking sound next to her caused her to scan the shed, but she couldn't tell where it was coming from.

Something brushed her ankle and her hand that was resting on the floor. Aspen looked down and then leaped to her feet. Rats! The floor was covered with fat gray rats!

The squeaking became deafening. Aspen bolted for the door to the sound of shrill squeals when she stepped on unsuspecting rats.

"Mom! Dad! Mom!" Surprised escape was so easy; she ran screaming up the cobblestone path.

The shed door slammed shut, but Aspen didn't look back. She ran as hard as she could to the house and burst through the back door.

"I hate this place! I hate this place!" Aspen screamed.

"Aspen?" Mom jumped up from the table where she, Dad, and Noah were eating lunch. "What's the matter? What happened?"

"Another old man—" began Noah.

Aspen turned on her brother. "Rats! There are rats in that shed! Hundreds of them! Gray, ugly rats!"

"What were you doing in the shed?" Dad stood and hurried out the open door.

"Rats, Aspen?" Noah smirked.

"Enough, Noah," said Mom flatly.

Noah rolled his eyes and then followed Dad.

Mom pulled Aspen to an empty chair. "Sit down, Aspen. Are you hurt? Did they bite you?"

"No, Mom! They crawled all over me. I…I fell on the floor when—" She stopped, not wanting to say that she had seen the old man again. It didn't matter anyway because Dad would see the rats and the old man wouldn't matter. Sobbing, she buried her face in her hands

In minutes, Dad and Noah were back in the house. Dad knelt by Aspen. "Are you sure they were rats, Aspen?"

Aspen's eyes widened when she looked up at her father. "Dad! There were hundreds of them! Didn't you—didn't you see them?"

Dad shook his head, and Aspen suddenly became aware of the puzzled look on her dad's face. Mom and Noah were looking at her as though she had lost her mind.

"No, Aspen. I looked through the windows, and the shed's filled with gardening tools. That's all. Doesn't even look like they have been touched yet this year."

"Why didn't you go in? The rats are inside! I was in there with the rats, Dad!"

Dad's expression changed from puzzled to concern. "Aspen, the door is locked."

Fear gripped Aspen as she realized her dad did not believe her. "What?! The door is not locked, Dad! I was inside the shed!"

"Instead of imaginary people, now it's imaginary rats," Noah scoffed.

"Noah—" Dad stood, but before he could say anything else, Aspen jumped to her feet and slammed both fists on the table. "I hate you, Noah! Why are you such a creep?"

Noah glared at her, "Shut up Aspen. You and your stupid invisible—" He stammered for a second. "Things! Geez, you have totally lost it!"

"Enough!" Dad boomed. "You kids stop fighting. We have enough to deal with around here without the two of you acting like you are five years old!"

Tears streamed down Aspen's face as she turned to Mom then Dad and then Noah. The look on their faces was all she needed.

She turned and ran from the room. "I *hate* this place!" she screamed, "And I hate all of you!"

4

GRANDPA WAS RICH

ASPEN LAY CURLED IN a ball on her bed with Sprinkle cuddled close to her chest. She had closed the door and locked it. For a while, her family left her alone but then Mom, talking to her daughter through the door, convinced Aspen to open it.

Aspen didn't say much. Mom tried to console her about moving to Tennessee and tried to assure her that things would get better. She also asked Aspen why she didn't answer when Mom called her to lunch. Aspen said she didn't hear her.

Aspen asked why no one came when she screamed, and Mom assured her that they had not heard her either.

Mom started to question Aspen about the rats but seemed uncomfortable and obviously changed her mind. Staying just a few minutes, she patted Aspen's head, kissed her cheek, told her everything would be fine and then she was gone. Aspen couldn't help but feel that Mom was trying to convince herself as well as her daughter.

Aspen snuggled down inside her comforter, pulling Sprinkle even closer. She remembered other instances where she had seen people that no one else had.

People, not rats. Aspen shuddered as the image of long tails and little fat gray bodies fixed itself in the front of her mind. Suddenly feeling sick, she jumped out of bed and ran out of her room to the bathroom. Leaning over the toilet, she heaved over and over, but nothing came out, and she gagged as sweat poured from her temples.

"Aspen?" Mom was at her side. She put a cold washcloth on Aspen's neck and then sat on the floor and pulled Aspen's head into her lap.

Aspen sobbed. She wasn't sure how long she cried, she only remembered Mom offering to help her change her clothes and put the sheets on her bed, but Aspen resisted the sheets and Mom let it go. She left Aspen lying on the bed, the comforter wrapped around her.

Suzann closed her daughter's door and quietly leaned against it. Before the family moved here, she had the house painted to give it a new fresh feeling, but now she noticed little imperfections on the wall where the paint had not quite been able to hide tiny creases where old wallpaper had once been. Tears pricked the corners of her eyes, and she blinked them back. Fearing for Aspen's state of mind and Noah's sullen, angry mood swings, she wanted to gather them both in her arms like she had done when they were little, and protect them from the world around them. Maybe she should do just that. Take them both, leave Jackson, and go back home.

Her heart wrenched, and a tiny gasp clutched her chest. The thought of leaving her husband of twenty-two years was incomprehensible, for any reason, but the reality of the situation they were in loomed over the entire house, like a thundercloud threatening to drench everything in its path.

Suzann quickly brushed at the tears that now streaked her cheeks. She had no idea what to do about any of this. Her only direction seemed to be to stay, to face whatever lies ahead. She and Jackson had always been a team, but now it seemed they were on opposing sides. But of what? Why the division? Why the secrecy?

A dark image once again pierced her consciousness, and she wrapped her arms around her stomach in an effort to ease some of the pain.

"Suzann?"

She stood erect quickly and wiping away her tears. She rubbed the dampness from her hands and walked briskly down the hall.

"Coming, Jackson."

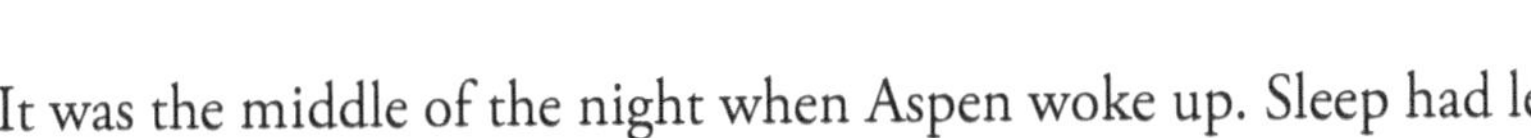

It was the middle of the night when Aspen woke up. Sleep had left her, and she stared at the ceiling.

Seeing people that no one else seemed to notice was not new to Aspen. In kindergarten, Sami showed up on the playground and played with Aspen every day at recess. None of the other kids talked to Sami and Aspen thought they were mean but when she asked them why they said they couldn't see anyone. Then one day, Sami said she was moving away, and Aspen never saw her again. The school had called Mom, and the vivid memory of her distraught mother arriving to pick her up that day had never left her—neither had she ever understood Mom's concern. Sami was as real to Aspen as any of her other friends, and she was sad that she was moving.

Then the time in a store when Aspen got lost and a tall lady with a blue dress stood with her until her mother came. No one else saw the lady in the blue dress.

And the time Aspen was caught in a riptide while surfing and could not keep her head above the water. An older man had lifted her onto her board and pushed her to the sand. Aspen didn't think about it until later, but the man just walked through the torrent water, calmly pushing Aspen's board. When she tried to show him to Noah and Krista, he was nowhere to be found.

Her family had always humored her when she told them about the people she could see, but now that she was sixteen, her experiences just seemed to irritate everyone. They seemed especially annoying to Dad, which is why Aspen had stopped sharing them with anyone but Krista. At least her best friend seemed to understand—anyway, she never laughed at Aspen.

Again tears stung Aspen's eyes. She shuddered at thoughts of the old man on the road and in the shed. She gagged when she thought of the rats. Her family now had good reason to believe she was crazy.

There was something else too. Not only did Aspen *see* the rats, but she could also *feel* their horrible fur. Thinking back, she realized that she had never actually touched Sami. The man in the ocean either and the lady in the blue dress just stood *next* to Aspen. And there was something else.

None of them scared me. I have never felt afraid—until now.

She wished Dad had given them their new cell phones so that she could call or text Krista.

Aspen rubbed the back of her hand under her nose and reached for some tissue. A sharp rap on the door pulled her out of her thoughts.

"Aspen?"

"Go away, Noah."

"Fine." She heard him slam his fist on the wall and then his footsteps going away from her door.

This is just great. My Mom and Dad have turned into Dr. Jekyll, and Mr. Hyde and my little sister is nuts!

After Aspen stormed out of the kitchen, Noah was overcome by guilt. He had treated Aspen badly for weeks. Maybe if he tried to understand her, they could at least communicate again. The reality is, he needed her. For whatever reason, Mom and Dad had left their family—not really, but emotionally—they were not communicating with their kids, or with each other. His or Aspen's needs seemed to be their least concern.

Noah fought the desire to cry. *I'm seventeen, not a baby.* Suddenly he didn't care if he was seventeen, he felt helpless, and that's what babies were. Helpless. Noah stormed back into his room and closed the door. He fell across his bed, buried his face in his pillow wept. *Why do I feel so afraid? What happened to our life?*

Aspen still had Sprinkle cuddled to her chest when she woke up. Sunlight flooded her room through her open blind, and she stretched out on her back. Sometime during the night, she had crawled under the comforter, and now she lay on the bare mattress. She had changed her clothes last night but had not showered, and now she felt grimy and uncomfortable. Collecting some clean clothes, she hurried to the bathroom before anyone else woke up. *One bathroom. This is going to be a challenge.*

Back in her room, Aspen unpacked her boxes and organized her drawers. She placed a picture of her and Krista on her dresser, making a mental note to ask Mom when the Internet would be hooked up and Dad when they would get their new cell phones.

A soft knock on the door startled her. "Aspen?" It was Noah again.

"What do you want?" Aspen snapped. She was not ready to forgive her brother for being such a jerk the entire trip to Tennessee and especially for last night.

"Fine." Just like before Noah slammed his fist against the wall, but this time, Aspen did not hear Noah retreat. After a few minutes, he opened the door just a crack. "Aspen?"

"What?" she mumbled and plopped down on her bed next to Sprinkle.

"Do you want to go with me to find the lake? Thought we could just check it out."

Aspen leaned up on her elbows. "Why?"

Noah shrugged. "Just forget it," he scowled, but he did not leave.

She wasn't sure why Noah was being so nice. She guessed it was because he did not want to go alone and it wasn't like he had a huge choice of companions. She rolled onto her back and rubbed her eyes, but she didn't say anything.

Noah walked in and over by her bed. "You look horrible."

"Thanks a lot," Aspen said dryly. She swung her legs over the opposite side of the bed from where Noah was standing, pulled herself to her feet and plunked Sprinkle on the window seat. She waited for a smart remark from Noah about her stuffed giraffe, but none came.

Relieved, she rubbed her wet hair vigorously with both hands and then shook her thick locks, letting them fall loosely down her back. Aspen wiped her face with her hands, breathed deeply and sighed as she blew the air out. "Okay."

Saying nothing, Noah turned on his heel, walked through the house and out the kitchen door. Aspen followed. Their parents were nowhere in sight.

She shuddered as they stepped out onto the cobblestone path that led to the shed. She scanned the ground for rats or any other rodent-type creatures. Seeing nothing, she hurried to catch Noah, relieved when they came to a wide concrete sidewalk that turned away from the house in another direction. She hadn't noticed it yesterday.

The sidewalk took them across the yard and into a forest of thick trees on the other side of the driveway. The path zigzagged as it began a gradual incline, becoming steeper as they walked deeper into the trees.

Aspen glanced back. The trees were so thick she could no longer see the servants' quarters. *Their house.* She looked around. In all directions—trees.

"Are you sure this is the right way?"

"No," said Noah flatly. "But this *is* the only path, and it goes up—Dad said the lake is up. I looked around a little bit this morning. This is the only way out of the yard except for a dirt path on the other side of the garage that goes down to that stream." Then he added, waving his hand to his left, "And the road-slash-driveway."

Aspen laughed a little, "Yeah, it is the longest driveway on the planet."

"Well, they probably had to hide the *servants'* quarters." Sarcasm was Noah's new trademark.

Suddenly Noah stopped and turned to face his sister. "Aspen?"

Aspen nodded, a little wary. "What?"

"That shed out there is kind of creepy. I mean, I'm not sure about the rats and all but—"

A cold chill rushed through Aspen's entire body. She searched for something to say that didn't reveal her apprehension. "There were rats, Noah. I don't care what you think. Did…did you try to go in?"

Noah scoffed, "No. Not even. It looked too creepy. I didn't want to get close."

"I—" Aspen stopped.

"You what?" Noah lowered his head, furrowed his brow and suspiciously eyed his sister. "What?"

Aspen raised her eyebrows, and her eyes widened. She shook her head. "Nothing."

Noah didn't look convinced. He stood firmly, his eyes scrutinizing her face but Aspen just stared back in mock aloofness. "Nothing, Noah. Let's get going before it gets too late. We might get lost."

Noah rolled his eyes. "We are on a *path*, Aspen." He turned and continued up the hill.

"True," Aspen mumbled. She followed her brother, continually checking behind her and the ground—for rats.

The path took a sharp left turn, and immediately, the incline became steeper. Now there was an iron handrail on both sides. Neither of them took hold of it, but Aspen assumed it had been placed there for the benefit of those who found the path too steep. The winding path narrowed and went from a path into long narrow cement steps that seemed to go straight up and were only wide enough for one person.

The rails that just seconds ago seemed obsolete to the two teenagers now became a welcome crutch, and the siblings held on with both hands as they climbed through the trees.

"I didn't think the hill was so steep," Noah huffed.

Aspen nodded. She knew Noah wasn't looking at her, but he didn't say anything else and neither did she.

For the rest of the climb, neither of them spoke. The steps finally ended, and they found themselves on a large concrete landing.

The landing had benches on two sides that faced each other, flanked by large molded concrete vases. A tall bush shaped like an upside-down teardrop in the center of each vase was surrounded at the base by a lush green vine dotted with little white flowers spilling over the edges.

The identical benches were made of ornamental iron that had been painted a dull red. The paint on the arms and the curved backs was worn but not peeling. The seats were made of wooden slats fitted close together.

Noah plopped down on one of them, "Whew. That. Was. Fun." He took a deep breath and let it out slowly "Good idea these benches," he patted the seat.

Aspen nodded in agreement and walked to the edge of the cement. The scene before her took her breath away. Three long wide steps opposite of where they had just climbed, descended from the patio to an expansive green carpet of grass. From the edges of the steps on both sides and bordering the entire short-cropped lawn, a variety of spring flowers filled a garden area about four feet wide. The flowers provided a perfect edging between the grass and the trees.

Six more benches, just like the one Noah was sitting on, were placed strategically several feet apart around the spacious grass area. There were no trees in the middle of the grass. It seemed as though someone had carved a big hole in the trees and plopped a house—a very large house—in the clearing.

She could see an opening in the trees opposite of where she was standing.

Aspen stuffed both hands into the back pockets of her jeans. "That is the biggest house I have ever seen."

Noah stood, walked out of the tree-covered landing, and joined his sister where the house and yard were in full view. A low whistle escaped through his teeth.

The back of the house had a cement patio like the one they were standing on only much larger. On either side of a wide set of steps, low brick planter boxes surrounded the entire patio, the same green vine with the tiny white flowers spilling over the sides. The flower gardens that encircled the grass butted up to steps on both sides.

Eight white iron chairs each with a round cushion surrounded a matching round table with a tightly bound umbrella protruding from the center hole. Four white iron lawn chairs, their thick, pale red pads matching the umbrella and chair cushions, sat in a neat row along the opposite edge of the patio. A small round iron table to the right of each lounge were tiny versions of the larger table.

To the right of the patio, a kidney-shaped pool with no diving board. Aspen thought it looked more like a very large hot tub. Around the pool sat neatly spaced little round tables next to lounges.

The entire back of the first floor was a span of six French doors.

The second story balcony doubled as a roof for the patio below.

More windows, blinds closed, stretched above the balcony and four chimneys reached skyward from the roof. Through the trees, the left side of the house was visible. Long windows on both levels of that side of the house also with closed blinds.

Aspen squinted. *This must be the side of the house I was looking at before. The blinds are closed.* She shuddered and dismissed the image of movement in an upper window the day before.

Clean white trim on the house appeared to have been freshly painted and added a pleasant contrast.

A thick hedge, perfectly trimmed, hugged the foundation. About four feet tall, it stopped just under the first-floor windows and where the cement patio met the French doors. It appeared to border the entire house.

"Well," Noah said absently, "I thought *Dad* had money."

"Yeah, no kidding."

Silently they both surmised the massive house, and grounds and then Noah said what Aspen was thinking, "How did our great-grandpa get so rich?"

5

LIGHTS IN THE LAKE

THE LAKE WAS BIGGER than Aspen had expected, considering her grandpa and the other homeowners had it built, at least that's what she was told. A stream on the other side flowed from the trees into the lake exiting near where they were standing. She guessed it was the same stream that led past the servants' house—*their house. The little house* and she smiled.

Noah's pleasant demeanor had disappeared, but she was getting used to his random mood swings.

They waded through the wildflowers on a path that had seen little use for some time.

Five other houses surrounded the lake. More thick forest made it hard to see the actual structures, but the roofs were visible above the trees, and each yard had an opening in the trees with a cement path leading away from the lake. The natural landscape was the same in every direction. At the treeline, there were colorful wildflowers, the dirt beach and the quiet lake in the center of it all.

On this side, a boardwalk protruded into the lake with a weathered swimming platform at the end of it. A boat dock on the opposite side was equally worn. A tire swing swayed gently in the breeze, and the tree that supported it stood majestically near the swimming platform.

Noah also observed the boat dock.

"Check out the *boats,*" he said sarcastically. "Ours could barely

30

turn around in this bathtub."

Several rowboats, canoes, and kayaks dotted the shore, but they were covered with dirt and did not appear to have been used in a while.

He's right. A yacht would never fit.

When Aspen didn't respond, he plopped down on a rock. "Whatever." He picked up a tiny pebble and tossed it into the water and then gave his sister a disparaging look. "It just doesn't make sense, Aspen. Dad has always worked from home and traveled when he needed to. Why the sudden urgency to move?"

Surprised by his sudden vulnerability Aspen shrugged. "Mom told you. They have to get this house ready to sell." She looked thoughtfully at her brother. "Noah?"

He turned to her but said nothing.

"Do you ever think Mom and Dad might get a divorce?"

He shook his head. "No, Aspen."

"But don't you think it's kind of weird when they stop talking, I should say *whispering* when we walk into a room. "

"Not really. Parents are supposed to act like that."

Aspen ignored his attempt to dodge the subject, "But Dad seems—different."

Noah was quiet for a minute, "I don't think Mom wanted to move."

"She is miserable," Aspen mumbled.

"*On guard* is more like it," Noah scoffed.

Suddenly he stood up and immediately changed the subject. irritating Aspen again. For as long as she could remember, Noah had tried to protect her. He had been doing that since they were little, but sometimes, like now, she didn't want to be protected.

Noah's mood lightened, and when Aspen looked at him, he motioned toward the swim platform and started towards it. "Let's go check out that tire swing."

Aspen glared at the back of her brother's head as he loped toward the swim dock. She decided to beat him there and darted past her unsuspecting brother.

When she reached the swim dock, she noticed a long wooden pole with a metal hook on the end, dangling from a low branch of the tree. The tire swing was hanging out over the lake, impossible to reach from the dock without the hook.

Retrieving the pole, she leaned out over the water, hooked the rope and pulled the swing to her. When it was close enough, she grasped the tire with one hand and tossed the pole behind her toward the dock, but it bounced off and into the water.

"Aspen!"

She laughed. "Sorry." She couldn't tell if Noah was irritated that the pole had fallen into the water or surprised that she had beaten him to the swing.

Aspen put one foot into the tire, and with her other foot, she pushed away from the dock. Leaning back, she bent her knees, pushed her feet into the tire, and straightened them again. She repeated the same motion until the swing was gliding back and forth over the water

The swinging caused a breeze that blew her hair away from her face, and a wave of contentment rushed over her. She laughed, leaning down so her fingers could skim through the cold, glassy liquid.

From out of nowhere, a huge wave came toward Aspen, and she jerked her hand out of the water. *What the—*

She looked around. No wind. No boats.

How did that happen?!

One wave became several and soon turned into a violent whirl-pool. Aspen pulled herself back up clinging to the rope with both hands. Frantically she scanned the water again looking for some craft that could have disturbed the otherwise peaceful water. Nothing was on the lake. She looked at Noah, who still laughed, seeming completely unaware.

Then she saw it—an image looming just beneath the surface. It was so bright she could almost see through it. She was frozen with fear when the swing stopped, suddenly nearly throwing her off.

She struggled to force the swing into motion and closer to the dock, but her legs that seconds ago propelled her effortlessly now felt like lead weights.

Noah stopped laughing. "Aspen?"

Aspen did not take her eyes from the churning water beneath her. "Aspen? You okay?"

Aspen croaked, "Just…no. Help me get off this thing."

"Get the swing going, so I can grab hold of your hand." He peered into the water below the dock. "You shouldn't have thrown the pole in the water!" he yelled.

To Aspen, Noah's voice sounded distorted like he was inside a tunnel.

"Noah!" Aspen screamed. She was terrified of falling in the whirlpool and scrambled to get her feet on top of the tire.

"Aspen, what are you doing?" Noah yelled. "Get the swing moving!"

"I…I'm trying!" The words barely escaped her throat as she desperately tried to get her feet as far from the water as she could.

Her eyes darted to Noah.

"Aspen?"

Now Noah sounded scared. He looked from her to the water beneath the dock. Falling onto his stomach, he plunged his arm into the water but then jumped up and dived in.

Aspen was still struggling to keep her feet on top of the tire when something firmly grasped her ankles. She tried to kick free of the invisible vise, but her efforts proved useless, and the tremendous force jerked her off the tire. The rope ripped through her hands, taking skin with it, and she plunged backward into the icy water. Kicking violently, she tried to get back to the surface, but to her horror, she could not move.

Relax. Aspen's instincts told her what to do when a wave plummeted her deep into the ocean. Relaxing would bring her to the surface quicker than trying to fight it.

As second nature water skills flashed through her mind, none of it seemed to matter. It was not the water that held her under. It was a force she could not see. Darkness closed in around her, but seconds later she was surrounded by tiny dancing lights. At that moment, a shock surged through her body, and she bolted straight out of the water.

"Noah!" Aspen gasped but sank again.

"I've got you!" Noah was beside her. He yanked on her arm and flipped her onto her back. He locked one arm around her neck, swimming confidently toward the dock with the other. They had both practiced this technique many times at the beginning of every summer in the junior lifeguard program in San Clemente.

Aspen struggled to breathe.

Grasping one of Aspen's hands, Noah released his grip on her neck. He struggled to get onto the ladder, locked his free arm around a rung and then sliding his hand down to her shoulder he locked his other arm underneath Aspen's arm and dragged her up the ladder. His muscles strained under her weight, but he managed to get her onto the dock while scraping her arm and ribs on the worn wooden steps.

Water belched violently from Aspen's nose, and throat and Noah rolled her onto her side and pounded between her shoulder blades. More water gushed from her mouth.

When she could finally breathe, she began sobbing and choking.

Noah's shaking arms pulled her to him. "What was *that* Aspen? This is just a stupid lake. Not even a wave or a tide to pull you under! You scared the—" He hugged her tighter.

No waves? What is he talking about?

Breathing was easier now, and her sobs subsided to soft whimpering. Her chest didn't hurt so much, but her throat was raw, and her eyes and nose felt like they were on fire.

Noah just held her while she cried. Finally, she pushed away from him. "Noah, didn't you see the waves? There were big waves—spinning—like a giant whirlpool."

Noah stared at his sister in silence as Aspen rushed on,

"Thanks…thanks for pushing me up, Noah." She fell back into his arms.

"Aspen?" This time Noah pushed her away and looked at his

sister who was staring at the water. She didn't respond. He turned to where she was looking. The tire was swinging gently at the end of the rope. The lake was still again; only tiny ripples lapped against the muddy shore.

"Aspen?" Noah raised his voice this time.

"I...I'm sorry, Noah." Her eyes were pleading when she looked at him. "Please don't tell Mom and—"

Noah's eyes looked puzzled.

"There were no waves, Aspen, and I didn't push you up. You just shot out of the water right when I got to you. It was...weird."

"You didn't? I...I...I don't know. It felt like...like I was shocked." Her eyes widened. "You won't tell Mom and Dad?"

"Are you kidding me? Why are you so worried about Mom and Dad knowing you fell off the stupid swing?" His brow furrowed. "How did you do that anyway? It was like you just decided to let go."

Aspen was shaking her head, but then she started to cry again. "I...I thought I saw—" she looked at her injured hands. Tiny bits of blood were coming to the surface now, and the burns from the rope were obvious. She started crying again.

"You thought you saw what?" Noah knelt and looked at her hands. "Aspen?" He took one of them, looking closer at the burns. "So, you did fall. Did you lose your balance or slip or something?"

"N...nothing. I don't know. The water was churning, like a whirlpool, like that big one in Hawaii we jumped into. It scared me." She looked at her brother. "Lakes are different than oceans."

Noah sat back a surprised look on his face. "Aspen, there were no waves. Honest! The water was still. Not even a breeze. The only movement was when you dragged your hand in it." As he talked, he stood and walked away from her to the edge of the dock. He peered at the water beneath the tire swing that now hung over the water too far out again to be reached without the hook. Shading his eyes with his hand, he searched the entire lake but then walked back to Aspen and pulled her to her feet.

He again tucked her head into his wet shoulder and gently patted her back. "It's okay. I'm just giving you a bad time. Sorry you fell." He looked back over the water and paused for a few seconds. "You have been crying a lot since we got to Tennessee."

"I hate this place! Please don't tell Mom and Dad, Noah," she said again.

"Like they are not going to notice we are soaked, not to mention freezing. Geez, why are you so worried about them finding out?"

"I just...I don't want them to know about this."

"I don't know, Aspen, you could have drowned."

Noah was not sure how to respond to Aspen.

Rats? Whirlpools? Geez, what next? Aspen is losing it.

He tugged on her arm. "C'mon, let's go." He shook his head in bewilderment as he helped her to her feet. "I still can't believe—" he sighed.

"What?"

"Nothing." Noah turned and started walking, still holding onto his sister's arm.

Aspen allowed her brother to pull her along the path back toward the trees and the little house. "They already think I'm crazy," she mumbled.

"No, they don't Aspen." He didn't look back, and his voice sounded far away.

Yes, they do, and now I'm starting to wonder about your sanity.

Noah felt sick. He knew he should tell their parents about the incident, but a strange sort of protection for his sister got in his way. He was honestly fearful of how they may react, especially Dad. He would play it by ear, not make any decision until he had to.

Aspen's head ached. What pulled her off the swing? What pushed her to the surface? She had felt two distinctly different forces. One thing she was sure of, the entire experience terrified her, and she had no idea how it had happened. She looked over her shoulder at the lake.

Nothing. Once again, the water was smooth as glass—the swing hung limply from the branch. An eerie silence permeated the air—the same strange silence as yesterday in the backyard.

She turned away, but as she did, something caught her attention. A mist began rising from the middle of the lake.

6

GIRL IN THE WINDOW

WHEN ASPEN AND NOAH entered the house through the kitchen door, they didn't see either of their parents. Still wet, but not dripping so much, they hurried through the kitchen, hoping to avoid having to explain.

They were stopped in the living room by a commotion in the front yard. The door was open, and Mom was standing just on the other side of it. They inched closer, staying back just far enough so their mother would not see them.

A man in an SUV appeared to be having a heated discussion with Dad. Aspen could hear them yelling. She couldn't understand what they were saying, but the looks on their faces painted an obvious picture. She crept closer to the open door.

The man jumped out of the SUV and lunged forward, shaking his fist in Dad's face. He yelled, "You will be sorry, Mr. Allen! I *will* get what is mine. You can be sure of that!"

Dad stepped toward the man his fists clenched at his sides. "You best get off this property!"

The driver stood still for a few seconds then he got back in his vehicle and threw the already running engine into reverse. He backed up so fast he nearly hit a tree, but then he jerked the wheel around and sped down the driveway.

Aspen and Noah were so engrossed in the action that Mom surprised them when she stepped through the door. The two exchanged a quick glance.

Noah opened his mouth to speak, but just then, Dad bolted through the door. He stopped abruptly when he saw his family.

Mom looked fearful as she threw a pleading look at her husband.

Dad took a deep breath. He looked first at his wife, then at each of his children. Then his anger turned to surprise. "Why are you two all wet?"

It seemed an odd question to Aspen after what had just happened, but she assumed the look their mother gave him stopped him from whatever he had started to say.

The siblings again exchanged a quick look, but it was Noah who spoke.

"Aspen, well she sort of fell off the dock." Noah wrinkled his brow. "I sort of pushed her…then…she sort of pulled me in with her."

Neither of their parents said anything, and the uncomfortable silence seemed to linger forever.

Aspen spoke up, "I don't think he meant for me to fall in, but I did. So I pulled him in with me."

Mom had a questioning look on her face, but Dad just shrugged. "Well, get changed. We are going up to the house." Dad started to walk past them. As he did, his eyes locked with Aspen's. She was startled that he looked—afraid?

"Who was that, Dad?" Noah blurted.

Dad turned around. He glanced at Mom when he spoke. "No one. No one you need to worry about." Then he turned and started to walk away.

"But what did he want?" Noah persisted.

"Noah!" Dad wheeled around. "I said it is nothing you need to worry about."

Noah shrank away from his dad. He didn't say anything more but stared after Dad as he disappeared into the kitchen.

Aspen was shivering. "Do we have to go? To…to the…the house?" She kept her hands to her sides, but the burns were killing her. Her side was throbbing, and her arm stung where it had scraped the ladder.

Mom followed their dad with her eyes. "Yes, we all need to go. Dad wants to show us through the house, so please go get dressed."

"I'm hungry," mumbled Noah. He glanced over at Aspen as he walked down the hall to his bedroom.

"I'll fix something. Just hurry up," Mom's voice trailed off as she went into the kitchen.

Aspen closed her bedroom door behind her and leaned against it. Through her window, she stared past Sprinkle to the trees and tried to comprehend all that had happened this morning. She couldn't make any sense of it. Her head felt like mush, and now more than ever, she longed to be home, in San Clemente—to call Krista and to go surfing.

She closed her eyes but then she heard Noah's bedroom door close, so trying not to irritate her painful hands, she quickly undressed using just her fingers to pull her clothes off. She slipped on her robe and hurried to the bathroom, but as she got closer, she could hear the shower. Noah had beaten her to it.

Outside the bathroom door, Aspen sank to the floor. She folded her arms around her knees and waited. "I hate my life," she said out loud.

Suzann stood by the kitchen door staring at her husband. With both hands on the counter, he was leaning forward, his head down.

"Jackson?"

He stiffened. "What?" he barked. "Who was that?"

"How the hell should I know? Obviously, an idiot if he would come onto my property and threaten me."

"But what—"

Jackson spun around. "Suzann! I don't know! How could I know any more than you do? You have been here as long as I have!"

Jackson rubbed his forehead with the back of his hand, and Suzann noticed beads of sweat on his temples. "Are you okay?" she asked.

"Yes, I'm fine." He dropped his head and took a deep breath. When he lifted his head, his temperament was immediately changed. "Were you going to fix some lunch before we go?"

Aspen explained her wounded hands by describing how she had fallen off the tire swing and to her relief, Mom didn't probe any further.

The gated entrance to the big house was some distance from the little house driveway, so Dad elected to drive. He pushed the remote control to open the gate and then guided the truck up the long U-shaped driveway, stopping in front of the porch. The *big* house sprawled in front of them.

A huge light hung above the massive double doors, and a walkway leading away from the front porch in both directions disappeared behind bushes on both sides. Well placed clumps of trees dotted the thick carpet of grass which was manicured with perfectly straight edges. The flower boxes along the front of the house were identical to those in the backyard and boasted the same green leafy plant with little white flowers. The grass extended to the black iron fence that spanned the entire length of the front yard.

"Looks like the painters finished," Mom said absently.

"I hope so, they were supposed to start on the inside today, but it doesn't appear anyone is here," said Dad.

"Maybe they are finished for the day," said Mom.

"Maybe," he huffed. "Pretty early to stop work."

Noah followed Mom and Dad up the wide front steps, but Aspen walked slower, hanging back a little. She wanted to walk around the side of the house, to look up at the window that she had seen yesterday, the one that someone had been looking out of.

She stopped walking when something caught her eye. It was in the front second-story window on the far right. She shaded her eyes from the late afternoon sun.

Nope. Nothing. The blind was closed. She started to walk again but glanced back at the window. The blind was open, had it been open before? No, it was closed, she was sure of it. She stood still staring at the window. Nothing. But the blind *was* open.

Aspen ran up the steps. "Dad, are you sure someone doesn't live here?"

"I'm sure, Aspen."

She pursed her lips, deciding not to say anything about the open blind that she was positive had been closed when she first got out of the truck. She followed her dad and Noah into the house. Mom was already inside.

Aspen, Noah, and Mom stopped just inside the door. They were all three visibly surprised by the tall entryway. The ceiling was the roof of the second story.

"This place is huge," breathed Noah.

Aspen nodded, but her attention was drawn to the huge paintings that hung in the front entry at the bottom of the stairs. About three feet off the floor, both extended halfway to the high ceiling.

The paintings were of two young couples. In the first one, the man was sitting, and the woman was standing. The lady in the picture had a high collar of ruffles around her neck. Aspen thought it looked like she was choking. Just looking at it made her swallow hard.

The second couple wore more normal clothes. The man wore a suit, much like the ones Dad wore, and the woman wore a long blue dress that fit her upper body but hung loosely from her waist.

Noah read out loud the words on the plaque fastened to the bottom of the first painting.

Allen Manor
Jackson Humphrey and
Faith Allen Est. 1948

And then he read the second:

Allen Manor
Jackson David and
Aspencia Allen Re-Est.
1970

Aspen looked closely at the second plaque. "Hey! That's my name, sort of." She had been told that she was named after her Grandma Allen, but Aspen had never seen her grandma's name written and she had just assumed her name was Aspen also.

"I didn't like Aspencia, so we shortened it to Aspen. I liked that better," said Mom.

"Me too," said Aspen.

"Jackson, I thought your grandma's name was Nina?" Mom was reading the plaque under the oldest painting.

Dad shrugged. "It was," He mumbled and absently turned his attention to some boxes on the floor of the entry.

Noah didn't seem to notice Dad's obvious avoidance of Mom's question. He was observing the entryway with its five different open archways branching off into other parts of the house. "It would be easy to get lost in here," he said. "And check out those stairs."

The staircase was longer and much wider than the one in their house in California. This one curved gracefully to the right and the hall at the top wasn't really a hall at all. It was more like a walkway with the stair banister bordering the entire length. Eight closed doors were visible from the entry. Dad pointed to the fourth door from the left. "That was my room," he explained.

Aspen was still studying the painting, "Did Grandma work?"

That question brought Dad back into the conversation, and he laughed. "Not ever! They used to entertain a lot. Dad was a pretty important figure in the community. In the community of Memphis, I mean. That made him pretty important in Sommerville, too."

Dad was looking up at his parent's portrait. "We had gardeners and maids and a cook."

Now "servants' quarters" makes more sense.

"Some of them lived in the house we're in now. They weren't here all the time, but several times a week. We used to have Christmas parties here with all of our cousins and the same thing in the summer on the Fourth of July. Most of my memories of this house—this place—are good."

Dad seemed lost in thought again, and it was the first time since they had come to Sommerville, that Aspen thought he seemed at all happy, but at the same time his eyes seemed strange and faraway. The same look she had seen in his eyes back in San Clemente when he had told them they were moving.

Mom interrupted everyone's thoughts. "*Most* of the memories?"

Dad appeared as though he didn't hear her, or maybe he ignored her. Aspen wasn't sure.

Mom's brow furrowed, but she motioned to the upper hallway. "There were six kids in Dad's family. Six bedrooms," she paused. "Hmm, there are eight doors."

Dad nodded. "One is a storage room." And continued his genealogy, "I was in the middle." Dad was counting with his fingers, "There was Sandra, Jim, Helen, Me, Rob, Dana and—"

Dad's thoughts seemed to drift away again, but then as though he realized they were all waiting for him to say more he smiled, stepped to Mom's side and put his arm around her waist.

"And what?" said Noah. "Uh, nothing. Just an extra room."

Aspen just wanted to escape. His actions did not seem genuine, not like they used to be, and that bothered her. "Okay if we go upstairs?" she asked. She didn't wait for an answer and Noah joined her. Neither spoke as they ascended the stairs. Aspen looked back.

Mom and Dad were talking in hushed tones as Dad put his hand on her back and guided her into another room.

7

SHADOWS AND A CHIPPED TOOTH

AT THE TOP OF the stairs, huge paintings adorned the hallway and large leafy fake plants draped from long narrow wooden wall tables between each of the eight doors. The tables looked heavy and had curved legs with gold-colored metal on the bottom.

"Look at this place, Aspen. Grandpa and Grandma had some bucks." He observed the tables. "Do you think that's real gold?"

"Wouldn't doubt it. Hello, they had maids and servants." Aspen stopped in front of a large square painting with a wide gold-colored frame. The painting was of three children, two girls, and a boy. Something in the painting caused Aspen to stop and look closer. She froze, and the hair on her arms and neck seemed to stand straight up.

Did that painting move?

Aspen stared at the painting for a long time, but now it just looked like any other painting. She backed away slowly while taking a deep breath to silence her pounding heart. *Still nothing.* Rubbing her arms in an effort to get the goosebumps to disappear, she moved slowly away from the painting, stopping to look at each of the other old paintings that lined the wall of the long hallway.

One of a couple with pleasant smiles on their faces, one of the same couple with a little girl, maybe about three years old and another of that same girl and two younger children.

Each painting was kind of black and white but not really. They all had a brown tint to them, except for the one of the three children—it was in color.

Aspen walked back to that painting.

This is the one that… moved. She stood still. Geez, I really am crazy.

Aspen backed up and studied the littlest child in the painting. It looked like a boy, but he was wearing a shirt that could easily be a dress.

"Noah, look at this kid," she pointed to the picture. "Isn't that a boy? He's wearing a dress."

Noah chuckled. "Glad I wasn't born then."

"That is a boy, that's my grandpa."

Aspen and Noah jumped. They hadn't heard Dad come up the stairs. "That's just the way they dressed for pictures back then," he said.

"That's lame." Aspen stared at the picture. "So, who are the two girls?"

"My Aunt Riley and Aunt Jeanie."

"Who cares?" asked Noah. "Geez, Aspen, do you need a history lesson?"

Aspen glared at him.

Dad chuckled softly, and Aspen eagerly studied his face, but there was nothing else there. It was just a chuckle.

"Mom and I have to go through some papers downstairs. I just wanted to tell you two not to move anything. These are my parent's things, and we need to go through all of it. A lot of it has been here since *my* Grandpa and Grandma lived here," he pointed to a closed door. "And just for the record, you are not to go in that storage—it is locked, and I don't want you in there."

Aspen was suddenly puzzled. "But I thought you were taking us—"

Dad raised his hand to silence her, and Aspen finished her sentence to herself—*on a tour.*

Saying nothing more, Dad descended the stairs.

Noah was obviously not interested in what Dad was saying and was already at the door of their father's old bedroom. He went in, and Aspen followed.

In the center of the room stood a four-poster bed with a dark blue comforter and two large pillows that were also dark blue. The curtains were the same color and trimmed in a little lighter shade of blue. The carpet was the same color as the trim on the curtains. A large picture of their dad in a football uniform holding his helmet under his arm hung next to one of the windows. They had both seen a smaller version of that picture before. He had a broad grin on his face and his head kind of cocked to one side.

"You look like him, Noah," observed Aspen.

"Yeah, kinda," agreed Noah. "Looks like he's about my age."

"I don't look that much like Mom."

"That's because we both look more like Dad, that's all," said Noah as he opened the closet door. It seemed unusually small for a closet. It was more like a tiny square box—with a very high ceiling. There were a few boxes piled on the shelves and a bag with worn baseball bats poking out of the top. No clothes or hangers hung from the wooden closet rod.

Noah closed the door and walked up behind Aspen who had opened the window seat. "Look at all these pictures," she said.

The seat was filled all the way to the top with picture albums. Aspen flipped through the pages seeing lots of pictures of people she didn't know. She recognized her father in some, but not too many.

There was one picture of six kids all appearing to be in their teen years. "These must be Dad's brothers and sisters," said Aspen.

She recognized her dad as the third one from the right. She noticed the lake in the background of the picture and realized the people were standing in the backyard of this house. The lake was visible because the picture had been taken from above, most likely from the balcony, but the trees were not as dense as they were now.

She closed the album to put it back in the window seat, but as she did, she noticed a small picture protruding from another larger album. Aspen pulled it free. It was a very old picture of a man and a woman and two little girls. The little girls looked a lot alike.

She laid the picture on top of the albums, closed the lid and then followed Noah into the hallway.

Suddenly she remembered the open blind she had seen from the truck that first day. She glanced back into Dad's old room and proceeded to the next room. This one had two windows—one directly opposite the door and one on the wall to the right. Aspen went to that window, propped open the blinds with two fingers and looked out. She was looking down into the side yard where there was more grass, more lawn chairs, and small round tables. Aspen could see the pool from here. She turned and walked back into the hall, leaving Noah alone to investigate.

"Where are you going?" asked Noah

"I'll be right back." Aspen walked past her dad's door and to the next one.

She paused and looked at the locked door of the storage. Something about that room intrigued her, but an involuntary shiver tickled her neck, and she hurriedly turned away.

As if reading her thoughts, Noah called after her, "Wonder what's in there?"

Aspen shrugged, trying to dismiss an uneasy feeling and went into the next room. It had a window directly across from the door just like Dad's room, and so did the next room farther down the hall. Both had similar furnishings.

Aspen passed that room and went to the far end of the hall. At the end on the left was a large door. It was closed. It had a different latch, not a doorknob but it was locked, so she went into the room next to it, at the end of the hall.

Only one window was on the left wall, and from there, she could see part of the lake and a fenced-in garden similar to the one at the little house, only bigger.

She closed the door and walked into the last room where she found Noah was standing oddly still, his arms to his sides and one foot in front of the other as though he had stopped in mid-stride.

Aspen asked, "What's the matter with you?"

"Shhh!" said Noah softly. He did not move. Aspen stopped. "What?"

"Is there anyone else up here?"

She turned around in a circle and whispered, "No."

"Well someone touched me on the shoulder just a second ago." Neither of them moved for several seconds.

Finally, Aspen glanced around. "Noah, there is no one here." A shiver ran through her again. She whispered, "Noah?"

"What?" he had still not moved or looked at her. "Did you feel a…kind of a shiver?"

"No, I felt someone touch me."

"I know, but did you feel a shiver?"

"No, w-e-l-l maybe. Maybe I did. I don't know. Why?"

"'Cause I just felt the same shiver I felt when I—" She gulped, and the lump that had formed in her throat felt like a rock. She stopped before telling him about seeing someone in the window the day before.

"When you what?"

"N…nothing." Aspen became distracted by the unusual furnishings in the room. Next to the bed stood a very old wooden cradle and matching rocker. A bulky dresser supported more pictures, and the pictures on these walls seemed even older than the ones in Dad's room and the other bedrooms.

Lace curtains and the bedspread that possibly once were white were now a faded dismal yellow. For Aspen, the room had an uneasy presence. *And apparently for Noah.* She shuddered. *This stuff seems like it's way older than the furniture in the rest of the house.*

A picture on the dresser in a thick round frame caught Aspen's attention. It was the same as the painting in the hall, the one with the three kids and her grandpa in that stupid dress but it had the brown tint, not color like the larger one in the hall.

Aspen leaned forward a little and looked closer at the picture.

Something looked different. "Noah?"

"What?" Noah had still not moved.

Aspen moved next to him and grabbed his arm. "Ahhh!"

He yelled so loud Aspen jumped and started laughing. "Dang it, Aspen!"

But she was already heading for the hall. "I want to see something." She hurried to the painting of the three kids with Noah at her heels.

When she stopped to look at it closer, Noah was already halfway down the stairs.

Aspen stared at the painting—she was sure she saw a double or a shadow behind the oldest sister. She blinked. Now it was gone.

What the—

Aunt Riley or Aunt Jeanie? She blinked a few times and looked again. No, there was just one girl on the left and one girl on the right.

The oldest girl had a necklace on a single pendant with a flower on it. She was smiling ever so slightly but enough so that Aspen could see that she had perfectly straight teeth. She noticed that because her dad had perfectly straight teeth also. A feature, unfortunately, she had not inherited but had always wished she had.

Suddenly Aspen turned and ran back into the bedroom. "Yes!" she said out loud. The flower on this necklace in this painting was different, just a little, but different. The stem on this flower leaned the other way, but there was something else.

"Her teeth! She has a chip in her tooth!"

"Whom are you talking to?"

"M-m-o-o-m-m!" moaned Aspen. "You scared me!"

"I'm sorry, Noah said you were still up here, and Dad's already in the truck."

"Mom?" Aspen barely heard what her mother had said. "Mom, look at that picture. Look at Grandpa's big sister. The one on the left."

"And?"

"Now come with me." Aspen grabbed her mother's hand and dragged her into the hallway. "Look at that picture. Do you see something different?"

"N-o-o-o-o," said her mother slowly. "Should I?" Aspen heard the truck horn.

"Look at the necklace, Mom, and her teeth. Do you see a chip in her tooth?"

Mom leaned in a little closer. "No."

Aspen pulled her mother back into the bedroom. "Aspen, what are you doing?" asked Mom.

Dad honked again.

"Just look, Mom. Look at that picture. It's the same one, right?"

"Seems to be," said her mother.

"Well, do you see the flower? See how it's leaning?" Aspen had not let go of her mother's hand. "The flower is leaning the other way, and there is a chip in her tooth!"

This time Dad honked the horn twice—Aspen knew he was becoming impatient.

Mom looked closely at the picture. "I don't know Aspen. I'm sure it's just a blemish on the picture. They are pretty old, and this is most likely a reprint. When it was done, it might have reversed it, so it looks backward." She took Aspen by the shoulders and turned her towards the door. "Now let's go."

Aspen obediently walked out of the room, but as she passed the painting, there it was again—she could barely see it—but it was there—another figure behind the oldest girl.

A shadow?

Mom also glanced back at the painting, and Aspen did not miss the uneasy look on her mother's face.

8

STRATEGY

THE REST OF THE day was uneventful for Aspen. She spent most of it helping her mother organize the kitchen and trying to seize an opportunity to probe her mother for more information about why they moved to Tennessee.

But Mom didn't take the bait. She just kept steering the conversation to pots and pans, or where to put the dinner plates. Aspen finally gave up on her interrogation. She did ask about the Internet, and Mom said it would be hooked up the following Monday. The little house had never had Internet, totally primitive Aspen thought, and the company had to actually come out and install it.

Considering the generic afternoon, Aspen was completely unprepared for the announcement at dinner.

"Summer school!" Noah shoved his chair away from the table and jumped to his feet. "I hate this stupid place! Instead of surfing with my friends, I will be in summer school with a bunch of geeks!" He glared at his father and then at his mother. Neither reacted. Exasperated Noah stomped out of the kitchen and through the front door deliberately slamming it behind him.

Dad's eyes narrowed as he watched Noah leave the room.

Aspen didn't say anything. She twirled her fork in her spaghetti, but she did not lift it to her mouth.

His voice steady, but in a tone Aspen was unfamiliar with, Dad began speaking, "Mom and I have a lot of work to do on this house.

We won't be able to spend much time with you kids, and since we live so far from the city we thought it might be good for you to meet some of the kids around here, make some new friends. Maybe it will help make this a little easier for you and Noah." He was not asking for anyone to agree with him. He was simply making a statement that didn't require, or leave room for, any discussion.

Aspen motioned toward the door Noah had slammed. "I don't know if anything will help Noah, Dad. But I was wondering—why we can't help with the house?"

Dad began, "There are things— Never mind. You are going to school."

There was silence, and then Aspen spoke again, "But—"

Mom sighed, "It isn't really school, Aspen. It's more like projects. They do art, writing, things like that."

"Still, Mom. Do we have—"

Both parents stopped eating and looked at her.

"What if we don't want to…go…to summer school or art school, or whatever it is?"

Dad stiffened. "It's not up for discussion," he said dryly.

His response left Aspen with a hole in the pit of her stomach. She had never heard her dad sound so cold. In the past, everything was up for discussion. They always talked things out before a decision was made. Obviously, those days were gone.

Aspen decided against asking about the cell phones instead gladly retreated to her room staying there until she went to bed.

Suzann woke up early after yet another fitful night's sleep. As she showered and dressed, she mulled over the overwhelming feeling of… She wasn't even sure what she felt! Maybe anxious. When Aspen had shown her the painting, and the picture, the feeling that came over her was anxious. And that startled her.

She was still plagued by it when she drove the kids into town to register for summer school. She understood that they didn't want to go, but her attempts at convincing Jackson there may be other alternatives had failed miserably. Besides, she decided, they did need to meet new friends,

There had been no one else at the school, just a curt lady with a tiny pointed nose that seemed a perfect perch for her tiny round glasses. Not a good start for her two unimpressed kids.

On the way back to the little house, Mom drove past the big house. Aspen noticed two trucks in the driveway with ladders and tools in the back.

She could not take her eyes off the house. After the conversation at dinner last night, she thought of an idea, and she hoped Noah might be interested. He had not contributed to the conversation the entire trip to and from the school, so it was impossible to read him right now.

Summer school started the third Monday in May and lasted six weeks. They would be there five days a week from eight am till noon, leaving plenty of time in the afternoon for her plan. Aspen knew hoping Noah would join her was a long shot, but she figured there was no harm in asking. If he said no, she would just pursue the idea on her own.

Their other two family cars were delivered while they were at the school. Mom's silver BMW, that even Dad rarely drove, and the 1989 red Chevrolet Iroc convertible was Noah's. He had fallen in love with the Iroc two summers ago when a neighbor put it up for sale. Dad and Mom surprised him with it, a combination Christmas and birthday present since his birthday was the end of November.

At the time, Noah was working at the food stand on the beach and then right after his sixteenth birthday, he started his job as a lifeguard. The job made it easy for him to comply with the agreement he had with his parents, which was to pay half of the cost of the car back to his parents, pay his own insurance and buy his gas.

It was a good set up for Noah for the past year, but now in Sommerville, Aspen wondered how it was going to work.

But even the arrival of the Iroc didn't seem to shake Noah out of his slump. After lunch, he and Aspen sat on the front steps of the *servants' quarters,* as Noah referred to it. Aspen just called it *the little house.* It was hard to call it *home.*

"It's good your car is here."

"I won't have money for gas anyway. Where can I lifeguard here?" Then he sarcastically added, "At the *lake?*"

"Well, you saved me." Aspen took a bite out of an apple. She crunched it slowly, purposely letting the juice run down her chin. Noah hated that, and she was hoping to get a reaction from him, just to break the ice before she presented her plan. Her ploy worked.

"Maybe I should have let you drown." He rolled his eyes at her. "Why do you insist on eating apples that way?"

"To annoy you, of course."

Noah shook his head but said nothing. He picked tiny leaves from a nearby bush tossing them one by one onto the sidewalk.

They sat in silence for some time while Aspen finished her apple. She ate everything but the stem and tossed it into the flower garden, watching it land next to a tiny pebble. Her mother used to tell her if she kept eating the seeds, she would have apples growing in her stomach. At eight, she had concluded that was never going to happen and continued the practice.

Aspen leaned her elbows on her knees, her chin in her hands and waited for the right moment to pop her idea to Noah.

"Aspen?"

"Humm?"

"I have been wondering what made you fall off that swing?"

This is perfect. He is starting the conversation.

Aspen stared at the cement below her feet. She didn't respond at first. When she did, her question surprised Noah. "So, do you believe me. You know, about the old man?"

Noah looked at her in bewilderment. "What does that have to do with— No Aspen. I mean, I don't know. I don't think you are a liar if that's what you mean, you're just a little kooky. What does falling off the swing have to do with the old man you think you saw?"

She continued to stare at the cement. "I don't know. I just wondered what you thought…about that…the old man."

"Have you—seen him again?" Noah seemed to choose his words carefully.

Aspen hesitated. "N…no. I don't know. I'm not sure." Her head still down she turned just enough to peer up at her brother. He looked unconvinced.

"Oh, well, okay," he said, then a long pause. "But *that* I don't believe." Then he hurried to clarify, "About the old man, I mean, yeah maybe, but I mean I don't believe that you have not seen him again, you know, if he really exists," his voice trailed off. "Forget it. I don't know what I mean."

Aspen eyed him carefully before she spoke, "I want to go to the big house *without* Mom and Dad."

Noah opened his mouth, seemingly surprised at the new conversation direction. He sighed instead, "Yeah, well, that idea is out." He mocked Dad, "Do not touch anything."

"Well…they won't have to know. That house is huge." The rest of the sentence rushed from her lips, "We could sneak in, and they would never even know we are there."

Noah raised one eyebrow and scrutinized his younger sister. "Wow. Who is this Aspen? Miss 'I never break a rule.'"

Taking in a deep breath, Aspen hunched her shoulders, "It's the new me." She grinned, "The new Tennessee me. There are some things I want to find out that's all."

"Like what?"

"I'm not sure. Just stuff."

"Oh, well, that will make a great adventure. Looking for nothing."

"Not looking for nothing; looking for something, just not sure what." She looked directly into her brother's eyes. "You *said* you felt something touch you, right?"

Noah shuddered but nodded. "So—"

"Well, this place is a little strange, Noah. You felt someone touch you, I saw an old man, *and* I fell off the swing, *and* I saw…I saw rats."

"Falling off that swing was just weird." He hesitated. "And the rats? Even weirder." Noah turned away. He voluntarily shuddered, puffing his cheeks and blowing air through his lips. "I knew that shed was creepy." He raised his eyebrows.

"How did you get in?"

"The door was unlocked, Noah. I was just looking at stuff."

"Well when Dad I went out there it was locked. I won't go near that place. It made me feel creepy when I was ten feet from it." He shuddered again only this time it seemed involuntary. "What was in there anyway?"

"Just gardening tools, lawnmower, garbage cans. Stuff like that."

Noah twisted his mouth. "Hmmm. And rats?"

"Yes." Aspen leaned forward and looked up into Noah's face. "So, when do we start?"

"Start what?"

"Investigating?"

"Oh. Well—"

"Are you afraid?"

"Afraid? No, I'm not afraid." His face looked indignant. "Not of your dumb ghosts; of Dad. He will kill us."

"Dad will never know," Aspen said quietly.

The corners of Noah's lips curled up. "Hope you're right. 'Cause if you're not, it isn't going to be pretty." He stood and stretched. "We will have a hard time getting away tomorrow. It's Sunday, and Dad wanted to go into Memphis for lunch or something."

"Well, who knows if that will happen? He was also going to take us on a tour of Grandma and Grandpa's house, remember? And that ended the second we got there. Anyway, school starts on Monday, so Mom and Dad will probably start working in the house too."

Noah groaned. "School. I cannot believe we are going to summer school."

"Yeah, but it might not be so bad. At least we can meet some people before we actually start school in the fall."

Noah groaned. "I'm hoping to be out of here before school starts."

Aspen started to challenge that, but instead, she quickly brought him back to her plan. "We can go to the house after school."

"Maybe." Noah yawned and stretched. "We can try."

Aspen could sense his apprehension returning. Even though he did seem somewhat interested, she knew how quickly his mind could change, and in a heartbeat, she could again return to his new public enemy number one, the *little* sister.

Noah was still wrestling with telling his parents about the accident at the lake, but the right time had not presented itself. He left Aspen on the front porch to plan their assault on the big house and went into their own house. He walked straight to the kitchen to the large window that looked out over the backyard.

He tried to see the shed, but the cobblestone path turned just past the garden, and anything beyond there, was blocked from view by trees.

It mortified him to think that he and his sister had to go to any kind of school or program or whatever it was. To Noah, it was just another word for jail.

He contemplated Aspen's proposal. He knew they would be in a lot of trouble if Dad found out and he was surprised that Aspen was so ready and willing to take the chance. Aspen was pretty much an obedient kid. Actually, they both were. They had no reason not to be.

Mom and Dad had always been upfront and open with the two of them...until now.

9

SUMMER SCHOOL

THE REST OF THE weekend was spent finishing the unpacking, and Mom and Dad spent some time in the big house. It had been boring, and Aspen was glad when Monday morning arrived. At least they had an agenda, although Noah still did not share her enthusiasm.

Aspen looked across the classroom at Noah, who was still standing by the door. He had not moved from that spot since they had arrived at school half an hour earlier.

This was not exactly what Aspen had expected this Summer School to be like. Instead of computers or art supplies, when they arrived, they were directed by that same pointy-nosed lady to a musty storage room. The room was filled with old wooden desks with chairs attached and a few tables. The other fourteen students in the room seemed as baffled as she was and at first glance, she thought they all seemed pretty normal, contrary to what Noah had predicted.

The teacher, Mr. Fielden, stood at the front of the class. He was kind of quirky looking. His brown hair jutted in all directions from beneath a Broncos cap which was backward. He wore a white sort of overcoat, more like a scrub from a hospital. The front pocket sagged from the weight of his cell phone and two pens. Underneath, he had on a brown tank top and jeans. He wore Converse tennis shoes with no socks. His eyes constantly moved behind bulky, square black-rimmed glasses, seeming to notice everything going on around him.

Aspen wondered if he dressed like that during the regular school year. She couldn't help but think how well he would fit in in California. This thought made her smile.

"Gather people, new students, Aspen, and Noah Allen. They hail from the sunny beaches of Southern California, and I am positive they are *thrilled* to be here. Get acquainted. Make them feel part of the *family*,"

That comment brought a little waive of chuckles from the small group.

"Now I realize this is not what you had planned for the first day of *Summer School*," Mr. Fielden put particular emphasis on the last two words. "But I told Mr. Gibbons," he turned to Aspen and Noah as if to acknowledge they did not know who Mr. Gibbons was, "our principal, that we would clean this room. Apparently, an antique dealer is interested in some old stuff which could mean some bucks for the school." He rested one hand on one of the desks drumming it with his fingers. "And this stuff is *old*."

"More like ancient," whispered a voice behind Aspen. She turned to see whom it belonged to.

The owner of the voice grinned at Aspen. "I'm serious," she whispered, leaning right up to Aspen's shoulder. "Some of these desks were here when my grandparent's went to school here."

"You are right about that Kiryn," Mr. Fielden looked in their direction as he spoke.

Kiryn straightened up, her long blonde hair whipping Aspen's face when she whirled to face Mr. Fielden. Her cobalt eyes widened, and she pursed her lips. "Oops, sorry," she said lightly holding up one hand in defense.

"Nothing to be sorry about," Mr. Fielden grimaced. "But why don't you share that with the rest of us. Secrets are so…unfair." He lowered his eyes and furrowed his brow.

Kiryn lifted her chin. "Well, I was just saying that some of these desks were here when my grandparents went to this school." She wrinkled her forehead. "And they would be like sixty or something."

"I'll go you one better Miss Whittaker. Some of these desks were here when your *great*-grandparents went to this school." His eyes twinkled a kind of wild, curious sparkle.

"Well, the school is ancient," said another voice belonging to a boy. The entire class, Aspen included, laughed in agreement.

Noah's face was as sullen as ever. "So what do we have to do?" His question surprised Aspen considering his obvious disinterest of the situation.

Mr. Fielden looked squarely at Noah. "What, Mr. Allen? Not excited about our *old stuff?*"

Noah shrugged. "Not really. Just what do we do?"

Mr. Fielden walked over and stood directly in front of Noah. "Know how to get an A in this class?" he said loudly, as though posing the question to everyone. His eyes, however, were fixed on Noah.

Noah didn't change his position but stammered his answer, "Uh, n...no."

Mr. Fielden slid his glasses to the end of his nose. He looked to his right and then to his left before his eyes found Noah's again. There was a disturbing silence, and Aspen sensed a sort of anticipation from the class.

Mr. Fielden threw his arms in the air, and spun in a circle on his heels, taking both Noah and Aspen by surprise, causing Noah to shrink closer to the wall.

The other students joined in the revelry and laughed along with Mr. Fielden. "Humor me! Humor me, people! I am less excited to be here than you are. I would rather be water skiing."

Noah and Aspen exchanged a look that expressed both bewilderment and relief.

Mr. Fielden extended a hand to Noah. Noah hesitated before taking it.

Mr. Fielden vigorously shook Noah's hand. "Humor me, Mr. Allen."

Noah laughed nervously. "Sure, I can humor."

The class laughed, and Aspen noticed Kiryn was giggling the

loudest. She was looking at Noah with evident admiration. The vibe in the room immediately relaxed, and the students moved among the desks.

"Here are rags, water and furniture polish. Clean these suckers up." Mr. Fielden motioned to a table at the front of the room. "I'll go out for snacks." He then disappeared into the hall.

Noah stared after him. *What a complete moron! He sounds as goofy as everyone else here. What's with the accent? We haven't moved to Tennessee, we have moved to the outer limits.*

He shook his head and strolled toward Aspen, who was talking to the girl who said her name was Kiryn.

She's pretty but a little strange. Ha! She and Aspen will be great friends.

His thoughts drifted to a girl back home. *I wonder if...*

Noah was surprised by a sudden catch in his throat.

Now standing next to Aspen he said, "Snacks? Is he for real?" Noah was talking to Aspen, but it was Kiryn who answered.

"Totally. Mr. Fielden's a riot. You won't mind this summer school." She grinned at the siblings. "I'm Kiryn Whittaker, a junior. And you are Aspen and Noah?"

"Yes." Aspen pointed to herself, "Junior." Then to Noah, "Senior."

Noah nodded. He motioned over his shoulder with his thumb, referring to Mr. Fielden. "He is weird. He probably doesn't really water ski. Is there even a lake big enough for that around here?"

"Oh, yes, he does. He has an awesome boat. I'm sure he will take us on it this summer, he always does. He usually goes to Lake Matthews. And yes, it's *way* big—not the ocean of course, but it will do."

"So, are you a *regular* at summer school?" Noah was borderline rude.

"Pretty much. Mr. Fielden is kind of like—my dad."

"*Your dad?*" Noah's cheeks reddened, and Aspen shook her head, embarrassed for her brother.

"Well, not exactly my dad. My uncle. But he is my dad. He has raised me since I was four after my parents were killed. So yes, he is *like* my dad. But not really, if you know what I mean."

Aspen and Noah were staring at Kiryn.

"So, do you call him Uncle Mr. Fielden?" Noah smirked.

Kiryn's face twisted and her eyes narrowed. "No, Dad and sometimes Uncle Rocky, but I don't call him either at school. He is just Mr. Fielden.

"Rocky? What kind of a name—"

"Noah!" Aspen blurted. "Geez."

Kiryn seemed oblivious and just rattled on, "Well, his name is Rockefeller or some dumb thing like that—who would do that to a kid? So, he shortened it to Rocky forever ago." Kiryn abruptly directed the conversation away from herself. "So, you guys are the," she made quotation marks in the air with her fingers, "Allen family."

"What does that mean?" Aspen scrunched her face into a questioning look.

"Well, you have a rep to protect in these here parts," quipped Kiryn. "Legend has it that your family is the wealthiest in Sommerville history, *maybe* in Memphis history."

"Legend?" Noah smirked. "I doubt that. Isn't Elvis from Memphis?"

"Okay," conceded Kiryn. "Except for Elvis." She rolled her eyes, "But I'll bet it is a pretty close race."

Noah chuckled, obviously satisfied with his statement of that fact.

Aspen barely heard Noah's last comment when the classroom door opened and quite possibly the most gorgeous guy she had ever seen strolled toward them.

"Well, that is because you don't really *know*." The guy was saying.

Easily six-four with chin-length almost black hair and emerald green eyes that were so distracting Aspen had to look away. His T-shirt hugged biceps that had spent considerable time in a weight room.

Aspen's thoughts surprised even her when suddenly she pictured that guy *without* the T-shirt—on the beach in California. She wanted to quiet the rush of butterflies in her stomach, but her heart was pounding so loud she was sure he could hear it. She felt completely out of control, and just gaped at him.

10

FLYING DESK

As the boy approached them, he smiled. His skin was very dark, but Aspen wasn't sure what ethnicity he was.

The boy repeated, "It's because you think you don't actually know."

"And you do?" The sarcasm was dripping in Noah's voice and he was visibly annoyed at Aspen's starstruck look.

"I do." The boy smiled. "I'm Gavin." He was looking directly at Aspen but reached for Noah's hand.

When Noah ignored the gesture, Gavin turned his full attention on Aspen.

Noah scowled and looked at his sister. He rolled his eyes behind Gavin's back but made sure Aspen could see him.

"How's that?" Noah's tone was flat as well as demanding.

Gavin turned from Kiryn to face Noah. "What's up with you, man? It is a simple fact, one that we all know about your family, but obviously, you *don't* know."

Noah's nostrils flared. "I know all I need to know. I don't need you to tell me about *my family*." He grabbed Aspen's arm and pulled her a few inches closer to him.

"Well, apparently, you do." Gavin brushed Noah off with his casual comment. He turned, winked at Aspen, and then walked away, seemingly disinterested.

Kiryn broke the awkward silence, "Well if you want to know more." She waved her hand from one side of the room to the other,

"Any of us will be glad to fill you in."

Some of the students standing nearby gave quick agreeable nods. "I'm interested," began Aspen, but she stopped when she caught Noah's disapproving look. She would address that subject later, right now, Noah was not only her brother but also the only person in this room that she actually *knew*.

Kiryn gave her an understanding smile. "Later," she whispered and Aspen nodded. Noah didn't notice. He was too busy being irritated.

Aspen retrieved a towel and a bottle of furniture polish from the table. Noah did too, but he retreated from the group, selecting a lone desk that was pushed up against the far wall.

Aspen started toward her brother but changed her mind. She sighed, and being careful not to annoy Noah more, she steered clear of Gavin too. She went to the desks next to the window.

Avoiding Kiryn on the other hand was a totally different challenge—even if Aspen had wanted to avoid her. Aspen immediately liked this chatty pretty girl.

"Hey, Aspen look at this." Kiryn was sitting on the floor looking up at the underside of a desk.

Aspen leaned down. "What?"

"This guy carved his name in this desk."

"So did these two people," the voice belonged to a short, stocky girl with bubbly pink cheeks. She giggled. "We would get in major trouble for scratching up our desks." She giggled again. "Hi, I'm Roxy."

Aspen smiled. "Hi—"

"Yep, that would be called vandalism," Gavin said and glanced at Aspen who turned away quickly but not before she smiled.

The carving in the desk piqued Aspen's curiosity. She casually wiped the dust off the top of a desk which was near her, but she scanned other desks close by for names of her grandparents. She looked across the room again to ask if Noah might be interested in helping her, but he was not looking in her direction, so she continued checking desks.

When Aspen wasn't looking, Noah scowled at her. *What a bunch of dimwits.* It irritated him that he was bothered by this seemingly quick connection Aspen had made with this new girl. Noah had never made friends as quickly as Aspen, and it appeared Tennessee would be no exception. He was irritated too by the way this Kiryn girl made him feel.

He glared at Gavin annoyed by the guy's self-confidence. Noah didn't like the way he coolly approached Aspen either.

Who does Romeo think he is telling us he knows more about our family than we do? This guy is a pain in the butt, and he had better stay away from my sister.

Aspen observed several desks that surrounded her. The wooden desks were all the same size, each with an attached chair.

Aspen lifted the top of one of the desks to find an empty cubby. A quick glance told her there was nothing carved inside. She closed the lid and began inspecting the next desk, cleaning as she went. She carefully checked each desk, hoping to find one of her grandparent's names. She found Benson, Kirk and a ton of Dixons but no Allen's.

Aspen started toward another group of desks, passing a single desk that was separated from the others. As she brushed by it, she felt a twinge in the back of her neck.

She paused, turning back to that desk. She bent over when she noticed a name carved on the front. *Kenneth Lloyd Dixon.* There was that twinge again. She stared at the name, but it meant nothing to her, so she dismissed the feeling and moved on.

She walked closer to the windows. Five desks had been pushed together, forming a misshapen circle.

In one window, a shadow of a person caught her eye—hesitating only for a second—she walked directly to the window to see what—or who—caused it. She leaned on the window sill, observing the spacious courtyard. Not even a tree, which was odd considering they were in the land of trees and the entire high school was surrounded by them.

But the shadow was there, all right. However Aspen couldn't see anything—inside or out—that would cast a shadow like that. She looked up at the cloudless sky and shrugged.

Wow, Noah is right. I am becoming a basket case. We are on the second story of the school. Who could be looking in a window up here?

She tried to ignore it and lifted the lid on another desk. It creaked a little as she took the piece of wood that was inside and propped the top open. Aspen leaned over and looked closely inside the cubby.

Laughter.

Aspen froze. Listening. A rustling sound and a breeze coming from the same closed window lifted her hair from her shoulders.

Instinctively, Aspen again started toward the window, but then she stopped and looked around the room. No one was paying any attention. Even chatty Kiryn was busily shining the only metal on one of the desks.

Drawn to the window, she walked quickly now, anxious to get over to it before anyone noticed her odd behavior. Her back to the window, she surveyed the students in the room. Not one person was even looking in her direction. Nor were they *laughing*—at least not this particular laughter.

She turned and stared through the glass. *Laughter and a breeze from a closed widow—I am a total idiot. No wonder Mom and Dad think I am crazy.*

A loud scraping sound from behind her caused Aspen to spin around just as a random desk slammed into her hip and sent her sprawling. She rolled over onto her back as the desk crashed onto the wood floor right next to her head.

"Aspen!" Noah was by her side almost immediately. She moaned when he hauled her up from the floor and helped her stand. "What happened?"

Aspen didn't know what to say. The look on Noah's face was the same as everyone else in the room—bewilderment.

Kiryn and one of the other boys were standing the fallen desk upright.

"Who pushed that desk?" Kiryn demanded but then answered her own question. "It's like it just flew across the floor and smacked right into you."

Aspen rubbed her hip. "I didn't see anyone push the desk. It was…it was just…there."

"Do you want to sit down, Aspen?" Kiryn plopped a chair in front of her.

Aspen sank into it and gave her new friend a weak smile. "That was embarrassing," she mumbled

Noah stood motionless next to his sister. He scanned the room.

Everyone was staring at Aspen. No one said anything.

The door flew open, and Mr. Fielden breezed into the room, supporting a large box. "I have soda and snacks!" he announced but then he stopped. "What's going on?" He dropped the box on the table with a loud thump and walked into the middle of the group.

"Aspen fell, well she didn't fall, well a desk made her fall, but—"

Mr. Fielden held up both hands palms forward to stop Kiryn's incessant chatter. Kiryn clamped her mouth shut and stared wide-eyed at their teacher. Mr. Fielden turned to Noah, "What happened?"

Noah looked at Aspen then jabbed his thumb in Kiryn's direction. "Pretty much what she said."

Mr. Fielden pursed his lips. "That's it?"

"Pretty much," Aspen confirmed. "It was just an accident." Then she mumbled, looking at Noah, "I seem to have a lot of those lately."

"Are you okay?" Mr. Fielden knelt down on one knee beside Aspen. Without looking back, he waved his hand. "Okay people, back to business."

She nodded. The crowd dispersed, heading directly for the box of snacks.

Undiscernible comments drifted through the air from all directions as the students grabbed their coveted snacks and went back to the task of cleaning the old desks.

Aspen stood. "Ohhhhh," she moaned. Noah gently pushed her shoulders, sitting her back on the chair. She sighed. "Thanks, Noah. I'm good."

"I know," said Noah. "But I am beginning to wonder if you are going to survive Tennessee." He took a deep breath letting the air escape making a kind of flapping sound with his lips. He walked away and returned seconds later. He put a Coke and a small bag of cookies on a desk near his sister. Noah looked at her intently for a few seconds and then walked away again.

Kiryn had been unusually quiet—at least considering how much she had talked up until now. She was sitting on a desk next to Aspen swinging her legs, her arms crossed over her chest. "So."

Aspen looked up. "What?"

"I like you! I'm glad you moved here." She grinned, and her eyes sparkled. She jumped off the desk and crossed the room to the snack box.

I'm not.

Aspen twisted stretching her leg and wounded hip as she looked curiously at the desk that had hit her. A flash of a teenage boy sitting in the chair caught her off guard, and she closed her eyes. *What? Why?*

"So, you're okay, right?"

Aspen jumped at the sound of Gavin's voice, and she opened her eyes. *The desk was...just a desk. No boy.*

Gavin stood right next to her.

"I'm fine. Clumsy but fine." She could feel her cheeks getting hot, and she knew she was blushing. She hated that she blushed so easily.

Gavin had two sodas and a bag of potato chips. He lifted one bottle of Coke. "I didn't know you already had one."

"Oh, yeah. Thanks. Noah got it for me."

Aspen found it difficult to look directly into Gavin's eyes. They were the most striking color of green she had ever seen, almost iridescent. She glanced absently at the window where the breeze, the shadow, and the laughter came from.

When she turned back, Gavin had the most curious look on his face, and his engaging eyes studied her.

As though being pulled back from some distant thought, he said, "I see that. Okay, well—" he suddenly seemed anxious. "Better clean a desk for the team." He smiled and placed the Coke on the desk next to her other one. "Injured girls get two."

Kiryn stood at Aspen's side again, and they watched Gavin walk away. She turned to Aspen, and as though reading her thoughts, she said, "I know, I know. Soooo good looking."

Embarrassed, Aspen laughed nervously. "Has he lived here his whole life too? What grade is he in?" The questions rushed out. Aspen realized it and tried to look nonchalant, waiting for Kiryn to answer.

Kiryn laughed. "Pretty much. His family actually has two houses. One here and another in Memphis. The one here is on Mystic Lake, near your grandpa's place, you know the 'Allen Manor.' She made quotation marks in the air with her fingers. They bought that house about five years ago."

"Wait, what? Really?" Aspen's eyebrows shot up, and her eyes widened.

"Which should I answer first?" Kiryn continued noticeably amused by Aspen's obvious confusion. "Well, first of all the Allen Manor is *your* house, I mean you know the big house, the *family* house. As for Gavin, when he was twelve his parents got a divorce, and his mom married a guy with twin boys who are three years older than Gavin. They are both in college now, so Gavin and his mom spend more time here. By the way, he is a senior. He just turned seventeen." She paused as if waiting to see if Aspen was keeping up, then she continued, "Rocky is his dad."

"So wait. He is your brother? No, cousin?"

Aspen's surprised look made Kiryn laugh. "He is actually no blood relation to me. My mom is Rocky's sister. So he is my kinda, sorta cousin."

Aspen's eyes widened. "Your cous—" But then her mind went a different direction. "And that's another thing? Mystic Lake?"

Kiryn laughed easily. "Lot's to learn, huh? It's just a name that the people around here made up. It's been called that for as long as I can remember though. Sometimes in the early morning, actually before it gets light, a kind of mist comes off the lake. It's kind of strange because it doesn't happen all the time and no one knows what causes it. It's like steam more than a mist, and it is like the lake is hot, but it isn't. I heard there was a search once for an underground thermal spring or something, but they didn't find anything. It's private property, so the city doesn't get involved. Everyone tells stories about the lake, but no one has ever proven any of it."

Aspen shuddered. *I saw that mist.*

Kiryn gestured with her hand. "You know, mist. Mysterious, mystic kind of came from all of it. You might have seen it."

Kiryn's voice seemed far away to Aspen. She shook her head, "Uh, no. I have only been to the lake once."

A cold chill swept over Aspen. What did it mean? Why was this happening to her? What, if anything did it have to do with her falling off the swing? And the laughter—the soft, soothing laughter. Who was that, and why could she hear it?

"Hey? Hello?"

Aspen became aware of Kiryn lightly tapping her shoulder. "S… sorry. I…was just thinking."

"Obviously." Kiryn jumped off the desk and picked up her towel. "We had better get to work." Then she added quickly, "Sure you're okay?"

Aspen nodded. She tried to process all of the new information. Allen Manor? Mystic Lake? Mr. Fielden is Gavin's dad? She picked up her wet towel and began wiping down the desk next to her. She bent down to wash the front and gasped. "Noah!"

Everyone looked up.

Aspen quickly dispelled any notion there was something wrong. "No, it's nothing. I mean, it's something." She shook her head as if to clear her thoughts. "Noah, I found Grandpa's desk."

Noah crossed the room, and Aspen noticed the glare he gave Gavin as he did.

Aspen read the name.

"Jackson Humphrey Allen."

The name was scrawled rather than written. Aspen ran her hand across the grooves in the wood that had been made by the carving.

"Aspen, that isn't Grandpa's desk. He was David Jackson Allen. This must be our *great*-grandpa's desk." Noah gave a low whistle, "These desks really are ancient."

"Told you," Kiryn said, and Aspen grinned. She was watching Noah, amused that he suddenly seemed intrigued.

Feeling someone looking at her, she looked over her shoulder. It was Gavin. He smiled, and his incredible green eyes seemed to look right into her soul. Her entire body tingled, and she felt beads of sweat forming on the back of her neck.

The boy Gavin—now he is worth the move to Sommerville.

She smiled back, but she did not look at Noah. For just this second, she didn't care what he thought.

11

BRICK WALL

WHEN SCHOOL ENDED, ASPEN and Noah drove straight home, and after grabbing a bottle of water, they started up the path. This time, Aspen ran ahead of Noah. Her hip hurt, but it wasn't killing her. Besides, her ribs, arm, and hands hurt too, so it was not a big deal. She was getting used to all of her flesh wounds.

She was grateful Mom and Dad were not home after school, so she did not have to explain more injuries. It wouldn't have been that big of a deal she guessed, but this was her second mishap in a week—uncharacteristic for her normal athletic abilities. In fact, she couldn't think of any injuries she had in the past, none significant anyway.

When they reached the base of the steps, her hip started to ache. She had not even checked to see if she had a bruise. She leaned against the railing, opened her water bottle, and chugged half of it down without stopping.

Noah had stopped at the last turn and was just walking up to meet her. "Everyone talks funny."

Aspen wrinkled her nose. "I know, it's just their accent though. I think it's kind of cute."

"Of course you do." He eyed her for a second, then shrugged. "How do you plan to get in the house?" Noah opened his water and drank the entire thing. Then he crushed the plastic bottle in his hand and dropped it next to the path.

"Noah, that is evidence."

He rolled his eyes. "For who? The FBI? Geez, Aspen, get a grip. No one even lives out here but us and no one—okay except maybe Dad—even cares if we are up here." He motioned toward the bottle. "I will pick it up on the way back. How do you plan to get into the house?"

Aspen scowled at him. She hadn't given much thought about how to get in. "I just figure the doors will be open. Mom and Dad are in there." She started up the steps."

"Uh-huh. Just going to march through the front door," it was a statement, not a question. But then Noah changed the subject, "Did you get your phone?" With that, he gave a low grunt and followed Aspen. Then he added, "I hate these steps."

"Me too." She grabbed the rails with both hands and lunged forward. "And yes, my phone was on my bed. A letter from Krista too."

"A letter? That's weird."

"I know. Actually, it's a card. Maybe because I haven't answered any emails. But still, good point."

"Well, it helps to have connections with the outside world. Without our phones or the Internet, it's like we're living on another planet. What did Krista have to say?"

"Mom said we should have Internet by the end of the week," she was trying to talk and breathe at the same time. "I didn't read it yet." She paused for a second, realizing she had set the all-important letter aside, a little surprised for doing so. "I wanted to wait until tonight when I am not in a hurry."

"Well, you have your phone now. You could just call her."

"Yeah. It should be charged a little when we get back. What is California like two or three hours behind us?"

"Two, I think."

Aspen stopped halfway up the steps. "Ohhhh," she moaned. "Do you hear that?"

Noah came up beside her. "Lawnmowers. Wouldn't you know it?

Guess Monday is the gardeners' day."

Aspen twisted her mouth. "I hadn't thought of anything like this."

"You haven't thought of much—" her scowl stopped him in mid-sentence.

"Well, we can't go that way. I don't want anyone telling Dad we were up here."

"Any other ideas, Sherlock?" Noah teased.

Aspen's scowl only intensified. She was irritable. She hadn't sat down at all since school. She envisioned a long hot bath, assuming she could get the bathroom to herself that long.

Noah turned and walked off the path into the trees. "I don't think we will have to go far. The trees are so thick—won't take much to be inconspicuous. Exactly *who* are we hiding from?"

Aspen didn't answer. She just followed him into the trees.

The ground immediately inclined. The dirt was black and damp with a sprinkle of leaves and sticks, but the trees were close enough that they could grab onto some of the lower limbs to pull themselves along.

It wasn't long until they came to a clearing, but the trees on the other side of it were so thick. Aspen moaned and collapsed on the ground.

Noah looked down at her. "Wait here."

She just nodded and massaged her sore hip.

Noah disappeared into the trees, but she could still hear him. In a few minutes, he was back. "It's practically straight up."

She thought of the steps. *Of course, it is.*

Aspen moaned, but she suddenly felt a wave of anger. "How in the heck did that desk hit me anyway?"

The tone of her voice must have surprised Noah, and he turned around. "That is the question of the hour."

His mood suddenly turned sour, and Aspen was sorry she brought it up.

"Someone pushed it. There is no other explanation, but the coward didn't own up." He picked up a big stick and chucked it like a spear into the trees. Aspen heard it clatter before it fell to the ground. "Probably that Gavin guy."

Aspen took a deep breath. "Oh, Noah. It wasn't Gavin."

"Figured you would say that. A pretty face does not make a good guy, Aspen. You should know that."

It doesn't make a bad guy either.

This argument would go nowhere fast, and Aspen knew it. She held out her hand to Noah. "Help me up?"

He eyed her suspiciously. "What? No retaliation?" He grabbed her arm and pulled her to her feet.

"No. Not today." Aspen brushed the dirt off the back of her shorts. "You actually like that freak, don't you?"

"How could I like him? I don't even know him. You just don't like him because he has long hair."

"That's stupid. *I* have long hair." Noah turned and walked into the trees.

Aspen followed. "Yeah, but now you're not unique."

"Like I care about that."

But Aspen knew she had hit a nerve.

Noah didn't look at her, and neither of them spoke as they climbed.

Within minutes they were at the top of the hill.

"I don't care about the dude's long hair okay?" Noah blurted. "I just think he's a wise guy."

"Okay."

Noah scowled, but Aspen didn't respond. He turned and walked out of the trees, and she followed.

They were on the side of the house where Aspen had seen the garden plot from the window. There was a door half-hidden by overgrown vines and a tree that grew close to the house. It seemed odd that the hedge had been allowed to cover the door as all the other bushes were neatly trimmed.

Noah slid past her. "Let me go first. I can move quicker." He looked at her hip, raised his eyebrows, and nodded quickly. "Right now, I mean."

Aspen nodded. "Whatever," she conceded.

He darted past the garden plot and along the edge of the patio. He glanced back to make sure Aspen was watching and then over-dramatized the whole thing, acting like he was in a scene from an action movie. He ducked behind a tall potted plant and then dived behind lawn furniture. Rolling from his stomach to his back and then his stomach again, crawling low across the patio. When he reached the house, he plastered himself against it and peeking through a bush he parted with both hands, he gave her a thumbs-up, motioning for Aspen to come.

She got to her feet, rolled her eyes, and walked deliberately across the middle of the patio. When she was next to Noah, she folded her arms across her chest. "Very funny." She pretended to be annoyed, but his playfulness made her smile. "What next?"

Noah laughed. "Just setting the mood little sister. Setting the mood."

"Whatever."

The door was to their left. They exchanged a quick glance, and then Noah stepped around her and reached for the doorknob. "Well, let's just go in." He grinned.

Please, please, please be open. Aspen stopped her pleading thoughts. Oh, wow, I am pathetic. The world is in turmoil, and I am praying for a stupid door to open. But then she silently pleaded again.

Noah's eyes widened when the knob easily rotated, but then his face fell when it just spun in his hand. Aspen scooted next to him, looking over his shoulder. Noah pushed on the door. It moved slightly. "We need something to pry it open."

They both looked around.

"Wait here, I want to check something." Noah ran toward the front of the house but returned almost immediately. "Bad idea," he said as he passed her and went to the back of the house. He crouched behind the hedge peering over it and then, bracing himself on a tree with one hand he leaped over the hedge and disappeared.

Beads of sweat trickled down Aspen's face and neck and made a river down the middle of her back.

Why am I so afraid of Dad finding out? I'm not afraid of my own Dad? Well, I didn't use to be, but he's different now. Noah, hurry up!

Just then he came from the back of the house.

"Why didn't you jump the hedge again?" she teased although relieved to see him.

"Turns out there is a path." Noah grinned. He held up the spoils of his venture, a small garden shovel, and a screwdriver. "Found these on the patio back there. No one was around. There were too many guys in the front yard. Looks like they are loading their trucks," his loud whisper was more like a hiss.

"Good job," she patted his shoulder and Noah frowned down his nose at her.

He skirted around her to the door. "Hope this works." He dropped the shovel in the dirt next to a bush.

Noah stepped back and looked at the doorframe. "What the— This door opens out. How weird is that? Entrance doors open in, not out."

"Pull then."

Noah looked back at her. "Do ya think?" He grasped the door handle again and pulled. The door didn't budge.

"Hurry, Noah."

"I *am*." Using the screwdriver, he pried at the metal around the doorknob.

The metal was so old it creased easily, but getting the screwdriver under it without completely destroying it wasn't so simple.

Aspen started to feel as though someone was looking at them and cautiously turned around. Nothing. She breathed deeply, keeping her body turned at an angle now so that she could keep watch for anyone that may approach. She kept looking from Noah to the backyard, then to the front yard and back again. It seemed like it was taking forever. "Can I help?"

"Nope," Noah's answer was barely audible.

Click.

They both froze for a brief second staring at each other's surprised faces.

"Lucky this door is so old, I was able to wiggle it enough to unlock it." Noah used his thumb and the screwdriver to press the creased metal back into place. It was *mostly* fixed, but it was scratched, and close inspection would reveal it had been tampered with.

Noah pulled on the doorknob. It was tight. He ran his fingers along the edges. "It's been painted shut. Remember when Mom did that to the cabinets in the garage?"

Aspen did remember. Dad teased Mom for weeks. Noah and Dad had to use razor blades to cut through the paint, separating the doors from the cabinets to get them open.

Noah worked the end of the screwdriver between the door and the frame and pulled down in short strokes, loosening the paint as it went.

Aspen could see that razor blades would be much easier, and cleaner.

"Get the shovel, Aspen. Do the same on the bottom of the door."

Obediently Aspen got down on her knees and wiggled the point of the shovel under the door. "It is so quiet around here. Makes me nervous." Even the lawnmowers were quiet now.

"Yeah," said Noah absently. "Kind of eerie." Then without looking down. "Focus Aspen."

"K." She again wiggled the shovel and slowly worked it under the door. It grated along the cement as she worked it between the door and the metal on the threshold. When she was about halfway across the bottom, the door lurched toward her. She crawled backward, moving out of Noah's way so he could open it.

Noah wiped his forehead with the back of his hand. The late afternoon sun had not dropped behind the trees yet, and the bushes next to the house provided little relief. They were both dripping with sweat.

"We should have brought more water. I didn't think this would be so hard or take so long," Aspen said absently. "It's so humid here."

Noah nodded but kept his attention on the door. "Obviously, this door is not used regularly—" He jerked it, and the door flew open. "Or *ever*."

Aspen's gasp was more like a shriek as their elation turned to immediate disappointment. Behind the door was a solid brick wall.

"What is *this* all about?" Aspen wasn't asking Noah, she just threw the question out into the air. It felt like her heart sank all the way down to her knees.

"Anything I can help you with?"

12

THE GARDNER

ASPEN'S HIGH-PITCHED SCREECH scared Noah almost as much as the husky voice behind them. Aspen dropped the shovel and lunged into Noah, clinging to his arm with both hands. They both whirled around to face a huge muscular man.

Dark sunglasses made it impossible to read his expression, but the corners of his mouth turned down. He stood with his feet wide apart his thick arms folded across his chest. Shaggy dishwater blonde hair protruded from the sweat-stained blue bandana tied around his head. His clothes were covered with grass and dirt, his hands were dirty, and sweat ran freely down the sides of his face and neck.

Neither Aspen nor Noah spoke. They just stared into the dark sunglasses of this unwelcome arrival.

"I *said*, anything I can help you with?"

Noah opened his mouth to answer, but men's voices approaching from the backyard distracted him, and his mouth clamped shut.

Aspen felt as though she would pass out. She glanced quickly around. There was no place to run, and besides, how would they ever get away from this guy?

Her stomach was reeling, and her mouth felt as though it were stuffed with cotton. Clinging to Noah's arm, her fingernails dug into his skin. He didn't even flinch.

Without taking his eyes from the frightened kids, the man turned his head and yelled in the direction of the voices.

"Sean?"

"Yep?" called one of the voices, but they continued to move closer. "You and Blake gather up those tools back there and take them around to the truck." The big man's eyes darted between Aspen and Noah, and he still did not look toward the voices.

"Sure thing," called the same voice and the footsteps retreated. "Okay, now—" began the man.

"Drew!" called the same voice, and the running footsteps came back towards the side of the house.

"What?" the big man yelled, clearly annoyed. "Are we done for the day?"

"Yeah. Wrap it up!"

The footsteps stopped and started again; only they were going away. Aspen listened until she couldn't hear them anymore. Sweat ran into the corners of Aspen's mouth, stinging her eyes, and she squeezed them shut.

Drew breathed deeply, "Well?" He twisted his mouth, but he did not budge from his stance.

Again Noah opened his mouth to speak.

Footsteps again, only this time they were coming from the front of the house. The suspense was unbelievable to Aspen. She wanted to scream, but she was afraid that if she moved even a tiny bit, she would pass out or throw up or both.

Drew mumbled something unintelligible under his breath and looked toward the sound. His expression changed immediately. He lunged forward, and with one sweep of his big arm, he moved Aspen and Noah aside.

Aspen stumbled, but Noah caught her. Still holding her arm, he moved her against the house and then stepped in front of her.

The big man quickly closed the door, turned and casually leaned against it. He scooped up the small garden shovel and motioned for Noah to drop the screwdriver on the ground.

Noah obeyed.

"Don't say anything," the man hissed.

"Oh, it's you, Drew."

Dad! Dad? Oh. My. Gosh! We are so in trouble! Aspen shrieked, but no sound came out of her throat. She looked from Noah to Drew. "That's our D—"

"Shhhh," Drew hissed. His expression did not change, and Aspen hated that she could not see his eyes.

Aspen gulped the words back, and they felt like huge metal balls forcing their way down her throat.

Noah stood like a statue.

Apparently, Dad had seen Drew, but bushes must have blocked his view of his kids.

"Mr. J." Drew grinned. "Look what I found." He jerked his thumb toward Noah and Aspen.

"Hey, Dad," it was barely a whisper. Noah lifted his hand and waved.

Dad stopped. His expression was one of confusion and aggravation. "What are you two doing up here?" He looked directly at Aspen. "Did you scream a moment ago?"

Aspen nodded.

"A huge spider. We were just—"

Drew interrupted Noah, "I saw them walking around the back." He turned to Aspen. "Then I heard her scream. I just found out who they were," he lied. "Could have guessed though. We all knew you had two kids."

Aspen nodded absently. *Are we lying to Dad?*

Drew continued, "I was doing some work over here and grabbed this guy," he nodded in Noah's direction. "He was just going to help me bring the big ladder around," the lie continued.

Dad eyed them all suspiciously, "Did you fall?" He was looking at Aspen's dirty knees.

"Yes, we were—"

"Aspen, are you okay?" Dad studied her face.

Aspen nodded. "It's so hot, and I fell when we were… when we—"

Noah said, "We were hiking through the trees. It's a pretty good hike from the servants' quarters to here." He brushed dirt from his knees.

Dad didn't look convinced and he said to Aspen, "You seem to be falling a lot lately." He turned to Noah, "Maybe you shouldn't be dragging her up the hill."

Aspen quickly objected when she realized Dad was blaming Noah. "No, it was my idea. It was just steeper than I expected. I should have worn jeans."

"Yeah, well you're not in *California* anymore," Dad scoffed and turned to Drew. "Aren't there any *men* working with you today?"

Dad's California statement dripped with sarcasm.

"Yes, sir. They were just all tied up at the time. Just thought I would get to know the kids."

"Well, they have other things to do." Dad scowled at both of them. "At *home*."

Noah sighed. "Yep, we do. Just looking around, Dad." Noah didn't seem as fearful now. "You didn't seem to mind when we went to the lake," he challenged.

Aspen winced at his sudden boldness.

Dad studied Noah for a few seconds before he said anything.

"I didn't mind *that*, but I don't see any reason for you to be poking around here, and I don't want you nosing around the house. I told you there are things I don't want moved."

"Okay, Dad," Noah said flatly.

Aspen's mind was racing watching the exchange between her dad and her brother. It was like watching two strangers, and it made her heart ache.

Dad nodded toward Drew. "And you kids don't need to bother folks."

"No bother at all, Mr. J. Nice kids." Drew seemed all too willing to convince their dad that everything was okay.

Why is he calling him Mr. J?

"We were actually wondering about—" Noah turned to look squarely at Drew who was looking directly at him.

Drew's lips formed a thin line, and he ever so slightly shook his head.

"About what?" Dad was getting agitated.

"About…about working for him," Noah motioned toward Drew.

"I need to make some money to pay for my car."

Dad shook his head. "We'll figure that out. You don't need to work for Drew. He already has plenty of help with the yard."

Aspen had barely breathed from the second Noah challenged their dad, but now she slowly let the air out of her chest, hoping Dad would not notice.

Noah shrugged. "Just a thought."

"Think of something else." Dad gave Drew a wary look and turned to walk away. He stopped and turned around. "Does Mom know you are up here?"

"Probably not. She wasn't home when we left. Isn't she with you?" said Noah.

"No. Well, she should be inside. I had to run to Memphis." He turned again. "Better go in and tell her you're here. She'll probably want to hear how school went." He stopped to look at Drew. "If you are through with them, of course," he added dryly.

Drew twisted his mouth and nodded. "Yep." He flicked one hand toward Dad, almost a half salute. "Later Mr. J."

Dad's eyes narrowed. "Just call me Jackson. You can lose the Mr. J. stuff."

Drew nodded. "Whatever you say," and under his breath, *"Mr. J."*

"I say," Dad snapped, and he turned to walk away. "You kids need to get some water," he called over his shoulder.

"Hey, Dad?" Aspen called after him.

Dad looked back but didn't stop walking.

"Thanks for the cell phones."

Dad waved again, and they all waited until he had disappeared around the corner.

13

CARD FROM KRISTA

"Who are you?" Noah demanded. "And why are you calling our dad Mr. J.?"

"Drew," the big man said flatly. He picked up the screwdriver and shovel and thrust them toward Noah. "That's none of your business."

When Drew lifted his hand, Aspen saw something she had not noticed before. The pinky finger on his left hand was missing down to the knuckle. It made her shiver.

"Those are yours." Noah shoved both hands in his pockets and kept them there.

Drew looked surprised, and a low chuckle escaped his throat. "Oh yeah." He dropped his hand to his side with the tools still in it and then checked the door. "No need to lock it, I'm sure it's broken anyway." His face wore a wry smile. He turned and strolled across the patio towards the backyard.

"Hey." Noah took two steps toward Drew. Aspen grabbed his arm.

Drew stopped and slowly turned around. "Leave it alone, kid." He waved his free hand toward the house. "Your mom wants you." He disappeared behind the bushes.

Noah brushed Aspen's hand away, his own hands clenched into tight fists. "Who does that guy—?"

"Not who? What?" Aspen's voice was quivering. "What was he— Why did he cover for us?"

Noah didn't respond.

Aspen started to walk toward the front of the house, pulling Noah along by his arm, wishing the sick feeling in her stomach would go away.

Noah shrugged her hand off again but walked with her, "What a jerk."

"Well, he didn't throw us under the bus. That is something."

"Whatever. He was covering for himself, not us. I don't trust that guy."

"He may not have been so nice if Dad hadn't shown up." Aspen gave a forced shiver. "I thought he was going to tell Dad we were trying to get into the house."

"Naw, that dude is up to something." Noah narrowed his eyes, and his jaw tightened. "And I—"

Aspen looked at him sideways. "We."

"*We* are going to find out what it is."

That satisfied Aspen, but it did not quiet her unsettled stomach.

They rounded the corner of the house. There was only one truck in the driveway, and no one was in the front yard. The relief Aspen felt rushed through her like a calming, cool breeze.

"Guess we had better go talk to Mom," Noah spoke the words slow and deliberate. He leaped onto the front porch and plopped down on the step.

"So why are we sitting here? Mom's probably inside."

"I don't *want* to talk to Mom," he said flatly.

Aspen stepped onto the porch, aware now that the ache in her hip was still there. "Noah, Mom hasn't done anything."

He sighed loudly. "Really? She let Dad move us here." He shrugged. "Okay, I know." He motioned to her hip, "You are not going to be able to hide that from her."

Aspen nodded. "I know."

"What is our next move?'

She looked toward the front door of the house. "Talk to Mom."

They both looked toward the truck in the driveway when the engine started. It was Drew. He cast them a side-glance, put his finger to his lips as if to say "shhh," then he laughed and drove away.

Jackson went inside the house, but instead of finding Suzann, he went quickly into the library and closed the door. He turned the tiny key in the lock, rifled through some papers and finally pulled a small box from the bottom desk drawer.

He unfolded the letter and read, again, from the middle of the second page:

Seriously, Jackson, I don't know what you're hiding from. You haven't been to see Mom and Dad, or me for that matter, in years. At this point, I am your only living relative, and I have done more than my share around here. Grandpa had his hands in so many things in this town, and Dad didn't settle half of them. Many people seem to think they are entitled to something, although I am not sure what that is. I have never gotten involved in Dad's business affairs.

You understand this stuff better than I do and Jerry wants nothing to do with it.

There are a lot of unanswered questions that you could probably to get to the bottom of.

Again, I have no idea why you are so afraid to come to Sommerville, but you are long overdue. It's your turn.

Jackson felt beads of sweat forming on the back of his neck and face. He mopped his forehead with his sleeve and then stared up at two large paintings on the opposite wall—his grandfather and his dad.

"I wish you would have listened to me when I was a little kid, Dad, but you didn't. I had to escape this place to get away from the crap I was living with." His eyes shifted to the painting of his grandfather. "This had to have started with you, Granddad. I hate

Sommerville, and I think I hate you."

"Jackson?"

Jackson straightened and took a deep breath. He tucked the letter back inside the box and buried it in the bottom of the drawer and quickly locked it.

"I'm...in here, Suzann!"

Aspen curled up on her bed. Her hot bath felt wonderful, and now her bruised hip rested on an ice pack.

Telling Mom had not been as stressful as they had thought it would be. Both she and Noah were surprised by Mom's almost apathetic response. She sympathized with Aspen's badly bruised hip, but somehow misunderstood and thought Aspen fell over the desk. Aspen chose not to clarify just to avoid confusion or trying to explain something she did not even understand herself.

Mom didn't seem to be concerned that she and Noah were at the big house, even though they did not have permission. Although it was not clear that they actually *needed* permission, they purposefully had not been upfront with their parents.

Noah drove Aspen to the little house in Mom's BMW, and he didn't even complain about having to wait to take his shower. She knew he was all wrapped up in the Drew issue, and she couldn't help but feel happy, in a weird sort of way, that Noah now had his own interest in the house, but right now she didn't care about any of it. She was so tired all she wanted to do was rest.

She picked up the square white envelope from Krista and ran her fingernail under the edge then pulled out the card. The picture on the front of two little girls sitting on the beach playing with shovels and a sand bucket made her laugh. Krista had scrawled *Miss My Favorite Sand Buddy* across the front of the card.

A sudden rush of tears stung Aspen's eyes. She piled her pillows up on her bed, stretched out on her back, and leaned against them. When she was comfortable, she opened the card and started to read.

Hey Aspen,

So I am pretty sure you are not getting any of my emails. Did you move to another planet or something?

Miss you so much! I have no idea what I am going to do this summer. Everything seems so empty without you. I am not very excited to go surfing ,and the Junior Lifeguard program doesn't even sound fun, but I'm going anyway. ☹ It starts tomorrow.

I cannot believe you moved! PLEASE PLEASE PLEASE!! Come back! We have been BFFs since we were two or something like that. Wahhh! I hate this!

Mom said maybe I could come and visit when you guys get settled.

That would be cool, huh?

Well, just CALL ME!!! I know you will have a phone soon, RIGHT??? Do you have a new number? Oh duh, you must, since the other one does not work. Why did you guys change numbers anyway? Were you trying to disappear or something!

Oh BTW, Justin was asking about you. He didn't believe you were really moving!! HAHA

K well bye. Love your face! Call me! Xoxoxo

Aspen let the tears run freely down her cheeks and onto her pajama top. The ache in her stomach felt like a ball that kept getting bigger and bigger. One layer for the old man, another for *rats*, another for Drew, a bunch of layers for Dad and Mom now a new one for Krista. Who knew how many layers would be added as the summer lingered?

Moaning, she rolled onto her stomach. Her insides felt like they were on fire, and she was sure this is what it felt like to have a broken heart. It had to be, or else why did it hurt so much?

She just wanted to go back home, to be with her friends and for her parents to act normal again. She was sure she had never felt this horrible. Aspen buried her face in her pillow, quiet tears turning into uncontrollable sobs. She didn't try to stop them, to be brave, or grown-up to impress her parents or Noah. The pain she felt was real, it hurt, and she wanted it to go away. She cried and cried until there were no more tears, and then she slept.

When Aspen woke up, it was getting dark outside. The light from the full moon spilled through her window and across her bed. Her side was so stiff she felt like she had been asleep for days. Her pillowcase was wet, and crinkled and her eyes felt swollen.

She rolled to the hip that didn't hurt and slowly sat up, letting her legs hang off the side of the bed and resting her feet on the soft thick rug. She wiggled her toes, pushed on the bed with her hands, and stood up.

Her movement caused the envelope which contained the card from Krista to fall onto the floor. Aspen bent over, and picked it up. A small crinkled picture landed at her feet.

She bent over slowly and picked it up and then walked to the light switch and flipped it on. A sticky note covered the picture.

Hey Aspen, the day after you left, I felt sorry for myself so I went over and sat on your front steps to cry. ☹ I found this laying in the ground cover next to that bush your mom planted when you were born. This is all there was, but it has a Tennessee address on it (I Googled it) ☺ so I thought maybe it might be something important, so here it is. Maybe it's nothing.

XOXO ☺

Aspen pulled the sticky note off the picture.

She gasped, and the picture fluttered to the floor when both hands flew to her mouth.

She picked it up. The thin crease down the center where it was folded left white where bits of the color had disappeared.

The picture was the body and legs of a man, but the head and one arm were missing. She turned it over. The address was their little house.

Puzzled and still searching every detail, her eyes found the one unmistakable clue. It was half-hidden, like the man in the picture unconsciously kept it from view.

Immediately the knot in her stomach felt like a vise was tightening around it, and her head started spinning.

Noah stayed in his room most of the afternoon fiddling with his phone. It always took so long to charge new phones, but he had enough power to make a phone call, so he called Derrick. He didn't expect him to answer knowing he was probably at the beach, but he left Derrick a message. Then he called Mick and Danny. No answers there either.

He boiled inside, thinking of all he was missing at home and how totally miserable life was now.

Noah really wanted to talk to Derrick. He was at the beach the day Aspen told him and Krista about some random man who had pushed her and her surfboard in when she got caught in a riptide. He had never discussed it with Derrick, but now Noah wondered if maybe Derrick had seen the guy Aspen was talking about. Noah felt like he needed to do anything he could to dispel Mom and Dad's—and his own—fears about his sister.

Besides that, he needed to talk to a friend. Life in this stupid town was a joke, and he needed someone to understand.

It drove him crazy the way Mom seemed so disconnected with all of them, but she did cook their meals, and right now she wanted him and Aspen to come to dinner.

14

NO ANSWER

"Aspen?" Noah knocked on her door, but then without waiting, he opened it, bumping into her.

"Oh, sorry. I am supposed to wake you up."

Saying nothing, she thrust the picture in Noah's face. He pulled back, squinting.

Aspen pushed it toward him again. Noah's eyes widened as he focused on the disheveled picture.

He lifted his eyes and stared at his sister his expression blank. "Where did you get this?"

Aspen picked up the sticky note and handed it to him. Noah read it. "What the—"

"I know. Can you believe this?" Aspen jabbed her finger at the picture, pointing out the one unmistakable clue. The man's hands were on his hips, so they could have easily missed it had they not just seen this man today.

Aspen turned abruptly grabbing her phone from her dresser, limped over and plopped down on her bed. She said absently, "It's about half charged," and she slid her finger down the blank screen.

Noah was turning the picture over and over in his hands. He didn't take his eyes off of it before sitting down by Aspen. First, he would read the note, stare at the image, and then repeat the same activity.

"Noah? Aspen?" They both jumped at the sound of Mom's voice.

She was coming down the hall.

"Be right there, Mom. Aspen was asleep!" called Noah.

"I am just sending a text to Krista. We're coming," added Aspen.

"Okay, but come now, please." They heard her going away from the room.

Aspen typed a few more lines on her phone and pushed *send.*

They both stood and started for the door, but Noah stopped suddenly and turned around. Aspen bumped into him, but before she could say anything, he held up the photograph.

"Where can we put this?"

"Well, shouldn't we ask Mom and Dad about it?"

Noah looked at the floor. He reminded Aspen of Dad with his eyebrows furrowed that way.

He shook his head. "No, not yet. It bothers me that Dad seemed to know that guy. Well, if this is him." Noah motioned to the picture.

"It is him. His finger is a dead giveaway, and anyway, it isn't so unusual that Dad would know him. He works at the house. Dad is sure to have met him."

"That's true, but it was the way Drew acted that bothers me the most." He thrust the picture at her, "Hide this."

Aspen didn't react at first.

"Aspen! Noah!" This time when Mom called, Aspen felt a rush of anxiety.

Noah jutted a finger at her and whispered, "Hide it." He disappeared into the hall calling to Mom, "She'll be here in a sec. She got a card from Krista today, and she is sending her a text."

Aspen took the picture and put it between her mattress and box springs. A rush of guilt consumed her. She hesitated but then hurried out of the room.

At the table, she slid into her seat and began dishing up some leafy green salad onto her plate. "So, Dad, do you know that guy? That Drew guy?" she blurted.

The look Noah shot across the table made her wish she could swallow the words back down along with her barbequed chicken.

Dad didn't seem ruffled by the question at all, but Mom quickly stood. She lifted the water picture from the table and walked over to the fridge and began adding ice to it.

Aspen thought that seemed a strange thing for Mom to do as the picture was half full of ice and water already, but she turned her attention back to what Dad was saying.

"Just met him. He has been on the job taking care of the grounds for about two months," said Dad.

"So is he new? I mean, was there another gardener before him?" asked Noah.

"I guess so." Dad took another piece of chicken and took a bite out of it. He chewed for a minute. "I believe Aunt Dana mentioned they fired the other man just before they moved."

"Fired him?" Mom was sitting again.

"I guess. The other gardeners who are still there worked for him. His name was Anthony, I think. He has worked on the house grounds for more than ten years."

"Wow, that sucks." Noah stuffed a roll into his mouth.

Aspen asked, "How come they fired him? Did he do something wrong?"

Dad placed his fork on his plate and ignored Aspen's question. "Why the sudden interest in Drew?"

"No reason," said Noah. "We just met him today. Seems like a nice enough guy," he lied.

"Well, we don't know anything about him, so it's best if you kids stay away from him." Mom didn't look at any of them as she spoke.

"Why does he call you 'Mr. J.'?"

Dad's eyes narrowed as they had earlier. "Have no idea," he mumbled. Aspen decided she had said enough.

No one said anything for a few minutes. They all finished eating about the same time.

Mom asked Aspen about her hip, reminded Noah it was his turn for the dishes, and then told Dad she wanted to take a bath and asked if any of them needed anything in the bathroom before she did.

Aspen and Noah said no, and Dad shook his head. He pulled out his cell phone and began scrolling the screen.

Aspen's hip had stiffened again after sitting. She pulled herself up and hobbled to her room. Gingerly she climbed onto her bed and picked up her cell phone.

No answer from Krista.

She thought sure she would have heard back from her right away. She reached in her backpack and found her little notebook with phone numbers and addresses of her friends in San Clemente. Krista's was right on the top of the list. She checked the number to make sure it was right and then she pushed the numbers and waited. Her heart leaped when Krista picked up but then she realized it was just her message.

Hey, this is Krista. I can't answer right now, but you know I'll call back in a sec. See ya!

"Ugh." Aspen couldn't hide her disappointment even if there was no one there to see her. She scrolled down the phone for a second and then pushed messages. She scanned over the one she had sent Krista.

Hey, I got ur card. Thanks! So cute! I miss u so much! That would b totally cool if u could come out this summer! Beg ur mom! So call me, but hey I was wondering abt that pic u sent. So strange. O well, we can talk when we talk. Hugs!

Aspen walked over to her dresser and plugged her phone back in to finish charging it. She reached under the mattress to check for the picture.

Still there.

Then she opened her window a little to let the breeze blow through her room. She didn't think she'd be tired because she'd slept all afternoon, but she was. Aspen checked the phone again to make sure the volume was all the way up so that she would hear when Krista called or sent her a text.

Aspen climbed between her sheets and pulled her comforter up to her chin. She turned her lamp off and snuggled into her pillows. She heard Noah's bedroom door shut and wondered if Mom was okay.

The day's events became tiny jumbled fragments and then multicolored swirls, and she slept.

15

TERROR IN THE PARKING LOT

MORNING CAME TOO EARLY for Aspen. She fell into the bucket seat of the Iroc, glad that Noah had the top down. He gunned the engine, and with the radio blaring, he spun the car around speeding down the long driveway. Aspen was sure if Dad was watching he would not be happy about Noah's driving but judging from Noah's aloofness, he probably didn't really care.

Neither of them had brought up the picture.

When they pulled out onto the road, Noah turned the radio off. "Did you hear from Krista?"

Aspen couldn't hide her disappointment. "No," she said sadly. "I tried to call her again, but she didn't answer."

"That's weird." He shrugged and changed the subject, "I've been thinking."

"That's a novel idea," Aspen laughed at her humor.

Noah rolled his eyes, "We are just going to walk in the front door today. Quietly."

"And go where?"

"To find where that door goes—went—was supposed to go."

Aspen was thoughtful for a minute. "Okay, I guess. Do you think that's smart?"

"I don't know, and I don't care. I hate the way Mom and Dad are acting. I don't trust them," Noah snapped.

"Noah—" she quickly decided not to haggle with him about their parents. Besides, she pretty much agreed. Instead, she said,

"Yeah, okay, but I want to get into that room upstairs, the one that was locked."

"The storage? Why?"

"I'm not sure. I just have a feeling, that's all."

Noah kept his eyes on the road. "There's a lot of things going on here, Aspen. It's confusing, but I think Dad is hiding something."

The familiar sick feeling rushed through Aspen, and she took a deep breath and released it with a sigh.

"Well?" Noah looked at her when she didn't answer. He turned the car into a parking space in the student parking lot, held the button while the top closed and locked it into place. He turned to her again when he got out of the car.

Aspen winced. "I guess I just don't want to believe that."

Kiryn bounced across the parking lot and pulled the door open. "Hey! Nice wheels."

"It's Noah's car." Aspen glanced at her brother who was still eying her as he walked around the front of the car.

"Who cares whose it is. You're riding in it." Kiryn turned to Noah. "How are you anyway?" She squinted her eyes and nervously twisted her mouth.

Noah gave her a puzzled look. "Uh, I'm good." He walked up the steps and opened the door. He started to go in and then turned around.

Kiryn was right behind Noah and she nearly bumped into him. "Good," she nodded, still twisting her mouth.

"Coming Gimp?" Noah still held the door open.

"Wow, your leg must really hurt. Was that from the desk?" Kiryn said observing, Aspen walk. "Do you need some help?"

"Yes, it is, and no, I'm coming. It only hurts for a minute after I have been sitting for a while." Aspen answered all three questions in one sentence then called to Noah, "Oh wait, Noah, unlock the car. I forgot my phone. I want to text Krista one more time."

Noah pointed his keys at the Iroc and Aspen heard the locks click. She heard Kiryn ask Noah, "Who's Krista?"

Aspen said, "You guys go on in. Be there in a second." She

couldn't help but notice the look of satisfaction on Noah's face when Kiryn brushed past him on the way. Kiryn immediately turned and headed for the door. It made her smile.

Noah was happy to walk into the school with Kiryn. He was telling her about Krista when he noticed Gavin leaning against the wall; both hands shoved in his pockets. A pretty brunette had one arm linked through one of his, and she was stroking his arm with her free hand.

Good. He has a girlfriend. She wasn't here yesterday. At least he won't be bugging my sister.

At that moment, the girl left Gavin and joined another guy who was walking past them. She linked arms with him as well.

Noah sighed. *Or not.*

Absently, he glanced over his shoulder, wondering what was taking Aspen so long. His thoughts were interrupted when the girl whom he had seen with Gavin was suddenly in front of him.

"Hi! I'm Cassie."

Aspen leaned inside the car, grabbed her phone, and backed out. As she did, goosebumps appeared on her arms, and a cold shiver ran down her back. She felt sweat forming on her temples.

She whirled around and was relieved to see no one there and laughed nervously at herself. Taking a deep breath, she wiped the back of her hand across her forehead and squeezed her eyes shut.

Get a grip. You're turning into a nut case.

She blew the air out of her lungs and opened her eyes. The old man was standing less than a foot from her!

Aspen stumbled backward and fell inside the car. She jerked on the door, but just before it closed, her cell phone slipped from her hand, landing on the pavement out of reach.

It's okay. It's okay. Noah will notice I'm missing and come out. It's okay.

Panic seized her. *NO! I need my phone. I need to call him.*

She scanned the parking lot. No one. She looked up at the old man. He hadn't moved. He just stared at her, his deep-set eyes squinted almost closed, his mouth a thin line.

Carefully, she inched the door open just a little and squeezed her hand through the crack. Keeping her eyes glued to the old man, she caught the phone between two fingers and wiggled it into the car. She pulled the door shut and slammed the lock down.

Aspen punched at the numbers on her phone. Nothing.

The screen is locked!

She kept glancing at the old man as she dragged her finger down the face of the phone. The main screen popped up.

Noah's number was programmed into her instant contacts.

"Push 3! Push 3!" She verbally tried to tell her hands to do what they seemed to have forgotten. *Nothing.* She pushed the flat screen over and over, but her hands were shaking so hard she could hardly hold onto it.

Suddenly she realized the problem. She had not programmed her new phone. "No auto dial! Oh what is his number?!"

Movement by the window caused her to look up. The man was moving closer to the car. Shaking uncontrollably, she screamed, "Please! Please come out, Noah! Someone, please!"

She scanned the parking lot again. Still, there was no one in sight except for the old man. He was now moving around to the other side of the car.

"Oh my—" Aspen's eyes suddenly focused. The driver's door was unlocked! She had locked her door manually instead of using the auto-lock. Without turning away from the old man, she reached behind her fumbling for the button, but she couldn't find it, and he was getting closer. He leaned down and looked through the window, his gnarly hand reaching for the door handle.

Aspen threw herself across the seat and jammed the lock down just as his hand touched the door.

She peered up at him. His face was nearly touching the glass, his hand firmly gripping the door handle. He pulled on it. When it didn't open, he shook it violently causing the car to rock.

"Go away! Go away! What do you want?" Aspen screamed. She frantically looked around again. "Noah! Noah! Someone!"

The screen on her phone was covered with sweat and was locked again. *911! Call 911!*

She wiped her hands on her jeans and tried to scroll down the face to unlock it but to no avail.

The old man stepped back now and reached one hand into his pocket.

"What are you doing? Please, please leave me alone!"

The horn! Aspen lunged across the seat and mashed the center of the steering wheel with the heel of her hand. The sound was deafening, but the old man did not move. "Noah! Noah!! Help! Someone help!"

"Aspen? Aspen!!"

Aspen whirled to see Noah coming out of the school. In seconds he was next to the car pulling the door open.

"Noah he's here!" Letting go of the horn she jerked her head around and thrust her hand toward the driver door. "The old man is—"

Gone! He is gone!

16

POLICE

"Aspen?"

Aspen flung herself out of the car and into Noah's arms. Sobbing, she buried her face in his shoulder. "He was here! He was here, Noah! By the car, right after you went in!"

"Who?"

"The old man! The old man from the road!" She was hysterical now and Noah shook her shoulders.

"Aspen!" He held her away from him and looked at her. "He was *here*?"

"Right here!" she sobbed. "He tried to get in the car!" She collapsed against him again.

"Where did he go? Which way? Was he running?"

Noah was still holding his sobbing sister when Kiryn and Gavin came out of the school.

"What happened?" Kiryn took over for Noah and Aspen fell into her arms.

Noah looked at Gavin. "She said a man tried to get in the car."

"I'll go this way," Gavin thrust his thumb over his shoulder.

"What does he look like?"

Noah took off in the other direction. "She just said he is old!"

"We should probably tell Mr. Fielden." Kiryn put her arm through Aspen's but didn't move. Aspen was crying too hard, so Kiryn pulled her across the sidewalk, and they sank onto the grass.

"We need to get some help, Aspen. I'll be right back."

"No! Don't leave me!" Aspen got to her feet, and the two girls went inside the school where Mr. Fielden met them.

"Oh good, you found her." Mr. Fielden's tone changed when he saw Aspen, "What happened to you?"

Aspen winced. That was the second time Mr. Fielden had asked her that same question in as many days.

He took Aspen from Kiryn. "What's going on?"

Mr. Fielden guided Aspen into a vacant classroom where they both sat down. Aspen started crying again, and Mr. Fielden looked to Kiryn for an explanation.

Kiryn shook her head, "I'm not sure. She said a man tried to get in the car." She motioned to the door. "Gavin and Noah went to look for him."

Mr. Fielden stood immediately, "Not a good idea. Kiryn, call the police. I will find the boys."

Aspen thought about protesting but changed her mind. She was scared, and she was sorry she had not told Mom and Dad about the old man in the shed.

Kiryn pulled her cell phone out of her pocket and punched in some numbers and then waited. "Hi, Claudia, it's Kiryn. I'm calling for Mr. Fielden at the high school. Could you send an officer please? Some guy tried to get in a girl's car." She paused, "Just a minute." She turned to Aspen, "What did he look like?"

Aspen sniffed. "Uh, he is old. Really old."

Kiryn related the information, and then she paused again, "Okay." She turned to Aspen again, "What was he driving? Or—"

"He wasn't driving. At least I didn't see a car or anything. He was just standing there," said Aspen. She wiped her eyes and nose with tissues Kiryn thrust in her hand.

Kiryn was still speaking into her phone, "Yes, her name is Aspen Allen. Yes, *the* Allen's." She covered her phone, "They want you to call your parents."

The Allen's?

Commotion and the sound of mixed male voices from the hall

drew Aspen's attention. She recognized all of them. Noah, Gavin, Mr. Fielden, and Dad. She figured Noah must have called Dad, but she didn't care anymore. Now maybe he would believe her.

Aspen looked up to see the four come through the door along with two police officers. More commotion caused Mr. Fielden to walk back out into the hall.

"People, people. Chill out." She heard him say. His voice drifted off as he herded the voices away from the room. She assumed it was the other students in her class.

"That was fast," Kiryn said to the officers. She put the cell phone back up to her ear, "Thanks, Claudia. They're here."

"We were just down the street," one of the officers responded to Kiryn's statement.

"Aspen?" Dad knelt next to his daughter.

She threw her arms around his neck. Seeing her dad caused the tears to erupt again.

Dad didn't say anything for a few seconds, but then he abruptly stood and turned to one of the policemen, "What do you need from us?

"We need a description, Mr. Allen." The taller officer spoke up.

"Did you see him, Noah?" asked Dad

Noah shook his head. "No, but she said it was the same old guy she saw on the road the other day.'

"The one she thought I was going to run over?" Dad looked and sounded astonished. He turned to Aspen, his face twisted in confusion.

"Yes," Noah said evenly.

Dad still stared at his daughter, "Aspen is that true?" Aspen nodded through short gasps.

Noah quickly turned to Gavin, "You didn't see anyone did you?" Gavin gave Aspen an apologetic look and shook his head.

Aspen was surprised that even with all the commotion, his intense green eyes could still cause her heart to flutter unexpectedly.

"Nope. No one." Gavin looked down at the floor, but then his head jerked up. "Wait. That girl standing by the door. Maybe she saw something."

"What girl?" Noah seemed perplexed.

With all eyes on him, Gavin began explaining, "That girl standing by the door. She had long blonde hair. You didn't see her?"

Noah's face was blank. "No clue. Did she come inside the school?"

"Yes, in front of us. She stopped and looked in this room. I wasn't paying attention to where she went after that. I assumed she came in here." Gavin raised his eyebrows and twisted his mouth to one side. "Guess not."

Dad pulled Aspen to him again and gently patted her back, and then he released her and stood up. He glanced at Noah, then at Gavin and then Kiryn.

Kiryn smiled, and her eyes widened.

Kiryn had a way of making everything seem, well, lighter. Not so foreboding.

"Can we get this done?" Dad didn't sound impatient, but he seemed rushed. Aspen wasn't sure if there was a difference, but to her, where Dad was concerned, it seemed like there was. He did not seem agitated and to Aspen that also meant impatient, but he seemed like he was in a hurry to leave.

"It would be helpful if we could find the girl you saw," the officer directed his statement to Gavin. "Maybe she saw the man."

"I'll go see if she is in one of the classes. Shouldn't be too hard. There aren't that many people here." Gavin disappeared into the hall.

Aspen answered a myriad of questions from her father, the police and Mr. Fielden who had returned moments earlier.

One of the police officers asked her dad if he had seen the man Aspen was describing. Dad responded with an emphatic no and did not expound at all. The officer studied Dad for a few seconds but then went onto more questions directed at Aspen.

Gavin returned a few minutes later. He didn't have any luck. He had checked the choir room, Mr. Fielden's classroom, and the main office to see if maybe she was a new student. All the other rooms were locked, and it didn't appear there was anyone else in the school.

Noah sat on the desk Aspen was seated, and Gavin sat on a desk across from them. Kiryn stayed too, but she chatted with one of the officers. It seemed to Aspen that Kiryn knew everybody. Now that she thought about it, *everyone* seemed to know everyone else in Sommerville. That was so different than in San Clemente.

Kiryn called the policemen by their first names, Ben and Hank. Aspen couldn't think of one policeman whom she knew personally. During the conversation, she learned that Ben was a fourth-generation policeman in Sommerville. Hank had moved out from Memphis just six months ago. Already he too seemed to know everyone.

Students from Mr. Fielden's class kept drifting in and out of the classroom. Soon the mood lightened, and even Aspen was laughing. Gavin stayed in the room, but he appeared cautious, always glancing at Noah, who was ignoring him.

Noah hadn't even cracked a smile, but he stayed close to his sister unconsciously resting his hand on her shoulder.

Maybe it was because of all that had happened in five short days but right now Noah was acting more like the brother she grew up with. She wondered how long that would last.

17

COUSINS BUT NOT REALLY

THE POLICE ASSURED JACKSON that patrol cars were scouring the entire area and would continue the search until dark.

When Aspen gave her description to the police, Dad was visibly surprised that she seemed so sure of what he looked like. She told them he had a scraggly gray beard, eyes that looked almost black and he was wearing overalls with holes in the knees. He wore a wide-brimmed hat with wisps of gray hair that touched the collar of his plaid shirt. Lost in thought, Hank called her back to the task.

"Oh, sorry. I was just thinking."

"Something you haven't told us?" Hank looked up from his electronic notepad.

She shook her head.

He was wearing the same clothes when I saw him on the road and in the shed.

She kept that thought tucked in the corner of her mind. She might tell Noah later.

"It does seem a little puzzling that we haven't spotted him," Ben was saying to Dad, "considering his age." He turned to Aspen. "How old do you think he is?

"Old. *Really* old."

Noah rolled his eyes. Suddenly seemingly annoyed again. "Do you think he is older than Grandma Hanson because you think she is *really* old and she is only about sixty or something?"

Aspen thought for a minute. *Well sixty is old.* She mused. "No, he is *way* older than that."

"Really?" Ben seemed surprised. "Must be a spry old guy."

"Guess so," Aspen mumbled. She suddenly felt foolish. He was so old she could have easily run from him. Then why didn't it seem like she could? He *looked* really old, but somehow he didn't *seem* so old.

"Okay," Dad was saying, "If we're finished here—" He turned to Aspen. "Are you staying at school?" Before she could answer, he turned to Noah, "You'll be with her, right?"

Noah nodded. "Yes, Dad."

Aspen caught the negative vibe of Noah's reply. She wondered if Dad noticed. He didn't seem to, or maybe he was ignoring it.

Dad nodded and looked at his watch. "I'm sorry, Aspen, I have to go. Are you sure you'll be okay?"

Kiryn jumped in immediately, "Of course she will. I'll take care of her." She scooted over and laid her arm across Aspen's shoulders.

"I'm fine, Dad." It was right then, right that second, when she looked into her dad's eyes that she realized he thought she was imagining again.

Dad patted Aspen on the arm but then gave her a quick squeeze. He shook hands with Ben and Hank and then looked back at Aspen as though he had forgotten something. "How's that hip?"

"Fine. It's really fine." Aspen realized she had not even felt the pain in her hip.

"Oh, you're just so *fine*," Kiryn teased quietly.

Dad lightly punched Noah in the shoulder, thanked Mr. Fielden for his help and gave a quick nod to Gavin and Kiryn.

With a brisk wave to no one in particular, he was gone.

Noah was fuming inside but felt helpless. Embarrassed by his sister's constant issues, he worried what people were starting to think of her; and yet feeling somewhat sympathetic, he now began to wonder if she was really ill. *Mentally.* The thought made his heart ache, and yet it also made him angry. What was it about this place that caused her so much turmoil?

There wasn't much left of the school day, and Mr. Fielden relented to student's pleas to plan a water skiing trip. It was scheduled for a week from Friday right after *school.*

Aspen chuckled. *School.*

Mom was right. This was a far cry from any school Aspen had ever attended. On top of that, so many strange things had happened to her, and it was only Wednesday.

The slow day gave Aspen and Noah a chance to get to know their other classmates. Rand was the police chief's son and hated his real name. It was Randall or Randy like his mom insisted on calling him. Jamie and Jenny were twins. They were athletic, and Aspen marveled at both of their physics.

The new student body president, Cassie, was blonde with almond-shaped blue eyes, and she was thin and pretty. She always looked at Gavin when she talked, and Aspen noticed how everyone seemed to hang on her every word. Everyone, that is, but Gavin. Girls like that bugged Aspen, but it annoyed her even worse that everyone gave Cassie so much attention.

Maybe I'm jealous. Aspen wasn't plain by any means. Her round, dark eyes and glistening, long, brown hair had always been attention getters, but she was tall and not at all that shapely. No chest and really no waist. Just straight up and down. She was muscular, after all, she surfed, but she was not built like those twins and for sure not as pretty, or as—gooey—as Cassie.

Aspen suddenly felt anxious watching Cassie flirt with Gavin though he did not seem very interested. Still, Aspen decided not to like Cassie, at least for now. She felt a stab in her heart when Cassie casually brushed by Gavin, purposely bumping his shoulder and giving a silly giggle when he stepped out of her way. Cassie slipped her arm through Gavin's, and he did not pull away.

Now the stab actually hurt and Aspen turned away from them, assuming Cassie must be Gavin's girlfriend. Cassie had returned late last night from New York where she had been attending a dance convention.

Of course, she dances. That's just perfect. What Aspen did well was left in California, where there was an ocean.

Aspen glanced sideways at them. Cassie and Gavin were talking. *Cooing. Cassie is actually cooing. Ugh.*

Aspen shrugged, and even though she felt silly, she could not dismiss the anxiety that swept over her. It was hard for her to look away, but she turned her attention to the one person she simply could not figure out.

Joseph. He seemed angry all the time. She had noticed him the last couple of days but really hadn't given it much thought. Now studying him closer, she couldn't help but wonder about him. He seemed particularly sullen toward her and Noah, but maybe that was just because they were new. He was quiet too. He never contributed much to any of the class conversations. Aspen figured she would learn more about him later, or maybe not. She didn't need to know everything about everyone, but something about his angry expression and distant eyes made her uncomfortable. Cassie made her just as uncomfortable but in an entirely different way.

When they left school, Aspen offered Kiryn a ride home. Noah put the top down, and Aspen noticed a look of satisfaction cross his face when Kiryn climbed in the back seat behind Aspen.

Noah pulled the car out of the parking lot and started down the street when they saw Gavin walking alone along the sidewalk.

"Hey, Noah!" Kiryn tapped him on the shoulder. "Can we give him a ride?"

Noah didn't answer, but he pulled the car alongside Gavin. "Geez is every girl crazy about this guy?" he mumbled. He looked back at Kiryn. "Why, is he your *boyfriend*?" he asked dryly.

Aspen chuckled and looked sideways at Noah. "What?" Noah demanded.

Kiryn laughed heartedly. "No, he's my cousin."

"Slash-brother," added Aspen when she saw the look on Noah's face.

"Oh…oh…well, yeah." Noah turned back around in his seat and put both hands on the wheel as Aspen observed the color in his cheeks. He didn't ask for any further explanation.

Aspen leaned her seat forward, Kiryn scooted over, and Gavin climbed in next to Kiryn.

"Thanks, man," said Gavin.

Noah lifted his chin in acknowledgment, but Aspen saw the tiny smile on his lips. She guessed he was happy to hear that Gavin was *not* Kiryn's boyfriend.

They drove in silence with the stereo blasting and the wind blowing through their hair.

Aspen breathed deeply. She closed her eyes and laid her head back on the seat but opened them quickly when Gavin leaned up and said something to Noah. She couldn't help, but wonder where stupid Cassie was but she refrained from asking.

She closed her eyes again, allowing the warm air and music to lull her to sleep. She was surprised when she opened her eyes again, and they were pulling up in front of a fast food restaurant.

"Where are we?" Aspen sat up.

"Memphis." Noah turned off the engine and opened the door. "Gavin offered to buy lunch, and I never turn down free food."

Aspen stretched and opened the door. She looked around. "Isn't there any place to eat in Sommerville?"

Gavin got out after Noah and Kiryn scooted across the seat climbing out behind him. She followed Noah into the restaurant. Gavin stopped before he went inside and turned to Aspen, "Yep, Bill and Nada's."

"Then why—"

"I wanted to ride in his car." He grinned. "You coming in?"

"I'll get us a table out here."

"What do you want?"

"Ummm, fish tacos, and a Coke."

"Fish tacos?" Gavin winced.

Aspen laughed. "K, a burger and Coke."

"Fries?"

"And fries."

Gavin nodded and disappeared into the restaurant.

Minutes later the four were downing lunch around a molded plastic table with attached benches. The umbrella over the table was a welcome relief from the hot sun.

Noah leaned both elbows on the table, his eyes darting to Kiryn and then to Gavin.

"So, what is it that you all seem to know about our family that we don't?'

Gavin and Kiryn exchanged a quick glance. Neither of them spoke immediately.

Aspen was perplexed by their silence. "What?"

Noah's eyes narrowed. "You guys want to walk home?" Gavin chuckled. He looked at Kiryn and raised his eyebrows.

Kiryn took a deep breath. She blew it out through pursed lips.

With the last bit of air, she said, "Okay."

"Legend has it—" said Gavin.

18

ALLEN LEGEND

Kiryn grimaced at Gavin.

"I was just setting the stage." He laughed. Kiryn rolled her eyes.

"*What?!*" Noah and Aspen spoke exactly at the same time, and that made all of them laugh.

Kiryn leaned forward, furrowed her eyebrows, her eyes squinting, so the blue nearly disappeared, "Well, your great-grandpa Jackson something Allen."

"Humphrey?" Aspen interjected. She remembered the name from the painting at the big house.

"Maybe." Kiryn continued, "Anyway, he was a big political guy in Memphis. Owned a butt load of property, too."

"Oh, your grandpa hung out with Elvis," Gavin said. Again Kiryn shot him an annoyed look.

"I'm just sayin'—" He gave Noah a curt nod and then raised both hands in surrender.

"Well, that comes *much* later," said Kiryn. "And besides they had one stupid dinner together, they didn't *hang* out."

"That we know of. We weren't *there*."

Aspen giggled, and it made her happy to hear Noah chuckle at Gavin's random interjections.

Kiryn squinted at Gavin. "Back to the *great*-grandpa."

Gavin just grinned and winked at Aspen. Her heart jumped so high she was sure it had landed in her throat, and she tried to swallow it back down to her chest. She did not want to feel this way about Gavin or anyone else. She had taken pride in her reputation for being an athlete and not crazy about boys, and she was not about to make that change. Not until after she graduated anyway.

Kiryn continued, "There were a bunch of guys in his—" Again she made quotations in the air with her fingers like she had yesterday, "*rich political group*." She threw both hands out. "They owned everything around here, and they called the shots. For everybody."

Kiryn kept talking, and Gavin added to the story. He didn't know as much as Kiryn, but he knew enough to add some interesting thoughts.

They told Aspen and Noah that their Great-Grandpa Allen was one of the original six that purchased the land in Sommerville and it was also the same six that had the lake built. They divided the land into equal shares, and each built a house on the lake.

The Dixon family, mainly Kenneth Dixon, owned about as much land as their great-grandpa and the two of them were really good friends. It was rare that they were ever seen apart.

Aspen wrinkled her forehead and looked down at her hands. Kiryn stopped talking, "What?"

"That name. I saw it on one of the desks at school." She didn't mention the weird feeling she had when she saw the name.

"Dixon?" asked Gavin. Aspen nodded.

"Not surprising," said Kiryn. "Their family goes way back in Sommerville."

"My mom and step-dad bought the house on the lake next door to his," said Gavin.

"You live on the lake?" Noah was visibly surprised—or annoyed—Aspen wasn't sure.

Gavin answered Noah first, "Yeah. Well, part of the time. It's the house directly across from yours, on the other side of the lake." He then answered Aspen, "Yes, Kenneth Dixon, but it was someone else's house we bought, not his."

Noah didn't comment. He just raised his eyebrows and continued to listen.

"The whole town hated that the Dixon's and the Allen's hired poor people from down south to work for them. Dixon was a *shrewd* businessman, that's how Uncle Rocky describes him."

Kiryn's emphasis on the word *shrewd* amused Aspen.

"His idea was to bring workers in from poor areas of the south, give them room and board for two years, pay them below the minimum wage, put their earnings into an investment account to earn the company interest and then taking them back to their homes paying them their two years of wages in a lump sum."

"The company put the workers up in small homes, cottages really, around the outskirts of Sommerville. The workers grew their own food, and the company supplied them with beef and milk and stuff, but the workers were never allowed to socialize with any of the people in Sommerville."

"And they were not allowed to leave the city limits either," added Gavin.

"For two years? I'll bet some of them broke that rule," said Noah.

"Not really. If they were caught they were immediately shipped back home. They didn't want to lose their jobs. Some of the workers asked to stay longer, but it was never allowed. They were usually between the ages of fifteen and eighteen, and the owners did not want to have to worry about them getting married and staying in the area," said Kiryn.

Noah asked, "What about school?"

Kiryn shrugged. "I don't know. I guess they didn't go to school."

"They were slaves?" Aspen was horrified by the idea.

"No, not slaves. Slavery was abolished, of course, but they would work for way less than everyone else, so your great-grandpa and Kenneth Dixon hired them." Kiryn continued, "But a few years after they started that business, some of the guys they took back home never actually *got* home."

"What do you mean?"

Kiryn looked at Noah. "Not sure." She flipped her hands forward spreading her fingers and opening her palms. "They just disappeared."

"There was an FBI investigation and everything," said Gavin. "It was a pretty big deal."

"Scandal you mean," Kiryn added dryly.

"Did our great-grandfather go to jail or something?" Aspen hated the direction this story seemed to be heading.

"Nope." Gavin sat back, "They never pinned anything on them." He and Dixon came up totally clean."

A welcome relief flooded through Aspen and her eyes dropped to her hands.

"But then—" Gavin's voice made Aspen's head jerk up, "What?"

"Well, the details are pretty sketchy, but—"

Kiryn jumped in, "But the oldest daughter had some kind of fling with one of the workers and ran away with him."

"You mean Grandpa's sister," said Noah.

Kiryn nodded. "Yes. They searched for them for months and then your great-grandma had some sort of nervous breakdown."

"Wow," Aspen breathed.

"Yeah, she was in a hospital for a while and then I guess she died. She never came back," said Gavin

"The daughter was really popular. She was even the Junior Miss of Sommerville. She was to have an elaborate 'Coming-Out Party' when she was sixteen."

"What is a 'coming out party'?" asked Aspen.

"The rich people used to have these big parties when their daughters' turned sixteen. To kind of let people know they were available."

"That's lame," said Aspen flatly. "So did the girl ever come back?"

"Yeah, it's a lame thing, but it was a big deal then," Kiryn paused.

"Among the rich," she scoffed. "Anyway, it's really weird. The whole family changed according to the stories, and no, she didn't come back. At least not that we know of."

"Her dad probably beat her for humiliating the family," said Gavin.

Noah didn't like that comment. He looked disgusted. "Can't choose your relatives."

"Guess not," Aspen said quietly.

"Well, they were rich, and that makes *you* rich," said Gavin. "That can't be too bad."

Noah squinted and slowly shook his head. "No actually, I don't think my dad took any of the inherita—"

"Yet," Gavin interrupted him, but Noah scowled, and Gavin clamped his mouth shut.

Kiryn rolled her eyes at Gavin and turned to Noah, "Why do you think that?" she asked.

"Because he told us he didn't. He left here for some reason and went to San Diego. After college, he started his own business with his own money."

Gavin looked doubtful. "Why would anyone not want his share of the family fortune?"

Noah shrugged. "Maybe Grandpa didn't offer it to him. I don't think they got along very well."

"I didn't think of that," said Aspen. "Dad's story always made sense."

"We don't have any reason to think otherwise." Noah turned and flung a wadded hamburger wrapper into a nearby garbage can. He turned back to the small group, "Now what?"

19

MY FAMILY THINKS I'M CRAZY

Aspen tried to process the story of the *Allen Legend*, as Kiryn so fondly referred to it. She studied the faces of the three people huddled around the picnic table for the past hour.

Noah's face displayed obvious interest. He was twirling his straw. Every few seconds, he would absently suck on the straw, forcing air from his empty soda cup. Aspen wished she knew what he was thinking. *If he would just stop making that disgusting noise!*

Kiryn, her dramatic over-energetic new friend leaned forward, her elbows on the table. Her eyes darted from Aspen to Noah and back again. She had just told the supposed legend of the Allen family with the detail of an accomplished historian and now seemed to be waiting for some sort of comment from Aspen or Noah.

Gavin, whose electrifying eyes started hurricane gale winds in Aspen's stomach every time he looked at her, had both elbows on his knees, his hands dangling between them. She studied his sharp jawline and high cheekbones and the way his thick hair fell across his forehead with his head down like that. His calm demeanor made him even more appealing to Aspen.

Her heart raced.

Gavin's interest in the Allen legend was equally as intense as his cousin's, which was oddly appealing. Aspen sighed. She hated that Gavin distracted her so easily, especially since he and Cassie were obviously an item.

"Well—" Kiryn sounded anxious.

"So…" Aspen spoke slowly. She was asking Noah, but she just threw the question out, "Should we talk to Dad?"

"No," Noah's tone was unmistakably firm.

Aspen looked at Kiryn and both of their eyes widened. Gavin sat up and twisted on the bench to face the table. He looked intently at Noah. "Why not?"

Noah breathed in deeply. "I probably need to talk to Aspen. Alone."

Aspen rolled her eyes. "Why, Noah? Of the four people at this table you and I know the least about our family."

Noah nodded, but it was evident that fact bothered him. "Yeah, I guess."

Aspen studied her brother. "What do you want to talk to me about that they can't hear?"

Noah looked directly in his sister's eyes. "I'm not sure. I guess about Dad, and that picture that Krista sent you. A lot of stuff that does not add up."

Everyone was quiet again.

Hesitantly Kiryn asked, "What about your dad?"

Aspen furrowed her brow. "He is just not himself. He has never acted so…so…weird. He is almost—mean."

"Not really mean, Aspen. More like *disinterested*."

"Oh, *okay*," Aspen said flatly. "And Mom, she seems like she is in the twilight zone most of the time. She is really different."

"Today at the school was the most normal Dad has been for at least two months, and even that was not like he usually is," said Noah thoughtfully.

Gavin took a deep breath, and it was apparent he was choosing his words carefully. "Maybe, we could help."

Noah had not taken his eyes from the soda cup. Now he turned to Gavin. "How?"

"Why don't you tell us what is going on, what is it that you are trying to find out—and why?" said Gavin.

Again everyone was quiet.

Noah and Aspen looked at each other. Aspen nodded quickly.

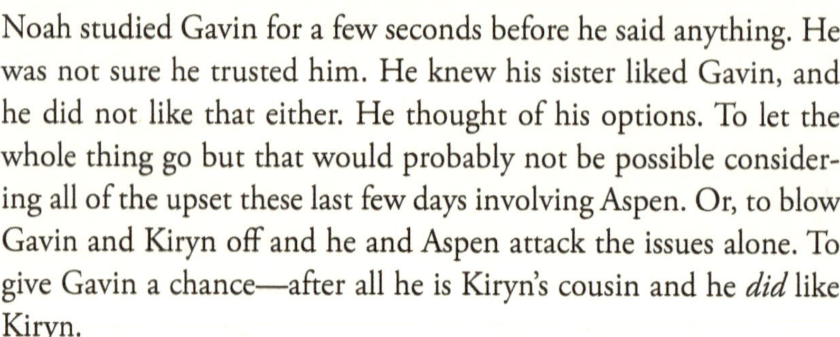

Noah studied Gavin for a few seconds before he said anything. He was not sure he trusted him. He knew his sister liked Gavin, and he did not like that either. He thought of his options. To let the whole thing go but that would probably not be possible considering all of the upset these last few days involving Aspen. Or, to blow Gavin and Kiryn off and he and Aspen attack the issues alone. To give Gavin a chance—after all he is Kiryn's cousin and he *did* like Kiryn.

Noah put his free hand to his face squeezing his temples between his thumb and fingers like he was trying to stop his head from hurting. Maybe he was. Aspen could understand if that were the case. When he looked up his face was sullen. "See, the thing is I— we—don't even know if there is a problem, but this guy Drew—"

"Drew—" Kiryn blurted. "The guy who takes care of the Allen Manor grounds?"

Aspen slowly shook her head at Kiryn. "I swear you know everybody."

"You will too after you have been around for a while." Kiryn grinned and scrunched her nose. "And you have to be snoopy— like me."

Noah chuckled and then answered Kiryn, "Yeah that guy. Aspen and I were trying to sneak in the big house—"

"Why? I mean, why sneak? Why not just—"

"Kiryn?" Gavin's voice was low and direct, "Why don't you let him tell us before you ask any questions."

"Oh, okay," Kiryn sighed. "You're right. Go ahead, Noah."

Noah started to say something but then just started laughing.

"This whole thing is crazy." He plopped his elbows on the table, dropping his head into his hands.

"Or not," Kiryn made a huge sweep across the table with her arm. "The floor is yours."

Noah continued, "So Drew, he caught us trying to get in the side door."

"There's a side—"

The three glowered at Kiryn, and she immediately clamped her mouth shut.

Noah went on, "He caught us and demanded to know what we were doing, but then when Dad came around the corner. This Drew guy jumped in front of the door and closed it acting like we were all friends or something." Noah paused, "And Dad knew him. He seemed annoyed with Drew, though."

"But," continued Aspen, "when Dad left, Drew was cold as ice and wouldn't answer any of Noah's questions. He just blew us off and told us to let it go. Then yesterday, I got this card from Krista, she is my friend from California," clarified Aspen. "In the card was a picture of what we think is that guy, Drew. Krista said she found it in the dirt by our front porch."

"She found it in California?" Gavin was visibly surprised. "Did you know him before?"

Kiryn asked, "Why do you think it was Drew? Didn't you say you just met him?"

"The picture didn't have a head," said Aspen.

"Then how—"

Aspen quickly added, "His finger, his pinky finger is cut off." Kiryn's eyes widened. "That's right," she said slowly.

"To answer your question, Gavin, no," Noah sounded frustrated.

"We didn't know him before—well Aspen and I didn't—and we don't know why the picture was at our house in San Clemente."

"I guess asking your dad is not an option?" said Gavin.

"I can't decide why not, but no, it doesn't feel right. I think Dad is the one who had the picture. Like Aspen said, it was obvious that

Dad knew Drew when he saw the three of us."

"Okay, why didn't you just walk in the front door?" Kiryn asked.

"Because Dad told us that he and Mom would be busy and that he didn't want us hanging around there. I don't know if he didn't want us in the house because he had never actually said that but then yesterday he did. Aspen wants to look in a locked room upstairs, and Dad specifically told us to stay out of the storage. We think the storage is the room that is locked. It must be, all of the other rooms are bedrooms. Of course, we *have* to get in a *locked* room." Noah chuckled softly, and stopped talking and again, everyone was silent.

Gavin changed the subject, "Hey Aspen, what about that old guy today? That was just weird."

Aspen felt her face getting hot, and a feeling she could only describe as *creepy* edged across her shoulders and spread down her back. A lump formed in her throat and stuck. She didn't try to speak, but then Noah spoke for her.

"That's another thing. Aspen has seen him twice. Once in—"

"Th…three times," Aspen croaked.

"What? When was the third?" Noah demanded.

Aspen blinked back the tears, but she didn't say anything.

"Aspen?" Noah's tone had softened. He didn't take his eyes off of his sister but explained to their friends, "Aspen saw an old man on the road the first day we moved here. Dad almost hit him."

"So, your dad saw him?" Kiryn's eyebrows shot up.

Noah squinted and twisted his mouth. "No, that was the guy he was talking about at the school today."

Tears trickled down Aspen's cheeks. "No, Dad didn't see him."

"Neither did Mom or Noah."

Kiryn and Gavin both looked at Noah who was shaking his head. "She's right. We didn't see him, but Asp—"

Aspen's dark look stopped him in mid-sentence. Kiryn stared at the siblings.

Gavin looked at the cement again.

Noah pulled the straw out of his cup and started chewing on it.

It seemed like the silence lasted forever, but finally, Aspen took a deep breath in and then blew it out until she had no air left. She flipped her hair behind her shoulders, taking a deep breath as she did. Placing both hands on the table in front of her, she said, "Okay, first of all let me state, that my family thinks I am crazy."

20

INVISIBLE GIRL

"W E   D O   N O T—"

"Noah, just shhh," Aspen held up her hand.

The corners of Gavin's lips turned up, and he grinned when Noah shot him a disconcerting look.

"Yes, you do, and that's fine. I have wondered that myself." Aspen sighed. "In a nutshell, when we got here last week, I saw an old man in the road. I thought Dad was going to hit him, but no one else even saw him. Then he was on the side of the road when we started driving again—"

"You didn't—"

Aspen stopped Noah again and then she confirmed what he had said. "He was *standing* on the side of the road." She purposely left out the part about how she was suddenly standing next to the old man, but then she continued, "Later that same day I went out in the backyard of the little house." She caught the questioning look on Kiryn's face, but didn't elaborate about her referral to their Tennessee home. "When I went inside this garden shed thing, I turned around, and he was there again only he scared the crap out of me that time."

Noah gave her an understanding look. "When you fell." It was a statement, not a question.

Both he and Aspen hesitated, and Aspen knew Noah was thinking about the rats. She gave him a *don't even think about it* look and went on.

"Yes, and then I saw him again today, by the car." Aspen turned to Kiryn, "The little house is what I call our house."

"Oh," Kiryn nodded.

"That's four times," said Gavin.

"Exactly! Why haven't you said anything, Aspen?" Noah's tone rose sharply as he jumped to his feet.

"Noah, sit down." Aspen saw that Noah was drawing attention from other people.

Noah glanced around and then slumped back down on the bench, "This has got to be someone from around here." Kiryn looked at Gavin for confirmation.

"You would think, but who? He doesn't sound like anyone we know." He turned to Aspen, "And why didn't anyone in your family see him?"

She shrugged. "I have no clue. He has gray hair and a beard. A hat, you know, with a wide brim, and he wears overalls and a plaid shirt."

"That's all? I mean is that what he is always wearing," asked Kiryn.

"Yes." Aspen wrinkled her nose with sudden realization.

"Strange, huh?"

"Just. A. Little," said Gavin.

Believing she was running the risk of losing the confidence of Gavin and Kiryn, Aspen purposely left out the incident at the lake. It had nothing to do with the old man anyway, and even though she knew she was forced off of the tire swing by something, it really made no sense even to her, so it seemed pointless to explain it to their new friends. She hadn't mentioned the shed being locked when Dad and Noah went out, and she didn't mention the rats either. Those two facts could be enough to put her over the crazy edge in their minds, so she kept those things to herself.

Out of the corner of her eye, she caught Noah looking at her, and somehow she knew he was thinking the same thing she was.

"Well—" Gavin sat up straight and then arched his back, stretching his arms over his head. "I think you guys could use some help."

Noah chewed on the edge of his lip for a second. "We don't know what we are looking for—or what we need help with—exactly."

Aspen studied the three faces around her. She was still struggling with keeping to herself some of the other things she hadn't told them.

There was more. The girl in the window; the painting that seemed to move—that *did* move.

No, I have told them enough for one day. Even Noah doesn't know everything.

Kiryn's eyes sparkled. "This is exciting."

Aspen did not feel the same exuberance, but she smiled anyway.

Noah said, "The police told Dad they would let him know if they find any information about the old man, but I would like to know what's up with that Drew guy and why there was a picture of him at our house in California."

Gavin and Kiryn exchanged a quick glance. "We know who to talk to," said Kiryn.

"And that would be?" Noah didn't look too convinced.

"My dad," said Gavin.

"Uncle Rocky," said Kiryn.

Noah laughed because they both spoke at the same time. "Well, we can talk to Mr. Fielden at school, when can we talk to your dad?" he asked Gavin.

Again Kiryn and Gavin exchanged a quick look only this time it was amusement.

"They are the same person," laughed Gavin.

"Mr. Fielden is your dad, *too?*" Noah looked confused when he turned to Kiryn.

"I said he was my sort of dad. He is my uncle," said Kiryn quickly. "But—well actually he is my guardian. He raised me."

Aspen could visualize the wheels turning in Noah's head as he tried to process what Kiryn had just explained.

"Rocky, uh Dad, is the one that told us about the Allen Legend," said Gavin. "There is probably a lot more that he *hasn't* told us."

As though he remembered something, he pulled his cell phone

out of his pocket, scrolling the front. "Wow, I better get going, I am supposed to meet my mom and step-dad for dinner." He slid the phone back in his pocket, then jerked his head up and looked past Aspen. "Hey!"

With one leap Gavin was over a low railing that divided the eating area from the drive-thru. "Wait!" He loped across the narrow road and onto the sidewalk.

"Where is he going?" Kiryn put her sunglasses back on and stared after Gavin.

"Who is he yelling at?" Noah slid into the driver's seat of the car and started the engine. He was still trying to process Rocky being both Kiryn and Gavin's dad.

Aspen, Kiryn, and Noah stared after Gavin. He stopped on the sidewalk, stood still for a couple of minutes, and then turned around and jogged back to the car. "Where did she go this time?"

"Who?" Aspen leaned forward and let him into the back seat.

"That girl that I saw at school this morning. She walked across the street and practically disappeared into those trees," he pointed across the street as he slid into his seat.

"I didn't see your invisible friend," Kiryn joked.

Gavin scowled, "She isn't invisible. She just doesn't answer. Actually, she does not even seem to notice me."

"That must be pretty deflating for a heartthrob like you," Noah chuckled, and Kiryn sympathetically slapped Gavin's shoulder.

"Aww, she probably didn't even see you."

Gavin glared at Noah and Kiryn but said nothing to either of them.

Aspen glanced over her shoulder. Gavin was still looking across the street. It bothered her that his interest in this girl tugged at her heart, making it feel like it was too large for her chest. First Cassie, now the invisible woman. She slumped down in her seat a little until she noticed Noah watching her. He squinted, pursed his lips and winked at her just before he dropped his sunglasses into place. His mouth wore a sheepish grin.

Noah winked at me? He is obviously delusional.

Aspen pulled her sunglasses from the top of her head and positioned them on her face. She knew he was pleased with his sarcastic comment to Gavin, but it annoyed her. Whatever Gavin was, he was not conceited.

She watched the trees rushing by on the side of the road as Noah turned the Iroc onto the highway toward Sommerville. She marveled at everything that had happened in the past few days, but she didn't want to think about everything.

She pushed the old man, the lake, Drew, the big house, the invisible girl, stupid gooey Cassie, and even Mom and Dad, to the very back of her mind leaving space for the only person she *wanted* to think about—Gavin.

Aspen allowed her thoughts to dwell only on his fantastic grin and his mesmerizing green eyes. She loved the way both stood out against his dark skin. She visualized him on the beach and surfing. She sighed and turned to look over her shoulder. Gavin was looking right at her.

The now-familiar rush of butterflies took her breath away.

21

BEST FRIENDS DON'T DIE

"Aspen?"

Aspen rolled over onto her side and scrunched her pillow under her cheek, trying to block the voice that was disturbing her sleep.

"Aspen wake up."

Aspen moaned and rubbed her eyes. She opened them a little and tried to focus. Her room was dark except for the beam of light coming from the hall.

"Mom?" Aspen croaked. "Is something wrong?"

Mom sat down on the edge of her bed just as Aspen became aware of Noah standing in her doorway.

Fully awake now, she pulled herself upright, "What's going on?"

"We just got a call from…from California." Mom's voice was barely a whisper.

"Grandma?" Aspen couldn't think of anyone else that would be calling in the middle of the night.

"No, Aspen." Mom fidgeted with the tissue in her hands.

Noah still stood in the doorway his form dark against the light behind him. Aspen couldn't see the details of his expression, but he was facing in her direction.

"Suzann?" Dad was coming down the hall, but when he got to the open door, he stopped by Noah.

Suddenly Aspen felt anxious. "Mom?" Tears welled up in her eyes, but she didn't know why.

"It's Krista, Aspen."

"Krista? I sent her a text last night, but she didn't—" Aspen searched her mother's face. "Mom? What about Krista?"

Noah moved across the room to his sister's bed, scooted her over, and sat down. He draped his arm across her shoulders.

Now Aspen could see his face clearly—he was crying. Noah never cried. His voice barely a whisper he pulled Aspen closer, "She was in an accident, Aspen. Surfing, and she's—"

"She's *what?*" Aspen searched their faces.

"She's…she's gone, Aspen." Dad's voice cracked, and he too crossed the room to her bedside.

The noise that escaped Aspen's throat sounded foreign to her ears. Tears gushed through her fingers when she buried her face in her hands. She felt like something had ripped her insides out.

Krista can't be dead! It's impossible! There must be some mistake! There has to be a mistake!

A heavy thickness closed around Aspen as silent screams shredded her insides with excruciating pain she had never experienced before.

Noah pulled Aspen to him, and Mom's weeping turned to sobs. She wrapped one arm around her children and clasped Dad's hand with the other.

Suddenly Aspen pulled away and gasped. "Mom…Mom, this can't be happening! If I would have been there—if we would have been together—I could have, maybe I could have—" She threw herself into her mother's waiting arms.

"Mom, I can't breathe. Please, Mom, please! Best friends don't die."

22

BURNIN' DAYLIGHT

DURING THE FLIGHT BACK to Tennessee from California, Aspen tried to sleep, but at best it was fitful. Every time she opened her eyes, she had to remind herself why she was on an airplane.

Noah slept next to her, his head resting in his hand, his elbow on the armrest.

The past three days had been grueling. Seeing all of their friends, the lifeguard team, the school, their house, and Krista's house. All of it had been overwhelming. The gloom hung heavy in the warm California air making it hard to enjoy seeing anyone.

Aspen pressed her forehead against the small oval window and stared into the black night sky. She let her thoughts drift back over the past three days and their unplanned visit home.

Grandma Hanson picked them up at the San Diego airport, took then to dinner and tucked them both into bed—just like she used to when they were little kids. Aspen was exhausted, and at some point, she fell asleep.

The next morning Grandma gave Noah the keys to the car so he and Aspen could drive themselves to San Clemente.

They were planning to go back to Grandma's house, but she put no pressure on them to do so. Grandma Hanson was great that way.

When Krista's mother insisted they stay with their family, it was an easy decision. Aspen and Noah slept on the sofas in the bonus room. Staying in Krista's room had not been offered nor would Aspen have accepted. After two days, she still could not bring herself to open Krista's closed bedroom door even though Krista's parents had given their permission.

The last evening with Krista's parents and two little sisters was one of tears and even some laughter as they sifted through twelve years of memories.

It was both good and bad for Aspen. Good because being in Krista's house felt so natural, this had been her home away from home while growing up.

Bad because Krista's visible absence was also a stark reality to Aspen that Krista was never coming back. That realization left her feeling lonely and empty—hollow even—a tremendous void in her chest that couldn't be satisfied.

Krista's father explained that the accident that took his daughter's life was simply that—an accident. Cutting into a wave, Krista's board caught an edge, flinging her into the water. She had popped back up so quickly, that the tip of the board hit her on the back of her head, knocking her unconscious. The torrent surf pulled Krista's unresisting body back into the sea, filling her lungs with deadly water.

Even though the lifeguards and members of her team had gotten to her within minutes, she did not respond to their lifesaving efforts.

Krista's life ended on the beach.

The next day it seemed everyone Aspen knew was at Krista's funeral—a bittersweet reunion for Aspen and Noah, having only left these lifelong friends just two weeks ago.

Aspen had imagined coming back home amid hugs and happiness. She and Krista spending every waking minute of sunshine at the beach.

There had been plenty of hugs, but the happiness was non-existent.

Suzann was stunned when Jackson suggested she go to California alone to attend Krista's funeral.

She flatly refused saying whatever Jackson's reasons were, they were not good enough to miss the funeral of their daughter's best friend and who had spent half of her life in their home.

Jackson conceded, saying nothing more.

Suzann did not sleep at all the night her children left for California. A part of her wanted to talk to her mother and see if the kids could stay there for the rest of the summer and if business weren't taken care of in Tennessee by fall, she would fly them back out.

The next morning she presented the idea to Jackson, and he answered with an emphatic *no*. He was not going to have his family separated at a time like this.

A time like what? Suzann had demanded, but Jackson left the subject hanging in the air lingering like sticky molasses. He simply said no and asked that she not challenge him on the subject.

Mom and Dad arrived in California the morning of the funeral and after staying the night with Grandma, left the next day to attend to the business they had in Tennessee. That surprised Aspen, but Mom explained to Krista's mother how they needed to go back. Suzann promised to come back soon and spend some quality time—she didn't say when—just soon.

The morning after the funeral, Aspen finally decided she needed to go into Krista's room. Just before she and Noah were about to leave Krista's house, she slipped quietly into the bedroom, softly closed the door behind her, and leaned against it allowing her eyes to tarry in a myriad of old memories. She had spent almost as much time here as she had in her own bedroom.

The walls were plastered with posters of their favorite surfers and collages of pictures of the two of them on the beach, at Sonny's pizza, on the pier, in grade school, middle school and high school. Aspen's entire life was in pictures on her friend's wall. The pictures had always been there, but the reality of their history had never occurred to Aspen—because, of course, best friends don't die.

A favorite picture of Krista and Aspen was taken at dusk. The two were posing on their surfboards—Krista had it blown up to poster size.

That wasn't there before. Krista must have made it after I left.

There was really nothing unique about it—the best friends were just floating on their surfboards at the end of one of those perfect days when everything went exactly right—the memory etched in both girls' minds forever. Aspen closed her eyes. She could almost smell the saltwater and hear Krista's laughter.

Aspen had a copy of that picture somewhere. She guessed maybe it was in the storage among other things they had left in California.

The silence in Krista's room was deafening to Aspen, and the familiar ache of the last few days settled in her stomach. Oozing into every crevice and magnifying the unbearable pain.

Aspen wandered the archives of memories with her dearest friend until tears blinded her vision, and she finally collapsed in a heap on the floor.

Aspen wasn't sure how long she cried. She heard someone approach the door and leave several times. She was glad whomever it was left her alone to mourn by herself.

When Aspen finally felt like she could leave, she picked herself up from the floor, whispered a prayer in her heart that she would be able to move on and blew a silent kiss to her absent friend.

Aspen opened the door and stepped out of the room. She was surprised to see Noah sitting on the floor at the end of the hall. His tear-streaked face beckoned Aspen, and she walked directly to him. He stood and hugged her to him, saying nothing.

Then they left.

That night, Aspen and Noah stayed with Noah's best friend, Derrick Stanton. The Junior Lifeguard team—most had grown up together at the beach—was holding a tribute for Krista the next morning—one week since her accident. It would start at 5 AM at the pier.

The entire city seemed to be aware of Krista's death, and even though many people showed up to surf that day, upon seeing and hearing what was going on, they stayed out of the water, allowing Krista's friends their time.

Derrick hauled Aspen and Noah's surfboards out of his garage, and they each carried their boards across the tracks.

Aspen saw Krista's parents, grandparents and two little sisters standing about halfway down the pier. She wanted to call out to them, but she couldn't form any words, so she simply lifted her arm and waved. Krista's parents waved back, and Aspen tried to imagine how they must feel. She honestly couldn't imagine that anyone could feel worse than she did right now, but she had no knowledge to weigh the difference.

Aspen and Noah were the last ones to arrive, and Noah immediately trotted down to the sand, but Aspen held back. Noah turned just before he stepped into the water. He waited, but she did not move.

Aspen had kept her emotions in control all morning but now the familiar overcast sky, the thick salty air filling her nostrils, the crashing waves, the Junior Lifeguard Team in red swimsuits and more than twenty of her other close friends in the water bobbing on their surfboards was too much for Aspen and sobs once again shook her body.

Noah dropped his board in the sand and trotted back to her. "You don't have to surf, Aspen, just paddle out with us."

"I can't Noah, I'm sorry. I just can't. Not without Krista. Not yet." Aspen rubbed her eyes with closed fists to stop the rush of tears, but it was no use. She dug her toes in the sand and shook her head. "I can't—" she whispered. "You go. Hurry, they are all waiting."

Noah reached down and squeezed her hand and then he walked, slower now, back to his board. Picking it up, he turned just before he reached the water and glanced over his shoulder at his sister.

Aspen waved, and Noah plopped on his board, paddling into the open sea. She shielded her eyes with her hand against the glistening water so she could see him more clearly and she watched then as they all turned and began paddling out. Some of them waved. Derrick threw her a kiss.

She tried to remember if she had ever surfed in these waters without Krista. If she had, she couldn't think of when.

The surf was up this morning, and the air was calm and warm—a perfect day. Krista would have loved that. She had a favorite saying that her dad had taken from a John Wayne movie and on a day like today, Krista would yell at the top of her lungs, "Surfs up! C'mon, we're burnin' daylight!" And every time she did Aspen would roll her eyes in mock annoyance and then join Krista in the race to the water.

Aspen's heart ached. How she longed to hear Krista say those words today.

It didn't take long before everyone was lined up in hopes of catching a wave together. That was the plan, but they knew it could take two or maybe three.

When Aspen saw the familiar swell building out beyond the surfers, she knew most of them would catch this one. She could almost feel the rush as they started to paddle in front of it. Just at the right time most of them, including Noah and Derrick, expertly jumped to their feet and dropped into the wave. Her heart soared as all of them curved lines in the waves—some tumbling from their boards, but most riding all the way in.

Those who didn't catch the first wave grabbed the next or the next. In less than an hour, all participants gathered on the beach, their surfboards standing on end in the sand to form a large circle. Aspen did the same, and then they joined hands.

Many different religions were represented in this group of young adults, ranging from thirteen to twenty-five, but even if they had no religious beliefs, when one of the senior lifeguards offered to pray, everyone bowed their heads.

He prayed for comfort for Krista's family, especially her two younger sisters. He prayed for all of those on the beach who loved

Krista to remember her and to maybe catch a wave for her now and then. That comment caused a low chuckle from some of her friends and made Aspen smile.

He prayed that this group would never have to suffer this kind of pain again in losing one of their own and he prayed that it would be years, if ever before the San Clemente waters took another life of any age or for any reason. He prayed that all those affected by Krista's death would be able to move on from this sadness and remember that when one door closes another opens.

He asked that Krista's best friend and soul sister, Aspen, could find peace especially since she would not be able to deal with her grief here, at the beach, among her friends. He closed his prayer with thanks that they were all of sound mind and body and had the blessing of enjoying one of God's creations, the oceans of this planet. Everyone joined in a chorus of "Amen."

Before Aspen had hardly lifted her head, Derrick and Noah simultaneously yelled, "Surf's up! C'mon everyone! We're burnin' daylight!"

Cheers burst from the group as they exchanged hugs with each other and with Aspen. Most grabbed their boards and charged back into the water. That is exactly what Krista would have wanted, for everyone to be in the water, not standing on the sand brooding over her.

Aspen noticed other surfers now descending from the parking lot and the pier, all here to enjoy this amazing day at the San Clemente beaches.

She saw Krista's family exiting the pier, her parent's arm-in-arm. Suddenly Krista's two little sisters broke from their grandparents grasp running straight toward Aspen. She caught them up in her outstretched arms and held them close. The tears once again tumbled freely down her cheeks and into the two girls' hair.

She stood them on the sand. Four-year-old Emily stretched up on tiptoes and kissed Aspen's cheek. "I love you, Aspen."

Six-year-old Mackenzie threw her arms around Aspen's waist, "I miss you, Aspen."

"I miss you too, and you both know I love you, right?"

They both nodded and turned to run back to their waiting grandparents. Krista's parents had already retreated to the parking lot.

Aspen watched until the girls were safely with their grandparents and then she turned around. Noah and Derrick were standing behind her, and the three sank into the sand, the boys on either side of Aspen.

"You okay?" Derrick lifted her hair away from her face. Aspen nodded. "Yes. I'm okay. Seems so, so—"

"Unreal," said Noah.

"Yeah. Unreal. Like I am going to wake up, and this will all have been a bad dream."

"Kind of like moving to Tennessee," Noah shook his head. "Two bad dreams in one month and we are not going to wake up from either of them, at least not any time soon."

Aspen sighed. "No kidding," She said quietly.

For several long minutes, the three sat silently peering at the water.

Finally, Aspen spoke, "What time does our plane leave?"

"Not till tomorrow at two, I think. "Dad changed the tickets when he found out about this today."

Aspen turned to Derrick, "Are you staying to surf?"

"If you guys are, I would kind of like to hang out with you while you're here."

Noah didn't say anything. He just looked at Aspen. Any other time he would not have cared what Aspen was thinking. She could have been dying on the beach, and Noah would have told her to just hang tight till he caught a few more waves.

Now patiently, almost sweetly, Aspen thought, he waited for her to respond. He would have freaked out if she had told him he was being sweet, so she kept that thought to herself.

Aspen said, "Why don't you guys surf for a while before we go back to San Diego? We should probably spend the evening with Grandma, don't you think?"

Noah stood, followed by Derrick, "Yep, we should. Okay, we only have a couple of hours here. If that, then we can take our boards back to Derrick's and grab some lunch before we go."

Aspen nodded. "Sounds good."

Noah and Derrick were off, and Aspen watched them until they were in the water. She opened her backpack and pulled out a towel and her sunglasses. She hadn't bothered to take her t-shirt off, but now she felt sticky from the muggy air, so she pulled it over her head, stuffing it in her backpack. She spread her towel on the sand and stretched out on her back.

It felt nice, so perfectly normal. She was exhausted. Soon the noise around her became a distant hum as the warm air, and the sound of the waves lulled her to sleep.

Aspen knew she was dreaming when she and Krista ran into the water. Krista's golden hair, dark eyes, and gleaming smile were exactly how she remembered. Her infectious laugh rang in Aspen's ears as they both rode their boards effortlessly to the beach, but just as they reached the sand, Krista abruptly turned and walked back into the water. She said nothing. She simply grinned and lifted her open hand to her friend, her soul sister. Then she turned and dived into the water, leaving Aspen alone on the shore.

23

COMFORT

I T HAD BEEN NEARLY a week since Krista's funeral. Aspen stayed home from school for two days, so Noah went without her. Kiryn came by to see her, but she hadn't felt like doing anything. She felt safe staying home.

The police had found no trace of the old man so Krista was pretty sure her parents still had the same concern as before—that their daughter might be a bit off track.

She didn't go into the backyard for fear of seeing the old man in the shed again. She hadn't heard any laughter, and thankfully, she saw no rats. Life, although boring, seemed pretty normal, at least compared to her first week in Sommerville.

Aspen had retrieved her boxes of pictures from their storage in California and had spent hours going through them. Pictures of family and friends, mainly Krista. She made a ton of journal entries about her soul sister and compiled a scrapbook containing all the highlights of their friendship. She laughed when she looked at the completed book.

It's huge! Then she sighed, *but* we *were huge.* And then she cried.

This morning Noah gave her no options. "Up and at 'em." He grinned through her open bedroom door. "We—I mean—I have a surprise for you."

Aspen gave him a wary look. "Should I be afraid?"

He laughed. "Be afraid. Be *very* afraid." He pulled her door shut and then opened it again. "Hurry up! You're burnin' daylight." He winked and closed the door.

Aspen smiled. *Yes, I guess we are.* She let her thoughts drift to Krista for only a second. She sighed. *Life goes on,* and she was able to stop the tears from coming this time. *Maybe being in Tennessee, it will be a little easier to get over Krista's dea—losing Krista.*

Sitting in the Iroc, she eyed Noah suspiciously. *What is up with him? That is the second time he has winked at me.*

When they pulled up in front of the school, Kiryn and Gavin were waiting on the steps.

Kiryn rushed to the car and pulled the door open. "I am so glad you came today!" She hauled Aspen out by her arm and gave her a huge hug.

"Me too." Aspen grinned, "I really am." She was surprised at how seeing Kiryn this time gave her a feeling of peace—or contentment—she wasn't sure, and seeing Gavin, well it was like a zillion butterflies burst their cocoons all at the same time.

Gavin grinned and slowly lifted his hand to wave, but he stayed where he was casually leaning against the school building.

Aspen had a sudden urge to run to him and throw her arms around him, but not quite sure if she would make a total fool of herself, she tried to remain…nonchalant.

Noah locked the car and followed the two girls into the school, and Gavin joined them.

It was good to be back at school. Everyone in the class was sympathetic and either said something kind or gave Aspen a hug. All except Joseph, who hung back away from Aspen, almost as if she were excreting poison—his actions still puzzled her.

Cassie was overwhelmingly annoying, but Aspen tried to be appreciative of her gushing attention even though Cassie watched Gavin from the corner of her eye while showering Aspen and Noah with insincere attention.

Ugh…she really, really bugs me, the pangs of pure jealously still alive and well.

School with Mr. Fielden was a welcome relief for Aspen. They spent the first hour re-planning the water skiing trip that was postponed in Noah and Aspen's absence.

Now they were watching a program about fishing in the Bering Sea. It was straight from the TV series, *Greatest Catch*. Mr. Fielden tied it to school because they were going to a lake and who knows, "There could be big fish." It made sense, considering who their teacher was. Aspen wondered if Mr. Fielden was as nutty in regular school. Probably not, she guessed, but his classes were still probably far from boring. He had announced today that they would be having three days of art lessons next week and Aspen was excited about that.

Mr. Fielden dismissed the class, and Kiryn was immediately at Aspen's side. They linked arms Kiryn chatting insensibly about nothing really and Aspen glad to have her there. She felt a warm friendship with Kiryn, even though they had only met less than a month ago.

When Aspen and Kiryn left the school building, Noah and Gavin were standing next to the Iroc. The top was already down and Gavin jumped in the back with Kiryn. Aspen locked her seatbelt and looked first at Noah, then at Kiryn and then Gavin.

"What's going on?"

"Dad and Mom are in Memphis." Noah pulled the Iroc out of the parking lot.

"And that means?" Aspen didn't get it.

"It means we can get into your grandpa's house without them there!" Kiryn sounded absolutely gleeful.

Aspen started to laugh. "What are we looking for? Do we have a plan at least?"

"We do." Gavin leaned up on the seat. "Noah and I will check out the side of the house where the door is, and you and Kiryn can go up to the locked room."

Aspen looked over her shoulder. Gavin's face was so close, she gasped. She held her breath when she felt her face flush. "Sorry," she whispered.

Gavin didn't even flinch. He just kept his eyes locked on hers and said something she didn't hear.

The car was speeding down the road, and the wind was loud. He yelled this time, "I have something to unlock the door!" Somehow she knew that was not what he said the first time.

Aspen's eyes widened when she looked over at Noah and yelled, "Are you sure about this?"

"Totally," Noah said flatly.

Gavin briefly touched her shoulder, sending tingles down to her toes, and then he sat back in his seat.

Aspen did not look at Noah even though she felt him looking at her.

"This will be great!" Kiryn squealed, making Aspen laugh.

She is not like Krista at all. She is so happy and, well Krista was happy, but Kiryn is more of a girlie girl *or something like that. Maybe that isn't it. She is just more* squealy. *Wow, is that even a word?*

Whatever Kiryn was, Aspen liked her. And clearly, so did Noah.

When they got to the house, the yard was vacant. Noah stopped outside the locked gates. "Oh—"

Whatever else he said, was under his breath. He looked back at Kiryn and Aspen, "You two wait here."

"Why?" Aspen asked.

Noah answered her, "I will park the car at the servants' quarters, and Gavin and I will go up the back way."

"Couldn't we just scale the fence?" Gavin asked.

"We could, but I don't want to leave the car parked out here. That would be too obvious. If it was in the driveway, we could just say we stopped to find Mom and Dad."

Aspen was a little annoyed at being eliminated from the hike. "Well, we can go—"

"I know you can, Aspen, but your hip is still bothering you, and it will be faster with two of us. We need to hurry." Noah got out and held the door open for Kiryn. Aspen climbed out the other side, and Gavin got into the front seat.

"I like rich friends." Gavin settled into the seat, leaned his head back and grinned.

Noah rolled his eyes. "Like you are so poor."

"Well, I don't have a sports car." Gavin smacked the side of the door. "Let's roll."

Noah turned the car around, and they sped over the hill out of sight. Aspen could hear Noah power shifting from here, and it made her laugh. She wondered what had made Gavin so comfortable with Noah all of a sudden. Maybe Noah had decided just to be his friend instead of trying to second-guess him all the time.

Aspen and Kiryn walked up to the gate. Kiryn asked, "Does your hip still hurt?"

"No. It's perfectly fine. The bruise is almost gone. Noah is being a dork."

Kiryn shrugged. "Well I don't think he's a dork. What steps is he talking about?"

Aspen's eyes narrowed, and then she laughed. "From the little house up to this house, they lead to the backyard and the lake." She sat on the cement and leaned back on a boulder next to the driveway entrance.

"Oh, are they steep or something?" Kiryn didn't sit down next to her.

"Yes, they are, but we could have all gone. I didn't want to argue with a dork." She grinned.

"Not today." Kiryn laughed.

"So, when did Gavin and Noah become BFF's?" Aspen asked.

"When Gavin jumped to your defense against Joseph."

"*What?* Why, what did Joseph do?"

"He made some comment in school the other day that Sommerville would be better off if you had died instead of your best friend."

That hurt Aspen's feelings even though she didn't know Joseph. "Really? Wow," she said quietly.

"Yeah, but Joseph can be a jerk. Noah said, 'Well maybe you would like to take *me* out.'" He leaped right over a desk to get to Joseph.

"*Are you kidding me?*"

"Nope. Then Gavin came between them, grabbed Joseph by the neck and pushed him up against a wall holding him there threatening to beat the crap out of him if he opened his blankity blank mouth again."

Aspen was speechless. She just stared at Kiryn.

"Seriously! Gavin held him until Rocky insisted he let Joseph go. I have never seen Gavin so mad." Kiryn nudged Aspen with her foot. "He likes you."

Aspen felt the blood rush into her cheeks.

"You like him too. I can see it," Kiryn teased as she dropped to the ground next to Aspen.

"Isn't he with Cassie?"

"Yeah, so what? All's fair in love and war. Hey!" Kiryn jumped right back up and started fiddling with the latch on the gate.

"Look—" Kiryn reached through the iron gate and lifted a small latch. The gate clicked, and one side of the gate moved just slightly toward them.

"Ahhh!" Aspen laughed. "Noah is going to freak out."

Kiryn proudly pushed the gate open, and the two girls marched through it.

Aspen's heart ached to hear Kiryn's confirmation about Cassie and Gavin.

24

LIVING CANVAS

KIRYN PULLED THE GATE shut and flipped the little latch back into place.

They both laughed as they walked up the driveway and onto the porch. Aspen went directly to the front door and pushed the thumb latch down. The door opened. "I can't believe this." She pushed on the door and the two went inside.

"Holy cow!" Kiryn was looking at the entry hall paintings of Aspen's grandparents and great-grandparents.

"I know huge. We don't even have a wall this big in San Clemente and the little house? Well, the entire thing could fit in this entryway."

"I doubt that," said Kiryn. Then she looked sideways at Aspen. "You guys have funny names for your house. The little house and servants' quarters. Why is that?"

"Okay, so it is a *little* bigger than this entry." Aspen shrugged. "I don't know. Noah hates that we live *down there in the servants' quarters* as he puts it and I just think it's a cute little house. It doesn't seem like home to us."

"Hmm. Well you do know that it *was* the servants' quarters, right?"

"Yeah, I know."

"Back in the day, the servants, usually a family, always lived on the grounds of the people they worked for."

"You mean slaves?" Aspen said sarcastically. "I cannot believe anyone ever owned another human being. It's so…. *medieval!*"

"I agree, but I am not talking about slaves. I just mean hired help. Usually the workers were a dad and mom. Each had a job at the house and sometimes their brothers and sisters too. By living on the grounds, they could have their children with them and be close to work. It just made sense in those days. They were usually very good friends with their *employers*."

"Okay, if you say so. I have never heard of such a thing. We had a cleaning lady, and Mom hires some women to help her when we have parties, but they live at their own houses and drive to ours to work, like any other normal person."

"It's just different, that's all." Kiryn walked over to the stairs. "Is that locked room up here?"

Aspen suddenly felt guilty for snapping at Kiryn. "Hey."

"What?" Kiryn looked back at her. "Sorry for sounding so irritated about the servant's thing. It's just—"

"No big deal. I don't understand fancy sports cars, surfing at the beach all day long and cleaning ladies either, so we are even!"

Aspen laughed. "Guess so." She hadn't considered Kiryn's perspective.

When the front door flew open, they both jumped.

"Hey! How did you get in here?" Noah stomped in with Gavin right behind him.

"Everything was unlocked." Kiryn laughed.

"How was the hike?"

"Whatever," said Noah and he rolled his eyes at Gavin who had a tiny smirk on his face.

"We were just going up to that room Aspen was talking about."

"Cool." Gavin pulled something out of his back pocket, "The magic entry tool."

Aspen came up behind Gavin. "What is that?"

"Have a friend from town whose dad is a locksmith." He raised his eyebrows. "Where is this room?" he said in a low even tone.

"Oh brother." said Kiryn. "Do you even know how to use that thing?"

"He showed me." Gavin wielded the tool like a sword. Noah went ahead of them. "We can figure it out."

In seconds they were all in the long hallway at the top of the stairs.

Kiryn began oohing and awing as she peered into each of the bedrooms. Gavin and Noah went to work on the locked door, and Aspen started toward the storage, but then she stopped in front of the painting—the one she had previously been drawn to.

She glanced quickly at Noah and their friends to see if they were watching her, but they weren't even looking in her direction.

Aspen turned slowly now to face the painting. It was the Allen children just as Kiryn had described in her history lesson. A girl of maybe thirteen or fourteen, a younger girl and a toddler boy, who she knew was her grandpa. They were raised in this house in the 1940s and 50s.

"You must be Riley," Aspen barely breathed the words. She reached out and lightly touched the cheek of the pleasant-looking teenager. She slid her hand down and touched the faces of the other two children, her eyes resting on the little boy, her grandfather she had never met. That dad had never made an effort for them to meet. Why?

Still touching the picture, she glanced over her shoulder. Gavin and Noah were busily trying to break into the room. Kiryn was looking curiously at a fake tree at the far end of the hall.

Aspen thought she heard Kiryn say, "Hey you guys," but then Kiryn turned and walked to the window talking as usual to anyone who was listening and right now none of them were.

Something in the painting moved under Aspen's hand, and she jerked her head around. She pulled her hand away and again, only more cautiously, she touched the canvas. It was moving—the tiny threads shifting ever so slightly. She could actually see them as well as feel them.

Aspen shivered and attempted to pull her hand away then suddenly she was looking out from—

Where am I? I'm, I'm…inside the painting?!

In an instant, Aspen faced the painting again, her fingers stuck to the canvas! She struggled to breathe as she anxiously kept trying to free them, but the pull of the painting held two of her fingers firmly in place. It felt much like when she had superglue on her fingers.

She looked over her shoulder. Noah, Gavin nor Kiryn were looking in her direction. A tiny panic rushed through her, and she tugged harder. This time, her fingers pulled free. Clasping her hand to her chest, she rubbed her fingers with the other hand, and quickly checked her body. Everything seemed normal. She stared at the painting. The tiny threads still seemed to be moving, especially right behind Riley. Aspen squinted and leaned closer to the painting. An image was forming.

A girl! Right behind Riley, another girl! Aspen's eyes widened, and she backed away.

She glanced again at Noah, Gavin, and Kiryn and turned back to the painting. Staying back a safe distance, she studied the image.

Riley and the girl in shadow *did* wear the same necklace. A tiny, long-stemmed flower, but the flower on the necklace of the girl in shadow faced the opposite direction.

Maybe Mom was right. Maybe she saw a reflection of the painting that was reversed, but then she saw what she had seen the first time she looked at this painting. It was barely noticeable, but it was there.

The teenage girl in the picture, the one called Riley, had perfectly straight teeth. The girl in the shadow had one chipped tooth, right in the front. This was a different girl!

Aspen whirled around. She wanted to say something, but what?

Noah and Gavin were getting frustrated with the door, and Kiryn was ambling towards Aspen. She was talking, but she sounded muffled like she was talking through a blanket.

Aspen suddenly felt anxious. *Why do I see this? Who is she if she is anybody at all? Why did I feel like I was in that painting? Maybe I really* am *crazy!*

She felt her chest tighten and she couldn't breathe, but right at that same instant, a soft breeze blew past the staircase towards her from the left side of the hallway. It was as though someone had just opened a window or turned a fan on low. Considering what had happened the last time she felt a breeze like that, she quickly scanned the hallway for anything that may suddenly hit her.

The breeze was coming from the direction of the room where the other picture was and where Noah thought someone touched him.

Time seemed to stop and then begin again only different, in slow motion.

At the end of that hall to her left, there was a girl with long dark hair, but she wasn't *totally* there. Aspen could see right through her. Her hair wafted about her shoulders, and her white dress whisked around her knees as though a fan was blowing on her. Her face was indiscernible, almost translucent.

This barely visible girl mesmerized Aspen.

Laughter.

Pulled out of the trance by the familiar whimsical sound, Aspen turned to look in the direction the laughter came from—the door where Noah and Gavin were struggling with the lock.

Gavin's hand was on the doorknob, and he said, "Here goes nothing."

Just as he spoke, Aspen saw a tall woman with dark skin and black hair. Aspen was stunned that neither of the boys seemed to notice her. Equally as surprising, Kiryn walked right past her heading directly for Aspen. The woman put her hand on top of Gavin's, the door opened, and then she was gone. Vanished. Just gone.

Aspen whirled and looked down the hall—the girl was coming toward her and Aspen backed away bumping into Kiryn.

Just as the girl reached the top of the stairs, she turned to go down. Instead, she took another step, and simply disappeared. It was as though she went through an invisible door.

"Hey? Are you okay?" Kiryn looked curiously at Aspen.

Aspen now realized that Kiryn, Gavin and Noah were all talking at the same time.

"What is so interesting about that painting?" Kiryn leaned over her shoulder.

"Yes!" Gavin was obviously pleased with himself.

Noah gave him a high five. "C'mon Aspen," he called over his shoulder.

"N...nothing," Aspen said to Kiryn. "That little kid is my grandpa." She glanced at the empty hallway where the girl had been.

"Hmm, cute." Kiryn glanced at the painting and then tugged on Aspen's arm. "C'mon, they got the door open."

Noah and Gavin stood in the hallway gaping through the open door.

"Why don't you go in?" Aspen walked up beside Noah and glanced over her shoulder. An empty hallway.

"Don't know, just had a strange feeling when that door opened," Noah whispered.

He looked directly at Aspen and she read his eyes. His face wore the same expression it had when he thought someone had touched him the last time they were in this house.

Aspen wondered if she should say anything about that day with Kiryn and Gavin there, so she just raised her eyebrows a bit. Noah shook his head, and she knew he picked up on her unspoken question.

Gavin stepped forward and pushed the door open a little more.

All four of them gasped. The room was pitch black. No windows.

"What do you make of this?" said Noah. "Every other room in this house has windows, big windows."

Their eyes had adjusted a little, and Noah reached for the inside wall of the room. He fumbled for a minute and then flipped a light switch. It surprised them all that the only lights in the room appeared to be two bare bulbs hanging on long cords from the center of the high A-shaped ceiling.

"The room seems so, so antique—" said Aspen.

"You mean ancient, don't you?" added Noah.

"It's kind of like they forgot about it," said Kiryn. "The rest of the house is more updated."

"Well, if it were just storage, it wouldn't have mattered," said Gavin as the four peered from the doorway.

Stacked trunks and shelves lined the walls. Lamps, suitcases, boxes, dresses folded and sealed in plastic, toys, *really* old toys, a guitar, shoes, shoes and more shoes, and paintings in old frames that were leaning against the wall one in front of the other.

A big round braided rug, much like the one in the little house, lay in the center of the room covering most of the wood-planked floor.

"Wow," Aspen breathed.

"Should we go in?" Kiryn's enthusiasm was not hard to notice, but still, she hesitated.

"Uh, yes—" Aspen stuttered.

"What's up with you?" Noah gave her an annoyed look. "I thought this is what you wanted."

"And we worked so *hard*," Gavin joked.

"I know. I'm...I'm sorry." Aspen glanced down the hall in both directions. Her eyes paused on the painting of the three children. Nothing.

She sighed. "Do you think Mom and Dad will be coming soon?"

"Nope," said Noah. "They told me this morning before we left for school." He looked at Aspen, "Before you got up, that they would be late. They are meeting some people for dinner at 7:30 after they get through with a bunch of legal stuff. That is in Memphis, so they have about a thirty-minute drive after that."

"See! We are good," Kiryn smiled. "C'mon!" She tugged on Aspen's arm again and then gently pushed her into the room.

"Well, you two have at it. We're going to check out the door that goes to a wall." Gavin laughed.

"You think I'm kidding?" Noah started for the stairs. "No. Crazy," chided Gavin.

Noah rolled his eyes and loped down the stairs. Gavin followed.

Suzann watched her husband become angrier by the minute.

"So, what you're telling me is that you can't find the will? How can that happen? Who's in charge of this place anyway? I know your firm has made a lot of money off my grandfather, and my dad. So who is going to solve this problem?"

Jackson yelled at Corey Baker, the stout little man behind the massive glass-topped desk.

"Mr. Allen, I have no idea where that will is. Your sister came in here over two months ago with the same request. The firm changed hands nearly five years ago. I suppose it was lost in the shuffle." Corey pulled a handkerchief from his inside suit pocket and mopped his brow.

"Lost! How does a big firm like this lose a will? You have computers, don't you? Find it!"

"Mr. All—"

Jackson jumped to his feet, startling Suzann and Corey Baker. "Forget it! You can deal with my attorney—a real law firm—not one that's run by a bunch of irresponsible idiots!"

Jackson stomped out the door, and Suzann followed. When they reached the first floor, Jackson sank onto a bench near the elevator.

Suzann put her hand on his shoulder. "Jackson, are you okay?"

When he looked up at her, his face looked suddenly older than his forty-four years. The lines in his forehead and between his eyebrows seemed deeper, and the dark circles under his eyes caused his eyes to look sunken.

In this vulnerable state, her heart ached for the man she loved. She moved her hand to the back of his neck, gently massaging his tired muscles. For a second Jackson seemed to relax, but when the elevator doors opened, he stood quickly.

"Let's go."

25

MORE PAINTINGS

ASPEN LOOKED OVER HER shoulder again and down the hall in both directions. Cautiously, she walked farther into the room.

"Are you okay?" Kiryn quickly looked around the hallway before she stepped in, and her eyes widened. "That old guy isn't *here*, is he?"

Aspen shook her head. "No…not yet."

Kiryn's eyes squinted almost shut. "Don't mess with me, Aspen."

"I'm not," she teased and pulled her friend inside.

No old man was there, but who were all of these other people?

Aspen stared in disbelief. A half dozen people were milling about the room. Some acknowledged her with a smile or a nod. Most did not seem to notice her.

Kiryn was oblivious to the entire scene. She rattled on about the dull gray walls and the floor made of wide wooden planks. "Look how it's not varnished and shiny, it just has a thin coat of finish over it. It's hardly worn at all."

"Hey? Anybody home?" Kiryn tapped her knuckles on Aspen's head.

"I'm, sorry, I just—" When Aspen spoke the people all turned and walked directly toward her and Kiryn. They passed right through them both and into the hallway.

Aspen whirled around, staring after them. Where she and Kiryn stood, the top of the staircase was in full view. Each of the people turned to go down the staircase, but instead, one at a time, they simply vanished—just as the girl had.

"Sooo—" Kiryn twisted her mouth and squinted at Aspen. "What are you looking at?"

Aspen slowly turned to Kiryn. "I…I'm not…sure."

Kiryn had already turned her attention back to the storage room. "So do you think Noah was right? This room was missed in the update of the rest of the house?"

"Ummm, yeah. Yeah, but—" Aspen looked at her friend and then spoke more directly to avoid any more of Kiryn's questions. "I don't think the house has been updated. I think this room just missed the original building!" Aspen quickly glanced around. She and Kiryn were alone.

I think.

The two girls walked into the middle of the room. "Where do we start?" Kiryn picked up a box and then set it back down. "What exactly are we looking for?"

Aspen took a deep breath. She looked around one more time and deciding the people were really gone—if they had ever been there at all. She clasped her hands, threading her fingers together. "Pictures."

"Pictures or paintings? Those leaning against the wall?"

"Let's start there."

There were several stacks of pictures, but what drew Aspen's attention were the six large paintings leaning against the wall.

One matched the one in the entry of her grandparents. Only it was smaller. The rest of the paintings were of many different couples with children.

A large group family painting was particularly interesting to Aspen. The last one was of one family. Aspen recognized the three children. Her great-grandparents family. None of them were smiling much.

"Well, that's a happy group," quipped Kiryn, and she busied herself with some boxes on the floor.

"I think that's just how they posed for pictures back then."

"Lame."

Aspen turned her attention back to the painting of the couples with children. In the center of the group was an older couple seated side by side. Their clothes depicted a family with money.

The women and girls wore dresses made of shiny fabric. Aspen guessed satin. Ruffles on the sleeves and neck and yards of lace at the bottom hid the presence of shoes. Each dress had that same high collar look that her great-grandmother wore in the painting in the entry hall, the kind that made Aspen's throat feel tight. Even worse were the sashes that gathered the yards of fabric snug to tiny waists.

Fancy suits, tuxedos really, with cummerbunds and coats with tails adorned all the men. Their pants were normal enough but with unusually wide cuffs, and each wore shiny black shoes.

Every boy, even the teenagers, wore a jacket with a lacy white shirt. Their pants were short like knickers and to Aspen's chagrin, white tights and the same style of shiny black dress shoes.

"Can you see Noah and Gavin dressed in those clothes? Too funny," Aspen chuckled.

Kiryn leaned toward Aspen. "Well, in today's world, they would look like total freaks. Actually, in that world too! Look at all of these other pictures. Everyone is dressed in normal jeans and pants."

"Dad said something about this is how they dressed for pictures."

Kiryn scoffed, "I guess if you were rich. My grandparents were wearing overalls and house dresses in their pictures!"

They both laughed, and Aspen scanned the painting, locating her great-grandparents and her grandpa, who was seated next to his mother. He appeared to be three or four years old. His older sister was standing behind him, her hand on her mother's arm. On the other side was the teenage daughter. Her face wore a pleasant smile. She was standing just behind her father, her hand on his shoulder. In front of her, hiding part of her dress, was a large potted-plant.

Aspen absently rubbed her fingers across the painting. Her eyes drifted back to the teenage daughter.

"Hey, look." Kiryn pulled the painting away from the wall

drawing Aspen's attention to the smaller duplicate painting of just Aspen's great-grandparents and their three children.

"Looks like it is a copy of Great-Grandpa's family from the big painting."

The two girls moved the larger painting from in front of the smaller one and Kiryn leaned closer, inspecting the smaller painting. "That's odd."

"What?"

With her fingernail, Kiryn lifted a tiny chip of paint from the potted plant. "The paint is peeling." Kiryn looked at the family painting and then with her fingernail, she chipped at the pot in that painting. Tiny flakes of paint fell on the floor.

"Weird. Is that normal for paint to come off the canvas?"

"I don't know. Cheap canvas?" Kiryn smirked and peeled another tiny piece.

"Or old canvas." Aspen moved Kiryn's hand to the side. "If we are going to mess it up, better me than you." She scraped the paint with her fingernail, and a small piece came off. She moved to Grandpa's suit coat and tried to peel the paint. Nothing. Then she tried a few more spots on the painting—still nothing. Moving back to the potted plant, she flipped up some more tiny flecks with her fingernail. "I wonder how come that spot is peeling."

"I don't know." Kiryn shrugged. "But it almost seems like the plant was painted later. Look." She leaned the painting forward so that they could see it from a side angle. "The paint on the plant is thicker." She stopped talking and looked closer at the smaller one. "It is on this one too."

"It is?" said Aspen thoughtfully.

"Totally weird." Kiryn curled her legs underneath her, sat on the floor, and turned her attention to the pictures she had taken out of a box.

"Did you find anything?" Aspen was still studying the paintings.

"Like what? It would be nice to know what I am searching for."

Kiryn flipped through the pictures. "These are mostly pictures of kids."

Aspen joined Kiryn on the braided rug and they passed pictures back and forth. Aspen kept coming back to a small picture of two girls who were about the same age, another girl a little younger and baby. She finally held the picture up to the large family painting.

"Do either of these girls look like she could be this girl?" She held it next to the teenage girls head.

Kiryn shrugged. "I guess it could be, but those little girls are so young, and the pictures aren't very good."

Without saying a word, Aspen suddenly stood and ran from the room.

Aspen's actions startled Kiryn, and she jumped to follow her.

Aspen went straight to the window seat in her dad's old room, opened it, and picked up the picture she put back just a few days earlier.

"Look," she thrust it in Kiryn's face.

Kiryn leaned back away from the picture. "What?'

"Do these girls—" Aspen pointed to the toddlers in the picture she had just picked up. "Look like these girls?" she pointed to the picture with the four kids.

Kiryn looked back and forth between the two pictures, "They could be, I guess."

"One of the girls is much smaller than the other. Maybe they are not the same age in this picture," said Aspen. She held up the picture of the two toddlers. "But here they look the same—like they are the same age."

"What are you getting at?" Kiryn looked confused.

Aspen was exasperated. "I don't know! It's just a feeling that I have."

They were distracted by footsteps on the stairs. "Aspen! Kiryn!" Noah hissed their names.

The two girls hurried out of the bedroom. Noah and Gavin were running toward them.

"What's the matter?" Aspen whispered.

"We have to get out of here. A car just pulled up to the house."

Gavin stopped at the top of the stairs and looked down to the front door. "Sounds like it's driving away."

They all relaxed.

"I wonder who that—"

The front door flew open and heavy footsteps clamored across the entry to the stairs.

26

INTRUDERS

THEY HEARD TWO MEN'S voices.

"Quick, in that room," Kiryn pushed Gavin and Noah toward the storage room where she and Aspen had just been. Aspen, however, turned around and ran back into the bedroom. She shut the window seat but kept the picture. She ran back out of the bedroom just in time to see the storage room door shut and the tops of two men's heads coming up the stairs. One of them was Drew.

What is he doing here?

The only place for her to go was back into the bedroom, but there was no time to close the door. She fell to the floor and slid under the bed.

"I put it in this drawer," one of the men said. It wasn't Drew.

They walked past the open door and stopped.

Aspen heard them open a drawer she assumed was in one of the hall tables. She could hear them rustling with some papers and then it sounded like they knelt down on the carpet.

"Where do you think this is?" It was Drew's voice.

"I'm not sure. It could be nothing, but it looks like, I don't know. A tunnel?" That was the other man speaking.

"I don't know either. I've searched all over this damn house, and I can't find anything. This is an old handmade map, and there have been a lot of improvements since this thing was drawn."

From the hallway, Aspen could hear what sounded like paper

being rolled or folded.

"I just want to find that box. It has to be in this house somewhere." Drew sounded agitated. "At least Aunt Beth told me the box was in this house."

"Well, at least it's easier to be here while the Allen's are in and out all the time." He paused for a few seconds. "How did you know the house would be open anyway?"

"I didn't." laughed Drew. "I came back when everyone was leaving last night. I waited in the pantry until everyone was gone and then I unlocked the front door and disengaged the electric gate. Mr. J keeps this place locked up tighter than a drum but I knew he wasn't going to be here today. "

They both laughed.

"So that's why you had Randy take the truck? So it wouldn't be parked in the driveway?"

"Yeah, I told them to be back by eight. Hey, don't let me forget to set the gate again."

Eight o'clock?! Anxiety rushed over Aspen.

"So we have about six hours," said one of the men.

"Yep. We better get busy. Let's start in the old man's bedroom."

The two men started back down the hall, but first one of them walked into the bedroom where Aspen was hiding. She held her breath.

"Why is this door open?" Drew pulled it shut, and relief flooded through Aspen as beads of sweat emerged on her forehead and neck.

She heard the men walking but then they stopped again. One of them tried a doorknob.

The storage?!

She propped up on her elbows to hear better. The top of her head pushing into the box springs. Her heart was pounding so hard she could only take tiny short breaths.

"What is up with this room?" the other man said.

"Dunno. It's been locked for as long as I have worked here."

It sounded like one of the men hit the door with his hand as they walked away from it.

"Another day, another dollar," Drew laughed.

"Oh, I think the Allen's have a lot more than a dollar for you." Their laughing got quieter as they moved farther down the hall.

"Holy cow!" hissed Noah. Gavin and Kiryn nodded.

"Who are they?" whispered Gavin.

"One of them sounded like Drew, but I can't be sure. I wonder what they want."

"Money," said Gavin whispering even more softly than before.

"We need to see if Aspen's okay," Kiryn said so quietly the two boys barely heard her.

"She's probably okay. She's hiding I'm sure." Noah opened the door a crack. He could only see the stair railing. He softly pulled it shut.

Kiryn walked over to the pile of small boxes on the floor. "I can't stand this. I have to do something if we are staying in here."

"Let's give it a few minutes and see if Aspen comes to us. I don't want to attract those guys attention." Noah sank down next to the door.

Gavin still stood leaning against the wall. "Yeah, sounds like they are just down the hall."

Aspen could still hear the men's muffled voices, so she held perfectly still. After what seemed like millennia, she felt sure they were staying where they were for a while, and she opted to make a run for the storage room.

She slid from under the bed, stood and tiptoed to the door but was terrified to open it. By pressing her ear against the door, she could hear muffled mumblings of the two men.

Aspen leaned against the door until her breathing slowed to a somewhat normal pace, and then she cracked the door open and peered out. She could see past the stairs but not into the hall where she thought the men had gone. She listened for a minute. It sounded like they were still down that hall as she suspected.

The storage room was two doors away. Aspen would have to lean out into the hall to see it. Rubbing her sweaty hands on her jeans, she took a deep breath and slowly opened the door wider. It didn't look that far. She gingerly stepped into the hallway—

"HEY!"

Aspen's heart went straight to her throat as she scrambled back through the open bedroom door. Heavy footsteps tromped in her direction as she closed the door to a tiny slit.

She slowly turned the doorknob to depress the latch until the door was completely closed and then she carefully engaged the latch.

Every fiber of her body was shaking, her heart was racing, and her throat was so dry she couldn't swallow.

"Go out there and tell that idiot to shut up. Better yet, tell him to come back when I told him to," Drew yelled as the other man ran down the stairs.

She heard the front door open, two voices arguing, and then the door slammed shut. The man was running back up the stairs. The sound of his heavy footsteps finally stopped, and she heard the door down the hall close again.

She sighed heavily and raked her fingers through her hair. She was trapped in the room, and she did not know how to get to Noah and the others.

She crouched behind the door, trying to sort things out.

"Aspen!" The door opened, and she jumped to her feet, clamping her hands over her mouth to suppress her scream.

"Gavin!" she hissed.

He put his finger to his lips as he slid into the room. "Shhh," he quietly closed the door behind him.

"Where are—"

"Shhh," he said, again his voice softer than the first time. "But how did—"

Gavin finally put his hand over Aspen's mouth. "Geez—"

Aspen's eyes widened. "Just be quiet—"

Aspen nodded, and he lowered his hand. He backed to the door and motioned for her to follow. Gavin opened it just a bit, and they both peered out. Without warning, he turned, put his hand under her chin, and lifted her face to his.

She melted under Gavin's emerald gaze as his other hand cupped the back of her head, and he pressed his lips firmly against hers.

Aspen's heart was racing when he released his kiss. With his lips brushing her cheek, he whispered, "I have wanted to do that since that first day at school."

He turned and cracked the door open. Aspen's head was still spinning when he pulled her into the hallway. Elation and apprehension wrestled with her emotions.

"C'mon." He closed the bedroom door and keeping her close, they covered the distance to the storage room door.

Gavin closed the door and locked it. Once inside, he released Aspen's hand.

Noah gave Aspen a curious look and the minute he did she realized her face felt flushed. Fumbling for words she blurted, "Did you hear those guys?"

"Not very well. We were trying," said Noah.

"They are searching for a box or something. There is something in it that his aunt told him about."

"Whose aunt?" Noah looked confused.

"Drew's! That was Drew."

Noah nodded to Gavin. "I thought that was his voice." He again looked curiously at his sister, "You okay?"

Aspen started to answer, but Gavin stepped in, "She was just scared. Found her behind the bedroom door." He turned slightly from Noah and Kiryn's view and winked at her.

Aspen nodded quickly, "He said the Allen's owe him a lot. They…they are the men that left the house unlocked."

Gavin reached for Aspen's hand again, and even though her entire body tingled, she deliberately pulled away.

Suddenly she was angry. If Gavin was with Cassie, why did he kiss her? She didn't like being second best to anybody. Not that she had a lot of experience being first but still!

"I thought we were dead when they tried to get in here. Figured they had a key," said Noah.

"I—I thought you were dead, too." Aspen was still holding the small picture in her hand.

"What's that?" asked Gavin.

"A picture of two little girls," Aspen said flatly and glared at him.

Gavin looked surprised. "That's what you went back for?"

"Yes." They were all looking at her so she snatched the small picture that Kiryn was still holding. "Don't they look like they could be the same kids?"

"Yeah, so?" Noah looked a little perplexed.

"Could be." Gavin glanced at the two pictures but then dismissed the subject and looked toward the door. "Should we try to get out of here now?

"*I* would still like to look around." Aspen turned on her heel crossing the floor to Kiryn.

Gavin shrugged. "It's your neck," he murmured. "Well, all of our necks."

"What?" Aspen stopped and glared at him. "If you don't want to be—"

"Geez, Aspen lighten up." Noah pulled a face. "What's up with you?"

Aspen ignored all of their questioning looks and sat on the floor next to Kiryn.

Kiryn glanced at Gavin, who was still standing motionless by the door. She turned back to the boxes surrounding her and lifted a book from one of them.

Her blue eyes sparkled. "Check this out."

SECRETS IN PRINT

Now it was Gavin's turn for confusion. *What's up with her? I thought she liked me.* He picked up a small notebook and sat on the other side of Kiryn. He didn't bother to look at Aspen. He was baffled by her sudden coolness.

Noah studied both of them, but neither Gavin nor Aspen acknowledged him.

Kiryn had a suede-covered book sitting in front of her. It had a little lock in the center of the front cover and a flap with the other side of the lock that held it in place. The cover was battered and worn, and the leather flap had been cut, leaving the lock engaged. Loose papers stuck out of the top and bottom of the book. The initials JHA were imprinted on the bottom right corner.

Noah was sitting across from Kiryn who turned the book so that he could read it.

They all spoke in hushed tones.

"Where did you get this?" Aspen peered at the initials on the cover. "Is this our great-great grandpa's?"

"I think so." Noah turned to the first page and whispered, "Problem is there are a ton of loose pages. Some of them don't even look like they belong to this book."

"But every page has your great-grandpa's initials at the bottom," said Kiryn

Noah picked up one of the papers and read:

Life couldn't be better. We moved the family into the manor on the lake just in time for Thanksgiving and Christmas.

JHA Nov 1948

"But then look at this." Noah held the page in front of Aspen. "A word or words were scribbled out."

"Exactly," Added Kiryn. "We can't read the first word but the second definitely said *is*. It has been replaced with *are*."

"We *are* so excited," read Aspen.

"Correct," said Noah. "But if the second word was once *is*, then *we* doesn't make sense. We *is* so excited?"

"Hmm." Aspen shrugged. "I don't know. Maybe he just made a mistake."

"Maybe," agreed Noah.

"I can't find any more pages that make sense after that entry," said Kiryn. "But then look at this one."

Aspen took the page from Kiryn and read:

This morning our daughter was missing. Her bed had not been slept in, and after searching until dark, one of my hired workers came to me and told me he thought she might have run away with his brother. He said they had talked about it, but he did not think they would actually do it.

I will kill that kid.

JHA April 4, 1957

Aspen put her hand on the book to stop Noah. "So there was another daughter? Besides Riley?" Immediately she thought of the girl in the hallway.

"Aspen?"

"What? I mean so…so, what do you think?"

Noah eyed her suspiciously. "I was just saying that I don't think there was another daughter." Noah glanced at the painting Aspen and Kiryn had propped in front of the other paintings. He pointed to their grandfather's family in the painting. "She looks like she is maybe fifteen, must have been done before she ran away."

Aspen thought of the other people she had seen in this room earlier, and she looked toward that wall.

Noah turned to where Aspen had been looking, "What is so interesting over there?"

"N…nothing." There was no way Aspen was telling the other three that there had been several people in this room earlier and that all of them just vanished.

Kiryn waited for Aspen to respond to Noah's question. When she didn't, she said, "I wonder if she ever did come back." Her voice was so quiet it was hard to hear her, "It makes me sad."

"Yeah, this is depressing," said Gavin. He leaned back, resting his forearms on his bent knees and looked at the floor, turning the small notebook over and over in his hands.

"What's that?" Noah reached for it, but Gavin pulled it back with a grin.

Noah sighed. "Where did you get it?"

"It was in the same box the book was in." He motioned to a wooden box on the floor next to Kiryn.

Kiryn explained for Aspen's benefit, "I found this box, and Noah got the lock off."

"Looks like you had to break it," said Aspen.

"Pretty much." Noah turned back to Gavin. "So what's in the notebook?"

"A map or drawing or something," Gavin dropped the notebook on top of the open journal they had been reading.

Aspen picked it up. "To where?"

"I thought you and Noah could tell us." Gavin didn't hide his sarcasm.

Noah eyed Aspen first and then Gavin but said nothing.

They all leaned over the notebook. It was a sketch of what looked like the upper hallway of the house and one room on the lower level, at least it looked like a room, but it had odd angles and seemed small.

"Bring it with us," said Noah.

Aspen seemed hesitant. "Are we stealing?"

"I think we are way past stealing. Let's say breaking and entering—"

Kiryn twisted her mouth. "Oh Gavin, we didn't break or enter anything. We just walked in the front door."

"Without permission. So just entering," said Gavin.

Noah looked at the broken lock on the box Kiryn had found and the band he had cut to open the locked book. He pursed his lips. "Yeah, we are way past stealing. We'll just take it."

"What did you cut it with?" Aspen asked.

Gavin reached behind him and revealed a pocketknife. "Figured it might come in handy."

Noah shrugged when Aspen gave him a why-didn't-you-think-of-that look. "Gavin is a lot better burglar than I am."

Gavin rolled his eyes, "You got that right. I am tired of whispering, though. Let's get out of here."

28

RECOGNITION

Noah went to the door, turned the deadbolt from the inside, and carefully cracked the door open. They all crowded behind him.

Faint voices of the two men came from behind a closed door.

Noah whispered, "You guys go. Be really quiet. Go out through the kitchen, not the front door."

"Aren't you coming?" Then Aspen added, "I'll wait with you."

"No, I'm coming. I will lock the door and be right behind you." Aspen nodded. "Okay." She picked up the journal.

"Wait." Kiryn lifted the box, closed the lid, and carefully placed the journal right where she had first found it, placing some loose papers back on top of it.

Noah helped Aspen put the large painting behind the other paintings leaving the room looking as undisturbed as possible.

Aspen placed the two pictures she and Kiryn had found between some pages of the journal and closed it. She scanned the room for any images of the people she had seen earlier—no one, not even the girl.

Noah opened the door and peeked out. He motioned to Gavin and then held the door open to let him through.

Gavin crept across the hallway. By the time he reached the stairs, Kiryn was on her way with Aspen close behind.

When Aspen passed the painting where she had seen the image

of the girl, she felt a tiny shiver on the back of her neck. She paused and glanced down the hall.

When she hesitated by the painting, Noah pushed on her back. "Hurry up," he breathed.

Within minutes they were all four running across the back lawn to the steps leading down to the little house.

Noah checked his phone for the time. "It's only four o'clock. Those idiots messed up everything."

"Not everything," said Gavin. "Why don't we get something to eat and come back after those guys leave? We could check out the cabinets."

"Is that all you think about is food?" said Kiryn.

"Well someone has to. I'm starving."

"We could fix something." Aspen looked at Noah.

"Naw. Let's try that Bill and Nada's place," Noah suddenly stopped. "Wait, how will we get back in the house?"

Noah motioned for Gavin to follow him and started running back up the steps.

While the girls waited, Aspen pulled a loose paper from the journal and read aloud:

There was a time when I thought she was a gift. When she gave me my son.

JHA June 16, 1998

My heart aches for you, my beloved sweet Ronda. I loved you, more than you could ever know.

JHA June 21, 1998

Aspen turned to Kiryn whose eyes were huge. "Wow," mouthed Kiryn.

Noah and Gavin clamored down the steps but stopped when they saw the look on both girls' faces.

"What?" Noah said.

"Noah, Great-Grandpa had an affair!" Aspen stared wide-eyed at her brother.

"Yeah, and it seems as though your grandpa was not your great-grandma's kid," added Kiryn.

"Well affairs aren't that unusual," Gavin said nonchalantly.

"Well, they are in our family." Aspen slapped her open hand on the journal.

"Like you know so much about your family," Gavin said dryly.

Kiryn stood abruptly, "Okay, I don't know what's wrong with you two but give it a rest already!"

Aspen and Gavin locked eyes and then both turned away. "He—he must have been fearful of it ruining his business or his life. Maybe because it sounds like the lady left him," said Aspen.

"What about his *marriage*?" Noah rolled his eyes.

"We should probably read a little more of it before we accuse him of adultery," said Gavin.

Aspen got the feeling Noah was not too excited to find out more about their great-grandfather's past. How could she blame him? It just kept getting worse.

When no one responded, Gavin sighed, "Okay, well, we left a window unlocked, and now we need to eat."

Aspen and Kiryn stood. When they did, Aspen's phone fell out of her back pocket. The jolt brought the main screen up.

Gavin picked it up, but before he handed it to her, he stopped and stared at the screen. His face looked confused. "Who is that?"

Aspen took it from him and made the picture bigger. "Krista."

"Krista?"

"Yes, Gavin. Krista. Her friend that…that died in California."

"Where have you been?" Kiryn was visibly annoyed.

Gavin held his open hand toward Aspen, and she reluctantly placed the phone in it. He studied the screen more closely and then slowly handed it back to Aspen.

"What?" Aspen clicked the screen off.

When Gavin spoke, it was just a casual comment, "She's very pretty."

The three of them stared at Gavin.

Aspen's irritation was obvious when she snapped, "Yeah she is—was."

29

BILL AND NADA'S

FRESH HOT BREAD AND apple pie, two of Bill and Nada's specialties, wafted through the door when the kids arrived. Booth lined walls and tables crowded in the middle of the floor. The crowded cafe was bursting at the seams with comfort food appeal. It wasn't hard to understand what made it such a popular spot in Sommerville.

Bill and Nada's opened in 1968, when the owners were fresh out of high school. Now, both in their mid-sixties, they still greeted each guest and oversaw the daily creation of their famous home-cooked meals to the delight of customers both old and new.

Today, Noah and Aspen being, the new, and Kiryn and Gavin, along with Mr. Fielden, who had unexpectedly stopped in for lunch, being among the old.

"So, what are you kids doing?"

"Hey, Rocky." Kiryn jumped up and kissed him on the cheek.

"Hi, Dad. I would jump up and give you a kiss too, but I'm stuck in the back of this booth." He glanced over at Aspen, but she was not looking at him.

"I'll bet you would." Mr. Fielden turned to Aspen and Noah, "You two managed to hook up with the wildest kids in this town."

Aspen laughed. "Hi, Mr. Fielden."

Mr. Fielden scowled. "I'm Mr. Fielden on the school grounds. Out in the world, I am just plain Rocky."

Kiryn and Gavin slid over, and Mr. Fielden sat down. He took one of Kiryn's remaining French fries. "Hear any more about that old guy that was bugging you?"

Aspen blushed. "No, nothing."

"Haven't seen him again?"

"Nope." Aspen felt uncomfortable talking about it.

Gavin glanced at Aspen and then jumped in, "Hey Dad, we have some things we would like to talk to you about."

"Okay, what?"

"Actually, a lot of stuff." Gavin lowered his voice.

"Mr. Field—"

He raised his hand to stop Noah. "Rocky."

"Rocky." Noah started again, "We have a lot going on. We really need to talk to someone."

"We suggested you," Kiryn said with satisfaction.

Rocky eyed Kiryn and then turned to Noah. "What about your parents?"

"Not possible. Not right now. They have not been the same since we got here. Mom acts like she is on guard around Dad."

"And stressed," added Aspen.

"Yeah, that too, and Dad is just not himself."

"Well, a move can do that to parents—" Rocky seemed to change his mind about what he was about to say.

Aspen continued as though she hadn't heard Rocky, "But he is mean or just in a bad mood all the time."

"Moving can be stressful," repeated Rocky.

"We know, but this is different. There is something wrong, and every time we ask questions about anything, we are either ignored, or they jump down our throats. And when Aspen hurt her hip, Mom would normally be all over that stuff, but she hardly seemed to notice."

"I'm sorry." Rocky was sympathetic. He turned to Aspen, "How is your hip anyway?"

"It's fine. Perfect."

"How are you doing, I mean, after losing your friend?"

Immediately tears stung her eyes, but she quickly blinked them back, "I hate it."

"Do you think it might be easier being here, though without the constant reminder that she is gone?" said Rocky.

Aspen nodded. "Yeah." She looked across the table at Gavin but then quickly looked away. His electric green eyes threatened to suck her in, and she was not ready to go there. His kiss had caught her off guard, and the last thing she needed was any more confusion.

Then she caught Kiryn's eye. As usual, her grin was as big as Montana. Once again, Aspen was glad she had met this perpetual happy girl.

Rocky changed the subject, "What are you kid's doing tonight? You must have homework, you know with school being so hard and all."

They all grinned ,and Rocky raised one eyebrow, "I get that you are not going to tell me what you're doing."

They all shook their heads.

"But we'll be done by ten." Gavin laughed but then his brow furrowed when he saw nothing in Aspen's expression.

"Why ten?"

"Our parents will be home then." Noah assumed that was what Gavin was referring to.

"Should I be worried?"

"No." Everyone but Aspen spoke up at the same time. Rocky looked at her. "Should I?"

Aspen squinted. "No, but we will tell you after we get done."

"Maybe," said Gavin.

Rocky pulled his cell phone out of his front pocket. "You'll be in town, right?"

They all nodded.

"Then I will expect you by ten-fifteen, fair?"

"Expect us where?" said Aspen.

"Why at my house, of course. Kiryn and Gavin know the way," he joked.

He snatched another of Kiryn's fries and then stood, "I think we have ice cream." He looked at Kiryn.

"Unless you ate it all." She laughed.

"Ten-fifteen," he called over his shoulder. "And I am a very strict parent." He stopped for a second and turned around, "And Aspen? I really am sorry about your friend."

"Thanks, Mr.—Rocky." Aspen smiled.

"Ten-fifteen."

Gavin saluted. "Roger."

Rocky walked to the door and then turned around again. "Hey, Allen, don't be hot-rodding around in that car. I have friends at the station." He laughed and waved before he let the door close behind him.

Noah twisted his mouth. "Can't get away with anything in this town."

30

UNLIKELY DAD

"Is he Strict? Your dad, I mean?" asked Noah.

"Actually he is. About keeping rules, not breaking laws, that kind of stuff," said Gavin.

"And curfew. But if he knows where we are, he is okay. Just has us text him all the time," added Kiryn.

"Sometimes he seems to worry about things I don't understand at all." Gavin sounded a little distant.

"And yes, he knows everyone, except of course Aspen's strange old man and Gavin's elusive blonde," said Kiryn.

That made everyone squirm a little, especially Aspen.

"So what does he worry about that you don't understand?" Aspen's voice showed signs of hesitancy.

"Mostly people. There are some people that he won't allow me to associate with," said Gavin.

"Like who?" asked Noah.

Gavin turned to Kiryn, "Remember that family that moved in a while ago? The Munoz's or something like that?"

"It was Munoa and yes. They were only here a month, and then they moved back to Memphis," said Kiryn.

"Yeah, I know, but we ran into them in the store one day, and when we were back in the car, Dad firmly told me not to associate with them."

"Aren't they related to your mom somehow?" said Kiryn.

"Maybe—"

"Well, then that makes sense. He is not particularly fond of your mom's family." Kiryn turned to Noah and Aspen and explained, "Not his mom. They get along great, but Rocky never did like the rest of her family."

"Does your mom care if you associate with them?" asked Noah.

"She backs Dad one hundred percent in that area. Not in everything but when it comes to people, yes."

"So is your mom Rocky's sister?" Aspen asked.

Kiryn stood, nodded briefly but abruptly changed the subject, "On that note! We need to read that book. We should go to your house."

Aspen looked at her curiously and then said, "Yeah, we should," and followed Kiryn out of the booth.

Gavin drained his soda cup and then followed the group. "Still seems a little weird to me. I have never even spoken to my mom's family, except for my grandma, and she died a few years ago." He shrugged. "Anyway, about the house, we should check to see if those guys are gone."

"They won't be. Drew said eight o'clock," Noah objected.

"Well, we can hope." Gavin stood with one hand on the passenger door, eyeing Noah.

Noah pulled the keys out of his pocket. He looked over at Gavin. "Don't even think about it."

Gavin laughed. "I won't, but I have always wanted to do that."

"What?' Kiryn climbed in the back seat.

"He wanted to leap over the door without opening it," explained Aspen. "Yeah, Noah would probably kill you."

"No probably about it," Noah said flatly.

When they were all in the car Noah unexpectedly asked, "Can you guys show us where Drew lives?" Then before either of them could answer, he said to Aspen, "Maybe we should call Mom and Dad and see if it's okay if we go to Rocky's tonight."

"Like they will care. At least we won't be home to bother them," Aspen said absently.

Noah glared at her. "*Okay*," Aspen conceded.

Gavin looked from Aspen to Noah. "Drew lives out on the county road. Turn right at the light," he said.

They drove past the school in the opposite direction from the little house and turned onto a road that took them away from the town.

The scenery was about the same as their side of town. Trees, trees, and more trees, but the houses weren't as big. They were nice homes but not mansions like the ones around the lake. Aspen was starting to understand a little more about the Allen reputation.

"I have never seen so many trees," said Aspen. "Anything could be hiding out here."

No one commented on the obvious.

It took about ten minutes to get to Drew's house. The modest home stood on about two acres of ground. Surrounded by a white picket fence, the part of the yard that wasn't covered in trees was covered in grass.

A huge garden plot that had been plowed and planted lay on the south side.

"What is up with Drew? Why do you suppose he thinks he is entitled to money from our dad?" Aspen was asking anyone who was listening.

Gavin answered her random question, "Don't know, but he must have a pretty good reason for all the trouble he is going to. Besides, it's probably from your grandparents, not your dad. My dad said the gardener who worked at your grandparent's house had been there for ten years and one day he just up and quit. Then before you know it, Drew took over. Hey, Noah, slow down here."

"Hmm. Dad said he was fired," said Aspen Gavin gave her a questioning look.

Noah looked over at him, "Why am I slowing down?" Gavin pointed at the house.

Aspen was surprised to see Joseph walk out the front door. "His dad is Drew?"

Gavin nodded. "He usually stays to himself, but his attitude toward you guys has brought out a whole new person."

"We've known him forever, but he has never acted like he does around the two of you," said Kiryn.

"Great, I don't want him to think we came out here to harass him." Noah started to speed up. "We should just turn around before he sees us."

"No, just keep driving. No law says we can't be on this road. It doesn't mean we were coming specifically here."

Joseph disappeared around the side of the house, they heard the roar of a motorcycle engine, and within seconds, he drove out of the driveway and turned onto the road right towards them. At first, it didn't look like Joseph noticed them, but when he passed the car, he suddenly looked back over his shoulder. It was hard to see any note of recognition behind his helmet.

"Maybe he didn't see us," said Aspen.

"Yeah, like this car is so hard to notice," Kiryn laughed.

"I heard about your fight with Joseph, Gavin. Thanks," Aspen turned to face him, and her heart jumped. She didn't like that, and she quickly looked away.

"I just didn't want Noah to get the crap kicked out of him." Gavin was still looking at Aspen.

"Yeah, right." Noah shook his head. His eyebrows furrowed, and his mouth twisted to one side.

Gavin laughed, "Just kidding."

Noah gave him a wary smile.

"So why did you want to come out here, Noah?" said Aspen.

"I don't know. Guess I hoped to see—I'm not even sure," Noah suddenly sounded exasperated.

"The lake is out here," In her best gleeful tone, Kiryn changed the subject.

"Where you water ski?" said Aspen.

"Yep. What is it Gavin about ten miles?"

Gavin nodded. "Do you want to drive out there?"

"Sure." Noah was looking in the rearview mirror. "Hey, a truck just turned into Drew's driveway."

Gavin looked back. "That's Blake Simmons truck."

"Blake. Noah that was one of the names Drew said the other day," said Aspen.

"Sure was."

"When?" asked Gavin.

Aspen answered, "At the house when we found the door. Some guy called to Drew from the backyard and Drew called him Blake."

Noah turned the car around in the middle of the road and drove back toward Drew's. It was easy to stay out of sight with so many trees between them and the house.

"Stop here. We can go over to the side of the house. They will never see us. Hurry before they get out of the truck."

Aspen was surprised Noah wasn't putting up any resistance to Gavin's orders. She guessed it was because Gavin knew more about this area than he did, or maybe he just decided he was his friend. Whatever the reason, it appeared that a little of the chip had fallen off Noah's shoulder.

Noah and Gavin were gone about five minutes. When they came back, they had decided to go back to the little house and wait until eight o'clock instead of driving out to the lake.

"We heard Drew tell Blake they would only be a few minutes. They just had to make some copies then they would go back."

Noah started the car and drove quickly past Drew's house and back toward town.

"We assume back to the house," Gavin answered the question Aspen was about to ask then he added, "Drew was carrying a black folder, you know one of those that has an elastic thing around it to hold it together."

Aspen barely heard Gavin. She was trying to put her thoughts in order. Everything seemed to be in little pieces scattered everywhere, and none of them seemed to fit.

On top of everything else, why did Kiryn dismiss her question about Gavin's mother being Rocky's sister, and what had at first been an electrifying attraction to Gavin, now weighed heavy on her heart. Maybe it was her insecurities, but she had no idea where she fit in Gavin's crowded mind where Cassie and the blonde girl definitely claimed some space.

She suddenly felt tired and wasn't sure she wanted to do anything. Unconsciously she rubbed her hand across the cover of the worn journal.

31

"AM I CRAZY?"

THE LATE AFTERNOON SUN made riding in the convertible nice—just enough of a breeze so that it was not too hot. That, combined with the top down made it difficult to carry on a conversation.

Aspen could see Gavin in the side mirror. He was looking ahead of them, drumming the side of the car with his fingers.

Noah kept looking in the rearview mirror like he was expecting something. She assumed he was looking for Blake's truck.

She looked back at Kiryn. Her head was against the seat, her eyes closed. Aspen sighed. Her thoughts flashed immediately to Krista and what they would be doing on an afternoon like this. The familiar lump formed in her throat and she tried to swallow it back down. She sank back into her seat but then lurched forward.

"Noah!"

Noah slammed on the brakes. He was driving fast, and the car fishtailed several times before skidding sideways to a stop.

"He's right there!" Aspen screamed. She threw the door open and jumped out, running frantically into the road in front of the car.

"Aspen!" She heard the chorus of voices, but she kept running toward the old man standing in the middle of the road. "What do you want?" she screamed, but the old man did not react.

Gavin, Noah, and Kiryn were all coming toward her.

"Can't you see him?" She stopped to look back at them as she thrust her hand in the direction of the old man, and then she turned and began running again but stopped.

Gone? Again he is gone!

Aspen stared at the empty road when she felt Noah's hand on her shoulder. "Aspen?"

She didn't turn around. Everything she had been keeping inside suddenly burst like the open floodgates of a dam. "He was there," she wailed. She pointed at the air in front of her, "Right there." She started walking, screaming at the empty road. "What do you want from me!?"

Noah ran up behind her, and grabbed her arm pulling her off balance.

Aspen fell, and Noah quickly put his hands under her arms, lifting her back to her feet.

"Aspen!" Noah yelled.

She felt her body weaken and sobbing she covered her face with her hands. "Noah? Am I crazy?" Through her tears, she looked up at Kiryn and then Gavin. "Am I? You both must think so by now."

Noah put his arm around his sister, but she pulled away. "Noah! Answer me!"

"No, Aspen, you are not crazy." He wiped her face with his hand and put his arm around her again. "C'mon."

This time Aspen let him lead her back to the car.

"Here, I'll sit in the back next to her." Gavin pulled the seat forward.

Noah didn't protest, but Aspen stopped short, glaring at Gavin through watery eyes.

"I just think we should get out of the middle of the road," said Gavin.

Reluctantly she climbed in and slid to the opposite side of the seat sobs still racking her body.

Gavin climbed in next to her. She felt him touch her shoulder, "Hey."

She looked over, and he held his arms open, but she didn't move.

How she wanted to slide over next to him, but she couldn't

make herself move from the security of the corner of the seat.

Unexpectedly, Gavin took hold of her wrist and gently pulled her to him. This time Aspen did not resist. She slid across the seat and buried her face in his shoulder, weeping unashamedly. She was tired and frustrated, and she hated the old man.

The Iroc sped down the road, and the only sound besides the car engine was the sound of Aspen's crying. When they arrived at the little house, Noah shut off the engine, but no one moved.

Aspen wasn't crying as hard, but tears still rolled down her cheeks. She could feel Gavin's heart beating against her shoulder, and she knew his shirt was soaking wet, but she didn't care. She just wanted all the weirdness to go away.

Kiryn reached down on the floor under her feet to retrieve a buzzing cell phone. "Is this your phone, Aspen? It says, MOM?" She placed it in Noah's outstretched hand.

Aspen sat up and rubbed her eyes, pressing her hand against her forehead. Gavin slid his hand to the back of her neck, massaging her neck and shoulders.

Aspen moaned softly as she leaned into his hand, unable to resist his touch or the welcome relief it brought.

Noah answered the phone, "Hey, Mom. Yeah, she did—huh? Oh, she just went into the house. She left her phone on the seat, but I saw it was you. Hey, she was calling to ask, since you and Dad will be late—"

Kiryn's eyes suddenly brightened. She touched Noah's shoulder, "Ask her if you guys can stay the night."

Noah winced at Kiryn, "We uh…we are going over to Mr. Fielden's. Did you know he is Kiryn and Gavin's dad?"

Noah was quiet for a minute. "Well, a few of the kids from school are going over for ice cream." Noah looked over at Kiryn, and Aspen was looking at her too. Kiryn's eyes were now even wider, making the blue stand out even more than normal.

"They—Kiryn and Gavin—wondered if we could just stay the night," he paused. "Yes, Mom, Mr. Fielden will be home." He rolled his eyes.

"We are going water skiing tomorrow after school so we will get our stuff and go from his place."

Again he was quiet.

"Okay, we will. Love you too."

Noah scrolled the front of the phone, "Okay, done. What will Rocky say?"

"He won't care." Kiryn smiled. "Now we can talk all night!" She seemed pleased with herself.

Aspen moaned, "My head hurts."

"Do you want to talk, Aspen. I mean seriously, I do believe you, but I can't figure this out. It is making me a little…scared…for you, I mean." Noah's brow was furrowed, and his eyes clouded, "I'm worried about you."

Tears ran freely down Aspen's cheeks. "I know, your sister is a freak."

"Not…really," The look on Gavin's face caused all of them to turn to him.

"What is that supposed to mean?" asked Noah.

Gavin took a deep breath and sighed, but he quickly changed the subject, "Noah, why don't you and I go up to the house and see if we can make sure a window is unlocked?"

Noah looked apprehensive. "I don't know. Aspen, will you be okay?"

Aspen sighed, but Kiryn quickly spoke up, "She'll be fine. I'm here."

"Okay with you, Aspen?" Noah turned back to his sister.

Aspen was relieved to have the attention taken away from her.

She nodded. "Sounds good. Besides, I need something for this awful headache."

"Hmm, my massage didn't work?"

Aspen turned quickly in his direction, "No. I mean yes. It was great. Thank you." And she quickly got out of the car.

32

MAN IN THE TREES

GAVIN CLIMBED IN THE front seat, and Noah sped out of the driveway. He stared after Aspen wondering at his feelings for this new seemingly troubled girl. His attraction to her hit him suddenly the minute she walked into school that first day, and he struggled with his emotions ever since. He and Cassie had been together off and on for nearly two years, but their relationship had waned somewhat over the last six months. Maybe it was because they were facing graduation and the future was so undecided. Cassie had started pushing marriage or at least moving in together, and Gavin wasn't interested in either. He wanted to go to school. To get out of Sommerville. He had always wanted to travel, to see the world, to do something big, something important. On the other hand, Cassie was content to give up her dancing opportunities and settle down with Gavin. He wanted no part of that, but he didn't know how to relate that to Cassie without hurting her feelings.

He shrugged when images of the blonde girls flashing smile and dimpled cheek rooted suddenly in his mind. He closed his eyes against it, but she wouldn't go away. Who was she? Why was he so captivated by her?

He followed Noah to the back of the big house, making just enough conversation to hopefully stop Noah from asking questions, but it didn't work.

They were back in the car but Noah had not started the engine. "What's on your mind?"

Gavin turned to Noah, whose look was intent.

"Something you're not telling me? Because you're pretty quiet," Gavin shrugged. "Naw. Just—"

"My sister?"

Gavin was surprised by Noah's direct hit, but he slowly nodded. "Maybe a little."

Noah turned in his seat to face Gavin squarely. "Look. I know you like her and she is totally sappy about you, but I don't know if—if she's okay and she doesn't need—"

Gavin was looking at the floor but held up one hand in protest, "Noah."

Noah's mouth clamped shut, and he slumped back in his seat.

"I know." Gavin continued, "I can't pretend I don't like her, but I know. I can see things are not quite right, with any of you."

His head jerked up.

"I—I mean I can see there are some things you guys have to deal with."

Noah started the Iroc, choosing to ignore Gavin's obvious slip of the tongue. "We're good then? You understand where I'm coming from?"

Gavin nodded. "Absolutely."

Noah gave Gavin a curt nod, and in seconds they were back on the road headed toward the little house.

Gavin thought of the man in the road that Aspen had seen. He thought of the elusive blonde girl, and then his thoughts turned to Cassie, but unable to resist, both Cassie and the blonde girl faded, and images of Aspen flooded his already crowded consciousness.

Undeniably, Aspen was spending more and more time in his

thoughts, and whether he liked to admit it or not, she was consuming his heart.

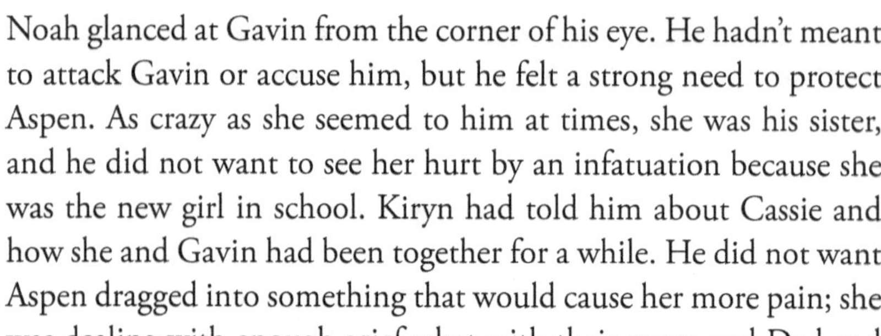

Noah glanced at Gavin from the corner of his eye. He hadn't meant to attack Gavin or accuse him, but he felt a strong need to protect Aspen. As crazy as she seemed to him at times, she was his sister, and he did not want to see her hurt by an infatuation because she was the new girl in school. Kiryn had told him about Cassie and how she and Gavin had been together for a while. He did not want Aspen dragged into something that would cause her more pain; she was dealing with enough grief what with their move and Dad and Mom and most of all losing Krista. All of that weighed heavy on his mind so he could only imagine how Aspen must feel.

Aspen was mentally exhausted. One more encounter with the old man, and now firmly believing that some part of her was really crazy, she just wanted to think about anything but Sommerville. She put the journal and notebook under some clothes in her drawer, slammed it shut and plopped down on her bed.

Kiryn watched Aspen's face light up when she talked about Krista. Since meeting Aspen, she had hoped the two would become best friends, but she never imagined anything like this happening. She had visualized Krista being Aspen's California best friend and her being Aspen's Tennessee best friend. It saddened her to know Aspen's heart was aching, and she hoped that by being a good friend, she could maybe ease some of that pain.

She asked to see the scrapbook Aspen had compiled of her and Krista, and the two girls giggled and cried while Aspen shared stories about growing up at the beach with her best friend.

It made Aspen feel good to talk about Krista, and soon she was so sleepy she couldn't keep her eyes open. It wasn't long before she and Kiryn were both asleep on her bed, the scrapbook open between them.

Again Aspen knew she was dreaming. She wondered why when she dreamed about Krista, she was clearly aware that she was in fact, dreaming.

Krista was running towards her, and Aspen stood up from her warm place on the sand. Krista didn't speak but waved her arm for Aspen to follow. When she did follow her, they were running straight for the ocean but just when Aspen felt damp sand beneath her feet, the ocean was gone, and they were running through thousands of trees.

Aspen could not catch up with Krista, but she stayed close behind her. They ran through trees for some time, and then the trees turned into billowy clouds surrounded by clear, blue sky that extended in every direction. Their bare feet sank into the soft whiteness—it was like running through cotton.

In the distance Aspen could see a small grove of trees that seemed out of place amid the clouds. A man stood in the center of the tiny grove.

Krista stopped at the edge of the grove. She appeared to be looking at the man, but he was nearly engulfed in a mist that began rising from the clouds right around him.

Krista stopped and turned around, and Aspen stopped too.

Krista folded her arms and frowned. She held up one finger and shook it side to side, like Aspen's mother used to do when she scolded her.

Suddenly Krista looked into the grove of trees. She pointed toward the figure with her left hand, her right hand still shaking her finger side to side. She turned back to Aspen, still slowly shaking her head from side to side, but the expression on her face now turned anxious.

Aspen tried to understand what Krista was telling her as once again, Krista pointed toward the man in the grove.

Slowly the man turned around.

He seemed familiar to Aspen. His gray hair was smooth and neatly trimmed. He wore a white suit, but his feet were bare. His face was calm, and even though he seemed old, he didn't have many wrinkles, and his gray beard was also neat and trimmed. Aspen gazed upon him for some time. He smiled, and she smiled back. Who was this man, and why did it seem as though she knew him.

Was it Grandpa?

Puzzled, she looked at Krista who was now walking away from her, away from the trees and away from the man. Aspen tried to follow, but Krista looked back and held up her open hand to stop Aspen, and then Krista again turned toward the man again. She stopped for a second, smiled at Aspen but once again shook her head and her finger side to side.

Aspen turned back to the man in the trees. He was no longer smiling, no longer wearing a white suit. His neatly trimmed beard now looked unkempt, and his bare feet wore boots. The white suit replaced with overalls and a plaid shirt, his hair protruded from a wide-brimmed hat. The steel eyes glared back at her. Aspen froze.

Her eyes jerked open, and she stared at the ceiling of her room. She could hear Kiryn's shallow breathing at the bottom of her bed. She picked up her phone. Noah and Gavin had been gone for almost two hours.

She took a deep breath and just held it for a second and then she released it slowly until it felt as though her lungs were empty, and then she closed her eyes and thought about the dream.

She sighed. It was just a dream. Anything can happen in dreams, but it seemed so real! Why did the man who seemed to be her grandpa suddenly become the old man who tormented her? And Krista? It was as though she was right there, close enough for Aspen to touch yet just far enough away that she couldn't reach her.

Aspen rubbed her eyes. *Wow. I just want one day that is normal.*

She felt Kiryn stir and then abruptly sit up. "Aspen, I am so sorry. I must have fallen asleep."

"Well, I didn't notice because I just woke up too." Aspen scooted to the edge of the bed and stood. She stretched. "I needed that." She laughed. "Apparently, you did too."

Kiryn was still trying to wake up, and she nodded through a yawn. "How long have they been gone?"

"More than two hours. I hope they are okay." Then she started for the door. "Want a soda? I think we have some."

"Sure." Kiryn laughed. "So if our brothers are dead, we're okay with that?"

"I don't think Drew will kill them. Scare them to death maybe, but not kill them."

"Nice that you are so concerned," Noah's voice came from the kitchen.

The two girls laughed when they walked in to find their brothers downing soda and cookies.

"Sure glad you two weren't standing guard while our lives were hanging in the balance," said Gavin.

Kiryn rolled her eyes and picked up the chocolate chip cookie bag. "So, did you find anything?"

"Actually we did." An impish smile crossed Noah's lips, and he stood and walked out of the room. "Let's get our stuff for the lake, Aspen. We have a lot to tell you. Gavin already called Rocky, and he is expecting us any time."

"Yeah, we were just waiting for the two princesses to wake up," snickered Gavin.

"Oh whatever." Aspen snatched a cookie from his hand and followed Noah.

33

I BELIEVE YOU

ASPEN LIKED ROCKY'S HOUSE immediately. The kitchen was painted white and yellow with black appliances and had a corner window nook with benches on two sides of a small square table and a chair on each of the other two sides.

The walls boasted pictures of Gavin and Kiryn at different stages of their lives. How different this family was than hers. Kiryn living with an uncle after her parents were killed and the uncle being Gavin's dad. Gavin, having another set of parents that he lived with part of the time. She picked up a picture of Rocky with Gavin and Kiryn on a boat, each holding a fish. They appeared to be about nine or ten years old.

Aspen smiled. Families can be so different and yet still be families.

Rocky's fireplace in the den was much like the one in the little house. It covered an entire wall only it was made of old brick instead of rock. The thick mantle stretched the entire length. The hearth was probably a foot and a half wide and made of the same brick as the rest of the fireplace. The room was cozy and inviting.

Rocky had pushed three overstuffed chairs and a small sofa together to make a circle around the coffee table. There were five paper plates, bottled water, and an assortment of Chinese food containers.

"I figured you kids would be hungry so when I went out to gas up the boat I grabbed some grub," Rocky grinned. "Help yourselves."

"Oh man, I was hoping for ice cream," teased Kiryn. Rocky plopped in a chair and picked up a plate. "Later."

"Thanks, Mr.—I mean, Rocky." Aspen grinned.

"Yeah, thanks," both Noah and Gavin chimed in.

"You guys are just trying to stay on his good side. You know you wanted ice cream." Kiryn filled her plate and sat down on the sofa. Noah and Gavin each took a chair, and Aspen sat beside Kiryn. They all began dishing up food. When the plates were full, and everyone was seated, Rocky looked at Noah.

"Now, what is on your mind?"

Noah looked first to Aspen and then Rocky.

"This all started the first day we came into Sommerville," began Noah and then he turned to his sister. "Do you want to start Aspen?"

She nodded and began to explain how she had seen an old man on the road and also on the side of the road, but no one else had seen him. Rocky asked her if she often saw people no one else could see, and Aspen told him that she had her entire life, but the incidents were far and few between and no one paid much attention to her when she told them.

"Except Krista. If she didn't really believe me, she made me think she did." She looked at Noah, "Unlike my *family*."

"Krista was just being nice." Noah's lips curved into a soft smile.

Aspen ignored him. She went on to explain that this was the first time she had this type of experience more than once where she saw the same person, and this was also the first time she had been afraid.

"I did see a girl in kindergarten every day, but in the same place on the playground. Mostly I just saw people once, and that was it."

"We have always kind of teased Aspen about her invisible people. Mom and Dad never took her seriously, and I just thought she was nuts." He grinned at Aspen who pulled a face at him.

"Very funny." Aspen continued telling them about going out to the shed and the old man being there and how she fell and how he stood still and just stared at her but then he backed out and disappeared. She explained how she had heard a sort of laughter that brought a peaceful feeling, how she had left the shed and ran back to the house.

"Could someone have been inside?" Kiryn asked.

"Not if she had just come out—" Noah began. "Unless someone went in while your back was turned—while you were walking away."

"That's a possibility," agreed Rocky.

Aspen said she hadn't walked that far, but she agreed that it might have been possible, but no one else was around. She started to tell them about the lake, but Noah stepped in.

"It was the weirdest thing I have ever seen," he said. "Aspen was on the tire swing just going back and forth, and then the swing just stopped, and she looked like she had just seen the Loch Ness monster. She tried to get on top of the tire, but then all of a sudden she just fell off, like straight down but then she fell back."

"Did you slip?" asked Rocky.

"No. I did not slip. I felt someone or some*thing* grab my ankles." She paused and looked at all of their faces. "I know that sounds so lame." She looked directly at Noah.

"You didn't tell me that." Noah looked surprised.

"I know. I didn't know how to tell you that. You said the water wasn't moving, but it was. There was a whirlpool underneath me when I fell." Aspen put her plate on the table. "I thought I was going to drown. I couldn't move. It was like something was holding me under the water and it was strange because under the water there was no current just still water."

"And you couldn't see anyone or feel anyone holding you?" This time it was Gavin who was asking the questions.

"No, just pressure or something, but then out of nowhere, I felt like an electric shock or…or something like that went through me, and then I was pushed to the surface."

"So, were you standing—upright?" asked Rocky.

"Yes!" Aspen blurted. "That is exactly right. I was standing, but my feet were not on the bottom of the lake."

Everyone, including Aspen, was quiet for a few minutes.

Noah broke the silence, "When she fell off the swing, I dived in to help her and just before I got to her she just shot—literally shot straight up out of the water."

He pushed his arm up in the air to demonstrate. "It was crazy. I pulled her to the dock, and she kept asking me not to tell Mom and Dad, and then she thanked me for pushing her out of the water." Noah looked right at Aspen and confirmed for her again, "I did not push you out of the water."

Aspen stared back at him. "Then who did?"

No one responded to that question. Rocky had his elbows resting on the arms of the chair, his hands folded in front of him. He didn't acknowledge Aspen's question but asked one of his own, "Why didn't you want Noah to tell your parents?"

Aspen took a deep breath, "About two months ago, Dad told us we had to move. Everything changed in our house. Mom became nervous and quiet. Dad was in such a bad mood, it was impossible to talk to him and Noah—" She looked at her brother, "Noah was just mad. It was awful."

"And it hasn't changed," Noah said quietly.

"Except you're not mad anymore," Kiryn grinned.

Noah sighed. "Yeah, not *so* mad anymore."

Gavin chuckled. Noah glanced at him warily but went on, "When we got home from the lake that day, Dad was fighting with some guy in the driveway."

"Any idea why or who he was?" asked Rocky.

"No, only that he told Dad that he would get his share," said Noah.

"Seems like everybody wants a piece of your family," said Gavin.

"What does that mean?" said Rocky.

"Oh, can we tell you that in a minute?" said Aspen.

Anxiety had replaced the anxious feelings, and she began wringing her hands. "See, there's some other stuff."

"Well, yeah, the stupid desk at school that hit you," said Kiryn.

"Yeah, that was strange," said Gavin.

"Noah thought you pushed it," said Aspen.

"Thanks," Gavin scowled at Noah.

"Well, I didn't know you, and you were standing the closest to her."

"Why would I push a desk at her or anyone else?" Gavin raised his voice.

Noah shrugged. "You probably wouldn't. Now that I know you."

"Probably not." Gavin let it drop.

Noah took a deep breath. "Sorry," he said as he let it out.

Gavin nodded. He turned to Aspen and winked. Kiryn saw that and kicked Aspen's foot.

Aspen kicked her back.

Rocky took a drink of water, raised his eyebrows at the four kids, and spoke in his schoolteacher tone, "Are we ready to move on?"

Noah nodded. "Yeah, Aspen and I wanted to go up to the big house. Dad told—"

"Wait. There is something else." They all looked at Aspen and waited.

"Dad and Mom took us up to the house after that guy in the driveway that afternoon. When I got out of the truck, I thought I saw someone in one of the upstairs windows, but when I looked a second time she—it was a girl—was gone, but then we went in the house."

Aspen told them how she had gone upstairs with Noah. How they had found the pictures in the window seat in the one bedroom, and how one of them, not in an album, was of four kids. For some reason, it was interesting to her, and she had left it on top of the other pictures when she closed the seat earlier. She told them how she had looked in the end room where she thought she saw the girl, but there was no one. When Rocky asked her if this scared her, she said no, it was just like the other people she had seen in the past. Then she told them how she went into a room, and Noah was just frozen there.

Noah interrupted her there, "I thought I felt someone. No, I did feel someone touch my shoulder. Just as plain as I am touching yours." He reached over and touched Kiryn's shoulder. "It was weird, and it gave me the creeps. Speaking of that, the shed Aspen went in gave me the creeps too, but I had brains enough not to go in. Besides," and he eyed Aspen, "when Dad and I went out there, the door was locked." He shook his head at Aspen, who was glaring at him, and Noah did not mention the rats, which was a relief to her.

Aspen waited for him to finish, and then she continued. She told them they didn't know what touched Noah but that it did scare him, but, she told them before that happened she was looking at a painting of their grandpa and his two sisters. When she looked at it, the canvas seemed to move, and she thought she saw another girl behind the oldest girl. She explained that there is another smaller picture just like it in one of the bedrooms, but in that picture, the girl had a chipped tooth, but in the big picture she didn't, and she had a necklace on, but the one in the bedroom was reversed.

"It, the necklace, was a flower, and the one in the bedroom faced the other way. I was going to show Noah, but he was already running downstairs. Mom had come up to get me. When I showed her the picture, she said maybe the picture was a copy that it reversed when they made it, but that didn't make sense because the other two kids looked the same in both the painting and the picture, but I think Mom kind of believed me because she had a funny look on her face when we went downstairs. She didn't know that I saw her look back at the painting though."

She left out the part where she thought she was inside the painting or that she was standing on the side of the road by the old man.

Everyone was staring at Aspen. She looked at each of them, her eyes darting from one to the other.

Rocky simply smiled.

"Aspen, what else haven't you told me?" Noah actually sounded kind of sad.

"I just didn't know how to tell you all of this, Noah. I really do think Mom and Dad think I am a little crazy, and I don't want them to have any proof!"

"Is there more?" asked Rocky. Kiryn sat quiet and wide-eyed.

Gavin was quiet, his eyes down, drawing little circles on his jeans with his finger.

"You mean about the girl or what?"

"I mean about anything," said Rocky.

"Well, about the picture. When the four of us went to the house, I looked at the big painting again, and the canvas did move, and I did see a shadow of a girl behind the oldest girl, I guess her name is Riley, and at the same time I felt a breeze, kind of, from the hall and when I looked, I saw a dark-haired girl standing at the end of the hall."

"Did she do anything?" asked Gavin, but he did not look up.

"No, but when you and Noah were trying to get into the storage room, I saw another girl—actually a lady. She had dark hair, and she put her hand on your hand right when the door opened, and just before that, I heard someone laughing. That's what made me look at you two. It came from where you were."

"Well, I just got goosebumps all over my entire body," said Kiryn, and she hugged herself, rubbing her arms with her hands.

Noah picked up a fortune cookie, opened it, and broke it in two. He threw the fortune on the table without reading it and popped the cookie into his mouth. "Why did I feel someone touch my shoulder, but nothing else and Aspen has all of this stuff going on?"

Rocky took a deep breath and then sighed. "My guess, Noah, is that you are not receptive like Aspen is. Whoever—"

"Or *what*ever," Noah interjected.

"Umm, I think this would be a, *whoever* situation. Anyway, I believe Aspen is easier to contact than you are."

"Well, that is just fine with me," Noah said emphatically. Then he went on, "That's when we decided we would go up to the big house *without* permission from Mom and Dad. That's when we met that Drew guy."

"Drew Dixon?" said Rocky. He was looking at Gavin. Gavin nodded.

Noah said, "That guy is weird. First, he acts like we are breaking some horrible rules, and then Dad appears, and he acts like we are his best new friends. That guy freaks me out."

Gavin jumped in, "They opened a door on the side of the house, Dad, and it opened into a brick wall."

Rocky raised his eyebrows and turned down the corners of his mouth. "Really?"

"Exactly," said Aspen.

"So, we didn't know—well, we still don't—what that is about, but Gavin and I have an idea."

Aspen reminded them about the old man by the car and how no one ever found him and how in a town this size where everyone seems to know everyone no one seems to know that old guy.

Rocky told them he had been checking around but didn't have any answers yet. He assured the kids that the police are still searching for him.

Kiryn said, "Well Aspen saw him again today, on the road by Drew's house."

Rocky's eyebrows shot up. "Why were you at Drew's house, and why didn't you call the police?" asked Rocky.

"We weren't actually at Drew's. We were near there, and Aspen saw the man in the road again, just like the first time," said Noah.

"Only this time, she jumped out of the car and ran into the middle of the road yelling at him."

Aspen dropped her head. "He was there," she said quietly.

"I believe you," said Rocky.

Aspen's head shot up, "You *do*?"

"I do. I don't think you are crazy, so I believe you, and that explains why none of you called the police."

"Oh," Aspen's voice fell. "But he disappeared—again. He always disappears." She looked up at Rocky, who was studying her face.

"There's more," said Kiryn. She looked at Noah, "The picture of Drew."

"Oh yeah. When Aspen got a card from Krista, she included a picture that she had found in a bush in our front yard. She sent it thinking it might be something we dropped," said Noah.

"This being your house in California?" Noah nodded.

"It was a picture of Drew?"

"Yes," said Gavin.

"Well, we are pretty sure it's Drew. The picture is torn—there is no head."

Rocky leaned back in his chair, a look of surprise on his face. "Why do you think it's Drew?"

"The guy has a missing pinky finger," said Noah flatly.

Rocky nodded. "Interesting," was all he said.

"The plot thickens," Kiryn squinted.

"It sure does," said Rocky. He motioned to Aspen, "So tell me about that book you brought with you."

"Wait, Dad," Gavin looked at his dad his green eyes a little clouded. "There is something I need to tell you. *All* of you."

34

GIFT OR CURSE?

EVERYONE'S ATTENTION WAS ON Gavin. He looked uneasy, apprehensive or maybe both. Aspen wasn't sure. His cool demeanor usually unaffected by anything right now was wavering.

He didn't say anything at first but turned to each one of them, his eyes resting on Aspen. "I just—" Then he stopped.

"You just what? What's on your mind, Gavin?" Rocky leaned toward his son, "Do you want to talk alone?"

"No, that won't work." He looked at Aspen, "She, actually, they," he motioned to both Aspen and Noah, "need to be here."

"Okay, then go on," Rocky said softly.

Aspen watched the face of this school teacher, father, and friend. He was not like most parents. So much of him seemed to be one of them, but in a forty-something body. He was aloof, more understanding, and more free-spirited than most adults she knew, including her own parents.

Gavin leaned back in his chair, putting one foot on the opposite knee. He rested his elbow on his thigh and twisted a loose thread at the bottom of his jeans. He took a deep breath, held it a few seconds then slowly let it out.

"Well, there are a couple of things. First," he turned to Aspen, "that woman you saw? I saw her too. I have seen her a lot."

Out of the corner of her eye, Aspen noticed Rocky stiffen. She glanced at him. His solemn expression fixed on Gavin.

"I have never said anything to you, Dad. When I first saw her, I just thought she was a woman who seemed to show up at different things, but one time I saw her on Christmas day when you and Mom got together to give me my presents. She was standing in the snow watching you and me have a snowball fight. I smiled at her, and she smiled back, but that's when I noticed that she was barefoot and wearing no coat and even though she was maybe ten feet from us, you didn't notice her. That day I realized she was someone only I could see."

"Did that frighten you at all?" asked Rocky.

"Yeah, it did, a little, although she is not a scary person. I just have no idea who she is. She looks a little like Mom. She has dark skin like us, but her eyes are green like mine, not brown like Mom's."

"So you saw her today when she opened the door," said Aspen.

Gavin nodded and then he grinned at Noah. "The tool wasn't so effective, I guess. When I saw her hand on mine, I knew she was probably the one who actually opened the door."

Noah shrugged. His face was hard for Aspen to read. It was somewhere between total disbelief and downright bewilderment. He did not look at her. "You…you didn't even say anything."

Gavin chuckled. "I didn't want you to think you had two crazies on your hands." He glanced at Aspen who simply glared at him and then he continued, "So she has been the only non-person—that's what I call her —that I have ever seen, that I am aware of. She seems to be around mostly when I am sick, hurt, sad, or in danger. That Christmas day was unusual."

"Not really," said Rocky. "Remember how sick you were that night?"

Gavin looked away for a minute as if remembering. "Oh yeah, I forgot. I woke up with a major earache that night."

"And had your tonsils out a month later," Rocky reminded him.

Gavin nodded, and then he went on, "Okay, so that is the story about her. Nothing earth-shattering."

"Except that you see dead people," said Noah.

"Well, I don't know if she's dead or just not living," Gavin's face twisted. "I mean, okay. That didn't make sense."

"No, it didn't." Aspen thought Kiryn almost looked frightened, and she was unusually serious now. She turned to Rocky, "What could it be?"

"Why don't we let Gavin finish before we speculate?" Rocky patted Kiryn's knee.

She rolled her eyes, folding her arms across her chest as she slumped deeper into the sofa.

Gavin gave her an annoyed look, but then he continued, "The other day when that guy was at the school, the one who tried to get into Aspen's car?"

Everyone nodded in succession.

"I saw a girl on the school steps. At first, I didn't think anything of it, but I was surprised that she was not in the school when I looked for her, but then when we were at McDonald's that afternoon, I saw her again. This time, I started thinking something was really not right. None of you guys saw her, but the weirdest part was that she just walked into the street in front of a car and then she was on the other side of the car going into the trees. The car coming at her didn't even swerve."

"And then she disappeared," said Kiryn.

"Not exactly. Before she went into the trees, she turned around and looked right at me. She had the most incredible dimples I have ever seen."

Aspen looked at Noah, and for a second, their eyes locked. "What color of hair did she have?" asked Noah.

"Blonde, long blonde thick hair. I noticed that because her hair was cut straight across the bottom. I don't know how to explain what I mean."

Aspen felt a twitch go through her. The image of Gavin looking at the picture of Krista on her phone flashed thorough her mind. She shook her head and immediately dismissed it.

That's impossible.

"But also today—" Gavin squinted and again seemed to be carefully choosing his words, "Today on the road, I saw the man you saw, Aspen. He was more like a…a shadow, but he was there. I could see right through him."

Tears sprang to Aspen's eyes. She looked at Noah. "So, I am not crazy. I'm not!"

Noah looked first at Gavin and then at Aspen. "No, you *both* are," he said flatly. What makes these two so special? How come I can't see any of this stuff? How come Kiryn can't? How come *you* can't?" He stood up as he pointed his finger at Rocky.

Rocky didn't answer. Instead, he spoke in a soft, even tone to Noah. "Why don't you sit down? Let's hear the whole thing."

Noah shook his head. He walked out of the room and into the kitchen. He was gone for about five minutes and no one said anything during that time.

When Noah came back, he fell into his chair. "Nothing about this place is normal. Everything has changed since we got here and now my sister sees ghosts or something and I find out the only person I thought could be my friend does too! This is just too weird. I just want to go home."

"Home?" Kiryn looked up at him.

"Home to *California*!" Noah yelled.

Kiryn's eyes filled with tears and Aspen scooted closer to her, draping her arm across her shoulders. "He can be a jerk," she whispered in Kiryn's ear, and she nodded.

Gavin rubbed his face with both hands and then sighed. "This is why I have not said anything." He motioned to Noah and then to Kiryn, "And what's worse, I think the girl is Aspen's friend," he blurted, taking all of them by surprise.

"What friend?" Her eyes widened, but then she understood. "You mean Krista?" Aspen was horrified. "What are you talking about? She *is* dead! This is not funny, Gavin."

Gavin jumped up. "Aspen, I knew that would be hard for you to take, but I had to tell you." He looked at Noah. "Both of you. You see what it means—at least what I think it means is that if I can see Krista and she really is dead, then the woman I am seeing is probably also dead, and that means—" he stopped and just stared at Aspen but then he started to move around the coffee table in her direction.

Aspen shrank away from Gavin's out-stretched hand by putting both of her hands behind her back.

"Aspen—" Noah stood up.

"You know what? I just need to think, okay—I just want to be alone for a minute."

Kiryn grabbed her arm before Aspen had a chance to resist. "C'mon, you can go in my room."

She led her away from the den and then turned down a short hall. She opened a door and gently pushed Aspen inside, "Just stay here till you want to talk." Kiryn bent over next to the bed and flipped a lamp on and then she turned to face Aspen, "Aspen, this whole thing is crazy weird—and, I know Gavin saying that had to upset you, but—" She left closing the door behind her.

Aspen jumped up, opened the door and called after Kiryn, "But what?"

Kiryn stopped, and without turning around, she said, "Gavin doesn't lie," and she continued down the hall.

Aspen didn't know whether to cry or scream, feel angry or relieved. All she knew was that this was the last straw. *How can Gavin claim to have seen Krista? If he thinks this is being my friend, he is crazy. I can't even think clearly anymore! I hate this! I hate this! I hate Mom and Dad, and I hate stupid Sommerville!*

She collapsed on Kiryn's bed. The tears came freely again, and she hugged her shoulders. She cried until her eyes felt swollen and then she lay on her side, staring at a wall of pictures. Aspen pulled herself up and sat on the edge of the bed. One of the pictures caught her eye, and she got up to see it more closely.

It was Kiryn. Her smile and sparkling eyes were impossible to mistake. She looked like she was about three or four-years-old and was sitting on a woman's lap. The man in the picture had his arms around both of them.

Kiryn's parents?

She gazed at the small family that looked so happy. She wondered how long before Kiryn's parents died, the picture had been taken.

Another picture of Kiryn's dad sitting in a little wading pool—Kiryn dumping water on his head from a red plastic bucket. She may have been two or three.

A third of Kiryn wearing high heels and wobbling toward her mother. She looked a little older in that one.

One that brought more tears to Aspen's eyes was of Kiryn cuddled on her mother's chest, obviously when she was first born.

More pictures—piggyback rides, baking cookies, and Christmas, but one particular picture struck Aspen the most. Kiryn was in a plastic swing, and the picture had been snapped when she was closest to the camera. On either side of her were her parents—both with looks of admiration as they gazed upon the giggling Kiryn.

Aspen suddenly felt foolish. How could she be so selfish? She had her parents and her brother. Kiryn had lost her whole family, and even though she and Rocky seemed to be doing great, how hard not to have your mother.

She thought of her own mom and longed for her to be the same mother she had been before they left California.

Then she thought of Krista. She would not want Aspen to be sad, she would want her to have new friends, and to be happy.

Aspen pulled some tissue out of the box on Kiryn's dresser, blew her nose and wiped her eyes. Everything was so confusing, but she knew no one here in this house meant her any harm. Still, she resented Gavin for saying the girl was Krista and she was not about to let this one slide. She shrugged, *I am not going to like him.* She slowly opened the door.

"Better now?" Kiryn startled Aspen. She was sitting on the floor just outside the door and giggled when she saw Aspen's hair. "You are a mess."

Aspen scowled, but she took Kiryn's extended hand, pulling her to her feet. "I'm fine." She caught Kiryn's sarcastic look, and it made her think of the day the old man had been there, and Aspen told Kiryn she was fine.

"Okay, I'm good and I…I know Gavin doesn't lie. I'm sorry, but

Kiryn, I can't believe Gavin said that. I'm having a hard time with that one."

"That's the only thing?" Kiryn grinned. "Forget it. You were just having a meltdown. You're entitled." She started toward the den again.

Aspen grabbed Kiryn's arm, turning her around to face her. "Kiryn? I'm sorry about your parents."

Kiryn sighed. "Me too." She gave Aspen a quick hug, turned quickly, and walked into the den.

Noah, Gavin, and Rocky were looking at the map in the little notebook. They looked up when the girls came in.

"Aspen, I'm—" Gavin stood up.

Aspen held her hands up in protest. "Nope, I'm sorry, Gavin. I'm just not ready to deal with that yet. Like Kiryn said, I am a mess."

Aspen didn't move toward Gavin, and he didn't come any closer. She sat down on the sofa, and Kiryn plopped down next to her. Gavin stood for another minute, but then he reluctantly sat in a chair across from them.

"Okay?" Noah's face was serious. He raised his eyebrows when Aspen didn't immediately answer.

"Yes, Noah. Sorry. I'm fine. It's just that something just occurred to me."

"What's that?" Rocky had been holding the notebook, but he put it on the table.

"Well, *assuming*," she glared at Gavin, "you can see Krista and, and she is dead, and we *both* can see the old man." She stopped, her eyebrows furrowed. She was looking at nothing really just processing her choice of words.

They all waited for her to go on.

Aspen scooted forward until she was sitting on the edge of the sofa. She picked up the journal and held it close to her chest. "If—" she looked over at Gavin, "*if* that is all true, does that mean the old man is real but…dead?"

SUMER

THE ROOM WAS ABSOLUTELY silent.

Finally, Rocky spoke up. "It would seem so," he said absently. Aspen watched his face change from intrigue to concern.

"Can you kids excuse me for a minute?" Rocky stood and started toward the staircase between the kitchen and the den. He put one foot on the bottom stair turned around, "Gavin did your mom leave for Florida today, or is she going tomorrow?"

"Today," said Gavin.

"Okay," said Rocky. Then he added absently, "There is ice cream," and he disappeared up the stairs.

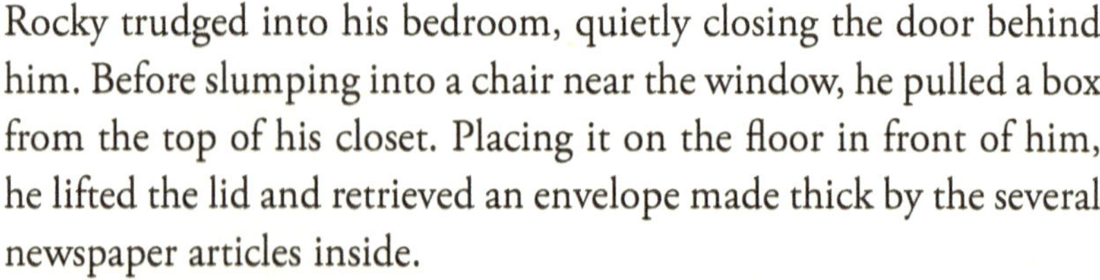

Rocky trudged into his bedroom, quietly closing the door behind him. Before slumping into a chair near the window, he pulled a box from the top of his closet. Placing it on the floor in front of him, he lifted the lid and retrieved an envelope made thick by the several newspaper articles inside.

He fumbled through the clippings until he came to the one he wanted. Carefully unfolding it, he stared at the yellowed paper. Three faces stared back at him, tugging at his heart. How he had dreaded this day. He had always envisioned Gavin's mother being with him and the three of them having a quiet conversation about

Gavin's start in life, but it was not to be that way.

Rocky lifted his cell phone from his pocket, noticing the lateness of the hour and realizing it was after one am in New York. He punched in Sara's number and waited.

Sara's voice came almost immediately through the speaker, "Rocky, is something wrong?"

The four went into the kitchen, and each filled a bowl with ice cream. They avoided talking any more about Krista.

When they got back to the den, Aspen again sat on the sofa. She was surprised when Gavin sat next to her. The sofa was so small that their shoulders were touching. He didn't say anything. He just looked right at her, giving her a quick smile and turned back to his ice cream.

Aspen looked across the table. Kiryn and Noah were both looking at Gavin. Noah shook his head, and Kiryn glowered at Gavin.

It wasn't long before Rocky joined them.

"I didn't dish any up for you. I wasn't sure how long you would be up there," said Kiryn.

"It's okay. I don't want any right now. Gavin, may I talk to you for a minute?"

It was easy to see that something was bothering Rocky. Gavin stood. Gavin stood. "Sure." He carried his ice cream and followed Rocky into the kitchen.

Noah and Aspen both turned to Kiryn. She shrugged. "Don't look at me. I have no idea."

Somehow Aspen knew Kiryn was holding out on them. When Rocky and Gavin returned, Gavin again sat down next to Aspen. His usual aloofness seemed a little more strained, and she wondered what Rocky had said to him.

Rocky sat down in the empty chair. His face looked tired now. He had his hand on his chin, his elbow on the arm of the chair. He looked at Gavin briefly and then stood again, crossed the floor to a cabinet opened a door and returned with a large brown envelope.

When he sat back down, he placed the envelope on the table. He looked at Kiryn and then at Gavin. He paused as if he was waiting for something.

Gavin nodded, and Rocky began.

"I needed Gavin's permission to tell you all—including him—something about his mother. Before I did that, I had to call his mom and explain some of what has happened since the two of you," he motioned to Aspen and Noah, "actually the Allen family, came to Sommerville. Sara agreed, Gavin, that I should probably tell you what we have waited your entire life to tell you."

Rocky paused, looking weary. "Considering all that has happened and the obvious involvement you have in this Aspen, I wanted to see if Gavin felt okay with me telling all of you. He said it is okay, but he has no idea what I am about to say."

Gavin sat back on the sofa and sighed. "It's okay Dad. We really need to figure all of this out and if you know something that will help we need to know too."

Rocky nodded. "Okay. I am not exactly sure where it fits nor do I know where to start with all of this information, but—"

Aspen's phone rang. She looked at Rocky. "I'm sorry," she mouthed and then she answered it quickly. "Hey, Mom." She was quiet for a minute. "We're here. Sure, just a second." She handed the phone to Rocky, "She wants to talk to you."

Aspen and Noah exchanged puzzled looks.

Rocky took the phone. "Hi, Mrs. Allen. Okay, Suzann."

Pause

"Yes, they are both here annoying me," he laughed. "We are all talking about the history of Sommerville. I have their undivided attention."

Pause

"Except for a short time in Memphis, my entire life."

Pause.

"Yes, I know the history." Rocky grinned at the four teenagers.

"Geez why all the questions?" Noah whispered.

Aspen shrugged. She felt anxious about the information they were waiting to hear and now even more anxious about this phone call.

Rocky listened for a couple of minutes, "Sure that is no problem at all. I will put them both to work."

Pause.

"Let me ask them." He put his phone on his lap. "Your parents have to leave town for a couple of days to go see your aunt in Oregon. She wants to know if you would want to stay here for the weekend or would you rather stay home."

"Home," said Noah.

"Here," said Aspen.

Aspen scowled at him. "Why?"

Noah looked at their two friends and then his sister, "No reason. Okay, here." He turned to Gavin, "Geez."

Gavin smiled. Of the four of them, he was the least outspoken, but right now, he was more quiet than normal.

"Good!" Kiryn blurted, but then she blushed. "I mean, cool! You can share my room, Aspen."

That made everyone laugh. Kiryn rolled her eyes.

"So, you good?" Rocky waited for Aspen and Noah to acknowledge.

They both nodded.

Rocky put the phone back to his ear, "Okay Suzann. They will stay here. They can go over and get some clothes after we get back from the lake tomorrow."

Pause

"It's fine with me. We have a lot to talk—learn about."

Pause

"Okay, so is everything okay with you and Mr. Allen?"

Long Pause.

"Okay, Suzann. I'll tell them. Be safe."

Rocky scrolled the face of the phone and handed it back to Aspen. "Your mom will call you in the morning. They have to go to your aunt's to pick up some keys or something."

All four teenagers exchanged quick looks.

Rocky squinted, and his eyebrows furrowed. "Why do I feel like I am being left out of something?"

"You first," said Gavin.

"What?" Rocky eyed his son.

"You tell us, and we'll tell you." Gavin grinned.

"Sounds fair." Rocky put his elbows on the arms of the chair, his hands in front of him, his fingers threaded.

He does that when he's thinking, observed Aspen.

Suddenly Rocky leaned forward and picked up the brown envelope. He took a deep breath and released it with the word, "Okay." He opened it and placed a picture in front of Gavin, which was also in front of Aspen.

"I wasn't going to start here, but may as well cut to the chase." He scrutinized Gavin's face.

Aspen stared at the picture of a woman. Her thick, shiny black hair hung loosely past her shoulders. Her perfect olive skin complimented her striking green eyes. Her white sleeveless shirt appeared to be silk and revealed fit, shapely arms. She was maybe twenty-years-old. A turquoise locket at the end of a silver chain hung around her neck. Her chin rested in her left hand, her head tipped just a little, and her lips parted into a soft smile.

Aspen had never seen Gavin's mother, but because of the obvious likeness, she assumed this was a younger picture of her.

She looked at Gavin. He was studying the picture closely. He looked from the picture to Rocky. "Dad, who is this?"

"Who do you think it is?

Gavin looked puzzled. "Is it Mom? When she was really young? Her eyes look more green than brown." Gavin picked the picture up and studied it more closely. "Actually—" Gavin hesitated, "Well, she looks like—the lady I keep seeing."

Rocky said nothing.

Aspen peered over Gavin's shoulder at the woman's neatly trimmed nails and the silver band on her left hand. Something looked very familiar, and suddenly an image flashed across her mind. *The hand, the same silver band, the same silky black hair.* This was the woman who had helped Gavin open the storage door.

Aspen's eyes widened, and she stared at Rocky.

36

HIDDEN PAST

Rocky spoke slowly, "When you were born, Gavin, there were some—problems." He paused, choosing his words carefully. "Your mother had a gift. She could see the future, people who had passed away, good things. She kept it mostly to herself, but she did share it with her sister and her parents."

"And that was a problem?" inquired Gavin.

"It wasn't until this happened. In one of her visions, your mother saw you—before you were born. She had just married. The man she married had been dating another woman for nearly five years. The woman was one of your mother's best friends in high school, but they had gone their separate ways and lost touch, but one sum-mer, the woman brought your father to Sommerville, and he met your mother—he was smitten. He broke off his relationship with the friend and started dating your mother. The ex-never got over it. She told them both—at their wedding no less—that she would make sure they regretted this day."

Aspen glanced at Gavin. He was leaning forward, his elbows on his knees, his chin in his hands. His eyes fixed on his dad.

"Your father was raised in Sommerville, so this is where they made their home. For the next year, your parents were the happiest couple in Sommerville."

"Why are you referring to you as 'father,' Dad?"

"I'm trying to explain. I'm honestly getting to that." Rocky paused for a second, waiting for Gavin to acknowledge him.

Gavin nodded.

"The day you were born, your father left you and your mother at the hospital and went home to shower and get some clean clothes—well that would make sense why he went home, no one knows for sure. Most likely, the last thing he expected was this woman to be waiting for him. He never had a chance. They found him not three feet inside the door, and it did not appear he had struggled."

"She *killed* him?" Kiryn blurted.

Rocky paused. He held one finger up to Kiryn. His eyes had not left Gavin's, but now he looked around the room, and so did Aspen. Everyone was mesmerized, including Aspen. She was so interested in this story that she almost felt guilty because this was apparently Gavin's parent's Rocky was talking about. She wondered how he must feel right now. She glanced at him out of the corner of her eye. His expression had not changed at all. He was staring at his dad.

Rocky turned to Kiryn and then back to Gavin. "Yes."

"How?" said Gavin, but there was no change in his expression. "Does this person have a name?"

"Her name was Mandi, and she shot him," said Rocky. Gavin didn't even flinch. "And Mom?"

"Apparently, Mandi had been planning this from the first day she learned that your mother was pregnant with you. She went from the house to the hospital. She posed as a nurse, and fortunately, your mother had fallen asleep, so they had already taken you back to the nursery. When the nurse returned, she found your mother. Mandi was found dead in her car in the hospital parking lot—wearing hospital scrubs."

"So she killed both of them and then herself?" Gavin's voice sounded hollow.

Rocky nodded.

Kiryn expressed exactly what Aspen was thinking, and from the look on Noah's face he felt the same way.

"I am so confused," said Kiryn.

"Do you think she was going to kill me?" Gavin asked quietly.

"Sure of it. She had a note in her car that she had written earlier. She said, and I quote, 'Today, I will rid the world of a witch and the only man I have ever loved. I will send them and their child to hell. Any offspring of hers must also be a 'witch'.'"

Gavin leaned back. He put his hands on his knees, stretched, and then relaxed. He looked at Kiryn. "So we are both orphans."

Kiryn smiled weakly. "Guess so."

"Gavin, I'm sorry," said Rocky, "We knew we would tell you someday, but we didn't know when. Tonight, hearing all of this, I knew it had to be now. It was hard for us considering the way your parents died. The more time passed, Mom and I just kept putting it off." He paused and studied Gavin's face. "You okay, Son?"

Gavin nodded. "Yeah. I don't even know those people." He picked up the picture of his mother. "So how did you and Mom get me?"

"Sara and I were already married, and your mother are sisters."

Rocky twisted his mouth. "I guess that's the easiest way to say that."

Gavin's eyebrows perked up. "Sisters? No wonder they look so much alike."

"I don't have any pictures of your father—he didn't mention the newspaper clipping—but your mom does. To answer your first question, we adopted you. You have been Sara and Rockefeller's son since you were just a few hours old. Of course, legally it took a little longer, but we took you home from the hospital that day. We couldn't have any children of our own. You were the most wonder-ful gift, Gavin."

Gavin grinned. He didn't say anything for a few seconds. Aspen couldn't read his expression. He seemed so calm about all of this news. She knew if it were her, she would be freaking out about now.

"So, who chose my name?" Gavin was looking at the picture. "Your mother did. She chose that name before you were even born. They called you Gavin from the minute they knew you were going to be a boy." The corners of Rocky's lips curved up. "You were supposed to be my nephew."

Gavin raised his eyebrows. He took a deep breath and then sighed with pursed lips. "Whew. That is a lot of information." His eyes widened, and he picked up the picture of his mother. "What is her name?"

"Sumer, and your dad was Juan. Sumer and Juan Munoa."

Aspen noticed Gavin flinch and then he looked at his dad. "The people in the store that day."

Rocky nodded. "I felt bad about that. I talked to them later. I was just worried about them telling you before your mom, and I did, but they assured me they didn't want to upset your life, although they probably would like to get to know you…now. They are your father's relatives. The woman in the store was your father's sister."

"I do have this picture, Gavin." Rocky reached inside the brown envelope again and pulled out a small snapshot. "Juan must have taken this of you and your mom. The camera was in his car."

"Awww…" Aspen leaned over Gavin's shoulder. Sumer's shining green eyes were looking directly at the camera. She looked tired but beautiful. Her jet black hair was such a contrast to the white hospital pillow. She cradled Gavin in her arms, his tiny face peeking out from a blue blanket. She had his cheek next to hers so that he was facing the camera. Glistening green peeked through the tiny slits in his eyes, the same green eyes as Sumer's. The same green as now.

"I was cute, huh?" Gavin smiled. "She really does look a lot like Mom." He looked at Rocky, and he nodded.

"So, this gift of seeing people—apparently dead people—I have the same thing?"

"It seems so. I have wondered if you would, but you have never said anything, so I just assumed it had passed you by. There is one more thing. Mandi conjured up a lot of stories about Sumer and spread them all over town. There are interesting stories on that side of the family—legends you will have to ask your mom to tell you about some time."

Rocky continued, "Mandi caused Sumer a lot of heartaches,

telling people that she was a witch. She had a lot of folks convinced too."

"How would she know? Did she know about the gift?" asked Kiryn.

Rocky nodded. "Because of their friendship when they were younger, Sumer confided in Mandi. So yes, she knew all about Sumer's gift. Part of what was hurtful to Sumer was that when they were in high school, she had been instrumental in locating Mandi's little brother who drowned when he was five years old. They dragged the river for days but found nothing until Sumer got involved, and then they found him in less than an hour. It was a brave thing for her to do because she knew it would expose her, but she came forward on her own."

Kiryn threw a fortune cookie at Noah. "You are awfully quiet."

"I am just trying to process all of this, and we haven't even started on Aspen, Grandpa's house and what we found today."

Rocky started to laugh. "We may need more food."

Gavin stayed seated when everyone else got up from the chairs. Aspen and Noah followed Rocky out onto the front porch, but Kiryn hung back. Aspen watched her through the open door. She sat down next to Gavin and put her arm around him. At first, he didn't move, but then he looked into Kiryn's face, and Aspen could see his eyes were moist. She noticed Rocky looking at them as well.

"He took that pretty well," said Noah.

"Yeah, but it has not hit him yet. Gavin's a tough kid—takes things in stride. He has a good heart. His parents are full-blood Native American, very quiet, unassuming people. He has a lot of that mannerism in him."

Aspen studied Gavin for a few seconds.

That makes sense. His skin is so dark, and he is so laid back all the time. He doesn't seem to have much of a temper. Except I guess with Joseph.

She smiled. It still warmed her heart that he had come to her and Noah's defense.

Gavin and Kiryn joined them on the porch.

"So Dad, we have to tell you what we found at the Allen house today." Gavin had now voluntarily changed the subject.

37

ALLEN-DIXON, INC.

"Okay, let's hear it." Rocky pulled a couple of patio chairs closer to the chaise lounge and the porch swing.

Aspen was happy Gavin was okay. At least he seems like he was for now.

Noah loped back in the den and picked up the small notebook. He came back and handed it to Rocky.

"Looks like some kind of a map," said Rocky.

"That's what I thought when I saw it." Gavin perked up. "We thought it looked like it starts—"

"Or ends," added Noah.

Gavin nodded. "In the kitchen. So after Drew left—"

"Drew? Am I missing something?" Now it was Rocky who looked puzzled.

"Yes, just a sec," said Gavin. "So, Noah and I found a small door behind the kitchen cabinets. We couldn't get it open but—" He turned to Noah, and his face lit up. "Dude! Your dad and mom are gone for two days. We can go over tomorrow afternoon."

"That's true, and we can go too." Kiryn grinned.

Gavin barely nodded at Kiryn but turned to Rocky, "We need to get through a wall upstairs, too, and we need to figure out how to get that door open."

"What about *Drew*?" asked Rocky. No one answered the question.

"Do you think the door under the cabinet leads to the door outside?" asked Aspen.

"Well, it's in the same vicinity, so it is entirely possible," said Noah.

"What do you think we will need to get through that wall?" Kiryn asked.

"Whoa slow down. What door? What wall? I don't think demolition of Mr. Allen's house is at all a good idea, and I still don't understand what Drew has to do with all of this. We are talking about Drew Dixon, aren't we?" inquired Rocky.

"Oh, yeah, Drew? My friend Krista, the one who died, sent me a card a day or so before she died. She included a picture of Drew. You know, the one we told you about that she found in the dirt by our front porch."

"Ahhh…" Rocky still seemed confused.

"Yes, in San Clemente," said Aspen. "She wrote on a sticky note that she thought it might be important, so she sent it to me."

Noah said, "Why was she on our front porch after we moved? I have been wondering that."

Aspen smiled. "She missed me."

Noah smiled. "Probably."

"Then there is the journal Aspen has." Gavin looked around. "Where is it?"

"And the old man, we still don't know what he is all about," added Kiryn.

"Except that he is dead," said Noah flatly.

"The journal is on the table. I'll get it." Aspen started to go in the house but Rocky stopped her.

"Before you get that, would you like to hear the Allen Legend?"

They all stopped talking at once and turned their attention back to Rocky.

Gavin shrugged and looked at the other three. "Sure."

"Yeah, sure," said Noah. "More about my wacky family."

Aspen turned around and slowly walked back to the group. Rocky, Noah and Gavin were sitting on three of the chairs. Aspen crossed her legs and sat down on the porch.

"Want to lean against this chair? Or do you want the chair?" Gavin started to stand up.

"She always sits on the floor," said Noah.

Aspen replied, "He's right, I do."

Noah just rolled his eyes and shook his head his mouth, twisting into a small smile.

Kiryn plopped down in the chair, and Aspen leaned against it.

"They know some of the legend. Gavin and I told them a little bit," said Kiryn.

"Good, then I can fill in the blanks." Rocky grinned. "Okay, kids. Storytime. So, do you know about the company your grandpa and Kenneth Dixon owned?"

The four nodded.

"Well, it was a really big operation. They were bringing in workers from all over the south, and people were standing in line to work for them. It was a good set up. They provided homes for the workers—nothing fancy but they were nice—and the workers had land to grow their own food. The ranch the company owned, provided beef, pork, and chicken for the families. The Richard's had a huge dairy farm—they still do—and the company paid them to provide an allotment of milk and eggs."

"Allen and Dixon put the money they would normally pay the workers into an account. The company earned interest on the money. It covered all of their expenses and earned them a fat paycheck at the end of each workers stint. At the end of the two years, the worker was paid the earnings he had accumulated and then flown back home."

"It was actually your grandpa's brainchild. He worked out the details so that the workers, though not paid top wage, were paid fairly and didn't have to put anything out of pocket to survive for those two years. It was designed to give the boys that came, a good start for making their own way when they got back home. Everybody liked Allen. He was a giving man and had a kind heart. He was well known for helping people less fortunate than he was."

"He does sound like a nice guy," said Kiryn. She threw a reassuring look at Noah and Aspen.

"However, Dixon did not have the same reputation. Rumor has it he was a shrewd man, and after a while, he decided he didn't agree with Allen. He thought the company should be taking a monthly *fee* out of the workers' pay as well as earning the interest, but Allen wouldn't hear of it. He didn't feel like they needed the extra because they were making plenty of money on the ranch, the crops of corn and soy and the interest on their investment, so he refused the 'fee' idea."

Rocky continued, "One of the six families that lived on the lake was named Tygert."

"That's my mom and step-dad's house," said Gavin.

Rocky nodded. "His step-dad is Doug." He smiled. "Nice guy if you like rich folk."

They all laughed, and Noah mocked. "I like having rich friends."

"Well, I don't have a sports car," said Gavin.

"Well, your dad is a mere teacher," said Rocky.

"A good one," said Aspen and she smiled at him.

"Kiss butt," said Gavin.

"Probably." She laughed.

"Hey, I'll take it as a compliment," laughed Rocky. He shielded his mouth with his hand and pretended to whisper to Aspen, "I'll pay you later."

"Okay," Aspen whispered back.

"Whatever," said Gavin.

Rocky continued, "Soon after Tygert moved, Dixon presented Allen with a new idea. He said that Tygert and his sons had opened a transport business and they came up with the idea of taking the workers home in groups, instead of buying them individual plane tickets. That way, they could transport a group of them to one location in each state and have relatives pick them up. At first, Allen resisted, but he wasn't stupid. He could see the huge savings that would be for the company to send them home by bus and in groups rather than buying them individual plane tickets, and it wouldn't really affect their workers either way. He finally agreed, and the Tygert Transportation Company added humans to their commodities."

"That went very well for a couple of years, but then there was a problem. Apparently, some of the workers came up missing."

"What does that mean?" said Gavin.

"They never made it home, just disappeared. An investigation went on for about a year. They turned Tygert, Dixon, and Allen inside out but they came up clean. The case was finally closed with the conclusion that the missing men—all about eighteen-years-old—once they got paid had just taken off on their own."

"The company never heard from the men's families, although Allen kept in touch with them now and again. None of the men ever showed up. After that, up to twenty workers would come up missing each year— sometimes as many as thirty—but these were poor folks and the authorities just chalked them up to runaways."

Noah asked, "So none of them were ever found?"

"They really never looked after the first five because right after that, Allen and Dixon had papers drawn up by their attorney's detailing that once the workers boarded that bus, they had been paid for their two years work and provided a way home and they were no longer the company's responsibility. Every kid had to sign it before they left Sommerville."

"Well, that was probably a good idea," said Noah.

"Of course it was," said Rocky. "That put the safety of the young men in the hands of the Tygert Transportation Company, but they also covered their butts by having their own attorney's draw up papers for them once the boys set foot off their bus, Tygert's Transportation responsibility ended."

"That sounds fair enough," said Gavin.

"It was assuming they made it off the bus, but there seemed to be a lot of unanswered questions."

"What questions?" said Kiryn.

"Well, the Tygert's were brought to trial several times over the next ten years by some of the families of missing men, but every single time, they were acquitted and went their merry way."

"So the Allen's and Dixon's were never put on trial again?" said Noah.

"Never. Not that is recorded anywhere," said Rocky.

"How do you know so much about all of this stuff?" said Noah.

Rocky smiled. "I'm a teacher. I read, and it's all in the history books of our little town. You just have to go to the library. Now you can find it on the Internet too."

Noah raised his eyebrows. "Oh."

Rocky went on, "The Allen family was the envy of the entire town. Old man Allen had a beautiful wife, two beautiful daughters and a son. He was in the best social circles and the highest political groups. He had the support of the entire town of Sommerville for governor, and most of Memphis too."

Rocky took a drink of water and sighed. "But then they had something happen that blasted the family right out of the water. They spiraled down fast. The strong foundations that the family seemed to have, crumbled like a deteriorating clay building."

"What was that?" Kiryn was as engrossed in the story as everyone else, and Aspen realized that Kiryn and Gavin were getting more details than they had known before about the "Allen Legend."

I can't believe our family has a legend.

"Well," Rocky continued. "Their oldest daughter ran away with one of the workers I have told you two that much. Now we are talking about workers who were forbidden to even socialize with the town folk, let alone with the Allen's. Poor Allen, he hired detectives and police, and they searched for I think, more than a year. She was never found, and she never came back."

"How sad," said Aspen.

"Did they find the guy?" said Noah.

"No, they didn't find either of them, and yes, I suppose it was pretty sad. Mrs. Allen actually had a nervous breakdown. She died within three months; I think it was."

Kiryn and Aspen exchanged a surprised look. "What?" Rocky looked puzzled.

"The journal. I'll get the journal." Aspen scrambled to her feet and jogged into the house. She was back in seconds. She plunked back down on the floor. Gavin was leaning over her, and Noah came over next to her as well. She found the spot where their grandpa had talked about putting his wife in a home and about how she had been there all these years.

"Do you know how old he was when he died, Rocky?" said Noah.

"Well, this journal has dates in it." Aspen scanned down the dates at the end. Her finger stopped on one date, and her eyes widened. She followed a date to the paragraph above it. "Look at this!" she read out loud.

I have been carrying so many burdens. I wish I had known what Tygert was doing with those kids. I don't know what I would have done. Looking back, was it all worth it?

JHA Jan 15, 1997

Aspen looked up, "What do you think that means?"

She didn't wait for an answer. She flipped back through the loose pages to where her finger held a spot and then she began reading again.

The sadness that fills my heart is impossible to describe, and the humiliation is becoming equally as great. My poor Nina has had a nervous breakdown, and I am admitting her to a hospital for a few days. I do not know what to tell the children. My political career is at risk along with our family fortune if I don't do something to save the Allen reputation, all will be lost. I am getting a lot of pressure from my business partner, Kenneth Dixon, to do something to smooth over the damage that has been done to the reputation of our family. We are beginning to appear as a family who is unstable, who will not be able to withstand the pressure of the public eye. I must make some difficult decisions.

JHA May 23, 1957

Socially I am alone. It is not proper for a man of my stature to be in public without a wife, and yet what am I to do? Nina is not improving. How could our lives have come to this? The longer our daughter is gone, the worse Nina's condition seems to get.

JHA June 15, 1957

Today has been seven months since our daughter has been gone. I have had to make some decisions that I have not wanted to make. I write them here so that by writing, maybe they will make more sense, seem more real. I have divorced my wife so that I can marry again. I have found a woman, an old friend, who has been a widow for a few years. She has no children. She will be a good mother and will represent me well in public. I do not love this woman—not like I do my Nina—but for the sake of our family, our reputation, and our future, I must continue my political pursuits. It will be a good thing, I hope. She will be good to my children.

JHA December 4, 1957

Aspen stopped reading and looked up at Rocky. The only sounds were the chirping of a few crickets and the soft rustle of the trees as the evening breeze passed through.

"Rocky, our great-grandma didn't die. At least not then," Noah was the first to speak.

"Well, he obviously made people think she did," added Aspen.

"Aspen, go to that part about paying the—women or ladies or whatever they were," said Kiryn.

Aspen scanned through the journal entries. When she found the place, Kiryn was talking about, and she began reading.

The women I paid to care for Nina are all gone now. They did their job well. It has been difficult finding their replacements. My Nina; my sweet young and beautiful Nina, who spent so many long lonely years in that miserable asylum. If only she could have made herself forget and keep quiet? What a terrible waste.

JHA May 11, 1996

"So where did she go?" Noah asked quietly.

Rocky shook his head. "Seems like he really loved his wife," said Rocky. "There must have been some pretty heavy pressures on him to do that."

"There is no excuse for pretending your wife is dead," said Noah.

"No, you are right about that," agreed Rocky. "But we only have bits and pieces of the story."

"We are going to read this whole journal," said Kiryn. "I'll bet we find out a lot of stuff."

"Listen to this, Rocky. Maybe this was his heavy pressure." Aspen dragged her finger down the page a little farther.

My heart aches for you, my beloved, sweet Ronda. I loved you, more than you could ever know. If only I could have let others know about you.

JHA Aug 1996

"Grandpa had an affair," said Aspen.

Rocky sat back in his chair. He rubbed his eyes. "Where did you get that journal?"

"In a locked room in the big house," said Noah. "Aspen just had to get in there."

Rocky's expression changed from questioning to understanding. "Ahhh, the door that—"

"Yes. The one that my—Sara—helped me open," Gavin finished Rocky's thought.

"There were other people in there," Aspen blurted.

They all stared at her, and then finally, Rocky asked, "What do you mean?"

"I mean when we went in there, I saw other people. They just—some of them smiled at me—and then they—well they walked out the door, and they disappeared at the top of the stairs." She looked at her brother and two friends. "I—I didn't want you guys to leave, so I didn't tell you."

No one said anything as though no one knew what to say.

Rocky studied Aspen's face for a few seconds. "And that didn't frighten you, Aspen?"

Aspen slowly shook her head. "They just seem like regular people."

"Except that they disappear," blurted Noah.

"Well, yeah. There is that," said Aspen.

Rocky rubbed his eyes with both hands and then looked at his phone. He surprised all four of them when he abruptly ended their conversation. "Kids, it's after two am. Let's get to bed. We have a big day tomorrow. We can pick up where we left off tomorrow night."

"Are you avoiding this subject?" Kiryn stood up and stretched.

"Not exactly. I have some things I want to look at though before we continue."

"Why don't we go over to the house and look at that shaft—tunnel—whatever it is." Noah looked at Gavin.

"Yeah, we have some tools that will probably work." Gavin looked tired.

"Can that wait until tomorrow? I would rather you did not go at night," asked Rocky and the boys both nodded.

Noah quickly added, "I am not going at night."

Aspen reluctantly closed the journal. She and Kiryn had taken a nap, so they were not as tired as the other three.

"We can read it in my room," Kiryn whispered as she linked arms with Aspen.

She stood on tiptoe and kissed Rocky on the cheek when she

passed him. "You're awesome, Rocky."

Rocky smiled. "What do you want *now*?" and then he winked at her.

"Night you guys," said Aspen.

"Night." Called Noah and he headed for the stairs behind Gavin.

"Hey Gavin?" Rocky called to his son. "Could I have just a minute?"

"Sure." Gavin came back down the stairs. "It's the second door on the right, Noah. The bathroom is at the end of the hall."

"Thanks, night man."

As she turned down the hall toward Kiryn's bedroom, Aspen saw Rocky put his arms around Gavin. Just before she closed the door, she heard Gavin quietly crying.

38

DAY IN THE SUN

RIGHT AFTER ROCKY TOOK roll, he told everyone to load up and head to the lake.

The lake was a welcome day of fun for Aspen. Other than thoughts of Krista that popped into her thoughts now and then, she had been able to set everything else aside and enjoy the day. She and Noah had quickly picked up on kneeboarding, but Aspen especially liked to watch Kiryn wakeboard. Rocky connected the ski rope to a bridge attached to the boat, putting the ski rope high above the water and the boat. Rocky explained that having the rope so high gave the wakeboarder more of an advantage to clear the water and made jumping a lot more challenging and fun. Whatever it took, Kiryn was an expert at it.

Some of the kids cooked hamburgers and hot dogs over the grill while others were being pulled behind Rocky's boat on tubes, skis or the wakeboards, and still, others played in the water. There was plenty of food and snacks, and Aspen drank more soda and ate more brownies than she thought possible.

Rocky was true to his word. He was an expert waterskier, as was Gavin. Kiryn drove the boat while the two of them slalomed together. Cutting back and forth behind the boat, ducking to avoid the other's ski rope, they both jumped the wake and then traded sides again. When they were the farthest away from the boat, they practically lay on their sides, their shoulder nearest the water nearly skimming the surface.

235

Kiryn explained that Gavin had been on waterskis since he was three-years-old. It reminded Aspen of Noah and her on surfboards.

When it was Kiryn's turn to ski, she proved to be every bit as good as Gavin.

It was fun to watch her fly over the wake, her bright smile plastered across her face. She rode the single ski right into the shore and stepped out of it, her hair only wet because of the spray caused by the boat.

Aspen loved being in the sun, and she knew Noah did too. This was the closest thing to home they had experienced since arriving in Sommerville.

The group had been on the lake for nearly six hours, and everyone was starting to wind down. Aspen, Kiryn and most of the other girls were stretched out on towels wherever they could fit on the boat, and the boys were playing football. Even Joseph joined in.

About five o'clock, Rocky gave the "pack it in" signal.

Everyone helped clean up the picnic area, but they weren't quite so willing to cash in on the day, so it wasn't long before all of them were back in the water. Rocky watched them from the bow of his boat.

A favorite diving spot was a huge boulder about fifty feet out. A couple of the boys swam out to it, and the rest of the students soon followed.

Aspen and Kiryn were still enjoying the sundeck on the back of the boat.

"I love this," said Aspen. "Most of my life I have been in the sun nearly every day." She held her arm in front of Kiryn's face. "I'm losing my tan. Am I getting white?"

Kiryn leaned up on her elbows. "Are you kidding me? You are nearly as dark as Gavin, and I know you're not a Native American. This," she held her own arm up next to Aspen's, "is white."

They both laughed.

"Hey," Kiryn whispered. She pointed at Rocky. He was sitting on the bow, his elbows resting on his bent knees. "He is looking pretty dry." She giggled, and Aspen nodded.

They both stood up. "C'mon, Rocky. We're going to swim out to the rock," said Kiryn.

"You girls go ahead. I'm enjoying this nice warm sun."

"Okay," said Kiryn.

They crept toward Rocky on either side of the boat. Just as they stepped onto the bow, they nodded at each other. Aspen grabbed one of Rocky's arms, and Kiryn grabbed the other, but when they did, Rocky wrapped one of his arms around the legs of each girl and with one grunted heave, he tossed them both into the water.

They came up out of the water laughing. "Ha! Thanks, Rocky," said Aspen.

"I saw that coming." He grinned. "I wasn't born yesterday."

He leaned back through the divided windshield and looked at his phone. "You have 30 minutes gals. Then we are out of here."

"Race ya," said Kiryn and the two girls immediately started swimming to the boulder.

As she swam, Aspen noticed Gavin climbing to the top of the boulder. He was alone. She had spent most of her time with Kiryn and the other girls, so she and Gavin had not talked much. She resolved to make a point of talking to him when she got there. She wanted to ask him about the kiss.

Kiryn and Aspen were both laughing when they reached the boulder with the other kids.

"Does anyone every scuba dive around here?" Aspen asked as they climbed out of the water.

"I suppose they do." Kiryn pulled herself up onto the huge rock and sat down. "I never have, but I think Rocky has done some scuba diving. Why?"

"No reason, I was just wondering." Aspen climbed up next to Kiryn, but as she did, she saw something that made her stomach twist into a tight knot.

Cassie and the twins were walking towards Gavin. When they reached him, Cassie turned and sat on the rock between Gavin's legs. She scooted back so that she was leaning against him and draped one arm over each of Gavin's thighs.

Aspen realized she was gaping at Cassie when Kiryn looked up at her. "What's up?" Kiryn twisted so that she could see what Aspen was looking at. "Oh, that—"

Aspen quickly turned but not before she felt Gavin's eyes on her. He was wearing sunglasses, but she knew he was looking at her. She quickly sat next to Kiryn.

"Don't worry about her." Kiryn scowled. "She doesn't let go easily."

"I'm not. I just—"

"Yes, you are. Honest! Cassie and Gavin are over. Gavin is just too nice to be rude to her. He has given her plenty of hints."

Aspen turned and looked over her shoulder at Gavin, who was laughing with Cassie and the twins. "Yeah, looks like he is in real pain." She stood. "Ready to go back?" Not waiting for an answer she dived into the water and swam deliberately for the boat.

39

TROUBLED HEART

KIRYN RESPONDED TO A text from Rocky to get the boat trailer and drive it down to the ramp. Gavin had not made it back yet, and Joseph unexpectedly volunteered to help Kiryn.

What with Gavin being all up in Cassie's business. Aspen scowled, and she ran to catch up to Joseph and Kiryn. She was stopped cold by an icy stare from Joseph when he turned in her direction. Kiryn hadn't noticed her behind them and feeling a bit dejected, Aspen watched Kiryn and Joseph walk away.

Brandon Simmons pulled up next to her in his dad's truck. "Want a ride, Aspen."

The truck was crowded with kids, but there was room for Aspen in the back of the double cab truck. She hesitated.

"I'll take you to Rocky's. That's where all of us are going."

Aspen nodded and climbed in next to Paula, a short, bubbly girl who made everyone feel comfortable. As the truck drove away, she saw Noah watching her from the shore where he, Gavin, the twins, and Cassie were getting out of the water. His puzzled look tugged at Aspen's heart, and she wished she had not accepted the ride. She lifted her hand to wave just as Gavin approached Noah. They both watched as Brandon's truck drove out of sight.

Noah didn't say anything to Aspen about leaving with Brandon, but Gavin did. He caught her alone on the front porch after everyone had left.

"Aspen I…about Cassie…she…"

Aspen had been leaning over the porch railing, but now she spun around to face Gavin. "You don't have to explain. I get it. I'm not an idiot. It's plain to see that you two like each other."

"Well it's pretty much over—"

Aspen cut him off, "It's no big deal, Gavin." She turned on her heel coming face to face with Noah, who had just stepped through the door.

"Was that necessary?" he said quietly.

Aspen glared at him. "What do you care?" she hissed just as quietly and walked into the house. Kiryn was coming out of the kitchen, and Aspen took the opportunity to talk about something else. "Hey what was up with Joseph?"

Kiryn looked past Aspen to Noah and Gavin talking on the porch. She gave Aspen a questioning look, but she responded to her question. "He, uh, well actually he wanted to talk to Rocky."

"Really? Why?"

"I'm not sure, but as soon as we got back to the boat ramp, he went right over to Rocky. They talked for a few minutes, and then Joseph left with some of his friends." She paused for a minute. "I thought it was kind of weird that he asked to help me. I've been driving the trailer to the ramp for a long time after these parties, and he has never volunteered before."

"Guess he was nervous with me around. He gave me a look that could kill when I tried to catch up with you two."

"I'm sorry, Aspen. I didn't know. Is that why you left with Brandon?"

"Yeah, among other things."

Kiryn glanced again at their brothers and draped her arm across Aspen's shoulders. "Boys are stupid," she said flatly and her teasing eyes locked with Aspen's.

The tension dissipated, and they both laughed.

40

MYSTERY SHAFT

NOAH AND GAVIN HAD left the same window open when they left the day before. They went to the kitchen first and straight to the cabinet.

Kiryn and Aspen pulled out an assortment of pots, pans, cookie sheets, cake pans, and metal water pitchers. Gavin and Noah kept checking the front and the back of the house while the girls cleared the cabinet.

When it was empty, they changed places and the girls watched the doors.

Noah crawled in on his stomach. They could hear him hitting the back of the cabinet. "It's a solid wall all the way in," he called, and then he slid back out. "It doesn't go anywhere except to more cabinet."

They put everything back in place and headed upstairs to the hall. Rocky supplied two hammers and a handsaw. When they got to the end of the hall, they all stood and looked at the wall for a second.

"Let's hurry—before it gets dark," said Aspen. She had the distinct feeling they were being watched, but when she surveyed the hall, she saw no sign of Gavin's mother or the blonde girl that she had seen in the hall. Her eyes rested on the painting. Nothing. It looked like any other painting.

The image of the painting in the storeroom flashed through her mind, but she immediately dismissed it and turned back to the wall they were standing in front of, but then she looked one more time at the storage door and wondered if anyone was in there. Chills ran down her spine.

Noah clutched the edges of the large pot the imitation tree stood in and pulled. It did not even budge. He stepped back. "Geez, that thing is heavy."

"Then we all need to help." Aspen slid past Noah and braced herself against the wall.

Kiryn did the same on the other side, and Gavin and Noah each grabbed the pot on opposite sides.

"Use your feet," said Noah.

Both girls put one foot against the pot. "Okay push," said Noah.

Gavin and Noah pulled with everything they had, and Kiryn and Aspen pushed with their feet using the wall for leverage.

The massive pot slid about an inch.

"Keep pushing," Gavin grunted. The pot started to steadily move a tiny inch at a time.

Aspen took a deep breath, pushed her hands against the wall, and gave a powerful heave with her foot. The pot slid, and at the same time, the wall gave way, and she fell backward right through the wall. She dropped straight down and then slid on metal until she hit a solid wall.

"Aspen!"

"Noah! What happened?!"

"You fell through the wall, Aspen. Just hold still till we get some light. Are you hurt?"

"No, I mean I bashed my head, but I'm okay."

Kiryn's voice sounded like she was in a tunnel when she yelled, "This is nuts, Aspen! There is a big hole in the wall. It looks like an air-conditioning shaft or something."

"I...I wish I could see you guys. It's really dark down here. I think this thing drops off. I'm afraid to move."

"Don't worry. Noah went to find a rope or—oh wait, here he is."

"Aspen, I have some sheets from one of the beds. I'm throwing them down to you." Noah sounded out of breath.

"Okay, is there a flashlight up there?"

"Gavin went to find one," said Kiryn.

The light from the hole was briefly blocked, and then the bed sheet flopped over the edge and slid down the shaft.

"Noah, I can barely see it, and I can't reach it."

"What?" Noah leaned through the hole.

"It's too short, and I don't dare try to turn and climb up."

"How short?"

"Maybe six feet."

"Okay, I'll go find another one."

Aspen heard him running down the hall.

"Is she okay?" She heard Gavin join Kiryn again. "Yeah, she seems fine," said Kiryn.

"Don't you guys get sick of asking if I'm okay?"

Gavin laughed. "Actually, it's the most excitement we've had around here since Jake's brother swore there were dead bodies buried under his dad's house. Here, I'm sending the light down."

Dead bodies? "Thanks for the visual, Gavin."

"Sorry." Gavin chuckled.

The flashlight clunked when it hit the metal and then it made a grating sound as it slid down the shaft. When it hit her foot, Aspen picked it up. She flipped the switch and pointed the weak beam into the air to her right. As she suspected, there was an abrupt drop off about six inches from where she was sitting. It was hard to tell how far the shaft dropped, but the black on one side made her think there was another shaft as well. She shuddered at that thought. The limited flashlight beam didn't give enough illumination to make out any details.

"Well?" Noah sounded impatient.

"Oh, sorry. I'm glad I didn't move. There is a drop-off, and I can't see the bottom, but I think it takes off in another direction. It's like an air-conditioning vent but bigger. Get me out of here!"

"We're working on it. Sounds like you are in a can," said Noah. "Here, this is ready."

The knotted sheet slid farther down the shaft this time, and when it was within her reach, Aspen cautiously twisted until she was on her back and could grasp it with both hands. "Ready!"

The sheet tightened, and she was dragged easily on the metal. She reached the bend in the shaft, and they tugged her until she was on the flat part just inside the jagged opening. She felt the shaft give under her weight, and she wiggled to get out faster. Noah and Gavin clutched her under each arm and pulled her out onto the floor.

Kiryn laughed. "You are dirty."

Aspen touched her hair and then looked at her hand. It was covered with gray dust, and so were her clothes and face.

"It must be pretty big," said Gavin.

"It is. I could sit up." She looked at the gaping hole in the wall. The fake wall was simply half-inch thick posterboard painted the same color as the walls. The wood frame around it gave the illusion that it had once been a door. "How are we going to fix that?"

"Tape." Gavin reached in his pocket. "I found it when I went for the flashlight."

"Scotch tape?" said Noah.

Gavin handed it to him. "Better than nothing." He picked up the two larger pieces of the posterboard and held them in place. "Tape," he ordered.

Noah obeyed and began securing them in place. "*Aspen.*"

"What?" Aspen turned around.

"I didn't say anything," said Kiryn.

"Oh, I thought you did." Aspen turned back to the wall in repair. "*Aspen.*"

41

STUCK BETWEEN WORLDS

THE HALL WAS DARK except for the soft beam cast from the light at the end of the hallway where Aspen was standing next to Kiryn, but the painting, the one where Aspen had seen the shadow of the girl, now seemed to produce its own light; though dim, it was enough to make the painting stand out from the rest.

Aspen clutched Kiryn's wrist and dragged her along as she slowly walked toward the painting. "Can you see that?" she whispered.

"See what? And why are you whispering?" But Kiryn went along willingly.

"Hey, we need help with this stupid tree," said Noah.

Aspen held her hand up to shush him and kept walking. She gazed at the glowing painting—it was as though it was pulling her to it.

Yes, it's doing it again.

"Aspen? Aspen, you're scaring me," Kiryn was whispering now.

"Just come with me. I want to show you something."

Kiryn gripped Aspen's arm but followed her anyway.

Aspen and Kiryn were now standing right in front of the painting. The tiny threads began to shift. She put the palm of her hand on the blank area behind the older girl, her grandpa's big sister. She could feel the painting moving under her hand.

"Aspen, what are you doing?" Noah said as he and Gavin approached them. She dropped Kiryn's wrist and again shushed

Noah, but she beckoned them to join her.

They were all four standing in front of the painting. Aspen kept her hand on the spot, and the threads in the canvas continued to move.

"It's moving," she whispered.

"What's moving?" said Gavin.

"The painting. Right under my hand."

The silence was like a morgue. Aspen glanced at the three of them. None of them looked convinced.

The painting stopped moving, and as it did, the image of the girl she had seen the first time slowly began to form under her hand. Aspen slowly pulled away, but the image continued to materialize.

"There is a girl. Right here, behind this girl." Aspen pointed to the older sister.

"A girl?" said Kiryn.

"Yes, I can see her. I have seen her before. She has a chipped tooth and see," she pointed to the tiny necklace on the older sister. "The girl has on a necklace like this one, but it faces the other way."

Aspen had not taken her eyes off the girl, but then there was that soft breeze again, and she turned to look down the hall. The same girl stood at the end of the hallway, her long brown hair blowing across her face just like before.

Aspen turned slightly to peer at the painting from the corner of her eye—the girl was still there. *How can she be?*

Suddenly Gavin was at her side, his hand on her elbow. "That's her. There is the girl I saw." He was looking toward the end of the hall as well.

Confused now, Aspen asked, "What color hair does she have?"

"Blonde."

"I can't see her. The girl I can see has brown hair. She...she is the same girl in the painting."

"It's your friend Krista. I am sure of it."

Suddenly Aspen's phone buzzed announcing a text. She pulled it from her pocket. The screen simply read KRISTA. The phone fell from Aspen's grasp and bounced across the carpet.

Noah picked it up and opened the text. His eyes widened as did Kiryn's when she read the text over Noah's shoulder. He thrust the phone toward Aspen.

"What does it say?" Aspen whispered.

Noah read, "It's me, Aspen. It's Krista. Gavin can see me."

Aspen looked from her phone to Gavin and then down the hall to the dark-haired girl. Her image began to fade.

"Wait!" Aspen's anxious command surprised even her. "Wait, who are you? Are you with Krista?"

The girl showed no indication that she could hear Aspen.

The girl standing next to Krista started to fade away, but when Aspen looked, she was still in the painting.

Kiryn and Noah looked down the empty hallway.

The cell phone screen was now dark. The three hadn't noticed that Aspen's hands were trembling and her shoulders shaking. The dark-haired girl was no longer in the hallway, and there was only a faint outline where she had been in the painting. It was only when Aspen slumped against the wall that Kiryn, Noah, and Gavin noticed that silent tears were streaming down her cheeks.

Noah handed the cell phone to Gavin and put his arm around his sister. "Aspen?"

"I—I don't know what I am supposed to do." She suddenly looked at Gavin. "Why can you see Krista and I can't? Why is she even here? What does that other girl want?"

"I have no idea," said Gavin quietly. "It was like Krista didn't even know the other girl was standing next to her. At least that's what you said."

"She was at the end of the hall, but it's like she isn't really looking at me. I can see her, but she looked past me." Aspen wiped her face with her hands. "Was Krista looking at you?"

Gavin nodded. "She looks right at me, but she doesn't say anything."

"Geez," breathed Kiryn. "Why are these people hanging around? What about the heaven and hell and paradise and stuff?"

That comment stopped everyone cold, and they all stared at Kiryn.

Her eyes widened. "Well! Why are they still here? Don't they have something more important to do? They are dead for crying out loud!"

Absolute silence.

It was Aspen who spoke first, "Yeah, what the heck are they bothering us for?"

Noah laughed, but only a quiet chuckle escaped Gavin's lips. "They need something. Actually, I think your girl needs something. I think, and I don't know of course, but I think Krista is here just so that you know you are not crazy. It's like she is your witness—and maybe that's why I can see her."

"Like you are a witness?" asked Noah.

Gavin shook his head. "No, it's Krista who is the witness. Aspen said Krista always believed in her. I think she comes to me so that someone else can see spirits, not just Aspen."

"But why can't Aspen see her?" Kiryn turned a sympathetic look toward Aspen.

"I don't know," Gavin said quietly. His eyes brightened. "But she texts only you."

Aspen thought about that for a second. "Yeah. she does."

"Okaaayyy," said Noah. "Can I say that this is just a little weird?"

"Everything is weird," said Kiryn. "It's like we have stepped into a different dimension or something."

"We haven't gone anywhere. They are coming to us," said Gavin.

Aspen was still covered with gray dust from the shaft she had fallen in and now mixed with tears, it was smeared all over her face. She sank to the floor.

"Can we just leave already?" said Noah.

"I just want to figure out what this is all about. I think Gavin is right. She wants something, but what?" Aspen sighed

"Maybe she is stuck, you know between worlds." Kiryn sank onto the carpet next to Aspen. The three were still waiting for her to go on. "Well you know, like that movie *Ghost*. Remember that guy was stuck between worlds because he had been murd—"

Her eyes suddenly widened. "Do you think?"

"That she was murdered?" Noah dismissed it. "No, that's a little melodramatic don't you think?"

Gavin and Aspen exchanged a quick glance. "It's possible," said Gavin.

"That just isn't normal everyday life," said Noah.

Gavin raised his eyebrows. "And this is?"

Noah pursed his lips. "True."

"Why would anyone murder her?" asked Aspen absently.

"Maybe that guy," said Kiryn. "You know the one the older sister ran away with."

"But that was Riley—" Aspen looked at all three of them. "Right?"

Everyone shrugged at the same time, but Gavin stood and walked to the painting. "Maybe there isn't another girl, Aspen. Maybe Riley appears to you behind herself—in the painting I mean."

Aspen stood now too. "Maybe. It's like her spirit is only in this house."

"So she is not only stuck between worlds but in just one house? For fifty years? That's horrible!"

Everyone laughed at Kiryn's dramatic expression.

"It seems something like that though, doesn't it?" Aspen sighed again. "It's all so confusing."

"Actually, there is a lot of crap going on here. Spirits, empty shafts, people trying to find stuff and get money from your family," surmised Gavin.

Noah winced. "How do you suppose Mom and Dad fit into all of this?"

"And Great-Grandma and Grandpa?" added Aspen.

No one offered any more possibilities. They managed to get the potted plant back into place, cleaned up the mess they had made, and decided to go back to Rocky's.

When they left through the kitchen, making sure a window was unlocked, Aspen paused and looked back.

"There is something very strange going on with this house," said Aspen.

"You mean that it is haunted?" said Noah. "Not haunted, that would be scary."

"What? This stuff is not scary?" said Kiryn.

"No. Well some of it, but mostly this house seems to have something that lets spirits get through," said Aspen.

"Well, that does not explain the old guy or that I could see Krista other places," said Gavin.

"Maybe that's the difference in our gifts. I can only see them here." She thought for a minute. "And in my dreams."

"But we can both see the old guy, and he is not here," said Gavin.

"Maybe he can't get in the house for some reason," said Noah.

Aspen looked at him in surprise. "Well, it makes sense. He is evil. This is not an evil house."

Noah looked thoughtful. "That's true. "What do you think, Kiryn?"

"I *want* to think that you are all nuts, but I *know* that you're not so I guess I will just join the crazies."

42

PLANS

"WHAT ARE YOU DOING with that?" Rocky called to Kiryn when she walked from the kitchen to the den with her laptop.

Kiryn plopped on the floor and put the laptop on the coffee table. "I am going to be the scribe, or historian or reporter. Call it what you want, someone needs to take notes."

"Good idea," said Noah, and he grinned at her.

Aspen held the journal on her lap. "So where do we start." But then she remembered something and turned to Noah. "Did you get that text message from Mom?"

"Yes, just did."

"What did it say?" said Kiryn.

"That they won't be home until Monday night," said Noah. "She said she had checked with you, Rocky."

He was just coming from the kitchen carrying three large pizza boxes from Bill and Nada's. "She did, and it's all good."

"Rocky, you're the best," said Aspen. "I'm starving."

"Well, I don't doubt it. It's been a big day."

"Soon you will be in the Guinness book of world records for the most accidents in a month." Noah opened a pizza box and lifted out a slice.

"In one day," said Kiryn.

"Whatever," said Aspen. "Anyway our parents aren't coming home tomorrow."

"Awesome." Gavin bit into a slice of sausage pizza. "That gives us two more days," he said with his mouth full.

Kiryn rolled her eyes. "Yesh, it doesh," she mocked him.

Rocky threw Gavin a bottle of water. "Here ya go. Wash that down."

Gavin caught it, twisted the lid off and gulped half the bottle. He wiped his mouth with the back of his hand. "Satisfied?" He glared at Kiryn.

Noah and Aspen were laughing.

That was the first time since she and Noah had met the two of them that they acted like the almost brother and sister that they were.

Aspen had the open journal on her lap. She took a bite of vegetable pizza and began scanning the pages, but Rocky interrupted her. "Would you be okay with waiting on that for a bit?"

Surprised by his request, Aspen closed the journal and waited for an explanation.

"I think that it may take a little time. I was thinking. We should probably go over to the house first."

Aspen glanced at Noah, who nodded.

She shrugged. "Okay," and she placed the journal on the coffee table.

"Joseph seemed anxious to talk to you, Rocky," said Kiryn.

Rocky leaned forward, his elbows on his knees. "He told me that he knows 'some stuff,' to use his words, but he is worried about hurting his dad."

"Why would he tell you that?" asked Gavin. "He seems to think it involves the Allen's."

"He didn't say how?"

Rocky shook his head. "Nope. He didn't tell me much, but there is something on his mind."

"Why would he tell you that but not tell you what?" said Noah.

"Good question." Rocky leaned back and stretched. He turned to Gavin. "Your mom is back in town tonight. I want you to see when she can come over so the three of us can talk."

"What about Doug?" Gavin smiled.

"He knows. Tell her we just need an hour or so." Gavin nodded. "Okay, I'll call her."

Aspen and Kiryn reappeared in the den after removing the remnants of what was once three pizzas.

Rocky motioned to Kiryn's laptop. "What do you have so far? I think we need some sort of plan to fit all the pieces together."

"I do too," said Aspen. "It kind of seems like everything that has happened should be connected or point to something or the same thing or—*Ahhh*. I don't know how to explain what I am trying to say."

"I know." Noah shook his head. "It really feels like we need to talk to Mom and Dad."

"Well, maybe we should when they get back," said Aspen.

"Why don't we see how much we can find out before then so that we have as much information as possible?" Rocky paused. "Or they will pull you out of my class."

"I doubt that." Noah laughed.

"I don't know. Spirits. Accidents, some old guy running around—prettttyyy strange stuff." Rocky rolled his eyes.

"This all started with Aspen, not you," said Noah.

Aspen glared at Noah and Rocky laughed. "True. Aspen, this is all your fault. Your parents should take you out of my class...to protect *me*," he chided.

"Funny," said Aspen and she scowled at both of them.

"So what have you got, Kiryn?" Rocky chuckled and changed the subject.

Kiryn had the laptop ready. "Here's what I have so far, so help me out if I have missed something."

Kiryn related all the notes she had put down, and Aspen and Noah filled in the blanks. When they finished, Gavin added, "Don't forget to mention that Joseph talked to Dad."

"Okay," said Kiryn. "And before that, he has seemed so hostile—toward Aspen and Noah that is."

"Seriously," said Aspen flatly.

"So tell me, Aspen, can we get in that shaft you were in?" The school-teacher Rocky brought them all back on task.

Aspen quickly sized-up everyone. Kiryn was about three inches shorter than Aspen, and she knew Noah was six-foot-three, and Gavin was about an inch taller than him. Rocky was the same height as Gavin. "Maybe, but it is not the most comfortable place. It drops off, and I am not sure where it goes."

"Would you be okay going down to see if you had better light?" Noah asked.

"Are you sure that's a good idea?" Gavin jumped in surprising all of them.

"Believe me, she is not afraid," said Noah.

"No, I can do it, but thanks, Gavin. I would feel better if someone were at the entrance or something." Then she looked at Noah, "I am kind of afraid. It's pretty creepy down there."

"What if we tied a rope around your ankle would that work?" Kiryn smiled.

"We could do that. You have a long rope, don't you, Rocky?" asked Gavin.

Rocky nodded and said, "Ski rope would be perfect."

43

STAIRCASES

ASPEN CHANGED INTO LONG jeans and a sweatshirt and replaced her flip-flops with tennis shoes. After they moved the potted tree, Rocky chuckled when he observed their attempted repair of the fake wall. "I'm not sure you kids would make it in the CSI."

They carefully removed the posterboard so they wouldn't cause any further damage and Rocky secured the rope around Aspen's ankle.

Gavin tied the rope around his waist, and when Kiryn chided him about being so cautious, Gavin was short with her. "We don't know what's down there. I—I mean we want to get her back out."

"Yes, *we* do," Kiryn teased.

With the rope secured around Gavin, Aspen easily slid back in the place she had originally ended up while Noah leaned into the shaft headfirst and held a second high beam flashlight for her.

Aspen inched to the edge of the where it dropped off and pointed the beam of light straight down. "Noah?"

"I'm here."

"It does go off in another direction—it just looks black. I can't really see anything. It smells musty."

"Like it's damp musty?"

"Kinda."

"Rocky?" Noah's voice sounded like he had turned away from her.

255

She leaned back and looked up. He wasn't visible, but the light was blocked, so she knew he was still in the shaft.

He turned around. "Aspen, are you okay with going down first or do you want to trade me places?"

"Are you coming with me?"

He grunted as he pushed himself over the bend in the shaft. "Yep." He walked his hands down the sides of the shaft to hold himself back from crashing into her. It was impossible to trade places with her. "Do you think I can drop from here without breaking my legs?" he asked.

"No, I think you better pull the rope up and let them lower you down. It looks like it's about a ten-foot drop."

Noah's eyes widened. "Really?"

"Don't die down there. Your parents will kill us," said Kiryn. Aspen chuckled nervously. "Okay."

Noah had to hold himself back out of the way so that Aspen could sit up.

"Take the rope off of your ankle and put it around your chest, under your arms."

Aspen nodded. She laid the flashlight next to the wall and untied the rope from her ankle. She put it around her chest and tied a secure double square knot.

Noah had been holding the flashlight on her. "Wow, I'm impressed. That lifeguard training really paid off."

Aspen rolled her eyes. "Who knew I would be using it in a tunnel?" Suddenly, San Clemente, the ocean and lifeguards seemed very distant to Aspen.

"Yeah, who would have thought." He wiggled the beam of light in her face. "Ready Sherlock?"

She took a deep breath and let it out slowly. "Ready." She handed her light to Noah.

"She's going, you guys."

"We've got it," Gavin called.

Aspen grasped Noah's arm and slowly inched around so that her feet were over the edge of the shaft. She lay on her stomach and then cautiously slid over the edge. When she let go of Noah's arm, she fully expected to drop a little, but the rope was so tight she just hung there.

"Can you give her some slack?" called Noah.

"Slack on the way," called Gavin and Aspen heard Kiryn laugh. Noah slid over to the edge so he could shine his light down the shaft.

As Aspen lowered, she tried to turn so that she was facing the opening at the bottom, but the rope forbid it, and she was forced to keep her back toward the black void.

"This gives me the creeps," she mumbled, but if Noah heard, her he didn't comment.

When her feet landed on the bottom, she pressed herself into the corner away from the opening and called to Noah to drop her flashlight.

He leaned over as far as he could and let it go. Aspen caught it easily. She shined the beam toward another shaft and a dark hole. Blackness. A dark, forbidding feeling coursed through her—trying to push it aside, she turned her attention to Noah.

"Coming down." Noah was using the rope for leverage and walking down the side of the shaft. He planted his feet next to Aspen, and then he called up to the others, "Can you guys hear me?"

"We can hear you," Gavin called back.

"Okay just checking." He turned the beam of his light toward the hole. He inched closer, and a low whistle escaped his lips.

"What?" Aspen moved a little closer so she could see what he was looking at.

"Check that out."

The hole was not quite as deep as this part of the shaft, and the bottom was made of wood planks. It was a small room rather than a shaft and on the side closest to where they were standing was a wooden ladder. It was fastened to the side of the shaft, which was also made of wood. The other three sides were metal. Other than that, the hole was empty.

"Does that look like a door?" Aspen was shining her light directly down on the ladder.

Noah leaned out a little further. "It does. Looks like a leather strap on it." He turned his face up again. "Hey, Gavin!"

"What?"

"Come on down here. There is a room at the bottom of this other shaft."

They could hear muffled voices and then Gavin's grunting as he wiggled himself into the shaft and slid down.

Aspen untied the rope from around her chest and coiled it on the floor.

"Wait for me!" Kiryn followed right after him. "Rocky is going to stay up here," she called.

"I hope so. We need to be able to get out of here," said Noah. "We'll go down the ladder to make room for you two."

"There's a ladder?" Gavin sounded surprised.

"Yeah, it goes all the way down." Noah handed Aspen his light. "I'm going first." He met no resistance.

"Be my guest." She pointed the beam down the hole illuminating the wooden floor. When he was down, she dropped both lights to him, and when she started down the ladder, Kiryn started down the rope.

Gavin quickly followed, and in minutes, the four of them were standing in the small room.

"What do you suppose this was used for?" Gavin was running his hand along the wooden planks behind the wall.

"Umm dunno. A secret passageway?" Noah was projecting his light, slowly inspecting every inch of the room.

Kiryn shivered. "Torture chamber comes to mind."

"Noooo Kiryn," teased Gavin. "This is too small for that."

"Where would they have put the rack?" Kiryn scowled. "Very funny."

"This is a little weird to have inside of a house," said Aspen. "I wonder if Dad knows about this."

"He lived here all while he was growing up. He probably does," said Gavin.

"Maybe." Aspen shrugged.

"Everything okay down there." Rocky sounded like he was a mile away.

Gavin quickly climbed to the top of the ladder. "We're okay, Dad. We are in some sort of room. There is a door. We're going to check it out."

Rocky called to them, "You kids be careful. Don't do anything stupid." Then he half mumbled, "It's a little late for that."

Gavin chuckled. "We won't." He scrambled back down the ladder skipping the last three rungs, he dropped to the floor.

Everyone felt the floor give when he did.

"Whoa. Did you feel that?" Aspen plastered herself against one wall, and Kiryn followed.

Noah bounced gently on the floor where he was standing. It didn't move. "Gavin do that again."

"Do you think that's a good idea?" Kiryn looked nervous.

"Well, if I fall through, throw me the rope." Gavin joked, and Kiryn and Aspen both glared at him.

"Relax." He scurried up the ladder and then jumped backward, landing in the same spot as he had before. Again the floor sank just a little but seemed more prominent right where he was standing.

The planks on the floor were so tightly fit there was no way to see between them to what might lie beneath, if anything. The ladder was attached to what was probably a door.

Noah turned his attention to the leather strap that appeared to have once been fastened on both ends and used to pull the door open. Three holes where it appeared screws had once been, but now only one screw held it in place. He gently pulled on it, and the door moved a little, but the screw threatened to fall out, so he worked his fingers between the door and the plank next to it and tried to grip the wood.

"Here." Aspen stepped up next to him and grasped the leather strap gently pulling as Noah worked the door open. It moved enough to get his hand around it, and he pulled.

The door was very heavy and protested as it creaked open.

"This door is four inches thick." Noah held his first finger and thumb away from it surmising the width.

"Like Kiryn said. Torture chamber." Aspen pointed to the ceiling. "No one up there can hear a thing from down here."

Gavin shook his head. "It is not a torture chamber." He shined the beam through the opening the door had provided. "It's an escape or something."

The four crowded around the open door. "Stairs?" Aspen looked at Noah.

A narrow winding staircase gently sloped and wound to the right, but they couldn't see the exit.

"Look at all the cobwebs," said Kiryn.

"Yeah, no one has been here for a while," Noah agreed. He looked at his three comrades. "Shall we?"

Gavin laughed. "Let's do it."

The girls didn't find it so humorous, but they were willing to go.

The staircase was only wide enough for one person. Noah led the way, followed by Aspen and Kiryn with Gavin taking up the rear.

Aspen kept close to Noah, peering over his shoulder. More cobwebs attacked their faces and stuck to their hair.

Another narrow door about halfway down the staircase caused them to stop.

"Let's come back to that," said Noah and no one objected.

The spiral staircase opened out into another room, larger than the first with doors on three sides.

Noah shined his flashlight on the ceiling. It was solid wood, much like the floor in the room they had just come from. There were no signs on the ceiling that the floor above them was sagging.

"Looks pretty solid to me."

"But that isn't high enough to be the floor of the other room," said Gavin.

"That's true. Maybe it was just a weak spot in the floor."

"Maybe."

They were all four in the room now. "Where do you suppose these doors go?"

"Let's find out." The doors all had doorknobs, and Noah grasped the one on the right, but it fell off in his hand. If it had once been a door, it was sealed shut.

Kiryn had already started to open another door. "Let's see—" That door creaked open, and Aspen gasped. Behind the door was a wall of brick.

"Noah! This must be the other side of the outside door that we found."

Noah ran his hand across the brick and then using the beam of his flashlight, he peered closer to the edges of the brick. "Yep, the brick just covers the door opening. It's wood on both sides." He looked at Aspen. "Weird."

"What about this door?" a wry smile crossed Aspen's face. "This is just like *Alice in Wonderland*."

Noah rolled his eyes. "Just waiting for the rabbit to appear, Aspen?"

She scowled as she turned the knob and pulled on the door, but she met with complete resistance. The door didn't budge. "Guess this one is locked." She smacked the door with her hand, and to everyone's surprise, her hand went right through the door all the way to her elbow.

Aspen gasped and jerked her hand back to her side. "What the—" Noah stared at her.

Aspen rubbed her hand against her jeans. "I—I don't know.

"Did—did my hand go *through* the door?" Noah nodded. "Did you guys see that?"

Kiryn hadn't moved. She was staring at Aspen, her startled eyes wide and blank.

Gavin's eyes narrowed. "What did that feel like, Aspen?"

"What?" Aspen felt nothing but confusion. "What do you mean?"

"What did it feel like? Did it hurt, was it soft, like air? What?"

Aspen looked at Noah and then Kiryn. They were waiting for her to respond to Gavin's question.

She took a deep breath. "Cold. It felt cold, and my hand—my

hand just went right through the wood like it wasn't even there—except it was really cold."

Gavin didn't say anything but knelt down and looked at the doorknob. "This isn't a real doorknob."

"What do you mean?" Kiryn was squatting next to him.

"Look." He pulled a pocketknife from his jeans pocket and worked the blade between the door and the metal knob. It started to give until it finally popped off, landing at his feet. "See, fake. Why would anyone put door knobs on doors that were never made to open in the first place?"

"Maybe they used to open," said Kiryn. "O—" she looked at Aspen. "Maybe whoever went in didn't *need* doors."

Noah gently put his hand on the door and pushed. Nothing.

Gavin did the same. Still nothing. He turned to Kiryn, and she held up both hands in protest. "That's okay, I'm good. That is just creepy."

Aspen tried not to let Kiryn's sudden sarcasm hurt her feelings. "Shhhh," Aspen held up her hand.

"What?" Noah whispered. "Listen."

"I hear it too." Gavin looked toward the stairs they had come from.

"Sounds like pounding or something," said Noah. "Maybe Rocky is trying to get our attention," said Kiryn.

"Why wouldn't he just yell?" said Gavin. He didn't wait for an answer. "I'll be right back." He disappeared up the winding staircase.

The other three followed him, and when they reached the door on the staircase, Noah turned the knob and pushed on the door. It creaked open. They shined all three flashlights up another set of stairs.

"Wait here," Noah ordered. With his flashlight to guide the way, he started up the long narrow staircase.

Aspen shined her light behind him. "You would think there would be lights in this place."

Kiryn scanned the entire room with her light. "You would think.

Can you see Noah?"

"Yes, the stairs just go straight up." She turned to her friend. "So what, now you think I'm creepy?"

Kiryn squirmed a little. "No—I said *that* was creepy—not *you* are creepy."

"But you are having doubts about me?"

"Not really doubts, Aspen, I just don't understand any of this. I feel like it is way out of my league, that's all."

Noah was back. "There is a small hallway at the top, maybe eight feet long and about three feet wide but that's it. The stairs just end there. No door. Nothing."

They heard someone coming, and Gavin reappeared at the bottom of the ladder just as the three emerged from the winding stairs.

"Something's wrong. The opening to the shaft is covered. I couldn't hear anything." Gavin sounded anxious.

"Maybe someone came, and Rocky tried to hide us," said Noah. "We'd better get up there."

"What if someone is waiting for us?" Kiryn looked scared. Noah looked at Gavin. "Did you call to him?"

"Yes, but he didn't answer."

"Let's go back up." Noah started up the winding stairs, followed by the girls and then Gavin."

Kiryn and Aspen exchanged a quick look before Kiryn stepped in front of her.

"She will be okay," Gavin whispered but Aspen didn't respond. She still felt the hurt Kiryn's look had caused her to feel.

They passed back through the smaller room. Aspen couldn't resist bouncing on the weak section of the floor. It moved under her weight. When Noah reached the top of the ladder, she followed.

Noah checked the rope to see that it was still taut. "Let me go first, then I can help the girls."

Gavin nodded.

They all couldn't fit in the shaft together, so they had to go up one at a time. Noah pulled Aspen up, and then she used the rope to pull herself up to the fake door. Kiryn came right behind her.

Aspen stopped when she got to the top. "Can you hear moaning?"

Kiryn nodded. "Rocky?" she called in a piercing whisper. The moaning got louder.

"What is it?" Noah called from behind them. "Not sure," Kiryn whispered.

Aspen pulled herself to the very top and pressed her ear against the posterboard. A chunk of it fell straight down and landed on the floor in the hallway. The potted tree was now pushed up against the opening.

Fear gripped Aspen's heart, and she hesitated. "Rocky?"

"Kiryn?"

"I'm right here, Daddy."

Aspen had never heard Kiryn call Rocky "dad" let alone "daddy". Kiryn anxiously pushed on Aspen's back. "Go!"

Aspen shoved the broken posterboard away and climbed directly into the tree with Kiryn right on her heels, and they both stumbled over the pot and tumbled onto the floor.

"Rocky?" Aspen shrieked when she saw him.

"Dad!?" Kiryn screamed.

44

ATTACK

Gavin and Noah were trying to get past the stubborn fake tree branches when Gavin saw his dad.

"What happened?" Gavin fell over the tree pot. He didn't bother getting to his feet. He scrambled across the floor to Rocky who lay in a heap under the window. Gavin lifted Rocky's head. "Dad?"

Rocky groaned again. He tried to open his eyes, but one eye was swollen almost shut. His face was badly cut and bruised, and his nose was bleeding.

Kiryn started to cry. "What happened to you?"

Rocky winced in pain as Gavin and Noah helped him roll to his back.

"Who did this?" Gavin looked across Rocky to Noah, his accusing tone unmistakable.

Noah was immediately defensive. "How should I know?"

Aspen went to the bathroom and returned with some damp washcloths. She handed them to Kiryn who wiped some of the blood from Rocky's face and hands.

"Is anything broken, Dad?" Gavin's eyes were moist as he and Noah helped Rocky sit up.

"Don't thi—don't think so. They punched my gut a few times, but I'm tough." He tried to smile but put his hand to his puffy lip. "Ouch."

"Who? Who punched you?" Gavin was upset, and Aspen put

265

her hand on his shoulder, but Gavin shrugged it off. "This is all because of you guys," he snapped.

Aspen drew her hand away immediately. "I'm—I'm sorry." Kiryn gave Aspen an understanding look. "Gavin didn't mean it."

"Yes, I did!" Gavin glared at Noah.

Rocky slowly brought his hand up and placed it on Gavin's shoulder. "No Gav, it isn't just about them." He nodded at Noah. "This involves our family too."

Rocky pushed his hands against the floor, and Gavin helped him slide closer to the wall. He leaned back and looked at Gavin. "Don't blame these kids or their family. They didn't ask for any of this, and neither did anyone else."

"What is that supposed to mean?" Gavin wasn't buying it. "Everything was pretty normal until they showed up."

"I mean it was bound to happen sometime. The Allen family coming here and the fact that the house is being sold—well it just drudged up a lot of buried feelings and, it appears, lies and deception." Rocky winced and tried to sit up a little straighter. "It's been like a pressure cooker—getting hotter and hotter over the years— just waiting for the lid to blow."

Aspen sank to the floor. "I'm totally confused."

"So am I." Kiryn gathered up the bloody cloths, and piled them behind her on the floor. She looked at Aspen, but she was talking to everyone. "And her hand went through the door."

Rocky looked surprised. "What?"

"Not now, Kiryn," snapped Gavin.

Aspen handed Rocky a fresh cloth, and he put it on his bulging lip. He studied the faces of the four teenagers, and then he sighed. "I don't know what that means, but we can talk more about it later. I did get a little research done before I was attacked and I think I may have a few answers—I just don't know all the questions."

Gavin was looking past Rocky at the potted tree. He seemed to purposely avoid Aspen's eyes. "How did you move that thing alone?"

Rocky chuckled. "It's amazing the strength you can find when you think your kids are in danger."

"What happened Rocky? Who did this?" Noah asked.

"Don't know who they were. I heard a truck pull up out front and then I heard the front door open. There were at least three men. I think one of them might have been Dylan."

"That's Drew's younger brother," Gavin explained without looking at Noah or Aspen.

"But," continued Rocky, "they had ski masks on when they attacked me." He paused, and a sarcastic laugh escaped. "Seriously, just like in the movies, and they didn't say a word, but I got a good bite on one of their hands."

Rocky poked his thumb in the air, making them all smile. "I didn't know why but I had a premonition to put that posterboard back up after you kids left, so I did that. I tried to move that lame pot, but it was so heavy I decided to let it be. I settled back to read Kiryn's notes."

Kiryn's eyes widened.

"No worries, I put the laptop in that bedroom." He reassured her and pointed to the nearest bedroom, the same one where Noah had found the bed sheets for the makeshift rope the day before.

Kiryn nodded and then as though she had a second thought, she jumped up.

"It's between the dresser and the wall," Rocky called after her.

Kiryn disappeared into the bedroom and returned moments later, hugging the laptop to her chest. Saying nothing, she sat down, but the relief on her face was obvious.

"So anyway, I heard these guys downstairs, so I figured I should probably move that pot. It wouldn't budge, but when I heard them coming up the stairs, I tried to push the stubborn thing again, and it still didn't move. They were so busy yacking they didn't notice me. They went straight down that hall." He pointed to the same hall where the two men had gone when the four kids were in the storage.

"But I knew I didn't have a prayer when they went back downstairs because they would be looking right at me and it wouldn't take a rocket scientist to see the wall was torn apart. So I sat on the floor and pushed it with my back. Almost killed me, but it moved." He chuckled, but again, his hand flew to his injured lip.

"So they heard that?" asked Noah.

"Yep, they sure did. They were on me like white on rice." Gavin chuckled. "Nice visual Dad."

"Do you need to go to the hospital?" asked Aspen.

"No, nothing's broken." He touched his face. "Well, maybe my nose but they can't do anything about that anyway."

Gavin looked straight at his dad. "Doesn't look crooked." He touched Rocky's nose.

Rocky grabbed Gavin's hand. "Ow! Right there. That's the tender spot."

"You look horrible, Dad. I'm so sorry this happened." Kiryn was now kneeling by him.

Aspen tried to avoid looking at Gavin or Kiryn as she began gathering up the disheveled pieces of posterboard and broken fake tree limbs. "I cannot believe you moved that tree, Rocky. It took all four of us," she spoke without looking up.

Rocky stretched out his arms and Gavin and Noah each grabbed one and pulled him to his feet. "Like I said, adrenalin takes over when your kids are involved. It slid like it was on ice," Rocky touched his back. "Man, I'm going to be sore."

45

PERSPECTIVE

Suzann Allen rubbed her eyes and sat on the edge of the bed, trying not to wake Jackson. She had been staring out the window into darkness for over two hours. Their trip to Oregon to see Jackson's sister, Dana, and hopefully, find their grandfathers will, proved futile.

She had taken the chance when she was alone with Dana to question her about the details of the will and the sale of the Allen Manor, hoping the conversation would lead to some hint as to why Jackson had been so upset about returning to Sommerville.

But her mild interrogation revealed nothing. It was not that Dana wasn't willing to share information, she was, but the only thing she knew was that Jackson had never really gotten along with their father and that Jackson was willing and ready to leave when he turned eighteen. No matter how hard their parents pleaded, they could not convince him to come back home.

Jackson had sent pictures and always sent their parents lavish gifts on their birthdays, Mother's Day, Father's Day and Christmas but other than that, he kept little contact with them. His leaving had not upset their mother as most kids go away to college, but his never returning broke her heart.

Suzann sighed and quietly slid into bed next to her sleeping husband. Lately, he slept restlessly—almost agitated, often crying out in his sleep, and she did not want to wake him.

Throughout their entire married life she could approach Jackson about anything—like now, she would have normally awakened him and rolled into his arms, and he would have responded by sharing what was on his mind—but those days had passed, at least for now. Jackson was so tight-lipped about what was bothering him that it had created a wall between them that seemed impossible to get through, and that made her sad.

Suzann scooted closer to Jackson, placed one hand softly on his shoulder and closed her eyes.

Jackson didn't stir.

Quiet tears leaked from the corners of her eyes as she stared at her husband's back.

"Rocky wants to relax in a hot tub for a while." Kiryn folded her legs and wiggled into a comfortable position on the porch swing with the laptop.

"I feel terrible that he got beat up." Aspen was absently thumbing through the journal. "Who would do that?"

"Someone that feels threatened," said Noah. "Has to be connected to Drew—you did say one of them sounded like his brother, right?"

"Yes, Dylan, he's kind of wacko." Gavin rubbed his face with both hands. "I'm starving. Are you guy's hungry?" Then without waiting for an answer. "Is Dad going to bed or coming back down here?"

No one responded to Gavin.

"Isn't he the one that was talking about something being buried under his dad's house?" said Aspen.

"Yes," said Kiryn, "but they searched everywhere. Nothing was ever found. "

"Why did he think that in the first place?" Noah stood up and added, "I'm hungry, too."

"He said he read some story about it." Gavin yawned. "No one knows. The guy is an idiot."

He said to Noah. "Let's go get some food before Dad—" he turned to Kiryn.

"Oh, sorry, Gavin. Yes, he said he's coming down."

Gavin nodded. "Before he gets down here then." He looked first at Aspen and then Kiryn. "You two want to go?"

"Wait a minute," Kiryn demanded. They all stopped and looked at her.

She continued, "I want to know why Aspen's hand went right through that door."

Noah's eyes were questioning but sympathetic—he said nothing. Gavin shrugged. "Well let's ask her." He looked directly at Aspen. "Why did your hand go through the door?"

Aspen was shocked. "What? How should I know? I—I have no idea!"

"Exactly." He said flatly.

"Well, that isn't an answer," said Kiryn.

"She doesn't know, Kiryn. How can she give us an answer when she doesn't know herself? What do you want from her?" He didn't try to hide his irritation.

"Well, what do you want from her?" Kiryn threw her hand in the air, motioning toward Aspen and Noah. "From them? You seem to blame them that Rocky got beat up."

Gavin sighed. "I don't blame them." He said quietly. "I just—I don't know."

Aspen said quietly, "I don't blame you if you think I am a freak, but Noah hasn't done anything."

Noah quickly jumped to his sister's defense. "Neither have you, Aspen. It's just—just who you are."

Aspen shrugged, trying to stop the tears that stung her eyes. Everyone was quiet.

"Aspen we are not blaming you—"

Aspen quickly stopped Gavin. "Yes you are, and that's okay. Weren't you going to get food?"

The tension in the air suddenly dissipated.

"I'll—we'll—wait here for Rocky." Kiryn turned to Aspen. "Will you stay here and go over these notes with me?"

Aspen's eyes narrowed. "Sure, I want to do that anyway. We only have one more day till Mom and Dad get back." She looked at Noah. "Did you hear from them today?"

Noah looked from Aspen to Kiryn and then said, "Good question." And he pulled his phone out of his pocket. "Oh, wow, yes. There are three texts and a missed call. I'll bet they called while we were in the—the cave."

Aspen checked her phone. "Same here. I'll call them. What are you guys going to get?"

"We'll surprise you." Gavin winked at her, but Aspen didn't even smile. She was still feeling the sting of Gavin's earlier comment and Kiryn's sudden hurtful remarks.

Gavin stood still for a second. He glanced at Noah and then at Kiryn and then abruptly walked across the floor to where Aspen was sitting. He placed both hands on the arms of her chair, putting his face within inches of hers.

Aspen looked up, and despite his cutting words and the perpetual knot in her stomach that feelings about Cassie causes, the butterflies were still there. She looked down at her hands.

With apparently no regard to the fact that Noah and Kiryn were surely watching him, Gavin lifted her chin with one hand, so he was looking right into her eyes. "Aspen I'm sorry. I didn't mean what I said. I really—I really care about you."

As hard as she tried, Aspen could not stop her eyes from brimming with tears. She nodded but said nothing though the look in his eyes convinced her that he was sincere.

Without warning, he leaned closer and gently kissed her forehead and then rested his own against hers for just a second and then he stood, but as he did, he took one of her hands in his.

Aspen quickly brushed a tear away.

Gavin squeezed her hand, released it, and then turned and walked directly down the steps and across the yard to the driveway. "You coming?" he said to Noah as he passed him.

Noah glanced at his sister. A wry smile crossed his face. He looked down, slightly shaking his head, and then he followed Gavin. "Yep," he mused.

Aspen looked at Kiryn anticipating a comment, but Kiryn only raised her eyebrows a bit and smiled. "Now, about that journal—" She sighed. "I'm sorry, Aspen. I just—"

"Don't understand me," Aspen finished the sentence for Kiryn and then she grinned. "I know—even I don't understand me." She picked up her phone and punched speed dial to call her parents but no answer.

"Why should you? My parents don't, Noah doesn't, nobody seems to so why should you guys?"

Kiryn winced. "Because you are my friend." She smiled weakly. "That's why."

They exchanged an understanding look, but neither said any more about it.

"Send your mom a text."

"No, I think I will leave her a message," and she punched speed dial one again.

"Hey, Mom it's Aspen. I'm sorry we missed your texts and calls today. We went over to the lake, so we left our phones in the car. I didn't even check my phone 'til now, and neither did Noah. We are good. Having lots of fun." She looked at Kiryn and rolled her eyes. "Are you guys still coming home tomorrow night? Do you want us to be there or come home Tuesday morning?" Her voice cracked, and she felt a tiny pang in her heart. "Love you, Mom, and tell Dad."

Kiryn laughed. "Now you're texting her?"

"Just to tell her I left her a message." She smiled. "Come over here. Let's go through this stuff."

"Okay, but could I get a Coke?"

"You're asking?"

"It's your house."

"If you ask again, I will have to hurt you. Bring me one too." Aspen returned with two bottles of Coke, and Kiryn read her the notes.

- You saw an old man on the road
- You saw someone in the window at the Mansion House
- You saw the same old man in the shed
- You were pulled under at Mystic Lake
- The desk hit you at school
- The same old man tried to get in your car at school
- Gavin saw Krista
- You saw Gavin's mom
- Gavin saw his mom
- We were in the storage
- Drew and that other guy were talking about some papers
- They took the papers from the house—they seemed to come from the master bedroom
- That painting in the storage
- The old man on the road by Drew's house
- You said there were more people in the storage
- We found your great-grandpa's journal
- We found that notebook with the map
- Old man at the lake
- Gavin saw the old man in the lake
- You saw that painting move
- You saw that blonde girl with the chipped tooth
- We found the shaft
- Rocky got beat up

"Aspen's hand went through a door," she said out loud as she typed.

She paused and then added, "Weird." And they both laughed. "It looks like you have everything."

"Okay, so now let's put down people in question."

"Oh, wait. Noah and I found that door and that guy yelling at Dad in the driveway."

Kiryn added the door to the brick wall and the guy yelling at Mr. Allen. She made a new category and typed:

- First person—Drew Dixon

"I'm going to put those in a spreadsheet; then we can add details."

"Good thinking." Aspen moved to the patio lounge and pulled her feet up. "What do you suppose is going on Kiryn?"

"I don't know, but I do think it's so interesting—and dangerous. So it's kind of exciting."

"And weird."

"Yes, and weird. Some of—well most of it freaks me out. I'm not really used to seeing a person's body part go through a door without the rest of the body attached."

Aspen nodded and chuckled lightly. "Me either." She stared at the bushes in front of the porch.

"You like Gavin a lot, don't you?" Kiryn didn't lift her head but peered at Aspen through her thick blonde eyelashes.

Aspen felt her face get hot. She knew Kiryn wouldn't leave the subject to rest for very long, "I really do." She paused and then added, "But I think I am afraid to like him too much, and then there is the Cassie issue."

Kiryn looked surprised. "Why?" Then she added, "Cassie is not an issue. You are *making* her an issue."

Aspen twisted the top off a Coke bottle, handed it to Kiryn and then opened her own and sat back on the lounge chair again. She curled her legs under her and took a drink.

Kiryn was still waiting for an answer.

"I am afraid because I don't know how long we'll be here. I really like him, and that scares me."

"You can't worry about that, Aspen. We only have one year of school left."

"Well, I don't want to get married or anything—there's college and—you know stuff after high school."

"Who says you have to?"

"Well no one, I just. I don't know. Yes! I do like Gavin very much."

Kiryn smiled. "Well, he obviously likes you!" She grinned but then suddenly looked a little embarrassed. "I think your brother is adorable."

"Adorable? Well, he is a pretty great guy but he can be a real jerk."

"So can Gavin." They both laughed.

"It's all in perspective."

"Yep—perspective." Kiryn took another drink of her Coke. "And from my perspective, your brother is awesome."

The girls looked up when Rocky walked out onto the porch.

"Rocky, you look…better," Aspen said.

"Nice try." Rocky laughed. His face was not bloody anymore but still cut, swollen and bruised. "I can open my eye a little bit." And then he added, "Am I interrupting boy talk?"

Aspen shot Kiryn a warning look.

"No, we were just saying how boys are stupid. You do look better, Rocky, but it still must hurt." Kiryn jumped up. "Want a soda? Gavin and Noah should be back any minute. They went to get food."

"Do we have any Mountain Dew?" Rocky slowly lowered himself into a chair.

"Do you want the lounge?" Aspen started to get up.

"Nope, the chair is perfect." He accepted the Mountain Dew from Kiryn and took a long drink. "What have you got?"

Kiryn handed him the laptop. "We were just starting to put down people who are issues."

Rocky read slowly through the notes and handed it back to her. "So you are adding people in question?"

"Yes. We started with Drew. He is obviously an issue. Then there is, I guess, that Dylan guy, and Joseph?" Aspen looked at Rocky. "Is that everyone?"

"We could include Gavin's parents," said Rocky.

"Why?" asked Kiryn.

"We'll get to that. I need to talk to Gavin and his mom." Kiryn shrugged. "K," and she briskly clicked the keys of her laptop.

Aspen heard the Iroc coming down the road, "There's the food."

46

YOU HAVE US

ASPEN FOUND NOAH SITTING on Rocky's front porch just as the sun was coming up. She walked out and sat down on the steps next to him. He looked over at her, smiled, and draped his arm across her shoulders. "So you and Gavin, huh?"

Aspen blushed, and to her surprise, Noah didn't have anything sarcastic to say.

Instead, he sighed. "This has been quite a ride."

"I know, and it's not over yet. I feel like we are right on the brink of something, but it's driving me crazy to know what it is." Aspen rested her chin in her hand. "I wonder if this is what an out of body experience feels like."

Noah chuckled. "Maybe, but we are still in our bodies."

Aspen winced. Thoughts of the side of the road and the painting in the hallway popped into her head, but she still didn't know how to explain it, so she hadn't tried.

She didn't have to now, Noah brought it up. "That thing with the door, Aspen?"

Aspen tensed. "What about it?"

"Has that ever happened before?"

Aspen shook her head. "Not, not like that, but—" her voice drifted off.

"What?"

"Well—it's like I project or go somewhere really fast and then

I'm back."

Noah looked puzzled.

"Like on the road the other day with the old man. I was sitting in the truck, but then I was standing next to him, and then I was back in the truck."

"I think I've heard of something like that. Actually, to be honest, I Googled some stuff last night. "I think it's like astral projection—which is basically an out of body experience."

"But don't you have to do that on purpose?"

"I'm not sure. It just makes sense though, Aspen."

He dropped his head and changed the subject leaving her to think about it. "You doing okay, I mean, with Krista and all? I can't believe you and Gavin can see her. Why do you think I can't?"

"A better question is why I *can*? I guess Gavin has some sort of gift, but I am just plain ol' me." She sighed. "And, yes, I'm okay. It seems like I have hardly had time to think about her being gone, and that makes me sad too."

Noah gave her shoulders an understanding squeeze, and then dropped his arm to his side. "You're anything but plain, Aspen. There is a lot more to you than I ever realized."

He cocked his head to one side as if to check himself. "Don't go thinking I'm going to be nice to you or anything. You are still my annoying little sister."

"I would never think that." Aspen smiled, and there was a long pause in their conversation as if neither knew where to take it.

Then Aspen said, "Noah, have you ever really thought about a—a spirit world?"

Noah turned to look at his sister. "Not really, I have never had a reason to think about it."

"So…now, have you thought about it now?"

Noah's head slowly bobbed up and down. "Yes, Aspen, there must be something else after we leave here, but what, I don't know. Obviously, people don't just die and disappear. They go somewhere else, but they must still exist or how would you and Gavin see them?"

Aspen turned away from Noah, took a deep breath, and let it slowly escape. She was silent for a few seconds and then turned moist eyes back to him.

"Thanks, Noah."

"For what?"

"For being my friend. For believing in me, even if it's just a little bit, and for—for being my brother. I guess the reality of this whole move is starting to get to me. Our parents have lost it, and all we have is each other, at least until they come back to the family."

Aspen's hands rested on the railing, and Noah covered both of hers with one of his. "You're my sister, aren't you? I don't think you're totally crazy—" He chuckled. "A little weird maybe, but you're right, we are all we have."

"You have us."

Aspen and Noah turned around to see Gavin and Kiryn standing in the doorway.

Aspen smiled. "Do we?" But then she quickly added, "Thanks Kiryn. We do know that." Aspen scooted closer to Noah so Kiryn could sit down.

Gavin stayed in the doorway. "What's on the agenda?" Noah stood up. "Back to the tunnel?"

"That's what I'm thinking, but my mom is coming over any minute now. Guess I need to talk with her and Dad."

"We'll wait," said Noah. "I can take these two out to breakfast since there is no school."

"How is Rocky feeling?" asked Aspen.

"He's pretty sore, but he won't admit it. I think being beat up is really pushing him, even more, to find out what's going on—made it more personal. He's pretty determined to talk to me with Mom, so I guess I will find out more then." Gavin sighed. "I'm starving."

The other three looked at him, and Gavin's eyes widened. "What?"

They all turned to the sound of a car turning into the driveway. It was a new white Lexus with gold wheels.

Noah rolled his eyes at Gavin. "I'm so poor, wish I had a sports car," he chided.

"Hey, that's not my car."

"Yeah, whatever." Noah laughed. "I guess that's our cue to leave."

"Bring me back some food." Gavin handed Kiryn a ten-dollar bill. "Wait, you guys need to meet my mom."

Aspen was startled at how much Gavin's mom looked like his birth mother. She reminded herself that they were sisters, but the resemblance was remarkable, more like twins. Sara had the same dark skin as Gavin, thick, silky black hair and a broad smile that set off her high, prominent cheekbones. Her eyes were blue and not quite as striking as Gavin's piercing green eyes but equally as warm and welcoming.

"Hey, Mom." She and Gavin embraced and then she immediately hugged Kiryn.

Kiryn whirled around and then as though presenting some sought after famous people, she thrust her open hand toward Noah and Aspen and said, "Here are Noah and Aspen."

Gavin laughed at Kiryn's enthusiasm.

Intrigued by this beautiful woman, Aspen reached for Sara's extended hand. Six or seven tiny loose silver bracelets fell to Sara's wrist and clinked.

"I've heard so much about you." Sara smiled and turned to Noah. "And you too. I am so happy to finally meet you both."

"I'll bet you have." Aspen cringed. "It's nice to meet you too. Gavin looks just like you."

Sara beamed. "Thank you, Aspen. I will take that as a compliment. How are you enjoying Sommerville so far?"

"Well, it's been interesting—" began Noah. "Lots of—lots of trees."

Sara laughed. "Yes, there are lots of trees." She motioned to the keys in Noah's hand. "Are you leaving?"

"Just going to get some breakfast—give you guys a chance to talk."

Sara's gaze fell on Gavin. "Yes, we do have much to talk about."

Her lips still smiled, but her eyes suddenly looked sad or pained, Aspen wasn't sure.

"Well, it was nice to meet you, Mrs. Mendell." Noah reached for her hand again.

"Please, call me Sara; Mrs. sounds so matronly."

Gavin rolled his eyes. "Okay, Mom." He took her arm, guiding her toward the front door. "Big breakfast, pancakes eggs, you know."

"I know, I know." Kiryn waved the $10 in the air. "Have you eaten Sara?"

"I'm fine." She called after them, and then she and Gavin disappeared into the house. Gavin popped back out the door. "I'll text you."

Kiryn waved. "He means he'll let us know when to come back."

Sara and Rocky were standing by Sara's car when they got back from breakfast. Rocky hugged her, she left, and he followed them into the house and went upstairs.

Gavin didn't come out of his room for nearly half an hour, and when he did, it was obvious that he had been crying. He joined them at the breakfast nook.

"Are you all right?" The concern showed on Kiryn's face.

"I'm actually fine. That was a good talk with Mom and Dad, and now I understand a lot of things about myself that I have always wondered. It was not an easy talk for them either." He searched all of their faces. "I really do want to tell you, but right now I don't think I can talk about it anymore."

"You don't ever have to tell us anything." Noah pushed the reheated plate of pancakes and eggs in front of Gavin. "Eat. You need nourishment."

Aspen could tell Gavin was uncomfortable. He was better at playing the in-control-tough-guy role. He pulled it off well, but now he seemed genuinely appreciative of Noah.

They all sat in silence for a few minutes while Gavin ate. Suddenly he said, "Hey man, I'm sorry about—you know—at the house.

Noah waived his hand. "No worries."

Suddenly Kiryn said, "Why do you suppose there are no lights in that shaft slash dungeon or whatever it is?" said Kiryn absently.

When no one responded, she looked up from the table to see everyone staring at her. She shrugged. "I was just wondering."

After what seemed like a full minute of silence, Gavin started to laugh and the other three joined in.

Kiryn was good at relieving tension. Aspen had learned that about her very early on.

"I don't know, Kiryn, but I agree with you," said Noah. "It does not make sense. I keep going over and over what the whole thing could possibly be about—don't know."

"I just want to get through the door we can't open." Gavin chugged down the last of a glass of milk. "Stuff like that drives me nuts."

"Maybe Aspen could walk through it." Noah laughed.

"You're too funny." Aspen was drumming her fingers on the table.

"What?" Noah gently pushed her shoulder.

Aspen twisted her mouth. "Umm, I think that long staircase, the one you went up, goes to the master bedroom, and that is where Drew and that guy were the other day. Maybe they don't know what to look for."

"And we do?" said Kiryn.

"Well, no, but we do know about the stairs, and let's face it, where else could they go? The master bedroom is the only room in that part of the house on that floor, and the stairs come right up from that door, you know the bricked one. Maybe all it used to be was an outside entrance to our great-grandparent's bedroom."

"The balcony in the back, on the second floor, how do we get to it?"

"Good question," said Aspen. "I have never seen a door to it, have any of you?"

They all shook their heads.

"Well, we aren't going to find out sitting here." Gavin stood up.

"Are we ready?"

They heard Rocky coming down the stairs, and he soon appeared in the doorway. He was carrying a box.

"What's that?" Kiryn was trying to read the front of the box.

"Walkie talkies—good ones—they may work to communicate with me."

"Rocky, you need to rest. You don't look like you feel very well." Kiryn put an arm around his waist. "You stay here. We'll be fine."

"I don't feel so great, but you kids are *not* going alone."

"Hey, Rocky? Noah just brought something up. How do we get to the balcony? There doesn't seem to be an entrance anywhere."

Rocky's eyebrows raised. "I don't know, but we should probably find out." He looked around. "Since it isn't obvious, but, one thing at a time."

47

SECRET PASSAGE

THEY HAD NEVER BEEN in the master suite of the big house and Aspen was nervous about it.

Gavin found Rocky a comfortable chair from one of the bedrooms and put it by the entrance to the shaft. Rocky elected to stay at the top of the staircase while the rest of them ventured down the hall.

The handle on the master bedroom door was different than on the other bedroom doors. It was a long brass handle much like would be found on an outside entrance door. They all concluded it *was* an entrance door handle complete with the push-down latch and the deadbolt lock.

"It's kind of overkill for a bedroom," said Aspen.

"I have a theory," Noah mused, "about this room." He tried the door, surprised that it was unlocked.

"Wow, that was unexpected." Kiryn expressed the same thought that Aspen had and from the looks on Gavin and Noah's faces they were surprised as well.

Gavin put the tool for unlocking doors back in his pocket.

The four silently stepped into the room saying nothing as they observed the grandeur of Jackson Humphrey and Faith Allen's bedroom.

The head of the king-sized bed sat directly under a full wall of the same narrow windows Aspen had observed from the outside.

The canopy above the bed was draped in heavy gold brocade fabric that matched the bedspread and pillow valances.

From each corner of the four-post canopy bed hung a thick gold braided rope with two long tassels at the ends. The bed was the only piece of furniture that sat on an enormous plush white circular rug that covered the entire center of the floor.

The wall to the right side of the bed boasted two armoires, sitting side by side, each easily nine feet tall. Stacked on the floor between the armoires and the windows, was a menagerie of old trunks and an overstuffed white sofa on the opposite side of the armoires. Next to the sofa and just inside the door stood a large potted plant, much like the heavy one at the end of the hall.

The end wall—the one directly across from the foot of the bed was nothing but bi-fold doors made of the same wood the floor was made from. A bathroom the size of Aspen's entire bedroom was located past the bi-fold doors and down a short hallway. It had obviously been modernized with a large jet tub, double sinks, and double shower-head, glass-enclosed shower.

However, the most impressive thing in the room was the ceiling-to-floor gun cabinets that lined the far wall to the left of the bed. The heavy top pieces sat on a base about a foot wider than the cabinets they supported. The wood's finish glistened where the sun bathed it through the partially open blinds, and the center of each individual door was a window etched in gold allowing admirers to see the guns but an intimidating gold lock secured each door to the cabinet.

"There must be fifty rifles in those cabinets," said Noah.

"Forty-two." They all looked at Kiryn. "I counted," she said matter-of-factly.

The extra width of the base from left to right boasted a row of inlaid boxes all which were lined with red velvet. Handsome polished handguns were protected under a glass shield just like the cabinet doors, and each individual door had an embedded gold key lock.

"There are *easily* fifty or sixty handguns in those boxes," said Gavin.

They all looked at Kiryn. She shrugged. "I didn't count."

"This would be a good reason why Drew wants to get in here," said Aspen.

"They *were* in here, and it does not appear they touched them." Noah referred to the embedded locks.

"Unless they had the key." Aspen raised her eyebrows, her lips formed a thin line, and then she mumbled, "No door to that staircase though."

"Yeah, I noticed that too." Kiryn ran her finger across the top of one of the glass doors leaving a light trace. She lifted her finger. "Dust. They didn't get into them, or we would know. So what was your theory, Noah?"

Noah was already studying the wall of closed bi-fold doors. He backed up toward the windows.

Gavin walked over next to him. "What are you thinking?"

Noah didn't answer but walked over and opened the end closet bi-fold revealing a row of men's suits in several different dull shades of blue, brown, black and gray. He bent down and crawled behind the racks but returned in seconds.

"What are you—" Aspen asked. She looked at Kiryn, who also looked confused.

Gavin's eyes lit up. "I know what he's doing."

He went to the opposite end of the closet doors and opened the first bi-fold. He turned to Aspen and Kiryn. "The fake wall," and then he started moving a stack of square file boxes from his end of the closet.

Aspen and Kiryn exchanged a puzzled look.

Noah started on the third set of doors as he explained. "Like the one by the tree. Maybe there is a fake wall that leads to that staircase. It's just a theory, but it makes sense."

The girls exchanged a quick glance and then immediately opened a set of doors.

"I was just thinking," Noah called from behind the clothes. "The stairs go to no place but a little hallway with no escape and if there was one fake wall—why not two?" He moved aside a section of evening gowns. "Wonder who wore those?"

"Well, grandmas *are* women." Aspen laughed.

"Hump." Noah shrugged. He dropped his hand and was again shrouded in a mass of fabric and lace.

Aspen and Kiryn faced racks of every color and style of women's high heels and rows of men's shoes in black brown and gray. They each grabbed hold of the ends of one of the shelves and tried to move it, but the stubborn shelf would not budge.

"These are attached to the wall," moaned Kiryn.

"Not this one." Gavin's voice was muffled. He peered from under a pale turquoise dress that seemed more of a house dress than the ones Noah was buried under.

"Check this out." Gavin lifted the dress and pushed a box out of the way. "This one has *wheels*." He put a strong emphasis on the word wheels.

Noah crawled out from under the evening gowns and then crawled next to Gavin. Together they tugged on the shelving unit.

The first jolt caused several pairs of shoes to tumble from the top shelves and Aspen, and Kiryn jumped out of the way.

The boys rolled the shelf forward until Noah could reach behind it. Aspen could hear his hand rubbing along the wall, but then it stopped.

"Bingo!" Noah then backed out of the closet. "Found it. We need to get this shelf all the way out."

"He likes that word, doesn't he?" said Kiryn and Aspen laughed.

"Wait." Aspen touched Noah's arm. "We know it only goes to the stairs, right?"

"Probably."

"Let's go down and see if we can find out where that other door goes first."

"I have an idea," said Kiryn. "Why don't you guys go down and if the door opens, we'll come down. We need to clean this stuff up anyway."

Gavin nodded. "That would work. No sense in all of us going down until we know."

"Exactly," said Kiryn

Rocky suddenly appeared in the doorway, "Drew is in the house." He said it so casually Aspen almost thought he was kidding, but when he stepped in, closed the door and then quietly turned the doorknob until the latch clicked, she knew he wasn't.

Rocky turned the deadbolt and put his pointer finger to his lips. "Shhh," he breathed.

"What—" But Rocky shushed Gavin with his raised open hand.

They could hear Drew and another man talking. One of them grabbed the door handle and pulled but met with immediate resistance.

"I told you to leave this door unlocked until Mr. J. gets back." It was Drew's voice, and he continued to spew a string of cuss words.

"I did." Another forceful tug on the door.

"Well, clearly, you didn't." Drew sounded angry. "Don't you have the key?"

"I *had* the key. I sent Blake to get a copy made so that I can put it back today."

One of them slugged the wall.

Probably Drew.

"Can't do anything right now. Might as well go get the yard finished. At least I'm getting paid for that."

The five in the bedroom each breathed a collective sigh of relief as the two men's footsteps descended away from the bedroom door.

"Where's your gun, Dad?" Gavin whispered.

"I put it in the bedroom when I put the chair in there. They surprised me when they came in the house, so I just hurried to tell you kids. My plan worked."

"What plan?" said Kiryn.

"Locking the door, of course." Rocky smiled.

Gavin laughed. "That was a fluke."

"You're right. I had no idea what I was doing," Rocky wiped his forehead with the back of his hand "But it still worked."

He slowly lowered his hand to his side when he caught sight of the gun cases along the opposite wall. A long, low whistle escaped his pursed lips.

"Exactly." Gavin grabbed Rocky's arm. "And check this out."

Noah and Gavin explained Noah's theory to Rocky that there could be a door behind a second "fake" wall that may lead to the stairs they found earlier.

"It could connect to this bedroom," said Noah.

Rocky raised his eyebrows and rubbed the back of his neck. "So many loose pieces of a very confusing puzzle."

Noah and Gavin explained that they were going to go down to the shaft and see if they could get the third door open while Kiryn and Aspen put the master bedroom back together.

"I have a better idea." Rocky disappeared. When he came back, he was carrying his rifle.

"Break through that wall and if you are right—you can go down this way."

"The wall on the other side looked solid," said Noah. "Are you sure?" asked Aspen. "I mean did you check it."

Noah shook his head. "No. Besides being creepy when I was up there *alone,* it didn't occur to me to check it. I just saw a small hall."

Gavin crawled back under the dresses. "Here I'll push, you guys pull this shelf farther out."

In minutes, the shelf was rolled to the edge of the closet—it was too wide to fit through the bi-fold doors, but the space left behind it was ample room for Noah and Gavin to remove the fake wall, if there was one. This time they were careful. They felt around until they found the perimeters of the posterboard then Gavin used his pocketknife to neatly cut along the edges of the wood frame. They removed the posterboard but were met with sections of two by fours.

Gavin sat back on his feet. "Maybe you were right."

Noah shined his flashlight at the top of the gaping hole. "Nope," he grabbed one of the two by fours and pulled. It resisted a little but then popped out. "I was wrong." He displayed the four-foot piece of wood for Gavin. The two by fours were lodged in the opening but were not nailed into place. Once removed, there was only a piece of posterboard about four feet in diameter.

Gavin grinned. "We hit the jackpot."

There were a total of five two by four's. Noah tested the wall behind them. It gave easily when he pushed on it.

Gavin again cut along the wood frame, and the posterboard fell into darkness.

Noah leaned through the hole with his flashlight. "I can't believe this."

"What?"

"We were right. It's the hall at the top of that long staircase." Gavin grinned. He poked his head around the shelves so he could see his dad and the girls. He whispered, "We'll be back in a few minutes."

Noah and Gavin used flashlights to make their way down the narrow staircase, which led them right to a winding staircase.

They were back in the master bedroom in less than ten minutes. They pushed the shoe rack back into place, and then they all double-checked to make sure the room was in order.

Rocky had been studying the gun cases. "This is an amazing collection. Weatherby, Winston, Browning. I wonder if this could be what Drew wants."

"We thought about that, but if that were the case, why didn't they take them?" asked Aspen.

"Probably doesn't have the keys." Rocky shrugged. "One thing for sure, they are worth a fortune."

They left the master bedroom, and since they had no key, they had to leave the door unlocked. That made Rocky chuckle.

"What?" Gavin eyed his dad.

"Oh, I was just thinking. Drew is going to think he is crazy when they come back and find the door unlocked."

48

CONFRONTATION

W HEN THEY REACHED THE main staircase, instead of going down, Aspen paused and then walked directly over to the painting and the others stopped with her.

The girl with the chipped tooth was very visible, not at all like the shadow she had been, more like she was standing in the background of the painting.

Gavin walked up behind Aspen and stood with her looking at the painting.

Aspen turned to look at him. "Can you see the girl in the painting?"

"No. I don't think I am supposed to see her."

Gavin stood there for a few more seconds. He touched her hand, and she looked at him. "Rocky is going downstairs. I am going down with him—you coming?"

"Not just yet, be down in a sec."

"Okay." Gavin and Noah left, and Kiryn joined Aspen.

Aspen gazed at the painting and then turned to Kiryn. "I need to look for something."

Kiryn nodded. "Okay." And she followed Aspen into the bedroom with the window seat full of pictures. Aspen pulled some albums out and put them on the floor.

"What are you looking for?" Kiryn knelt on the floor next to Aspen.

At first, Aspen didn't answer. She rapidly flipped through several albums while Kiryn patiently waited.

Finally, Aspen piled all of the albums back into the window seat and closed the lid. Exasperated, she turned to Kiryn. "I have this feeling, but nothing makes sense, so I am probably wrong."

They walked out of the room. Aspen looked at the painting. Nothing. She shuddered. She walked over to the storage door and pressed her hand firmly against it—she wondered if her hand would pass through it. Nothing. "Sometimes, I get so frustrated. I wish I knew what I am supposed to get or do from all of this."

Kiryn plopped her arm around her friend. "That wouldn't be any fun!" She laughed. "What feeling were you talking about? In there with the pictures?"

Aspen shrugged. "I—never mind. It's lame."

She was glad when Noah met them at the bottom of the stairs, so she did not have to try to explain what she didn't understand herself. How do you explain feelings, or intuition, or—promptings? That was it, promptings. She felt like she was getting promptings from—she had no idea where from.

Noah looked anxious as the girls approached. "Rocky is talking to Drew and Dylan. Come on."

He disappeared through the front door, but then he popped back in and looked directly at Aspen. "You won't believe who Dylan is."

Aspen and Kiryn hurried to catch up.

"Who?" Aspen yelled after him, but her question was immediately answered when she saw the three men.

Rocky and Gavin were standing next to Drew, and now she knew what Noah meant. The other man, who must be Dylan, was the same man that had been arguing with their dad in the driveway.

Aspen and Kiryn slowed to a walk behind Noah as they quietly approached the group. The three men were arguing but not yelling.

Rocky's shotgun lay across his chest, cradled in his arms. "What does Sumer have to do with any of this?"

Dylan stepped towards Rocky, his flexed fist in Rocky's face. "You know *exactly* what she has to do with this!" he hissed.

Drew's arm shot in front of Dylan. "Enough, Dylan."

Dylan turned to the side and spit tobacco juice on the ground causing Aspen's stomach to churn.

"Look, Rocky. We have some things we need to get from the house—" said Drew.

"Seems to me, you already got what you needed." Gavin stepped toward Drew, but the side barrel of Rocky's rifle caught Gavin across the chest, stopping him in his tracks.

"What is that supposed to mean?" Drew turned on Gavin.

"It doesn't matter." Rocky glowered at his son and Gavin backed away.

Aspen swallowed hard. She was sure Gavin was talking about the papers that Drew had taken from the house and copied—at least that is what they had assumed he had done.

"Let's go." Rocky motioned to the four teenagers to follow him. Dylan lunged forward and grabbed Rocky's shoulder.

Rocky called out in pain but swung around thrusting the nose of the gun barrel in Dylan's chest.

Dylan fell back into Drew, who was coming up behind him.

"Hell, Rocky! What did you do that for?" Drew was fuming and moved Dylan out of the way. He was a lot bigger than Rocky and that scared Aspen

Rocky didn't flinch. His eyes drifted to Dylan's left hand, and Aspen's eyes followed.

"Oh, I don't know, Drew? Got any ideas where he got that bite?" Rocky nodded toward Dylan's hand but did not move the rifle.

Drew held one hand behind him, letting Dylan know to stop, and Aspen watched as the color drained from their faces.

"Don't mess with me, Drew." Rocky's lips became a thin line. He stood perfectly still the gun still pointed at Dylan.

Drew didn't say anything instead, they walked across the grass and got into the same truck Aspen and Noah had seen in front of Drew's house. Someone else was at the wheel. The truck started and sped out of the driveway turning right onto the road. When it was out of sight, Rocky turned back to the four teenagers.

Aspen, Noah, and Kiryn stared in disbelief at Rocky, but Gavin was still simmering.

"Should have just shot the idiot, Dad. He was the guy who beat you up. I didn't even notice his hand until you pointed it out."

Rocky's face relaxed, and a small smile replaced the hard line on his lips. "Yeah, that would have been a great idea." He laughed. "Then your dad could go to prison. Wouldn't that be a great legacy for old Rockefeller?"

He put his hand on Gavin's shoulder. "C'mon. Let's go over to Bill and Nada's and get something to eat." He motioned to the other three. "We need a plan, and I need something more than a Mountain Dew."

They walked toward the parked cars.

"Wait." Noah turned back. "I didn't lock the doors."

"Did you leave the window unlocked?" asked Gavin.

Noah was already on the porch. "I will!" he called over his shoulder.

In minutes, Gavin was back, and they all piled in the Iroc. Rocky climbed up into his truck and started the engine.

Kiryn stood up and cupped her hands around her mouth. "Hey, Rocky?"

Rocky turned off the noisy diesel engine. "What?" he leaned over so he was closer to the open passenger window.

"I was—I—well that didn't seem like you—Dad?" Kiryn stammered.

Rocky winked at her then he scanned the faces of the other three. Looking back to Kiryn, he smiled.

"That *was* me—that *isn't* me." Rocky started the engine again and pulled away.

Kiryn looked bewildered when she sat back down.

Gavin looked over at her. "Guess we don't know Dad as well as we thought."

Noah started the car, but before he put it in gear, he looked at all of them. "Well, I think he's pretty cool. That was awesome."

Aspen rolled her eyes. "Of course, you would think that."

Noah laughed and sped out of the driveway. Outside the gate, he jumped out and put the lock on, jumped back in the car and laughed again as he drove away.

Rocky had a table for them, and they all crowded around munching on French fries, hamburgers, and shakes.

Gavin observed the half-full glass of Mountain Dew his dad was drinking. "I thought you needed something more than that."

Rocky smiled. "Yeah, I thought so too, but that *was* me too, that also *isn't* me now." He shrugged and dropped his eyes to the table, giving no further explanation and Gavin didn't press for one.

"Well, I have a question I have been wondering about," said Kiryn. "Why doesn't the gate at the house have an electric lock? Wouldn't that be more secure?"

"It did when we first got here." Noah looked thoughtful. "Remember, Aspen? Dad opened it with a remote that first day. Maybe it broke."

"Or maybe it was disabled," said Rocky.

"Why?" Kiryn took a long drink of her vanilla shake. "Umm it was—disabled, I mean."

Everyone looked at Aspen, and she explained. "I heard Drew talking about that when I was in the bedroom, you know when you guys were in the storage, but he said he was going to hook it back up again."

"Well, looks like they broke it, or maybe it is easier to use a lock with a key. Maybe your dad felt it would be more secure that way," said Rocky.

Aspen wiped her mouth with a napkin. "Maybe. I don't think Dad had anything to do with it, though."

"Well, that is the least of our concerns," said Gavin.

"Yes," agreed Noah. "We need to get through that door at the bottom of the stairs."

Rocky reached down and picked up a notepad that lay on the seat next to him.

"I have a couple of thoughts." He pushed empty fry containers and cups out of the way and laid the notepad on the table.

On the first page, was a crude drawing of the shaft, the stairs and the two rooms at the bottom of each. He had made a pretty good likeness from the kid's descriptions, considering he had not actually been down there.

Rocky pointed to a two-inch-thick black line. "This is the door to the brick wall and subsequently to the outside of the house."

He pointed to another thick line only it was blue. "This is the opening to the stairs that curve and go to the shaft, and this," he pointed to a thick green line on the spiral staircase, "is the staircase that leads to the bedroom."

He then pointed to the last line, which was red. "And this is the roadblock. The door that will not open."

Rocky put an "X" through the black, blue, and green lines. "We know where all of these go." He drew a circle around the red line. "This is the mystery, and I have a feeling it is one of our answers."

"To which question?" asked Noah.

Rocky shook his head and rubbed both hands through his curly black hair. "I don't know."

"Something has been bothering Aspen." Kiryn looked at her friend.

"What was on your mind at the house today? When we went to look at the pictures? You never did tell me."

"Well, we were interrupted by Wyatt Earp here." She laughed. "I'm just kidding Rocky. I still cannot believe that you were that—mean."

"No offense taken." Rocky smiled. "Didn't realize your old school teacher had a past."

Gavin looked at him. "There is a past?"

"A tiny one." Rocky blew it off and motioned to Aspen. "About the pictures."

"I'm not sure," said Aspen. "In my mind, I just keep going back to that picture I found of the two little girls, and oh, by the way," she looked at Noah, "I tried to put my hand through the storage door, and nothing happened."

"Why?" Noah shrugged, but he didn't wait for an answer. Instead, he said, "That could have been two cousins, two friends, two of anybody. It doesn't have much to do with anything." He looked around at the four faces staring at him. "Well, does it?"

"Portals," Rocky said without looking up at any of them.

"Huh?" Noah said what they were all thinking.

"Portals. Aspen can access portals into other dimensions—I think."

"That makes total sense." Gavin grinned.

Aspen shrugged and dismissed the subject. "Well I want to talk about the pictures—one of them had dimples."

They all seemed to sense her apprehension about the portals and let the subject drop.

Noah said, "So? A lot of kids have dimples. *We* have dimples."

Gavin sighed. "Who can be sure, but we probably shouldn't count out any theory yet. What are you wondering about the picture."

Aspen slowly shook her head. "It's just that—it seems like there are two different girls."

Noah drank the last of his shake. "What do you mean? In Great-Grandpa's family?"

"Yes. I have no idea why. It's just a feeling, nothing else."

"Well, it doesn't make sense at this point, but really what does?" said Kiryn.

Aspen sighed. "I guess."

"What do we have to go on?" Rocky had a pen ready to write on his notepad. "I'm just going to make some notes for Kiryn to add to her stuff."

"Well, we know Drew and Dylan want something from the house, that's a given," said Gavin.

"And we know that the old man is trying to interfere with Aspen. At least it sure seems like that," added Kiryn.

"We also know that Krista is trying to help us, but I am not sure how," said Aspen. "And the girl in the picture keeps appearing.

Who knows what she wants?"

"It would appear that Drew and Dylan have something they are holding over your dad's head," said Rocky.

Everyone was quiet at the mention of Jackson Allen.

"We really need to talk to Dad." Noah looked at Aspen, and she nodded. For a few seconds, the two of them studied each other's faces.

"I had a thought about that shaft," Kiryn broke the silence.

"And that is?" said Gavin.

"Remember when we studied old antebellum mansions? They all had what was called a 'dumb waiter.'"

"A what?" Aspen had no idea what she was talking about.

"A dumb waiter. It was a shaft—kind of like an elevator—that moved up and down from the main floor to the second or third story. They had ropes and pulleys that raised a shelf or platform or something up and down so that dishes, and other things I suppose, could be moved between the floors without using the stairs."

"Humm." Rocky's eyes widened. "That could be exactly what that was."

"But it curves. It does not go straight down," said Gavin.

"I know, and that's the part that doesn't fit, but when I was leaning on the top part, where it's flat just before the hole in the wall, it sank or dented or something. I was in such a hurry to get out to Rocky, I kind of forgot about it, but last night I remembered. That spot didn't feel as solid as the rest of the shaft," said Kiryn.

"Any theory is a good one until we prove it wrong," said Rocky. "We should check that out."

"Okay, but what would it prove?" Gavin looked from Noah to Kiryn and then back to Rocky.

"I have no idea." Kiryn laughed and then continued, "Noah mentioned the balcony."

"Oh yeah, how to get to it?"

"Isn't there a staircase from the back patio?" said Kiryn.

"Well, you would think so. To be honest, I haven't paid any attention."

Aspen shrugged. "It seems odd that you could only get to a second-story balcony from the outside."

"Good point," Rocky agreed.

Noah pulled his phone out of his pocket and scrolled the front. "It's twelve-thirty. Mom and Dad said they would be back in Memphis about ten."

"So are you staying with us tonight?" Kiryn looked from Noah to Aspen. "Okay?"

"Yes, we might as well." Aspen looked at Rocky. "If that's okay."

"Since you have come, I have almost been beaten to death, and I had to pull my gun out of storage. Why ruin the fun now?"

Aspen furrowed her brow. "I'm sorry."

"I'm kidding." Rocky stood and picked up the bill. "And you kids are costing me a fortune."

"We have money," said Noah.

"Again, I am kidding." Rocky walked to the counter and handed the bill to a short, plump, pleasant-looking lady that Aspen had learned was Nada who was the other half of Bill.

The kids walked past him. "So are we meeting at the house?" asked Gavin.

"Yep. I am going to run home and grab the laptop." Rocky followed them out the door.

"Why do we need that?" asked Kiryn

"A theory." He grinned. "And a pretty good one, I think."

49

THAT'S NOT OUR DAD

KIRYN'S THEORY PROVED RIGHT. They removed the flat piece of metal with a crowbar and a hammer. The shaft beneath it was about three feet square and dropped straight down. There were pulleys on two sides at the top of the shaft, but no ropes were attached.

Noah retrieved a book from one of the bedrooms and dropped it down the shaft—it fell into darkness and landed with a thud. He flooded the shaft with a beam from his flashlight. The book lay flat on the bottom having disturbed only sleeping dust.

"I wonder why someone added that other shaft onto this one?" said Aspen.

"Good question," said Gavin, "Maybe this one was added second, or maybe they were built at the same time."

Gavin turned to Noah, "Let's go down to the kitchen and see if we can find where that book landed."

"Might be hard to find. Looks like the sides of the shaft are solid." Noah followed Gavin down the stairs.

Aspen and Kiryn put the fake wall back in place. Since they were going in and out so much and with Rocky's assurance that Drew and Dylan may not come around too much now, they had made a unanimous decision to leave the tree by the window so they would not have to keep moving it. They decided a large chair in place of the tree might work, and they hoped Aspen's parents didn't notice the change.

Aspen whirled around and stared down the hall. She thought she heard someone say her name.

Kiryn looked wide-eyed at her friend. "What are you looking at?"

Aspen linked her arm thorough Kiryn's. "C'mon."

"Sure," whispered Kiryn. "I ain't afraid of no ghost."

Kiryn's face amused Aspen. Her eyes were wide and anxious.

Aspen squeezed her arm. "It's okay."

They walked slowly down the hallway toward the painting. "I wonder if we have both lost our minds. We are taking this spirit stuff way too casually," said Kiryn.

"They are just people—" Aspen stopped walking and looked at Kiryn.

"What?"

"People. They are just people. We know who Krista is and now we know who Sumer is. They are just people who used to live in this world—people who meant something to someone at one time—actually, they still do—mean something."

She paused as the words caught in her throat. "Now—now they live somewhere else."

"And just drop in to visit now and then?" Kiryn's whisper was nearly a shriek. "Well, I don't like it one bit."

Aspen chuckled, suddenly relaxed again. "Well, these are nice spirits. It's that old guy I don't want to see anymore." Aspen walked right up to the painting. She lifted her hand and placed her fingers on the canvas where the threads usually moved. Nothing.

Again, she thought she heard her name, only this time it was a piercing whisper.

Aspen jumped and turned around, causing Kiryn to stumble backward when Aspen bumped into her.

The girl was standing in front of the storage door. She was barely visible, but Aspen could see her. She seemed to be shaking her head. Aspen stared in her direction. She began to get goosebumps on her neck and arms.

The girl stared back at Aspen with no expression, but it was the image behind the girl that also drew Aspen's attention. Sumer was barely a shadow, but she was there, and almost as quickly as Aspen had seen her, she disappeared.

"What do you want me to do?" whispered Aspen, not sure whom she was asking.

Kiryn suddenly leaned into Aspen, linking arms with her. "Aspen! What is happening?"

Aspen was equally startled. The storage doorknob turned, and the door slowly opened. The girl did not move, and neither did Aspen or Kiryn, but Aspen could feel Kiryn's hands shaking.

Okay, I know that was Sumer, but why does she have to be invisible?

Aspen was frozen. She didn't know if she dared walk past the girl and go into the dark room. Kiryn still clung to her as they stood still for what seemed like forever, but Aspen knew it was only seconds.

What if we go in there and get locked in? Noah won't know where we are. And—and—what if—the other people are there again?

Aspen whirled around when she felt a gentle nudge on her back. She came face to face with Sumer whose face wore a faint smile, but there was a kind of pleading in her eyes. These were the same mystic green eyes that Aspen saw whenever she looked into Gavin's.

Sumer stood right next to Aspen, but suddenly she was standing at least ten feet away from her.

Sumer nodded slightly, and Aspen turned back to the open door. She took a step forward but was immediately stopped by Kiryn's clinging. Both arms laced through Aspen's one arm.

Aspen paused. Without taking her eyes from the girl, she whispered to Kiryn.

"It's okay. Just come with me."

Kiryn did not respond but still held tightly to Aspen's arm.

Aspen stepped forward again, this time meeting little resistance from Kiryn. They walked slowly to the open door.

The room was dark. Aspen fumbled for the light switch just inside the door as Noah had done. Her hand located it, and she flipped it on. The soft light on the wall illuminated the room only slightly.

It looked foreboding to Aspen, and she was not sure why, but as she stood there, she had the distinct feeling that this room held another vital clue to the mystery she and Noah, and now their two friends and Rocky had been thrown into.

Aspen looked back to where the image of the girl had been. She was gone. She looked back toward the painting. Sumer was gone as well.

Aspen turned back to the storage room. Kiryn clung so close she realized they could almost be one person. She gently tugged on Kiryn's arm, and they stepped inside the room.

The storage room was nothing like they had left it. The paintings they had been looking at a few days earlier, and had so carefully put back in place, were now strewn on the floor. The two girls stopped. Only one remained leaning against the wall—the painting of her great-grandfather, his wife, and their three children.

"What the—" whispered Kiryn.

"I don't know," Aspen whispered back.

Dragging Kiryn along, Aspen stepped around the paintings on the floor until she was standing in front of the one against the wall. She hadn't realized before how tall it was. Without the other paintings stacked around it, this one appeared to be about five feet tall and only a foot or so less in width.

Kiryn tugged on Aspen's arm, "Who did this?"

Aspen shook her head. "I don't know she said again." *But I have a pretty good idea.*

The parents in the painting sat straight up—the mother looked pleasant enough. She had her hand on her husband's knee, and his hand covered hers, their fingers laced together. She wore a long, white chiffon dress that fit her body to the knees but then fanned out the layers of chiffon draping to the floor in neat folds.

The tips of black shoes peeked from beneath the dress. She wore a black and white hat that sat kind of on the side of her blonde hair which was somehow secured on top of her head. The dress had a high neck, and little white buttons fell in a single row all the way down the front. The woman's face displayed a wide smile, but

Aspen thought her eyes looked distant and empty.

Aspen's great-grandfather wore a black suit. The front was cut short, but the back hung past the chair toward the floor. His white shirt had lace on the front and lace poked out from the sleeves of the jacket. His right hand held the front of his jacket where a thin watch-chain dangled from a slit pocket. His pose reminded Aspen of a picture she had seen of Napoleon. His dark brown hair was combed neatly in place, his wide grin sporting a long mustache that turned up at the ends. His eyes too, like his wife's, appeared distant and empty.

Aspen gazed at the parents for some time, but then she studied the eyes of each person.

The young boy, her grandfather, had deep dimples that stood out against his chubby cheeks and his brown eyes sparkled. His front teeth were awkwardly bigger than his other teeth, making Aspen think he was about seven-years-old when the painting was done.

He was kneeling on the ground, a hand resting on his father's knee. His suit and shirt were similar to his father's, but his pants came just below the knees and white long socks extended to his black shoes of which Aspen could only see the side of one. She shuddered. At least he wasn't wearing a dress.

Aspen paused for a minute, looking back at the boy's face. *Those dimples...*

Her eyes drifted to the youngest girl. Long brown hair hung in thick ringlets past her shoulders and brown eyes framed by long dark eyelashes stared back at Aspen. Her lips were barely parted and curved into a faint smile revealing perfect, straight teeth. Her pink dress dotted with little white flowers had puffy sleeves that gathered in at the wrists. A bibbed-front white pinafore covered the front of the dress to about mid-thigh length with yards of eyelet lace cascading to the floor. Aspen could only assume she had shoes hidden under all of that lace. The girl's left hand rested on her father's shoulder, and her right hand hung limp at her side.

The oldest daughter was standing to the left of her mother. Her dress was identical to her younger sister's except it was a pale lavender color. The front of her dress from about the top of her legs down was hidden behind a potted plant. Aspen was not sure why the plant annoyed her, but it did. It seemed out of place.

She looked back at the girl's face. The sides of her hair were pulled up on the top of her head and secured with a brown clip that was only partially visible. She too had long dark ringlets that hung over her shoulders nearly to her waist. Her lips were slightly turned up at the corners, but it was her round brown eyes that most intrigued Aspen.

Instinctively Aspen touched the face of the older sister. She felt Kiryn's arm relax and pull away from her, disturbing the quietness of Aspen's thoughts.

Kiryn leaned forward and touched the potted plant. "This bugs me. The paint is so thick on this pot." She ran her hand to the mother's dress. "And here too. I wonder what lame person painted this."

Aspen chuckled at Kiryn's criticism of the painting that was well over fifty years old. "Maybe the painter's spirit could come here, and you could teach him a thing or two."

Kiryn rolled her eyes. "That's okay. I am just fine with the spirits that surround you. I don't need any to come here specifically to see me."

Aspen had started to laugh when the two girls were startled by yelling coming from outside.

"Dad, Dad, wait!" It was Noah's voice. The front door of the house flew open.

Aspen's heart was suddenly in her throat. "That's my dad!" She turned and ran from the room, stumbling through the paintings on the floor. Kiryn was right behind her.

They peered over the railing into the foyer below.

"I have to get a call to tell me that the school teacher pulled a gun on a man while my kids were standing right there, and then I learn that you all have been in this house tearing apart the walls and doing who knows what?"

Aspen had never seen her dad so mad.

"Mr. Allen," Rocky reached toward Dad.

Dad spun on him. "Don't you, Mr. Allen me, Mr. Fielden! I will have you arrested, and you will never teach school in this place again!"

"What kind of a father are you to encourage this kind of nonsense? I think I have left my kids with a responsible adult while their mother and I took care of some important business but instead I have to come back to find all hell has broken loose!"

"Dad, Rocky—I mean Mr. Fielden was just trying—" Noah stammered.

It was at this moment that Aspen was not sure if she was looking at the same man she had known as her father for sixteen years.

Jackson Allen lunged at his son with both hands, shoving him back and throwing Noah to the floor. "Don't Dad me, you lying little—"

Gavin and Rocky both sprang toward Dad, each of them grabbing one of his arms, but he was so angry they could not contain him. He threw them both off and glancing at Noah who was still on the floor, he charged for the stairs.

Noah's face expressed the horror he must have felt. Their dad had never laid a hand on either of them or their mother.

Aspen gasped as she watched her dad take the stairs two at a time, cursing all the way to the top. He hesitated when he saw Aspen and Kiryn but only for a second and then he pushed past them heading directly for the wall at the end of the hall.

"What have you done? Why would you take out this wall? What do you think you are doing?"

Dad was yelling so loud Aspen froze against the railing. Everything around her seemed disconnected and confusing. Her heart was pounding, and she was finding it hard to breathe, and the more she tried to gulp air, the harder it was.

"Dad?"

Aspen heard Noah behind her, and in seconds Noah, Gavin, and Rocky were in front of her.

She tried to speak, "Don't—" but the words stuck in her throat.

Rocky stepped forward and put his arms around Aspen and Kiryn's shoulders.

Jackson Allen lunged towards them all. "Get your hands off my daughter."

"Dad?" Noah stepped in front of him.

Aspen was shocked. She was sure their dad would not push Noah again, but he proved her wrong. With one sweep of his arm, he moved Noah to the side and continued past them toward the master bedroom.

Aspen heard Dad struggle with the key in the lock, but then the bedroom door hit the wall when he pushed it open. He stood silent for a minute, and all Aspen could hear was his labored breathing. He was like a wild man, someone she did not recognize.

The pain in Noah's eyes was more than Aspen could stand, but when Noah started again toward their father, Rocky caught him by the shoulder.

"Let it be," he whispered.

Noah looked at Aspen. She watched the hurt turn into sadness, and he began to cry. Aspen reached for his hand, but he didn't respond. His head hung, and he covered his face with both hands.

Aspen heard her father coming toward them, and she looked away from Noah in Dad's direction.

Jackson's face twisted into an angry snarl, his eyes wild and sweat poured from his face and neck. He thrust a finger toward all of them. "I will deal with all of you later." He looked directly at Rocky. "You will be in jail today!"

Dad turned to go down the stairs, but he suddenly stopped, staring into the air in front of him. His face turned from anger to horror, and for a few seconds, he seemed paralyzed, his hands clutching the railing on both sides.

Aspen suddenly felt sorry for him, but it was impossible to discern why she felt that way or what was happening.

He looked directly at Aspen and then Noah. His wild, angry eyes were now filled with agony, causing both of his children to cry even more.

Dad turned back to the place he had been looking before. He choked and covered his face with both hands. Sobs suddenly racked his entire body. "No God, please no," he cried and grabbing the railing, he all but fell down the stairs.

"Dad!" screamed Aspen. She broke free from Rocky's arm and ran toward the stairs but was immediately stopped by Noah.

She fell against Noah's chest, their arms encircling each other while both wept openly.

Rocky wrapped his arms around them as their father's truck screeched out of the driveway.

Noah wanted to follow their dad, but Rocky wouldn't let him. "Let's give him some time, Noah."

When they arrived at Rocky's, Aspen and Noah's faces were swollen from crying. They both collapsed in the den, and Rocky brought bottled water to both of them.

Gavin and Kiryn had not said anything. They didn't even know Jackson Allen, so they were not sure if this was normal behavior for him or not.

Noah cleared that up in a hurry. "My dad has never so much as yelled at us. He laughs and jokes with us, surfs with us and loves us, and our mom. I do not know who that man was."

Tears streamed down Aspen's face. "Oh, why did we come here? Everything is such a mess."

Kiryn draped her arm across Aspen's shoulders. "We'll figure it out." She looked at Rocky. "Huh, Dad?"

Rocky sighed. "Well, there is obviously something really bothering your dad. There must be something going on that neither of you knows about."

"I'm sorry he was so mean to you." Noah looked up at Rocky through bloodshot eyes. "He didn't mean any of it."

Gavin looked at his dad, "I guess you'll know if you end up in jail."

"Oh, he meant that part." Rocky smiled. "But the police in this town know something is coming to a head. I have been filling them in on everything—" he grinned now. "That they need to know." He twisted the top off a bottle of water and downed the entire thing.

Noah's phone rang. He looked at it and then looked at Aspen. "It's Mom." He let it continue to ring.

"Well answer it!" Aspen almost screamed at him.

Noah quickly scrolled the front of the phone and put it to his ear. "Mom?" He had not taken his eyes from Aspen's. He whispered, "She's crying."

Aspen felt the anxiety immediately come back into her chest, and she wrapped both of her arms around herself. More tears spilled down her cheeks.

Noah was listening. "Where are you?" He was quiet again, "Okay, in Memphis?"

Again, he listened. "We'll go now, Mom. It will be okay. See you there in a while. Oh, uh how will you get home?" He listened again. "Okay. Yes, we love you, Mom."

Noah dropped his phone in his lap and buried his face in his hands. For a minute he was silent but then his body started shaking and sobs wrenched from his throat the next words tumbling rapidly over each other.

"Dad—Dad collapsed at the police station. He had a heart attack."

Aspen jumped to her feet. "Is he okay?"

"I don't know." He looked at Rocky, but he was already on his feet and said to all of them, "C'mon get in the truck."

Aspen and Noah stood outside the intensive care unit staring through the window at their father. He looked pale and harmless—not at all like the strange monster he had seemed just a couple of hours ago. His face was covered with an oxygen mask and tubes, and IV's were attached to both arms. A monitor clicked the unsteady beeps of his heartbeat.

Aspen buried her head in Noah's shoulder, more tears soaking his already wet T-shirt. "What if he dies?"

Noah hugged her tightly. "He's not going to die, Aspen," he whispered. "We still have a lot to do, to talk about."

"I want to leave Sommerville." Noah nodded. "I do too."

"You must be the Allen children." They looked up as a doctor approached them. He was tall and willowy, his blonde hair thinning on top. His blue eyes were kind, and his voice soft and reassuring.

They both nodded.

The doctor extended his hand. "I'm Doctor Winslow."

"Hi," mumbled Noah and he and Aspen shook the doctor's hand.

"Your dad had a pretty severe heart attack. We are going to stabilize him and then put a stent in his heart to open the blocked artery. His vitals were pretty bad when we got him in here, but he is doing better now."

"Is he going to die?" said Aspen.

"No—not if I can help it. He could have, though if he hadn't been where he received immediate help. He will have to spend a few days with us if all goes well."

"Our mother—"

The doctor put his hand on Noah's shoulder. "I talked to your mother about a half-hour ago. She knows what we are doing and has already given us permission if she does not make it before we need to do the surgery, but, we will hold off as long as we can."

Noah nodded. "Okay."

"Can we go in there?" Aspen motioned toward the room where Dad lay.

"Well, he is in and out of sleep. I'm not sure he will know you're there." Dr. Winslow stopped talking and studied the two teenagers. Then he sighed, "Yes, you can. Just please try not to upset him."

"Okay," said Aspen.

When they approached the bed, Aspen was startled by the

anguished look on her father's face. "He looks like he is in pain," she whispered, and she put her hand over one of Dad's.

Dad opened his eyes. He tried to say something, but no words came out. His eyes drifted from Aspen to Noah. He tried to lift his hand toward them, but Noah gently pushed it back down.

He leaned over his father. "I love you, Dad." Aspen saw his tears fall on their fathers face and Noah quickly dabbed them away with his fingers.

Dad's head slightly nodded. He looked into Noah's eyes and then to Aspen as tears trickled from the corners of his eyes. His eyelids slowly closed, and his breathing became shallow.

Aspen's hand flew to her mouth, and she gasped. "Is he dead, Noah?"

Noah pointed to the beeping monitor. "No, he is asleep." Aspen relaxed, but more tears came.

Noah took her hand. "C'mon, let's go."

"Shouldn't we stay with him?"

A nurse poked her head in. "I need to check your dad, could you step out here for a minute?"

They both nodded and walked past her as she came into the room. She pulled a curtain around the bed all but hiding their father from view. It was a few minutes before she came back out and she skirted past them to the phone on the wall.

They couldn't hear what she said, but when she hung up the phone, she turned around. "We are taking your dad into surgery now. You can wait in the visitor's lounge down the hall right next to the elevators."

"But our mom—" Noah began.

"I'm sorry. We can't wait any longer." The nurse's tone was apologetic, but she hurried past them into their dad's room. As she did, she pointed down the hall. "The waiting room is down there."

"O...okay." Aspen felt her heart quicken as Noah took her arm and led her away from the intensive care unit and into the hallway.

She hated hospitals. Everything looked so glum. Even the bright paintings that dotted the walls looked drab and lifeless right now.

When they entered the waiting room, they found Gavin, Rocky, and Kiryn there. Gavin immediately pulled Aspen into his arms and Noah went directly to Kiryn. They all hugged in silence.

"Why don't we go for a walk?" Rocky looked at the clock in the wall. "Your mom should be here soon." He looked over at Noah. "Sara is bringing her from the airport."

Relief washed over Aspen with that news. At least someone they knew was picking her up. Her mother hadn't had time to make any friends in Sommerville.

Suddenly she had a thought, "Why was Mom at the airport instead of with Dad?"

Rocky shrugged. "Apparently she was trying to get him to calm down before they left the airport, but he just got into the car and drove away without her."

Noah and Aspen's eyes locked, and Noah spoke for both of them, "That was not our dad."

50

EMPTY HOUSE

ASPEN AND NOAH DIDN'T talk about much of anything when Mom arrived at the hospital. She didn't appear to know anything about the confrontation between her husband and her children, and they did not bring it up.

Jackson was still in surgery—the doctor explained they were inserting a stint in the front part of his heart. He further explained that this particular heart attack that their dad had was often referred to as "the widowmaker" because without immediate help, it can take the victim's life.

They were instructed to wait, and they would be told when Dad had been taken to recovery. Aspen was terrified that her dad would die and she could not grasp anything that was happening. Everything seemed disjointed to her. She just lay with her head in her mother's lap and cried until she fell asleep.

It was nearly two more hours before Dr. Winslow came to tell them the surgery went well and that it may be a couple of hours before Dad was back in his room in intensive care.

While Dad was in surgery, Gavin had taken Noah to get his car and then he Kiryn and Rocky went home.

Noah, Mom, and Aspen waited until they were sure Dad was stabilized. When Dad was in his room, they went in for just a few minutes, but at the doctor's encouragement, they left for home.

314

The day had been long and grueling. Aspen and Noah had not been home since their parents left for Oregon. The little house seemed empty when they walked through the front door. It had never felt like home, but now it felt even more lifeless and unwelcome.

Aspen sank onto the sofa, and Noah sat in a chair across from her. Mom sat next to Aspen, curling her legs under her. She had not shed one tear since she had been back in Sommerville but now, sipping on a cup of tea, quiet tears trickled down her cheeks. She quickly brushed them away.

Aspen felt more in control now and scooted close to her mother and hugged her neck, and Mom patted her daughter's leg.

"Do you feel like talking, Mom?" Noah watched her face as he spoke.

Mom looked surprised. "About what?" Noah and Aspen exchanged puzzled looks.

"About Dad, Mom. About Dad."

Aspen was surprised at Mom's reaction. "He will be okay." She nervously traced the edges of the teacup with her finger.

Noah's face immediately hardened but when he caught Aspen's disparaging look, he softened again. "Okay, I hope so." He abruptly changed the subject. "So what did you and Dad have to go to Oregon for?"

Aspen still assumed that Mom knew nothing about why Dad had confronted the two of them.

"Oh." Mom set the teacup on the table in front of them, which was a relief to Aspen because it was driving her crazy watching her mother fiddle with it.

Mom folded her hands across her lap. "Well, there seems to be a major part of the will missing. We have to find it—at least that is what your father says. He says it fits all the pieces together." She sighed.

"But honestly, it is so frustrating. Even the part we have does not make sense, and we cannot find the name of the attorney firm that has been handling it all these years. We thought for sure if we went to Aunt Dana's and Uncle Jerry's, between the four of us we could find the papers."

"We thought maybe they had been packed by accident in one of the boxes Aunt Dana took with her. She had a lot of loose paperwork to be completed." Mom sighed again only this time, it was more labored, and she sounded more discouraged.

"What do Dylan and Drew have to do with all of this?" asked Noah.

Mom immediately looked uncomfortable. "Dylan who?" Aspen noticed the obvious omission of Drew's name.

Noah looked at Aspen. "What the heck is their last name?"

"Dixon, I think." Aspen looked at Mom. "You don't know them, Mom?"

Mom shook her head. "Never heard the name."

Noah leaned forward. "So you don't know Dylan *or* Drew?"

Again Aspen glowered at her brother.

"No, Noah." Mom stood up. "I'm tired, and you kids must be too. Why don't we get to bed so that we can go visit Dad after school tomorrow?"

She paused. "You do have school, right?"

They both nodded. Aspen couldn't see any reason to try to explain the events of the past few days to Mom. How they had gone to the lake, found the shaft, the journal, the paintings, Rocky being beat up and canceling school today, the old man—her thoughts drifted off.

What's the use? Mom is a total wreck.

Mom leaned over and kissed the top of Aspen's head. She walked around the table, bent down and kissed Noah's cheek and then she started down the hall.

"Love you, Mom," Noah mumbled after her.

Mom stopped. "I love the two of you more than you can imagine." She looked at each of them and then turned and plodded into her room.

51

WHISPERS

WHEN ASPEN WOKE UP, it was still dark outside. The large red numbers on her alarm clock seemed to glow brighter than usual.

Two twenty. Why am I so awake?

She swung her legs over the edge of her bed. Feeling eyes piercing her back, she slowly turned around but saw no one there. She stared into the dark through the open window; sure someone was watching her.

She shuddered, jumped up, and closed the blind wondering if she had just imagined it. Plopping onto her back on her bed, she began sorting through the difference in her feelings when she saw Sumer as opposed to the old man. One brought comfort and the other unmistakable fear. *Was he dead, too?* She let her thoughts tarry there for a few minutes.

Impossible.

Then how did she see them both? Of course, she did believe in good and evil, but was the old man actually evil? That thought caused her to chill right down to her bones. Was he? Could he? Be coming from...from... She refused to let the word even formulate in her mind. She just wanted the old man to be a figment of her imagination.

But could he be a figment of Gavin's imagination too?

Logic told her that was not possible, but somehow it made it easier for her to deal with the old man—to pretend that he was not real—that someone, somehow, was playing an elaborate trick on her, but why?

She dragged her fingers through her long hair, stood and shuffled into the hallway. Noah was snoring when she passed his room. She continued through the living room toward the kitchen. When she passed the hall leading to her parent's bedroom, she thought she heard someone talking.

Quietly she tiptoed to her parent's bedroom door. The thin beam of light beneath the door caused her to stay back. She wasn't sure why, except she assumed Mom would be asleep. Instead, Mom was talking to someone, and it obviously wasn't Dad. Aspen held her breath so that she could better hear the loud whispering.

"I don't know what you want me to do. We simply couldn't find it." Mom hissed. She sounded upset—afraid.

There was a long pause.

"You leave my kids out of this."

Aspen heard the phone drop to the floor and then her mother's muffled crying. She stood still for a long time just listening, too afraid to move. Mom's cries slowly gave way to shallow, even breathing, and Aspen was sure Mom had fallen asleep.

She quietly started back to her room, wide-awake now and wondering if she should wake Noah questioning too why she didn't feel like she could intrude on her mother at that time. It made her uneasy like there was a secret she was not supposed to be a part of. She thought of the picture of Drew, and Dad's heart attack and—confusion.

Our lives are nothing but confusion right now.

Back in her room, Aspen fumbled through her drawer for the journal. Flipping through some of the loose pages she stopped on the one she was looking for . . .

> Dixon called me to his hospital bed today. I did not want to go, but I did.
>
> I suppose because he is on his death bed, he thinks he needs to get right with God.

The things he confessed to me I will take to my grave.

All the money, this big house, all the prestige, and fame—mean nothing to me.

I can't believe he has lived with these lies all these years, and claiming to be my friend.

Of course, I have lived with my own demons—but this is too much. So much pain. I don't think I can bear to live with all of this much longer.

Drove by the hospital today. Didn't go in—can't go in—I can't. So many lies!

1995

Aspen turned the journal pages slowly. The ink on this page, in particular, was smeared. The page had been crinkled and had a tear nearly halfway down the middle. The ink ran in several places, and she wasn't sure why, but she knew the stains were from tears.

She placed the journal on her window seat and turned back to her bed but stopped and turned around. Reaching across the journal, she picked up Sprinkle. Holding her treasured stuffed giraffe in her arms, she climbed into bed, pulled her knees to her chest tightly hugging her snuggly childhood comforter.

Sleep was impossible with so many things chasing around in her head.

What did Dixon tell her grandpa? Why did he drive by the hospital? Who was Ronda, and why was she so important to him? What demons? What LIES?

And now Mom, who was she talking to in the middle of the night? Also, what did Sumer, Gavin's real mom, have to do with any of this?

Aspen rolled over and put Sprinkle on her pillow and then flopped onto her back. She propped her hands behind her head, staring at the ceiling fan. She watched it slowly spin, the blades methodically taking their turn drifting into the beam of light the moon cast across her room. Then each would disappear again into the shadows. The fan produced a soft hum that on any other night, would sooth Aspen and help her fall asleep, but tonight, it was only annoying

"Ugh!" Aspen jumped out of bed. She walked to the dresser, fumbling until she found her cell phone and then reached into her jeans pocket for the receipt from the hospital cafeteria. She called the number and waited. The answer came at the other end of the line, "*Sommerville Hospital.*"

"H—hi. Could I—um, I just wanted to check on my Dad."

"*Do you know what room he is in?*"

"He is in intensive care. I think the 3rd floor."

"*Oh, yes, Mr. Allen. I can connect you with the night nurse.*"

"Thank you."

"*Cardiac Intensive Care, this is Cecelia, how may I help you?*"

"Hi, I was just wondering...can you tell me how my dad is doing?"

"*Of course, may I ask whom I am speaking to?*"

"Aspen Allen. My Dad is Jackson Allen."

"*Yes, Aspen. Your dad is resting peacefully. He had a rough day today, but he's sleeping now.*"

Aspen sighed. "Oh, good. Thank you."

"*Aspen, would you like to speak to your mother?*"

That information startled Aspen. "My mom's there?"

"*Yes, just a minute.*"

There was a long pause.

"*Aspen?*"

"Mom?"

"*Aspen, what are you doing up?*"

"I couldn't sleep. I just wanted to check on Dad. I thought you were in bed."

"*I couldn't sleep either, so I drove over here to be with Dad.*"

Aspen's eyes brimmed with tears. "Mom, are you okay? I didn't even hear you leave."

"*I'm fine. I woke Noah and told him I would be home in the morning. I just didn't want to leave Dad alone all night.*"

Aspen choked, "Oh, okay."

"Aspen why are you crying?"

"Everything is just a mess, Mom, and now Dad." She was crying hard now and trying to talk between gasps for air.

"It will all be okay Aspen. I promise." Mom was quiet for a minute, allowing Aspen's crying to soften, and then she continued. *"We haven't had much time together since Krista died. I am so sorry, Aspen."*

"It's okay, Mom. You and Dad had things to do." Aspen felt her chest tighten and the familiar anxiety return. "I just have so much to tell—"

"We'll talk. Promise. We just need to get Dad better now. We have to think about that now." Mom's voice trailed off.

"Aspen?" Noah walked into her room.

She looked up at him. "It's Mom, she is at the—"

"I know."

"Oh yeah."

"Aspen it's nearly five. Why don't you and Noah get dressed and come and get me and we'll have some breakfast before you go to school? Unless you don't want to go to school."

"What are you going to do all day, Mom?"

"I am going to come home and shower and then come back to the hospital. You kids should go to school."

"Yeah, probably. Okay, I'll tell Noah. Love you, Mom. See you in a little while." Aspen stared at her phone as the screen went blank.

52

JOSEPH'S SURPRISE

"We were worried when we didn't see you at school." Kiryn threw her arms around Aspen. "How's your dad?"

"Good, I guess. He's still sleeping mostly." Aspen hugged Kiryn back.

"You guys look tired." Gavin bumped knuckles with Noah.

"Not much sleep," Noah yawned. "Sorry about school. Was Rocky mad?"

Gavin furrowed his brow and twisted his mouth. "No, this is Rocky we're talking about."

"True," Noah laughed.

"Where's your mom?" Kiryn asked.

"We took her home to get some sleep." Noah yawned again. "We are going to meet her here for dinner."

"At the hospital cafeteria?" Kiryn wrinkled her nose. Noah looked around. "Not a lot of choices."

"Yes, there is." Kiryn linked arms with Noah, which caught him by surprise. "You are all coming to our house."

Gavin grinned. "That's a great idea."

"Hey, by the way," Aspen touched Gavin's arm. "That was nice of Sara to bring Mom from the airport."

"She didn't mind. She wanted to meet your mom anyway." He stared into Aspen's eyes for a second, and Aspen felt the butterflies flitting widely in her stomach.

Gavin put one arm around her shoulders and pulled her close. "It's all good," he said softly and then released her.

Aspen stiffened. "Okay." She moved away and caught Gavin's puzzled look from the corner of her eye. She knew how easy it would be, with everything that had happened, to succumb to Gavin's attention, but there was still the Cassie issue and—that kiss—neither subject had been addressed.

They were interrupted when a truck turned into the hospital parking lot. Aspen was surprised to see it was Joseph Dixon. Without shutting off the engine, he put the truck in park, stepped out and walked around the back of the truck directly up to Noah.

"Hey, Joseph," said Kiryn.

He glanced at her. "Hey." He thrust a package loosely wrapped in brown paper toward Noah. "I—I thought you might want this."

"You'll see." Joseph looked down at the ground, and then he looked up at Aspen. He turned quickly and walked back to his truck, but then he turned around.

"Hey, my...my Dad, he didn't mean—I mean he was depending on that—and I'm sorry, my Uncle Dylan is a little crazy." He chewed his lip.

"Look I found it a long time ago, like when I was maybe ten. We, my dad and my uncle, we were moving some trees off my great-grandpa's property. I saw this—" he pointed to the package. "That. In a pile of dirt, and I sneaked it home—" he chuckled softly." I thought I had found a great treasure, but then when I started reading it, I hated your family and I had never even met you."

He looked at Gavin. "There was some stuff in there about your mom's sister, I think. I'm not sure, but it seemed like the woman must be your mom's sister. Just because of what I read in there."

He thrust his finger toward the package, and then he turned back toward his truck. Suddenly he whirled around. "But I just put the dumb thing away, till now, till you guys came. I dug it out. Now what I read made me sad—and mad—but," he looked at Noah and then Aspen. "Not at you."

Joseph stopped talking and looked at them. This time he got into his truck. "Just read it!" he called through the open window and then he drove away.

Aspen looked at Noah. He looked as bewildered as she felt. "What was that all about?"

Kiryn peered over Noah's shoulder. "This apparently." Noah lifted the package for all to see. "It feels like a book."

Noah placed the package on the trunk of the Iroc and carefully took the wrapping off. Bare threads that had once held the cover to the spine were broken and stretched. A few tiny spots where black dirt had been rubbed off, revealed evidence that in its better days, it may have been tan.

The bottom right-hand corner of the cover had been rubbed until a name was almost invisible.

Ke nh Ll y Dix

Gavin studied the name. "That's Dixon's old man. Well actually, grandfather." His eyes widened. "Wonder what's in *that* little book?"

"That's the guy who owned the company with my dad's grandpa?" Noah was still looking at the book.

"The same."

Aspen said, "I read some stuff in Grandpa's journal last night too."

"Last night?" Noah questioned Aspen.

"Couldn't sleep."

"Hmm, I could right now." Noah rubbed his eyes with his free hand.

"May I see that?" Kiryn reached for the book.

Noah handed it to her. "Yes. I need to sleep. I am so tired."

Gavin put his arm around Aspen. He moved her hair and put his hand on the back of her bare neck, sending tingles all the way down her spine. He guided her to the Iroc and opened the passenger door. "Why don't you two go home and get some sleep. Then you can bring your mom to our house for dinner and then after you see your dad later, you guys come back over."

Kiryn handed the journal back to Aspen. "Here, he gave this to you guys. You should look at it first."

Aspen nodded. "Okay."

Gavin quickly pointed to Kiryn and then himself, "In the meantime, we—" he repeated the motion, "We'll see if Dad found anything important."

He grinned as he closed the door for Aspen, looking quite satisfied with himself for his plan.

Noah sighed. "Sounds good to me." He took Kiryn's hand, squeezed it, then got in the car.

Gavin put both hands on the car door and leaned close to Aspen. "See you later."

Aspen's head was spinning. She was overtired, overwhelmed, and now butterflies fluttered through her stomach where so much anxiety had been just hours before. She smiled at Gavin and waved at Kiryn. "See ya."

Gavin walked over by Kiryn. He leaned against Rocky's truck, lifted his sunglasses off his nose, grinned at Aspen and then let them drop back into place.

Aspen waved again.

"You and Gavin are a perfect pair. You both roam with the walking dead."

"Yeah, perfect," she snapped.

Noah laughed. "Geez, I was just kidding. He's a nice enough guy."

"Oh, please, you like him." Aspen still did not look at Noah.

"So do you, and that's what I said. He's a nice enough guy."

"He is."

"Aspen?"

She breathed deeply. "I...I just don't— There is too much going on to think about that stuff."

Noah didn't respond so Aspen changed the subject. "And Kiryn?"

Noah shifted in his seat and suddenly became uncomfortable. "What?"

"Nothing. I just—"

"Noah, what?"

"I guess I never told you that I was always holding out for Krista."

Aspen was shocked. "No, you never did, and I would never have known that."

"Well, she was my little sister's best friend." He paused, the words catching in his throat. Turning away from her, he steered the Iroc from the curb. "She's been around since I was five or something—she—I just— I thought I would have more time, that's all."

Aspen stared at her brother, who was really struggling to talk. He had been emotional at Krista's funeral like all of their other friends, but this new upset was coming as a complete surprise.

"I'm sorry, Noah." Aspen didn't know what else to say.

"I— No big deal." Noah choked on the words. "Just not enough...enough time."

Noah's sunglasses hid his expression, but the tear that trickled down his cheek made Aspen's heart ache.

She reached over and quickly patted his shoulder. "Guess Kiryn is helping both of us," she said quietly.

Noah glanced at her and smiled. "Yeah. She's cool." Aspen settled back in her seat.

Yeah, she is.

After a few minutes of silence, Noah looked over at her. "Hey, Aspen?"

She turned toward him.

"Just wanted to say, Kiryn is not Krista, and I know that."

"Okay."

"Well, what I mean...is that...is that I do like Kiryn—for Kiryn. I really do."

Aspen nodded. "Okay." She said again.

"I just wanted you to know that."

Aspen grinned and again settled back in her seat, closed her eyes, and let the warm sun bathe her face.

I know that too.

When they got to the little house, their mother was still asleep. They waited about thirty minutes, but it was getting late in the afternoon, and they knew she wanted to see their dad before dinner, so Noah woke her up.

While they waited for her to shower, Aspen pulled out the battered journal Joseph had given her. She flipped through the pages reading aloud to Noah.

Business still doing great. Allen should be governor in the next election. Don't know how he will feel about moving his family from the lake to Memphis. Oh well, he will have to deal with it if he wants business to continue. We are meeting about the will today.

January 16, 1957

Allen signed the will. The agreement gives my estate 15% of all profits, and after his death, it will drop to 10%. My estate will go to my family.

January 27, 1957

Having a hard time living with myself. My grandsons are the same age now as those boys.

June 21, 1989

I am still not sure what Tygert did with those boys, but I have a pretty good idea. How could I—all those years—

I have to tell Allen about the girl.

July 16, 1989

"I wonder if that has anything to do with Drew and Dylan." Aspen looked up from the journal. She placed it on the coffee table in front of her and picked up a bottle of water.

"I doubt it, that was written a long time ago." Noah's puzzled look distracted Aspen. He was looking at the book.

"What?" Aspen followed Noah's eyes to the book, and she realized why Noah's face wore the look it did.

The pages were turning—not like a breeze that blows several pages, but one at a time like someone was purposely turning them.

Aspen reached for the book but a sensation in her fingertips that seemed to come from the book itself made her immediately pull away.

"What the—" Noah leaned back, sinking as far as he could into the sofa.

Neither of them moved as the pages slowly turned. After a few seconds, the pages stopped turning, and the book lay open on nearly the last page.

Aspen and Noah exchanged a quick glance, but both turned immediately back to the book.

Aspen scanned the room with her eyes. "Krista?" she whispered. She heard the familiar soft laughter.

Aspen looked over at Noah whose eyes were so wide he made Aspen laugh. "It's Sumer," she whispered so as not to startle him.

"What do you mean it's Sumer?" Noah hissed, but then his eyes widened even more. "Gavin's mother?"

Aspen nodded, but she couldn't help but be amused by the look on his face, and she realized that she was becoming somewhat comfortable with her newfound gift of—visions?

Noah shuddered, and Aspen laughed again. He leaned a little closer to the book, and then peered up at Aspen through his eyelashes and whispered, "Is Krista here?"

Aspen shook her head. "I don't know."

"Oh," and he looked back at the book.

Aspen was mesmerized by what she saw. The pages of the book were being smoothed from the center to the edges, over and over it seemed, in an attempt to get rid of some of the time-etched creases that made reading more difficult in some places.

Now the book was still.

Noah slid around the table and sat next to Aspen. One line on the page seemed darker than the rest of the writing. Aspen put her finger on that line and began reading.

I had no idea Tygert was actually—well not Tygert himself, but his company—was actually doing with those boys. I have lived with this nightmare for ten years. I have a son of my own that is the same age as those boys.

May 11, 1952

I have nightmares about them. He said under the house. Does that mean he killed them? Impossible! Even so, I have looked under the house he used to live in. I even looked under my house. Nothing.

I have made a decision. I don't know if it is the right decision, but I am going to do it anyway. I am going to tell Allen. It is the least I can do. Maybe it will put his mind at ease. He has been miserable for a long time.

January 19, 1991

Allen told everyone that Nina had died.

January 26, 1991

It has been four years. I still have not told Allen about Ronda.

April 2, 1995

Aspen and Noah noticed that the handwriting was getting very shaky. The next entry told them why.

In hospital. Don't think I will live much longer. Telling Allen today.

I told him. He is gone, but I still do not feel any peace. I am sure I will go to hell. His reaction was not what I expected. He just started to cry, and then he left.

August 6, 1995

Aspen leaned back against the sofa. "Wow." She rubbed her eyes.

"Who is Ronda?" Noah whispered.

Aspen's eyes widened. "The girl in Great-Grandpa's journal. The one he may have had an affair."

"Doesn't make sense."

"Why? He is all 'I'm so sad that you left me.' Or something like that."

Aspen sighed "What do you suppose Joseph meant when he mentioned Drew?"

"Wish I knew." Noah ran his hand through his chin-length brown hair. "This is getting crazier every—"

"Drew? The gardener?" Aspen jumped.

Mom surprised them both when she walked up behind them. "Yeah." Noah stammered. "His kid, Joseph, is in our class. Drew has a brother, Dylan, that told people there was something buried under his dad's house."

"His grandpa's house." Aspen corrected him. She looked at her mother, who was nervously scrolling through her phone. "Everything all right, Mom?" she asked.

"Yes, yes. Let's go see your dad. Thanks for letting me sleep." She walked briskly out the front door.

Aspen hurried behind her, but before she got to the porch steps, Mom had the engine running in the BMW.

Noah ran up behind Aspen. "Mom, we are going to Mr. Fielden's for dinner. Why don't you ride with us?"

Mom waved to her kids and called over the sound of the engine, "No, you kids may want to stay longer at your friends, and I have a couple of errands to do later. Meet you at the hospital."

Aspen shrugged. "Okay." She climbed in the Iroc, but her mother's actions left a raw empty hole in her stomach.

53

FINALLY WE MEET

ASPEN LEANED AGAINST THE wall watching her mom and Noah.

Mom was holding Dad's hand, her blank eyes gazing at his sleeping face.

Noah absently stroked Dad's other hand, his forehead resting on the bed.

The doctor had been in and explained to them they were keeping Dad in a drug-induced sleep—a sort of coma, just not as deep. They were not lowering his body temperature or anything like that. He told them that every time Dad woke up, he became agitated and was hallucinating, calling out to people in the room that no one else could see.

Dr. Winslow was concerned that Dad might have another heart attack. He said putting the stent in Dad's heart was a success. However, their dad had so much emotional anxiety that each time he woke up, they could not get him calmed down long enough to deal with any of it, so they elected to keep him asleep—at least for the time being.

Aspen's gaze drifted from the window to her dad's face. She really only heard one part of one sentence Dr. Winslow said—*calling out to people in the room that no one else could see.*

Dad looked pale—gray almost—and his face looked sad. She wished she could see his eyes, although the last time she did see them, they were wild, angry, and filled with agony. From what the doctor described, she suspected this time she would only see agony, but why? *If Gavin got his gift from his mother, is it possible—*

"Hey." Noah jolted Aspen out of her thoughts.

Her head jerked up—Mom was no longer in the room. "Are we leaving?"

"Yes, Mom is already out in the hall. She wanted to talk to the night nurse for a minute. I think she wants to come back later."

"Okay, I'll be right there." Aspen walked over next to her dad. She bent down and kissed his cheek. "I love you, Daddy," she whispered. "I—" she paused. She searched her father's face then sighed deeply. "I love you, Daddy," she repeated.

"Finally, we meet." Rocky grinned as he took Suzann's hand in both of his.

Gavin rolled his eyes. "Wow." He mouthed to Aspen, and she laughed, but she also saw another side to Rocky—a charming side.

Rocky outdid himself this time. He had a spread of crab and shrimp, something called twice-baked potatoes, that Aspen had never tasted, the biggest fruit plate that Bill and Nada's sold, and an assortment of soft drinks and water.

When they finished dinner, Rocky invited Suzann to sit on the front porch. He expressed concern for her husband and talked with her about the four teenagers he had spent the past few days with.

Mom was as surprised as Aspen and Noah had been to learn that Rocky was Gavin's dad and Kiryn's guardian.

Rocky seemed to be succeeding in helping Mom relax. She even laughed when Rocky gave her a few unimportant details about the past few days with their children.

After dinner was cleaned up, the four kids joined Rocky and Suzann on the porch where Gavin started the conversation Aspen silently hoped he wouldn't bring up while Mom was there.

"So they found some interesting stuff in that book Joseph gave to Noah today, Rocky."

Aspen swallowed hard, watching Mom's face. Rocky's interest was now piqued. "Like what?"

"Remember when Dylan was telling everyone there was something important buried under his grandpa's house and everyone thought he was nuts?"

Rocky nodded. "Go on."

"That little book says there actually *was* something buried under a house, so maybe he wasn't so crazy."

Noah asked, "What kind of something?"

"Well according to this," Kiryn produced the book Aspen had laid on the table. "Don't know. It's not very clear."

Noah blurted, "Could have something to do with Dylan and Drew acting so strange at the big house the other day?" The second he spoke he immediately turned to look at their mother and Aspen could see by the look on his face that he regretted bringing it up.

The color drained from Mom's face, and Noah took two steps toward her, but her hand shot up to stop him. She jumped to her feet, turned to Rocky, and thanked him for dinner, and then hurriedly disappeared into the house. She returned in seconds with her purse and headed for her car.

"I'm staying at the hospital with your dad tonight. You kids can stay here or go home. I will see you in the morning."

Aspen raced down the steps. "Mom!"

But her mother was already in the car. Aspen watched the top snap into place on the BMW as her mother sped out of the driveway. Mom glanced back for just a second, and Aspen wondered if she saw them all staring after her.

The BMW disappeared out of sight when Aspen noticed the bewildered look on Rocky's face.

"Well, that went well," he scoffed.

"Where do you think she's going?" Noah asked quietly.

"To the hospital?" said Kiryn.

Aspen didn't respond. The questions were not directed at her; they were just thrown out into the air.

"She seemed uncomfortable when we talked about Drew," said Aspen.

"Drew?" Gavin's head shot up.

Aspen's forehead wrinkled. "Yes, why?"

"Didn't you say Krista sent you a picture of Drew she found at your house in San Clemente?" said Gavin.

Aspen nodded.

"Do you think Drew could have meant the picture for her?" Gavin stood up.

Aspen looked at Noah, and she knew he was thinking the same thing she was. "Mom knows something about Drew, Noah."

Noah dug in his pockets for his keys. "C'mon, you guys. Let's follow her."

Rocky grabbed his shoulder. He tossed Gavin his truck keys. "Let Gavin drive. Your car is too easy to spot."

The four piled into Rocky's truck. "Be careful!" he yelled as Gavin sped out of the driveway.

"Let's go to Drew's house," said Noah

"Do you think she would go to his house?" Kiryn sounded unconvinced.

"Just a gut feeling."

It took nearly fifteen minutes to get to the road Drew's house was on. When they turned onto the dark street, the headlights of the truck caught the red taillights on a car that parked off the road near the fence about fifty yards from Drew's house.

Aspen gulped. It was her mother's BMW. A sick feeling settled in the pit of her stomach, and she wrapped her arms around her body. She felt Kiryn's hand on her shoulder. She looked at Gavin and then Noah.

Noah's eyes focused on Drew's house, his mouth formed into a thin line.

Gavin slowed down as they passed the car. It was empty, and they rolled slowly past. They were all looking at Drew's house.

Aspen looked over her shoulder at her mother's car. She thought she saw someone get in on the passenger's side.

"Gavin, stop!" Aspen hit Noah on the shoulder. "It's Mom, Noah, she is getting in her car."

Gavin stopped immediately when Aspen yelled at him, and Noah jumped out. Aspen threw her door open and followed.

In seconds, Noah was at the driver's side of their mother's car. He pulled the door open, and he and Aspen leaned down to look inside.

Mom was sobbing uncontrollably, and Aspen started to cry too.

Noah quickly moved around to the other side of the car, kneeled in the dirt and pulled his mother's face into his shoulder.

Aspen slid into the driver's seat. Neither of them spoke, and Mom cried harder.

It was several minutes before her crying subsided, and she slowly pulled away from Noah.

"Mom?" Tears rolled down Aspen's cheeks. She had never seen her mother like this.

Mom struggled to talk, "I'm so sorry and so…emba…embarrassed."

"Is it Dad?" Noah said softly.

"N…No." she suddenly looked up, her eyes swollen and red but with surprise in them. "I mean of c…course your…da…dad, but that is not what is wrong right now."

"Then what?" Noah looked puzzled.

Mom said nothing she just started sobbing again.

Noah again spoke softly to his mother, "Mom, we need to talk." Mom nodded.

"Does this concern Drew, Mom?" Aspen blurted it and was sorry the minute she did, but Mom's reaction surprised her.

She nodded.

Noah and Aspen exchanged a quick look.

"You guys okay?" Gavin was leaning down peering at Noah and his mother.

Kiryn leaned in as well. "Want to go back to our house?"

Noah and Aspen looked at their mother. She said nothing and made no indication one way or the other.

Noah nodded at Gavin. "You drive Aspen." He stood up and closed Mom's door.

The tiny sports car didn't have a back seat, so Noah followed Gavin and Kiryn back to the truck.

Aspen started the engine. When she did, the headlights flooded her brother and friends. Kiryn slid her arm around Noah's waist and leaned her head against his shoulder.

Noah did not resist. Instead, he put his arm across her shoulders.

The whole scene made Aspen feel warm inside, and if not for her upset mother sitting next to her, she would have thoroughly enjoyed the moment.

Instead, after she turned the car around and was heading down the dark road, she patted her mom's shoulder.

"Oh, Aspen, I have been so afraid."

"Of what, Mom?"

"That man."

Sudden fear coursed through Aspen but it quickly turned to anger. "Did someone hurt you, Mom?"

"No…no, but he threatened to hurt you and Noah."

An icy feeling replaced the anger, and Aspen felt her entire body tense.

"Drew? Do you mean Drew?"

Mom nodded. "Yes."

Aspen hesitated, but then she spoke choosing her words carefully. "Mom did…did he—Drew, send you a picture?"

Mom was looking directly at Aspen, and she scanned her mother's face.

The headlights on Rocky's truck behind them illuminated the entire car, casting eerie shadows across their faces.

Mom's eyes widened. "How? How did you know that?" Aspen shuddered. "Krista."

"Krista?" Mom's voice went up two octaves.

Aspen nodded. "She found the picture wadded up next to the front porch after we left. It was almost buried by a bush. She sent it to me with that card the day before—before her accident."

There was a distant look in Mom's eyes. "I must have dropped it. I meant to—to throw it away. I just—I forgot." She barely whispered the words.

Mom leaned wearily against the car window. Short gasps kept escaping her throat, and with her elbow propped on the door; she rested her forehead in her hand.

Aspen glanced at her mother, and anxiety coursed through every part of her body. She struggled to see the road through blinding tears—she was filled with fear, confusion, and sadness.

Mom didn't offer any more information the rest of the drive. When Aspen stopped the car in Rocky's driveway, Noah was immediately at his mother's door opening it and helping her out.

Kiryn had called ahead to alert Rocky, and he was standing with the front door propped open when the two vehicles drove in.

While Mom spent a few minutes in the bathroom, Noah called the hospital to check on Dad. There was no change, but at least he was no worse.

Mom settled onto the porch swing next to Aspen. "Okay," she began. She told them how just about a week before they moved, she received a special delivery package addressed only to her. When she opened it, there was a brief letter. It told her she needed to help Drew, get access to the Allen Manor, that there were some papers he needed and that he would make life miserable for her family if she didn't. He said he would involve her kids. The letter included the picture so Mom would know who Drew was and that he meant business. She said she was terrified when she found out he was working right on the property, but she still didn't dare tell Jackson or anyone else.

She also explained that Dad had been distant since he got the letter from Aunt Dana, so she didn't feel she could talk to him. She hoped to come to Sommerville, find the papers, and give them to Drew, sell Grandpa and Grandma's house and be done with it all. She had torn the picture in half and had thought she threw it away.

"What did you think he would do to us?" asked Noah.

"How should I know?" Mom shook her head, and more tears came. "He scared me. I thought when I found the papers he wanted, he would go away, but I couldn't find them. When Aunt Dana told us she had taken some boxes with her, I thought they might be there."

Aspen asked, "That's why you and Dad went to Oregon?"

"Partly, but we need to find the will, too. That is causing your father all kinds of problems."

Rocky had been quiet, but now he asked, "Do you know what papers he wants, Suzann?"

Mom twisted the bottom of her blouse. "Not exactly—but I believe they are like an amendment to the will or maybe the actual will. We are not even sure that we have the original. Drew wanted me to get him into the house, but I guess he figured that out himself when he got the job as the gardener."

"Well, that didn't get him in. We heard him tell someone he hid in the pantry when you and Dad left, and then he left the back door unlocked so that he could get in later," said Aspen.

Mom started to ask, "When were you—"

Rocky raised his hand in protest. "Suzann, there is way too much to tell you right now, you have enough on your plate with Jackson."

"Okay." Mom readily agreed.

Noah was less deterred, "What papers? Why—"

Mom cut Noah off. "It's a document that should accompany the will. Problem is—we can't find either. We only know that a will does exist. We have been working with Grandpa's tax people, but we cannot seem to find the attorneys that handled the estate."

Rocky looked puzzled. "So this is Jackson's father's will?"

"No, this is Jackson's Grandpa's will we are looking for. The only thing his father's will says is that when he dies, the will of Jackson Humphrey Allen needs to be read and enforced."

"So, it has never been read?" asked Gavin.

"I guess not. Jackson doesn't know anything about it."

"Mom, why didn't Dad ever come back here—I mean before now?" asked Aspen.

"I don't know, Aspen. I really don't. All I know is that he got a phone call, and then a letter from his sister and his entire world seemed to crumble."

Mom's voice cracked, and more tears rolled down her cheeks. "And so did ours." She peered through her wet eyelashes at Aspen and then Noah.

Aspen gave her a weak smile and slipped her arm around her mother's shoulders.

"Mom, we can figure this out." Noah leaned toward his mother and peered into her eyes.

Aspen thought Noah seemed to be trying to sound confident, but she also recognized the apprehension in his voice.

"How are you going to do that? Your dad is sick and—"

"Mom, we will." Aspen paused for a second, and then she asked, "Were you going to Drew's house, Mom, because that's what it looked like?"

"Not really. I mean, I did dial his number, but I never pushed send." She rolled her eyes. "I'm not very tough."

Rocky leaned forward, his elbows resting on his knees. "As I said, there is probably a lot that we need to tell you, Suzann." He scanned the faces of the four teenagers. "But first there are still some things we need to finish."

Again Aspen breathed a quiet sigh of relief. She did not want her mom to have any more to worry about or any more reason to think her only daughter was crazy.

Rocky continued, "But I will tell you that you do not have to worry about Drew anymore. He is not going to hurt anybody."

Mom looked surprised and doubtful. "Really? Why? What has changed?"

Rocky smiled. "Will you trust us?"

Mom laughed nervously, but Rocky continued motioning to the four teenagers, "We have found some interesting things, Suzann."

"Like what?" Mom sounded unconvinced.

Rocky took a deep breath and let it escape slowly. "Will you trust us?'

"It's Drew I don't trust," said Mom.

"Don't you worry any more about Drew, he won't bother you or the kids."

Mom looked directly at Rocky. "How can you be so sure? I have not delivered what he wanted."

Rocky started to say something but was distracted by the buzzing of Gavin's phone.

Rocky hurriedly finished his sentence, "Just trust us."

Aspen noticed the look on Gavin's face, but she tried not to draw attention to it.

Noah wasn't looking at Gavin, neither was Kiryn, but Rocky was, and Aspen knew he had seen Gavin's expression change as well.

Rocky stood. "There are some things I would like to check on tonight. Why don't you kids escort Suzann to the hospital," he looked at Mom. "Is that where you want to go?"

Mom nodded. "Yes. I keep thinking maybe he won't be so upset if I am there when he wakes up."

Gavin walked into the kitchen and motioned for Rocky to follow.

Mom gathered her things. "I really don't need an escort," she said to Noah.

"Yeah you do, Mom."

In minutes, Rocky and Gavin returned.

"Noah, why don't you drive your mom's car and the girls can follow you and give you a ride back."

"Okay." Noah didn't question Rocky, and Aspen saw that both Noah and Kiryn had now noticed the uneasiness on Gavin's face.

54

A Real Live Dead Man

The three teenagers couldn't get back fast enough. They found Gavin and Rocky perched in front of the computer.

"What is going on?" asked Aspen.

"Check this out." Gavin tossed Aspen his cell phone. "The last text."

Aspen unlocked the phone. The text was still on the screen.

OBITUARIES – AUG 8, 1995

Kenneth Lloyd Dixon

Aug 6, 1995

Aspen's eyes grew wide. "Oh my gosh!"

"What?" Noah snatched the phone from her hand. "What the?" he dropped the phone on the floor.

Kiryn picked it up.

"You, too?" Noah's expression was a cross between fear and bewilderment.

Kiryn seemed confused for a second, but then she seemed to suddenly realize, and her eyes widened. "Krista!"

"Exactly," said Noah.

"Who knows? How can any of this be?" Gavin answered Noah's question. "But look what we found."

341

Rocky was clicking all over the screen with the mouse. "Just a second. I want to make the picture larger."

They all peered at the screen, but when the image came up, Aspen's hands shot to her mouth. The old man's face stared back at her from the computer screen.

Everyone turned to look at Aspen, but her eyes were still fixed on the screen.

The confusion following the computer discovery took a few minutes to subside.

Aspen was upset that now for sure she knew the old man really was dead and all of them were shocked to learn that he was, in fact, the very Dixon that had been their great-grandpa's business partner.

"This puts some things into perspective." Rocky tried to assure them.

"But Rocky! A real live dead man—I mean well, that sounded lame, but you know what I mean—is trying to hurt me!"

"Maybe not hurt you, Aspen, so much as to *stop* you," said Noah

"From doing *what*?"

"Aspen you are borderline hysterical right now." Noah stepped toward her. "Calm down." He pumped the air with both hands like he was pushing something down.

"I am not hysterical, Noah! I just—just cannot believe this!"

"Well, who did you think it was?" Gavin was exhibiting his normally calm demeanor.

Aspen's mouth clamped shut, and she stared at Gavin. "Well—"

Gavin looked from Noah to Aspen. "Hey, could you marry her? No one has that effect on my sister."

Aspen glared at Noah. "Funny," she said flatly.

"I thought so." He chuckled.

Kiryn looked exasperated. "Okay. So we need to figure this out." She turned to Rocky. "Dad?"

Rocky's surprised look made everyone laugh. "So now I am the brain of the operation?"

"Well, geez—dead people who everyone can see but me!"

"Wait—I can't see dead people," said Noah.

Kiryn glared at him. "Whatever." She turned back to Rocky. "And dead people texting. What is that anyway?"

"A world we never knew existed, Kiryn, well almost." Rocky winked at Gavin. He looked back at Kiryn. "And by the way, I can't see dead people either."

Kiryn rolled her eyes and plopped into a chair. She put her elbows on the table and rested her head in her hands. "Well, they are all around us now, and someone has to take charge."

"Okay. Everyone into the den." Rocky picked up the laptop and herded the kids.

"Sit." He commanded. They all obeyed.

"Okay, let's go through the facts." He turned to Noah, "How is your mom?"

"Fine, I think. She seemed to be a little better when we got to Dad's room." As if anticipating Rocky's next question, he added, "Dad was sleeping."

"Good. She will be okay. They both will." Rocky smiled and then continued, "Let's go through the facts." He held up one finger. "So the dead man is Dixon and, per the journal Joseph gave you, he killed some girl that you kids think your grandpa was having an affair with, supposedly Ronda."

He waited for a response, and they all nodded.

Rocky held up two fingers. "Krista and Sumer, who are both dead, are obviously trying to help you, Aspen, for whatever reason."

Now he held up a third finger. "And Dylan and Drew, who are Dixon's grandsons, obviously want something from the house—and just to interject here—I don't think they know that their great-grandpa killed anyone."

"Why?" Gavin asked dryly.

"Well, because they may be a little rough around the edges, Gavin—"

"They beat the crap out of you, Dad."

"I know, I know, but I don't think they are murderers and they are a pretty tight family. I think they would be shocked to know there had been murder," Rocky added. "If, in fact, it did occur."

"But the journal—"

"Yes Kiryn, but still this is speculation. We don't have any facts."

"Not really." He sighed. "But I digress."

He now held up four fingers. "We know that there is a mysterious tunnel under the Allen house, which was hidden behind fake walls. We don't know if it has anything to do with anything."

"Except that it is weird," said Kiryn

"True it is that," Rocky agreed. "All of this seems to be pointing to something—"

Aspen had not really been listening, and Noah noticed. "Are you with us, Sherlock?"

Aspen squinted at him. "Yes, I'm here." Her mood was sullen. They all waited for her to continue.

"What is it, Aspen?" Rocky leaned in her direction.

"The girl. The girl that I can only see in the house, who never says anything."

"Okay?"

"It's all pointing to her. I know it is. At least I believe she is a key factor."

"Aspen has seen her in that picture with the other kids—" Kiryn paused for a second, but her eyes suddenly sparkled. "Wait!"

"Again? Okay," said Rocky.

"That painting up in that storage room. It has been bugging me."

Noah asked, "What about the painting?"

"It's the thick paint, isn't it?" said Aspen and her mood picked up.

"Yes!" Kiryn stood up.

"What are we missing?" Gavin and Noah exchanged puzzled looks.

"There is a huge painting in the storeroom. Kiryn and I found it the other day. The paint on the wife's dress and the flowerpot, which I might add is a *little* out of place, is a lot thicker. Like it was painted later or something."

"I would not have noticed it—well I did notice it chipping, but not that the paint was thicker—if it hadn't have been for Picasso here."

Kiryn laughed. "A few art classes do not make me a painter. You should see it, Dad if, you study it for a few minutes you can tell something is—wrong."

"Well, what does it have to do with anything?" asked Noah.

"Not sure," said Aspen. "It just seems like it does."

"We need to go check it out." Kiryn started to stand up.

"Whoa." Rocky pulled her back into her chair. "We have already destroyed the hallway and broken through the closet."

Gavin sighed. "Yeah, Mr. Allen is not going to like that."

Noah and Aspen exchanged a quick glance and then looked at Gavin.

"Wow, sorry you guys." Gavin's dark complexion turned a deep shade of red.

"It's fine, Gavin. Dad is going to be fine."

Aspen had to force back more tears, and everyone was silent for a few seconds.

Rocky changed the subject. "Okay look. We will go check out the painting. Do you think the girl Dixon is talking about is that Ronda—the one you believe your great-grandpa had an affair with?"

"*If* he had an affair," said Noah

"You don't think so?" Gavin looked surprised.

"I don't. Guess I just don't want to believe a grandpa of mine had an affair. I don't know why. It just doesn't sound right."

"Well, affairs never *sound* right because they never *are* right," said Kiryn sarcastically.

Rocky took a deep breath. "So, we need to figure out where that other door goes to —the one in the tunnel you kids found."

"Does it matter?" said Kiryn.

"I think it does," said Rocky.

Gavin was reading Dixon's obituary on the computer. "Did you read this, Dad?"

"No. I had just pulled up the picture when these guys got here."

"He killed himself."

"*What?*" Noah leaned over the computer. "*How?*"

"Says here self-inflicted gunshot wound."

"No kidding?" Rocky too leaned closer to read. He read out loud: "Mr. Dixon was being treated for cancer at the Sommerville Community Hospital. However, the cause of death was a self-inflicted gunshot wound. He was found dead in his hospital bed on August 7, 1995, at 3:00 am."

"Dang! This is getting crazier all the time," said Noah.

"Okay, so he did have a bunch of guilt going on. I agree with your mom. We need to find that will," said Rocky.

"How are we going to do that?" asked Aspen.

"I think I may pay a visit to Drew."

"Are you sure, Dad?" Gavin did not appear to like the idea.

"I have known Drew a long time. Maybe he can shed some light on the subject." Rocky ran his fingers through his curly hair, "Maybe we can work together."

Gavin rolled his eyes. "That's pretty optimistic."

"Not really, Gavin. Maybe they, he and Dylan, really don't know the truth."

"Maybe, but they threatened my mom." Noah scowled.

"They did, and that is the first thing I will address. I will take Hank with me."

"Okay, that makes me feel better." Gavin sighed.

It made Aspen feel better too, knowing the policeman she met at school would be with Rocky.

Rocky turned to Noah and then Aspen. "Do you kids have any idea how your dad may be involved—other than trying to get rid of the house for the estate?"

Noah and Aspen both shook their heads. "No clue," said Aspen.

"Nope," said Noah.

"Okay, we will assume then that his stress level has to do with the estate and the will they cannot locate." Rocky glanced at the clock on the fireplace mantle.

"It's getting late kids. Should we hold off on the painting until tomorrow? You actually need someone—a professional—to help with that painting, don't you?"

"No. Let's go now." Kiryn protested rather loudly, making the other three laugh. But then as though she just heard the rest of Rocky's question she said quietly, "Yes. I will call Miss Greenland in the morning. Maybe she will know someone."

Rocky nodded.

"We could go to sleep now and get up early—it's Saturday," said Noah. "Okay if we stay here, Rocky?"

"Of course." Rocky stretched. "Then I'm going to bed." He picked up the laptop.

"Does not look like he's going to bed." Noah looked sideways at Gavin.

Rocky gave the boys a wry smile. "Have a little checking I want to do."

"Uh-huh. Night Dad."

"Night Gavin." He kissed Kiryn as he walked past her. "Night kids." He waved and disappeared up the stairs.

55

MIDNIGHT MEETING

Aspen walked out onto the front porch and sat down on the steps. She pulled her phone out and punched in her mother's number.

She heard Kiryn talking to Noah and Gavin. "Anyone want to go get a shake?"

"Sure, you coming, Gavin?" said Noah.

"Go ahead. I'm going to go talk to Dad for a minute." Noah and Kiryn walked past Aspen.

"There you are. We're going for shakes, want to go?"

"No thanks, Noah, I'm going to call Mom."

"We can bring you one." Noah climbed in the Iroc. "Tell Mom I love her."

"Okay." Aspen looked up. "Raspberry."

Kiryn got in the passenger's side. She grinned at Aspen as the car sped away just as Mom answered her phone.

"Mom? Hi. How are you doing?"

"I'm good—tired."

"Are you sure you're okay?"

"I am Aspen. I need to think about your dad right now. I hope Mr. Fielden can help with Drew."

"He will Mom. He is going to go see him. Mom, you can call him Rocky." Aspen smiled.

"Okay."

"How is Dad?"

348

"Still sleeping. They brought a bed in for me."

"That's good. We are staying here tonight then we'll go over to Grandpa's house in the morning—early. Maybe we could get a key sometime. Noah or Gavin usually crawl through a window."

Mom laughed wearily. *"Oh, wow. Yes, I will give you a key."*

"I love you, Mom."

"Love you too, Aspen. Talk to you tomorrow."

"Night."

"Is your mom okay?"

Aspen jumped. "Oh, Gavin, I didn't hear you come out." He sat down next to her.

"I thought you were going to talk to your dad."

"He went to bed. Worked, didn't it?"

"What worked?"

"Getting ten minutes alone with you." Aspen felt her face getting hot. "Guess so."

Gavin lifted her long, dark hair off her shoulder and smoothed it down her back. He caressed her cheek with the back of his hand.

Aspen pulled away from him, but it didn't stop her heart from fluttering wildly as goosebumps spread across her neck.

Gavin didn't pull his hand away. Instead, he rested it on her shoulder. "So..."

Aspen turned, peering into his emerald eyes but she didn't say anything. Instead, she averted her eyes to her hands in her lap.

Gavin began again, "So, I just want you to tell me you don't care about me—more than a friend—and if that's the case then—"

Aspen heard the Iroc speeding toward Rocky's house. She quickly looked up at Gavin through her eyelashes. "I—"

The Iroc pulled to a stop in the driveway, and Kiryn climbed out carrying two paper bags. "We're back!"

Rocky went immediately to his desk by the window, opened the bottom drawer, and retrieved the journal. He had taken it from the table earlier without the kids noticing. He would have to put it back before he went to bed, but something about the girl the kids called Ronda was bothering him. He had a feeling—

Rocky flipped through the loose pages of the journal. Some were intact. Most were out of synch, haphazardly stuffed amid the fixed pages.

Using his finger, he scanned the pages, searching for the name Ronda. Becoming anxious when he did not readily find—what am I looking for?

It was just a hunch. Maybe he was wrong. He closed the book, turned, and stared through the window into the darkness.

Rocky sighed and turned back to his desk. Next to the closed journal lay a loose, wrinkled page from the book. He picked it up, flipped open the journal, and placed the paper between two pages. When he did, a sealed envelope fell onto the desk. It had nothing written on the front. Rocky picked it up, opened it, and read the short paragraph.

He felt his heart leap and quickly folded it and closed the journal.

Rocky nodded, satisfied with his find. He carefully put the letter back in the envelope and tucked it beneath some folders in the bottom drawer of his desk.

When to tell the kids? He wasn't sure. He only knew that Noah and Aspen didn't need anything else on their plate. He would wait until the right time, if such a time presented itself.

In stocking feet, Rocky slipped quietly from his bedroom and down the stairs. He had heard a car leave and now, peering through the railing, he could see that Aspen and Gavin were on the front porch.

Quickly he returned the journal to the coffee table and just as quickly was back up the stairs when he heard the car pull back into the driveway.

It had been three weeks since Dad's heart attack, and he was showing very little improvement. Mom was spending more and more time at the hospital. The doctor was not sure how to help him, explaining that most of his problems right now seemed to be emotional. They were keeping him sedated most of the time because every time he woke up, he became agitated and the doctors were afraid of another massive heart attack. They seemed unclear about what was making him so upset. Aspen and Noah visited every day, sometimes twice a day after they had dinner with their mother.

It was after one of these late visits that the call came from Rocky.

Aspen and Noah had been sitting in the hospital parking lot talking for over two hours.

"He wants us to come over."

"*Now?*" Aspen looked at her phone. "It's after midnight."

"Well, like we have anything else going."

Aspen sighed. "Yeah, no kidding."

Noah started the Iroc and turned out of the parking lot. "Must be something important."

They were surprised to see some extra cars in the driveway and to find several people already gathered in Rocky's den. Aspen recognized Drew, Dylan, Sara, and Joseph, she didn't know the man with Sara but assumed it was Gavin's step-dad, and the woman next to Joseph she assumed was his mother. Hank was there too, standing in the open doorway to the porch.

Aspen suddenly felt nervous. "What's—what is this all about?"

"Well, I think we're finally putting some facts together here," said Rocky. "Do you feel like hearing about it?"

Aspen glanced at Noah and he nodded. "We okay?" she asked.

"Yep, shoot. There is absolutely nothing anyone can tell me that would shock me."

Kiryn twisted her lips. "Ummm, I don't know about that," and she glanced at Rocky and Gavin.

As though Noah had just realized who was there, he flashed an angry look in Drew's direction. "What did you do to our mother?" he demanded.

Drew opened his mouth but clamped it shut when Rocky shot a warning look in his direction, and Aspen saw Hank do the same. At his outburst, everyone else turned in Noah's direction.

She looked at Sara. She truly was beautiful, and Aspen couldn't help but wonder if Rocky ever felt sad that they were no longer married.

Gavin's step-father was a handsome, well-dressed man. His perfect brown hair and his dark blue shirt tucked neatly into gray slacks made him look like a magazine model.

Sara and Rocky, at least from Aspen's point of view, were polar opposites.

Dylan sat slumped over in a chair, his chin resting in his hand, his eyes looking at the floor. He was wearing a T-shirt, jeans and a baseball cap. She couldn't see his expression, but it was obvious that he did not want to be here.

Drew sat next to him. He didn't seem so big and intimidating as he had when she and Noah first encountered him on the big house grounds. Drew sat upright, his arms folded across his chest just as they had been that day, but he was clean and wearing shorts, a T-shirt, and a baseball cap backward. His face wore a look of concern more than anything. He didn't seem so angry.

Joseph sat next to his dad. He was looking right at Aspen. He looked nervous and uncomfortable. Aspen smiled at him, but he only ducked his head and looked at the floor.

Hank seemed to be the most aloof. He leaned against the door and Aspen noted his black police belt with his gun tucked in the holster.

Rocky finally started to talk. "Noah?" Rocky sounded a little hesitant waiting for Noah to respond.

Aspen looked at Noah. Their eyes locked for a few seconds and then Noah nodded. "Sure," he said quietly, and he suddenly looked exhausted.

Rocky explained that he and Hank had gone over to Drew's to talk to him. In the course of the conversation, Drew and Dylan told Rocky their story, most of it Rocky knew, but some he did not, and Hank had only heard bits and pieces.

Drew and Dylan's parents were killed in a boating accident when they were fifteen and seventeen years old. After that, they lived with their grandpa and grandma.

Their grandfather, Kenneth Lloyd Dixon, was Great-Grandpa Allen's business partner. Drew and his grandfather had never really meshed, but Dylan followed his grandpa around like a puppy, hanging on his every word.

Then Drew got married.

At that point in the story, Rocky realized he had not introduced Leslie, Drew's wife, or Gavin's step-dad, Doug.

Joseph seemed to be more like his mother than his dad, Aspen thought. More quiet, not so brash.

Rocky went on to say that one night when Kenneth was drunk— Rocky paused and turned to Dylan, "Why don't *you* tell the kids what you told us?"

Dylan lifted his eyes but not his head. His mouth twitched uncomfortably, and he rubbed his forehead with one hand.

They waited.

Finally, Dylan sighed heavily, "One night, my grandpa came home late. I was watching a movie with—with Sumer." The mention of her name seemed to cause him pain.

Noah and Aspen exchanged a quick look.

That's why Dylan mentioned Sumer in the front yard of the big house that day.

Dylan continued, "Grandpa was really drunk. He started to tell me about how years earlier he had convinced old man Allen to put in his will that his heirs—meaning me and Drew because he had no other kids—would be rich. He said that he told Allen that if he didn't add them to the will, he would tell the FBI about what Tygert had done with the boys."

"The boys that the journal talks about?" Noah pointed to the book that lay on the coffee table.

"Yeah, those boys that Grandpa and Allen hired to work for Allen-Dixon, Inc."

"Well, what did he do with them?" Noah was becoming impatient, and Rocky reached over Kiryn's head to put a hand on Noah's shoulder.

"Calm down, Noah, you need to hear all of this."

Noah shrugged but didn't take his eyes off Dylan.

"Grandpa said that Gil Tygert, who owned Tygert Transport, had started out just taking the boys back to the state they came from—Allen-Dixon paid them to take each one home—but then, someone in Tygert's company got the idea to get rid of the boys and keep the wages Allen-Dixon paid the boys."

"*Get rid of them?*" Aspen's voice shot up two octaves.

"Yeah," Dylan said quietly.

"How?" Aspen's still stared wide-eyed at Dylan.

Dylan shrugged. "I don't know. Grandpa said he told Allen that he knew where the boys were and if Allen—see—well the thing is, Grandpa knew that Allen wouldn't protest, he had been through so much already losing his daughter and all, and then his wife." Dylan stopped for a second. "Grandpa also knew about Allen's first wife."

"What about her?" Noah leaned forward in his seat.

"Relax kid. It's not like you knew her or anything." Drew said dryly.

Noah shot out of his seat and stumbled around the coffee table but stopped when Hank yelled at him.

"Noah!" Hank boomed, and Aspen was surprised at the commanding sound of this otherwise mild-mannered man.

Noah stopped in mid-stride, his fists clenched and his face twisted into a snarl. He clenched his teeth. "She was my dad's grandma, you jerk," he hissed.

Drew shrank into his chair but said nothing.

"Sit down, Noah," Hank spoke again, softer now but equally as commanding and Noah retreated to his seat.

Kiryn slipped her arm around his leg and clasped her hands as though she could hold him there.

Dylan looked to Rocky for a signal to continue. When he got it, he went on. "Allen's wife lost it when their daughter disappeared. The girl ran away with some guy, and that really humiliated the upper-class Allen's. They were all highly respected in this area—high-class folks you know,—and they had a lot of money. Allen couldn't handle it."

"With pressure from your grandpa," said Aspen.

Dylan paused, "Yeah, I guess you're right about that. Anyway, Allen decided to commit his wife to an asylum, but the thing is, she really wasn't crazy or anything. Allen just didn't know how to deal with his wife, his daughter's disappearance and losing his grip on his political career, so Grandpa suggested they get with a doctor to keep her drugged for a while. Then it was easy to just leave her there, well once Allen realized he could marry Faith. She was ten years younger than him, and that seemed good, I guess."

Noah was staring at his folded hands in front of him, and Aspen's head was spinning. "Our great-grandpa was a real piece of work," she said.

"In all fairness, Aspen, public and political pressure can do a lot to change a person," said Rocky.

Aspen winced. "I guess," she said softly.

"When we came to the Allen house, we were just looking for what was ours. I only contacted your mom because we panicked when we found out you guys were coming here and were going to sell the house," said Drew. He almost sounded apologetic.

"What happened to the other gardener?" Noah spat.

"Now wait a minute." Drew stood up, shaking his finger at Noah, but he immediately sat back down when Hank's hand dropped to his gun. "We just talked to a few of the right people to get the job, that's all."

Noah scoffed, "I'll bet you did."

Aspen couldn't believe what she was hearing. The things in the journal were now taking on a life of their own. Before they seemed like stories— or legends—not really facts. At least it had been easier to deal with when she thought that. To kind of pretend it all wasn't real, but now—The entire thing made her feel sick inside. She noticed Noah, and he looked like she felt.

Aspen looked first at Drew and then Dylan. "Why didn't you just ask?"

A soft voice came from Drew's wife. "That's what I asked him," said Leslie.

Drew looked at her, and sighed but he had nothing to say.

Leslie added, "When I found out, I asked him that." She looked apologetically at Aspen. "I had no idea all of this was going on and right under my nose."

Dylan and Drew were now both shifting uncomfortably in their seats.

Joseph hadn't looked up from the floor.

"So that's about as far as we got," said Rocky.

"Wait, did you guys know about the guns? The ones in the master bedroom?" asked Gavin of Drew and Dylan.

They both shook their heads, and Drew answered, "No, we had never been in there. We aren't thieves; we didn't bother them."

"Not exactly," mumbled Noah sarcastically. If anyone heard that, they chose to ignore him.

"Yeah, I checked." Kiryn blurted and Drew furrowed his eyebrows at her.

Rocky shot Kiryn an annoyed look.

"Sorry," she whispered, but it made Aspen smile.

"So," began Rocky, "do either of you know what Tygert did with those boys?"

"Hell no, Rocky," said Drew. "There are nearly two hundred of them."

"Grandpa used to talk about burying something under a house—so we checked under his house, under Tygert's old house," he looked at Sara and Doug, and they both looked startled. "Never occurred to us he could be talking about people."

"Oh, Dylan, he wasn't talking about bodies." Drew shrugged it off but Dylan just raised his eyebrows and shook his head. Then Drew clarified, "We hoped it might be money."

Doug looked mortified. "Our house?"

"Well, before you bought it, of course."

Doug winced and turned to Sara. "Is there a basement under our house?"

"Not that I know of." Sara looked back at Drew.

Drew shook his head. "No, we went under the foundation and dug all over. It's just a crawl space. There was nothing there."

Gavin looked at Aspen—he seemed to be reading her mind, and she knew he was thinking the same thing she was.

The root cellar in the Manor.

Aspen looked down at Kiryn and then at Noah. She was sure they were all on the same page. "Do you still have the blueprints, Gavin?"

Gavin stood up. "Right here." He walked over to a cabinet and pulled them out of a drawer. He spread them out on the coffee table and tapped on the drawing where the root cellar was.

The entire room was quiet.

"Under the Allen house?" Rocky finally said almost in disbelief.

"It would be a perfect place," said Noah. "No one would ever suspect that."

"What's buried?" Noah asked.

"Maybe bodies," said Gavin.

"Wait a minute. This is a lot of speculation here. You got my grandpa tried and hanged and no proof!"

No one responded and Drew dropped his head to his hands and then rubbed his face. "This is a lot more complicated than I ever imagined."

"There's something else." Dylan's voice sounded as though he was going to start crying.

Surprised by that, everyone in the room waited for him to continue.

Dylan scanned their faces, and then he blurted, "Mandi didn't kill Sumer and Juan."

Sara gasped, and the color drained from Rocky's face. "What are you talking about, Dylan?"

He spoke slowly, carefully choosing his words, "Well, remember that I told you Grandpa came home and Sumer and I were there?" He didn't wait for anyone to answer.

"Sumer heard all of it. I think Grandpa forgot about her being there because he even forgot he had told me too until I reminded him later, but, about a year after Sumer and I broke up, she started dating Juan, and Mandi came over for a beer one night just to talk."

I knew Sumer could see things—you know, that other people couldn't see—she had found Mandi's little brother when we were all in high school." He turned to Aspen and Noah. "He was dead, though."

They both nodded, and Dylan continued, "Mandi hated Sumer then, she had just found out Mandi and Juan were getting married. She was drunk, and she made some comment about how she wished Sumer and Juan were dead."

"Anyway, Grandpa heard that." Dylan's voice had been in control until now, but he choked on his next words. "Grand—Grandpa hired someone to killed them, and then he set Mandi up."

"Dylan!" Drew grabbed his brother by the arm.

Aspen glanced at Hank. He stood erect, but he did not move from his spot by the door.

Dylan burst into tears. "Drew it's true! Grandpa told me about a month before he died. He was worried that Mandi would find the bodies and blow the whistle on him and Tygert."

Dylan dropped his head and began crying openly.

Drew ran his fingers through his hair, slowly shaking his head. His face bore sincere anguish when he looked at them all. "Why did they kill Juan too?" Drew breathed.

"They were going to kill him too," Dylan thrust his finger at Gavin, "because Mandi had been telling everyone that Sumer was a witch and that they all needed to die. It made more sense to kill them all. It would be easier to frame Mandi, but I guess it got messed up or something because the baby lived."

Gavin looked over at his mother. She was staring at Dylan as though he was crazy.

"Who killed Mandi?" asked Rocky.

"I don't know who killed any of them. I just know Grandpa hired it done. I guess the same person made it look like Mandi killed herself." Dylan was sobbing uncontrollably.

"He was my grandpa. I loved him. I hated that he told me all of that. I didn't want to know. It was bad enough that he told me about the boys, but at least he didn't kill *them*."

"What about the boys?" the question came from Hank.

Dylan shook his head. "I'm not sure, but I think Tygert may have killed at least some of them too. The stories are that they just disappeared."

Dylan leaned into Drew's shoulder and Drew wrapped his arm around his brother.

Drew's face was ashen gray, and he just stared straight ahead.

Dylan choked through whispers now, "Drew, Grandpa killed the only girl I ever loved."

"I know, I know," Drew whispered. "I'm so sorry little brother." Except for Dylan's muffled sobs, the room was deathly quiet.

A thousand thoughts tumbled over and over in Aspen's head.

No wonder Dylan had never gotten married. No wonder everyone thought he was wacky and different. After losing his parents, he found out that the grandpa he idolized was a murderer—even though he didn't pull the trigger. Dylan had been carrying that secret around all of these years.

Dylan's sobs subsided to short quiet gasps. He rubbed his face with his hands, but the tears kept silently falling.

Kiryn got up and retrieved him a box of Kleenex. Dylan took it without looking at her, and she quickly sat back down.

Quietly Gavin reached for Kenneth Lloyd Dixon's journal. He flipped through the pages until he came to the page that had been torn out. "Maybe it was all here. It looks like a few pages are missing,"

"Only two."

56

CONFESSION

"Joseph?" Drew's questioning eyes studied his son. "What do you mean?"

Joseph stuffed a hand into the pocket of his sweatshirt and retrieved some folded papers.

Aspen could see they were the same type of paper that was in the journal he had given them.

Visibly shaking, Joseph moved around the sofa and put the papers on the table in front of Aspen. "I think the answer you may be looking for is right there."

Aspen stared at the papers. She didn't want to know any more, and yet she did. With pleading eyes, she turned to Rocky. She could not bear one more piece of bad news, and she was sure that's what it would be.

"Dad," Joseph was standing in front of Drew. "Before they read that, I have had this for a long time. I'm the one that gave the journal to them." He thrust his thumb over his shoulder at whoever was behind him. "I—I found out about it eight years ago. remember when we moved that big tree off grandpa's property?"

Drew nodded, but his expression was complete bewilderment. "Well, I found it in the dirt when you and Uncle Dylan went to get a chain. I saw it had Great-Grandpa's name on it and I thought it was a treasure, so I put it in the attic in my room and then forgot about it. I got it out about a year ago and read it. I—I knew what happened to—to that girl."

"What girl?" Aspen blurted. "Riley?"

Joseph turned around to face Aspen, "N...no. I don't know about any Riley."

Aspen looked at Noah, then Gavin, Kiryn, and Rocky. They were all looking at Joseph.

"Just, just read it, Mr. Fielden." Joseph let out a labored sigh and sank into his chair. His mother scooted closer to him and put her arm around his shoulders, but Joseph did not look up.

Rocky picked up the papers and carefully unfolded them. He smoothed them out on the table. The ink was nearly worn off in some parts, but it was legible.

"Uh, before you read that," said Joseph, now his head jerked up, and he turned to Drew and Dylan, "I knew how much you admired your grandpa, Uncle Dylan and that you loved him, Dad. I just didn't want you to read that, but when the Allen family moved here, and all this trouble started, I—well I—"

Drew put his hand on Joseph's knee. "Whatever it is, Joseph, you did the right thing."

Joseph looked at his mother and again dropped his head. Rocky read the first page:

I am telling Allen today. I don't have much longer to live any-way—I am dying of cancer. The older I get, the more this whole thing haunts me. Funny, what you do for money, especially when you are young and stupid.

I have tried to tell Allen for four months, but every time he comes to visit, I just can't do it, but today I will, and then it will be over. All over.

He just walked in. He is gone.

August 5, 1995

Rocky looked at everyone. All the faces in the room bore the same look of confusion—all but Joseph.

Rocky moved the first page and began reading the second which was much longer:

I told him how his daughter and that kid heard Tygert and me talking down by the lake. They overheard Tygert telling me about his plan for the boys and offered to cut me in. I wanted to think about it.

I told Allen how after Tygert left me alone on the lake that night, I thought I heard someone in one of the rowboats.

Sure enough, it was her and that kid. They pleaded with me to leave them alone and that they wouldn't tell, but I had been drinking and my blood boiled at the sight of them.

Stupid kids were no matches for me even though they tried to fight. I pulled them out of the boat and held them under water until they stopped moving. I lodged them between the poles that held the dock in place and the next night Tygert, and I went to move them, but their bodies were gone. I ordered Tygert to find their body's and that I didn't care what he did with them but that no one had better find them or he would pay.

Money talks. I have no idea what he did with them.

I killed two kids. Looking back, I can't believe I did that. Up until that point in my life, I was a liar, but not a murderer. After that day, I was not only a cold-blooded murderer who took the life of two innocent kids, but I was a third-party to the senseless disappearance of nearly two hundred boys. No, I did not actually participate, but I knew about it.

I could have turned Tygert in and told Allen then and there but, instead, I tried to cover up the whole thing. And why? For money, political position, and what I thought was security. I knew Allen would fall apart, and I was not willing to give up all we had worked for, but if I had, Allen's daughter would still be alive, Tygert would be in prison (he is dead now anyway) and, life may not have been so black all those years. My dear family has no idea what I was involved in. Funny how greed works—makes it so easy to live a life of sin and evil.

It was nearly a week after I told Allen that I woke up in a cold sweat. I know both of those kids were in my room—maybe it was just a dream, but it was too real. For the rest of my life, I have been in fear every time I go to bed, but they have never come back.

Reality is, I am an evil man. I know my boy won't see this—hopefully, my grandsons won't either, and my Francine is dead. I will soon join her, but I fear I will not be in the same place she is.

How I wish I could change the past, but that is impossible. I will go to my maker and pay the dearest price for the life I lived. No for the life I bought.

Allen said nothing to me. He just cried, and then he left. I did not intend for life to be such a mess, but one lie leads to another and then another.

So now, for anyone who reads this, yes, I killed Ronda Allen and her boyfriend. I do not know where the bodies are.

August 5, 1995

Rocky had been holding an envelope the entire time. When he finished reading the journal, he opened it. "I found this in the journal the other night," he began. "I didn't want to add any more confusion, so I took it and the page it referred to, out of the journal." Now he read:

Rhonda—concerning Ronda and that kid—I never found them, Dixon. I don't know what happened to those bodies.

"So Tygert didn't bury them like he told Dixon?" said Gavin.

"I guess not. This letter was sealed. It didn't appear Dixon ever read it."

Aspen couldn't breathe. The room closed in on her, and she began gasping for air. Someone forcefully pushed her head between her knees and then nothing.

When Aspen woke up, she was laying on the sofa, and Gavin was sitting close by. Her mouth was dry as though it was full of cotton, and her head was reeling. She couldn't see her brother. "Where's Noah?"

"Aspen take this." She did not resist the welcome drink of the water Rocky offered, and she swallowed the tiny tablet he gave her as well.

Gavin leaned over her and brushed the hair from her face. She turned to Kiryn whose face now looked fuzzy. Noah seemed to be moving in slow motion as he sank onto the floor next to the sofa.

Aspen tried to touch Noah's shoulder, but her hand seemed detached from her body and would not do what she wanted it to do. She tried to keep focusing on Noah, but her eyes were too heavy—blackness.

57

RELENTLESS DREAM

ASPEN KNEW SHE WAS dreaming. She tried to wake up but could not make her eyes open. She was running away from something—something that was relentlessly pursuing her, and she ran harder, faster. The only sound was her heavy breathing as she tried to escape from—what?

She kept looking back to see what was chasing her, but she saw only blackness, and she ran harder.

Suddenly, as though the ground disappeared from beneath her feet, she was falling, not tumbling but dropping straight down. There seemed to be no end just falling, and she scratched at the air trying to grab something, but there was nothing to hold on to.

When she landed, the surface gave slightly under the impact of her weight, and she lay on her back. She tried to sit up, but as she did, she began sliding backward. She groped at the blackness around her, trying to grab something, anything! She slammed her hands on the surface beneath, but she continued to propel downward.

Then she just stopped. The smell was familiar—musty, damp. She ran her hand across the surface she was sitting on—wood, but where was she? Desperately she tried to focus through the thick darkness to see something, anything that might help her understand where she was. What she was sure of was that she was deep inside of some sort of hole.

She tried to call—no sound. She tried to stand and immediately found she was surrounded by an extremely bright light—no longer below the ground, but now above the earth, looking down. As though looking through the window of a plane, she could see through thin clouds, but all she could see was water, no not just water; it was the ocean.

The light made her relax, and she began searching her surroundings.

Someone was walking toward her, but then—

Running! Running away from something—something that was relentlessly pursuing her and she ran harder, faster, the only sound was her heavy breathing as she tried to escape.

She kept looking back to see what it was but saw only blackness and she ran harder.

This is the exact same dream! Wake up! Wake up! She screamed.

Again the ground disappeared, and she was falling—dropping straight down. Endless falling and she scratched at the air to grab something as before—nothing.

She landed on the same surface that gave slightly under the impact of her weight, and she lay on her back. She tried to sit up and again began sliding backward. She groped at the blackness—slammed her hands on the surface beneath her, but she continued to propel downward.

And again, an abrupt stop. The smell was familiar—musty, damp. She ran her hand across the surface. Again she was sitting on wood, but where was she? Desperately she tried to focus—she knew she was in the deep hole again.

This time she tried to stand more slowly.

Immediately, the same bright light—no longer below the ground, but now above the earth, looking down. The same as before, as though looking through the window of a plane, she could see through thin clouds, but all she could see was water. No, this was the ocean—her ocean—in California.

Just as before the light made her relax. She tried to breathe slowly, so maybe her heart would beat even slower, but again there was someone walking toward her, and then—

Running.

The dream repeated precisely as before two more times. Running, falling, standing, the light, someone coming toward her and then again—

Wake up! Wake up!

She felt as though she was trapped in an endless cycle that she would never escape from but this time, looking down at the ocean, the figure came up through the clouds toward her, this time he came closer.

Uncertain, Aspen backed away, thinking maybe now that something would be different if she just moved a little, maybe she would wake up, but she didn't.

She waited. Now she could see the figure was a man and he moved forward as if in a cloud, the cloud carried him closer and soon the clouds engulfed Aspen.

She studied his face. She had only seen pictures, but she knew it was her Great-Grandpa Allen!

His lips were slightly turned up, but his eyebrows were furrowed, his forehead creased with lines of worry.

Aspen could not look away from his eyes. They were pleading, sad.

For a second Aspen thought to run, but feeling no danger or fear, she lingered, looking into his eyes.

He came within a few feet of her and stopped. Surprised that he had come so close, Aspen gasped.

The lines in his forehead softened—his eyes dropped to his hands.

It was then that Aspen noticed he was carrying something. It was a small box about the size of a child's shoebox. Etched in gold, the box was made of wood. On the front was a small latch with a tiny gold padlock.

Her grandpa turned the box over. She could see a small indent in the bottom, and in the hollow space, there was a tiny gold key. He turned the box back over and extended his arms toward her the box sitting on his open palms.

58

RILEY OR RONDA

"Aspen, Aspen?" Someone was shaking her. "Noah?"

"Yeah, you…you were having some sort of nightmare." Noah's hands were on her shoulders.

Aspen looked around. Gavin, Kiryn, and Rocky were sitting around the coffee table.

"I…I was…I couldn't wake up." Aspen started to sit up, and Noah put his arm across her back to help her. "It was…the craziest dream ever."

Rocky stood up and walked over to her. "Are you okay, Sweetheart?"

Aspen nodded. She studied each of their faces. "Where did everyone go?"

"It was a pretty big night. Rocky gave you something to help you sleep. You weren't handling things very well," said Noah.

Aspen looked past all of them at the sunlight peering through the front windows. Surprised, she asked, "Did I sleep all night?"

Gavin nodded. "Well everyone didn't leave until almost three, so yes, you slept the rest of the night and then some. We have been awake for a couple of hours. It's nearly ten o'clock."

Anxiously Aspen asked, "Mom? Did you call Mom?"

"She was here earlier to check on you. Dad is awake, too. He has been working with some counselor guy this morning," said Noah.

"Did you go see him?" Aspen wasn't sure which was stronger,

the ache in her heart that her mom did not stay with her or the pangs of hunger attacking her stomach.

As though Kiryn read her mind, she said, "Do you feel like coming into the kitchen. I'll make you an omelet."

"Yes, I'm starving." Aspen started to stand up, and both Gavin and Noah jumped to steady her.

Aspen stopped. "I'm fine you guys." She took a couple of steps. "Okay I'm a little wobbly, but I'm fine."

"How about I just help you?" Kiryn cast a disparaging look at Noah and Gavin and put her arm through Aspen's and everyone filed into the kitchen.

"Did you go see Dad, Noah?" Aspen asked again.

"Not yet. He's having a pretty rough time. Mom is over there."

Aspen looked at Rocky, "I wasn't having a hard time, I just couldn't breathe—or stay awake."

Rocky stared at her.

"Okay, maybe a little hard time, but I mean I wasn't like going to freak out or anything."

"You were shaking pretty bad, Aspen, and twice you almost passed out," Noah reassured her.

"There was so much confusion going on with everyone else. I just thought it best if you could sleep. It had already been a long day, and then all of that new information—" Rocky's voice trailed off.

Kiryn placed the omelet and a glass of orange juice in front of Aspen, and they all crowded around the nook. While Aspen ate, they began rehashing the events of the night before.

"I can't believe Dixon actually killed whomever Ronda is," began Aspen.

"Ronda," began Gavin, "was Allen's daughter." He paused, waiting for Aspen to respond.

"You mean Riley?"

"He means *Ronda*." Rocky nodded in Gavin's direction.

Aspen stopped eating. "Oh yeah, he did say that." Her head was spinning again.

"It appears Grandpa had another daughter, possibly older than Riley," said Noah.

Aspen gasped, and she stared wide-eyed at the others. "The girl! The girl in the Mansion House, in the picture. The dark-haired girl!" The words tumbled out of Aspen's mouth so fast little bits of egg spilled out with them. She wiped her mouth with the back of her hand, "Sorry," she continued to stare at them.

Noah took a deep breath and let it slowly release before he spoke. "Apparently."

Aspen's fork clattered to her plate. She pressed her fingers against her temples and tried to conjure up the image of the girl. She couldn't. She simply could not see her.

"I can only see her in Grandpa's house—" She blurted. "That has got to mean something. She must be there."

Kiryn shuddered. "You mean her body?"

"No, I don't know. It's been what, fifty years?"

"More like sixty," said Noah.

"Okay, everyone calm down." Rocky stood and walked directly to the fridge. "He pulled out a bottle of Coke and held it up for the rest to see. "Anyone else want one of these?"

Everyone laughed.

"A Coke, Dad?" Gavin eyed him suspiciously.

"Just sounds good," said Rocky. He opened it and gulped down half the bottle, and then he walked back over to the nook holding the now half-empty bottle of Coke in front of him, "Relieves stress."

Rocky sat down. "I have been trying to process this all night." He turned to Aspen. "I made these kids go to bed."

"Like we got any sleep," said Gavin.

"You did, trust me. I was awake all night; you were sleeping." With his finger, Rocky made imaginary marks on the table. "One, there must be something buried in the root cellar—hopefully not people. Two, Ronda and her boyfriend were murdered. Three, somewhere there is a will that was supposed to leave money to the Dixon boys, Dylan and Drew. Four—"

"But isn't that like blood money?" blurted Kiryn.

Rocky's brow furrowed. "You watch too many movies. The thing is, it doesn't matter how or why apparently Allen gave a portion of his estate to the heirs of Dixon. They did nothing, and there is no one left to prosecute. It does not hurt anyone here today," he motioned to Aspen and Noah, "or your parents to find out what it is and do something about it. They obviously depended on it, and they loved their grandpa, they didn't have a hand in this."

Kiryn plopped her elbow on the table and rested her hand in her chin. "I guess so," she snarled.

Gavin squinted and eyed his sister. "Kiryn?"

"Well, it just seems awful to me! People get killed, and the guy who did it gets to leave money to his family. How is that right?"

Absently Noah said, "She has a point."

"Yes, she does," sighed Rocky. "It's really not our decision, is it?"

They all shook their heads in agreement. "No." Kiryn sighed.

Rocky went on, "I think it's important for us to keep in mind that we have no idea if Tygert or Dixon killed any of those boys. Seems like someone would have found out if that were true, so we need to be careful about jumping to conclusions."

No one responded.

Rocky was adamant. "Right?"

This time they all nodded, but Kiryn who rolled her eyes.

59

HIDDEN BEHIND THE PAINT

Mr. Weston had the painting propped on a large easel with the back of it toward the door.

Kiryn ran into the room. "What did you find, Mr. Weston?"

Kiryn's art teacher had recommended Mr. Weston to attempt to remove the thick paint from the painting and see if there was something under it. They found him sitting on a stool in front of the painting while cleaning residue from his hands. "I would never have believed this if I hadn't found it for myself."

Aspen was suddenly anxious about what she might see as she, Gavin and Noah joined Kiryn and Mr. Weston.

"Unbelievable," Gavin whispered as though he was only talking to himself.

Mr. Weston had completely removed the large potted plant and what was in its place was not what Aspen expected, but she really didn't know what she had expected.

It was another girl, who looked curiously like the oldest sister.

One detail immediately caught Aspen's eye.

A chipped tooth.

"This...this is the girl I keep seeing." She looked anxiously at Noah, who quickly stepped beside her and draped his arm across her shoulders.

Almost as shocking was the woman who now sat where Faith had been. Her beautiful pleasant features and endearing eyes were looking right back at Aspen.

Mr. Weston held up a large photograph he had taken of the painting before he started to work.

"Here is what the painting used to look like." He turned to Kiryn. "Is this what you expected?"

Kiryn shook her head. "Not even. I—we didn't know what to expect."

Kiryn pointed to the new girl and turned to Aspen. "So who do you think this is? Ronda, maybe?"

Aspen nodded but before she could say anything Mr. Weston spoke up.

"Beats me," said Mr. Weston. "But whoever did the work was a master with his paints. I couldn't believe the detail. The painting is over fifty years old, and apparently, no one even noticed."

"Or maybe they chose to ignore it," said Aspen.

"Maybe," said Mr. Weston. "But why?" He pointed to the signature at the bottom right corner of the original painting. "Sabrina." He rubbed the back of his neck and looked around the room.

"Someone has taken great care to make sure that it was kept clean from dust and just simple wear and tear." And then he repeated, "Amazing that no one noticed this before."

"They weren't supposed to," Gavin muttered, but Mr. Weston didn't seem to hear him, and for just a second, Aspen's eyes met with Gavin's. Amid all that was going on, his green eyes penetrated right into her soul and his ability to calm her, spread through her entire body. She smiled and again turned to the artwork before them.

Aspen pointed to the signature. "Do you recognize that name, Mr. Weston?"

He shook his head, "Nope. Have no idea who that painter was."

Aspen was amazed to see how someone had skillfully covered the girl with the potted plant but covering Nina with Faith was truly a masterpiece.

Faith was positioned exactly how Nina had been sitting, right down to the tilt of her head and the way her fingers weaved through

Great-Grandpa's fingers; her hand resting in his.

The girl was sitting on the floor next to Nina, and in front of Riley. Her dark brown hair pulled up in much the same style as Riley's, with long curls spilling over her shoulders. Her broad smile revealing the same deep dimples as her younger brother's.

Aspen could only assume this must be the Ronda mentioned in Dixon's journal. She must also be Grandpa's sister.

Ronda, who had not run away at all, but had been murdered. The thought still made Aspen shudder.

"She…she must be somewhere in this house. That must be why she only comes to me here." Aspen caught the curious look on Mr. Weston's face, and she tried to quickly think of a way to take back what she had just said, but Kiryn's next comment pretty much distracted from Aspen's.

"Do you honestly think Tygert would have put her right here in your grandpa's house?" Kiryn sounded shocked.

That's assuming what we think are the facts, actually are—the facts." Gavin was trying hard to cover for both Aspen and Kiryn while Mr. Weston's blank look spoke loudly to all of them.

Aspen heard Noah say quietly to Gavin, "What a ruthless bugger, burying her right here," his disgust evident.

Mr. Weston stood as he put the last of his tools into a small metal case. "This has been a most interesting task." He displayed a small notebook. "I'm going to give this to Dave over at the newspaper." He looked at Aspen. "If that's okay with you folks."

Rocky, who hadn't said much of anything up until now spoke up, "Could you hold off on that for a few days? There are a couple of things I would like to check out first."

Mr. Weston pushed his glasses back on his nose. "Sure, Mr. Fielden." I'm in no hurry, but it is hard to keep a secret like this, so don't take too long." He winked at Aspen. "An interesting legend, the Allen family, it gets more interesting every day."

If Mr. Weston said "interesting" one more time, Aspen would want to hit him, but instead, she just smiled. "Thanks so much for all that you've done."

She still hated the idea that their family was a legend of any kind and now to add murder to it, was almost too much.

"Yes, yes. I'll be going now." Mr. Weston skirted past all of them toward the door. He turned abruptly. "If I were you, folks, I would keep the door to this room locked." He patted the briefcase he had flung over his shoulder. "I left you a copy of the photo. I have mine in here. I also have a photo of the re-finished product." He disappeared into the hallway.

"Okay," said Aspen. "Well, thank you."

"Mr. Weston?" Noah called after him, and Mr. Weston popped his head back inside.

"What do we owe you?"

"Haven't figured it out yet. Okay, if I send you a bill?"

"Sure," said Noah as Mr. Weston disappeared and Aspen heard him trot down the stairs.

Rocky sighed. "Whew. Lots of information today." He walked over to the painting and stood between Kiryn and Aspen. "That is amazing. Do you think Allen did this? Or rather had it done?"

"Why?" said Kiryn.

"I don't know. To cover up for putting his first wife in an asylum?"

"Why else? I mean, geez, who could think of doing this, but then what other reason would there be?" Aspen sighed. "This whole thing gets weirder every day."

Find her.

"What?" Aspen turned around, but Noah and Gavin were still huddled in the corner talking, and Kiryn had already started toward them.

Rocky was comparing the photo of the painting before it had been restored. "Amazing," he mumbled.

Aspen turned back to the painting and stared into Ronda's eyes. "What? Did you…did you?" she whispered and then rubbed her face with her hands. She turned to say something to the others but changed her mind. This moment was hers—Ronda had spoken to her—finally.

Through misty eyes, she smiled—a huge smile—and she couldn't help but touch her tooth, the same one of Ronda's that was broken. Then she heard it again.

Find me.

60

PATRICE

After hearing Ronda's voice in the storage room, Aspen felt compelled to learn more about her gift and the fact that she could see—literally—dead people.

Rocky did not even hesitate. In fact, he had explained, that is exactly what he had talked to Sara and Gavin about a week ago. After obtaining permission from Aspen's mother, he had arranged a meeting with one of Sara and Sumer's aunts, who was a well-known expert in this sort of thing.

When Suzann questioned what they were meeting for, he explained that this person would help the kids deal with some of the issues Dylan had brought up. Rocky invited her to attend, but she declined, stating that she was not ready to add anything else to "deal" with right now.

Rocky was relieved. He didn't want to have to face her with all the details either.

Patrice Munoa was seated in one of four chairs on her front porch when Rocky, Sara, and the four kids arrived.

Aspen tried to see her clearly through the car window, but trees in the yard blocked her view. It had been raining, but it was not cold. However, Aspen could not stop shivering. She smiled when

Noah touched her hand and laughed when she looked at Kiryn.

"What?" Kiryn frowned at Aspen. "Why are you so nervous?"

"Seriously, Kiryn, you aren't the one who sees dead people," laughed Noah. "It's Aspen and Gavin who should be nervous."

The three piled out of the Iroc just as Rocky, Gavin, and Sara drove up in Rocky's truck.

"Well, I just hope it ends there. I hope that by us being here, Noah, you and I don't start seeing them too."

"I thought that's what you wanted," Aspen chided.

"Exactly! *Wanted.*I have changed my mind," said Kiryn with conviction.

Aspen laughed and linked arms with her friend.

"We ready for this?" Rocky put his arm around Aspen's shoulders as the group walked up the path to the front porch. He stopped and said to all of them, "Oh, by the way, I spoke to Hank this morning. The FBI has assigned a team to work the case."

"So, are they going to re-open the files?" asked Gavin.

"They are working on it. Two detectives, along with Hank, will meet with us on Thursday, if that works for everyone." Rocky laughed. "Can you kids clear your schedules?"

"We'll see if we can fit it in," said Noah. "How is your father, Noah?" asked Sara.

Noah shrugged. "About the same. He isn't getting any worse, so that's a good thing. He is meeting with counselors when they can keep him calm long enough, but he won't talk. He won't tell them what's wrong—what's bothering him."

Rocky added, "Their mother, Suzann, does not know anything about this gift that Aspen has been dealing with."

"Well, she does know that I see spirits—or images—she thinks they are my imagination, just like Dad thinks, and Noah thought. So she kinda knows, but she has no clue what has been happening since we got to Sommerville."

Sara nodded. "I'm so sorry, kids."

"Thanks," said Noah.

Then Sara said, "When do you plan to tell her?"

Noah shrugged. "We haven't figured that out yet."

Rocky stepped up onto the porch first and extended his hand to Patrice. "Thank you so much for seeing us today, Ms. Munoa."

Patrice smiled. "I am happy to! I have been waiting a long time for this family to contact me. I knew someone had to have this gift after Sumer left us. Just didn't know who was going to come forth. Scares some folks you know!" She laughed heartily.

"Do ya think?" mumbled Kiryn. Patrice stood and hugged her niece.

"Hi Aunt Patrice." Sara hugged her back and then introduced everyone.

Patrice welcomed them all and then motioned for Gavin to sit in one of the two empty chairs directly in front of her. She paused, looking over Aspen, Noah, and Kiryn. She motioned to Aspen, "And you, dear, you take the last chair." She pointed to some chairs along the railing. "Rocky could you, and the other youngsters bring a chair over as well?"

Aspen gave Patrice a puzzled look. "How, how did you know that I...I was the one with the gift?"

"The light. The lights around you are dancing. This tells me there is an active connection with you and beings that have gone beyond."

Aspen's eyes widened. "Does...does Gavin have lights?"

Patrice smiled. "All living creatures have lights. Some are just more active or more *intuitive* than others." She motioned to Kiryn, Noah, and Rocky. "All of you have lights."

"Well, thank goodness—I was starting to get a little jealous." Everyone laughed at Kiryn's comment.

"This is a funny girl," said Patrice.

"Yes, very funny." Rocky rolled his eyes.

Patrice laughed again. "It is best that we never take ourselves too seriously, my friends."

"May I ask a question?" said Noah. When Patrice nodded, he went on, "How old are you?"

"Noah!" Aspen was embarrassed.

"What? I asked if I could ask a question."

"It is fine. I don't care who knows my age. I am eighty-three." Everyone but Sara was surprised.

"How old did you think I was?"

Noah took a deep breath. "Honestly?"

"Honestly."

"I was thinking, maybe sixty."

They all nodded in agreement, and that obviously pleased Patrice. "I have been around a long time, but thank you, Noah." She placed her hands in her lap. "Why do you ask?"

Noah shrugged. "I was just wondering if you might have been around when our great-grandpa lived here."

A small smile and a slow nod. "Ahhh, I was." Aspen's heart leaped, and she quickly looked at Noah. Aspen asked, "Did…did you know them?"

Patrice closed her eyes. "Know them? I knew of them. I am very familiar with them all." Again Patrice slowly nodded her head. She opened her eyes and looked from Aspen to Gavin. She put both hands on her knees, "Now, should we get down to business?"

"So my friend, Gavin. I understand that you see your mother and also Aspen's friend who recently passed. How long have you been able to see your mother?"

"All my life, I guess."

"Can you tell me a little more about your experiences?"

Gavin explained how he had seen a woman for almost as long as he could remember—but that it wasn't until that one winter when he realized she must not be real. She was standing in the snow with bare feet, and his dad didn't even notice her, even though she was where he could easily have seen her. He said, looking back now, he wonders how many other people he may have seen that were possibly dead as well.

"And the old man?" Patrice was studying Gavin intently.

"Just the last few weeks," said Gavin. "But he is like a shadow. I can tell he is not a regular person. He is more like what you might expect a ghost to look like—you know—in the movies." Gavin explained further that when he sees Krista, it is like looking at Kiryn or Aspen but that Krista does not always acknowledge him.

"Do you know of any other people?"

Gavin thought for a minute. "I'm not sure, but I do know that I can't see the girl in the big house that Aspen keeps seeing. We—me and Aspen—were looking at the same spot in the hall and Aspen could see the girl, and I could see Krista, but neither of us could see the other person—uh—ghost or spirit."

"Creepy," mumbled Kiryn.

Patrice laughed, and so did everyone else. "Yes, it would seem so," said Patrice.

"I'm not sure how to explain what I mean," said Gavin.

"You explained it very well. Your gift Gavin, allows you to see people that have an emotional connection to you through either yourself or someone you care about. It is not likely that you will recognize that you are seeing them at first until you figure out the connection and they may appear to be regular living people until you realize that only you can see them."

"Most of the time, the people you see are there as some type of protection or specific reason that involves either you or the person you care about. Your gift makes it easy for spirits to contact you or make themselves visible to you once they know they can trust you. Your ability to see the shadow or outline of the man is your inner spirit trying to assist Aspen's inner spirit. It is that emotional connection working overtime, so to speak. In other words, those particular spirits would never contact you first."

Patrice looked at Aspen and then back to Gavin. "Is Aspen's friend the first person you have seen other than your mother?"

Gavin nodded. "Yes. At least I think so."

"Wrong," said Patrice. "There have been others—I'm sure of it—but you were not reachable at that particular time. You will now be more aware of it, and when someone tries to contact you, it will be clearer because you will be watching for, and expecting it."

"Expecting it?" said Gavin.

"Yes, well, at least you should. As with all spiritual gifts, you must expect them to happen. Be aware all the time that at any given second, you may be called upon for any number of reasons."

"Wow." Gavin looked at Rocky who smiled.

"May I say something?" asked Sara.

Patrice nodded, "Of course you may."

Sara looked at Gavin. "I don't have this gift Gavin, but as you know, your mother did. One of the reasons Rocky and I have been so hesitant to tell you about your mother and how she died was because if you had this gift, we didn't want you to be afraid. Your mother used her gift in many ways to help other people. She didn't tell many people about it because, well, except in certain circles, she appeared to be crazy."

Aspen chuckled, and so did Noah. "Right?" said Sara.

"Well, it's kind of hard not to think that. Some of the things Aspen has seen have been pretty…weird," said Noah.

Sara laughed. "I know. I was the sister with no gift just like you are the brother. It can be very frustrating at times. I have to admit, the older Gavin got, I didn't think he had inherited the gift, and I was relieved, but, of course, now we know that wasn't true at all."

"Well, he has always been a little strange," said Rocky.

"Thanks, Dad."

"No problem."

"So, Patrice, my mom was able to find people that were lost. I don't have that, right?" said Gavin.

"I'm sure that you do, but you must develop it. You would have to concentrate when an image comes to your mind, to see if it is just an image or an image that means something. One that is trying to contact you."

Gavin nodded. "This is kind of heavy stuff."

"Very heavy. A great responsibility. However, it is also your choice. You do not have to do anything with it. That, my young friend, is your choice and yours alone. Do you have any questions?"

"Not right this second."

Patrice nodded and turned to Aspen, "Now to you, my dear."

Aspen's heart started racing, and she sat forward in her chair.

"I believe your gift is a bit different from Gavin's. Can you tell me about it?"

Aspen explained how, since she was a little girl, she could see people that no one else seemed to notice. She said it had never really bothered her, but that it did seem to be a concern to her parents, and as they got older, to Noah.

She told Patrice that none of the people she had ever seen had scared her, but that the old man was terrifying and that he followed her and tried different ways to contact her. Aspen said there were other things too, but she did not expound any further.

Patrice sat back in her chair and closed her eyes for a few seconds. When she opened them, she leaned forward and looked directly into Aspen's eyes.

"The people who contact you need help directly from you. For example, the girl you have seen is trying to reach you to help her solve something, right?"

"She's stuck. Well, that's what we think," said Kiryn.

"Exactly! She is stuck. Either in another dimension or between here and the spirit world."

"What do you mean another dimension?" asked Aspen.

"Well, there are some spirits who are not truly spirits at all. They have moved on to another location but are still very much alive. I bring this up because this may be the case for you."

"Why?" Aspen sounded alarmed. "Why do you say that?"

"Well, when Sara contacted me, she also gave me information that Rocky had given her and from what I understand this young lady's body was never located?"

"We don't know that for sure, Patrice," said Rocky. "That is just the information we have from the journals. The man wrote in his journal that he killed the two kids, but he never did find the bodies after he drowned them. He hired someone else, however, to find and dispose of them. His journal indicates that he is not sure that ever happened."

Patrice smiled. "That is my point. On this one, we are not sure. You will have to do your own investigation."

"How do I do that?'

"You have seen many spirits, correct?" Aspen nodded.

"Have you seen them come and go?"

"What do you mean?"

"Have they vanished before your eyes? Like maybe walked through a wall?"

Aspen's eyes flashed, and Patrice noticed. "You remember something?"

"Uh, yes, a few things. There were some people—or I guess they were people—they seemed to be people, anyway, in the storage room. They all walked out into the hall, but when they started to go down the stairs, they just vanished."

"Go on." Patrice fixed her eyes on Aspen's face.

"Well I…I sort of put my hand through—well, I didn't actually put it through—it just went through—"

"Oh my gosh, Aspen—"

Kiryn turned to Patrice. "Aspen leaned against a door, and her hand went right through it. I saw it." Kiryn's voice rose. "We all saw it."

Suddenly she whirled around to Rocky. "Dad! That day on the stairs. He froze in the exact spot that those people and…and the girl vanished."

"A portal, maybe?" Patrice raised her eyebrows.

"I suppose, at least that's what I was thinking," said Rocky.

"Not suppose. It is," Patrice said as she smiled. "You can develop this gift—you can move through space—into other dimensions. You can go into those portals."

Aspen did not like the sound of this.

"How does she get back?" Noah sounded apprehensive.

"She will know how, although it can be challenging at first."

"Can she take other people with her?" asked Gavin.

"She can, but again, that can be very challenging, especially when she takes someone who has no particular connection at that time."

"So it's not advisable, right?" said Kiryn.

"It depends on the person. Aspen would have to make that decision."

"Wait! What if I don't want to go into portals or whatever they are?" Aspen's gaze dropped to her lap. She said almost in a whisper, "It's scary."

Kiryn sighed. "It was strange to see your arm disappear."

"I have. I mean I haven't gone into any portal, but have moved through space." She looked at Noah. "I'm sorry, Noah, this is the last thing—I promise—that I haven't told you about."

Everyone looked at Aspen.

"Well, that was random," said Kiryn.

Noah shook his head. "Just please don't tell me I am walking among the living dead. That *you* are a spirit."

Patrice laughed. "I can assure you, she is not."

"Okay, well good, at least I have that from an expert."

"Why don't you explain, Aspen." Gavin was obviously curious.

"The first day on the road—the old man—I somehow was standing right next to him on the road for just a few seconds." She looked at Noah. "I kind of told you about that one." She continued, "But the painting in the hallway, when you guys were trying to get in the storage room, I was inside the painting looking at all of you."

Noah jumped up, "Okay, that is just freaky! See Aspen! I don't think you should tell people this stuff! Someone will have you committed!"

Rocky pulled on Noah's arm. "Calm down. This is why we are here so that we can all understand."

Noah relented and sat back on his chair.

Kiryn reached over and patted his leg. Unexpectedly, Noah grabbed her hand and held onto it. Kiryn's surprised look made Aspen giggle.

"Does your sister look any different to you, Noah, since these happenings began?" asked Patrice.

Noah shook his head. "No, she is just as psychotic as ever." He smiled. "I'm just kidding. No, she looks the same."

"Exactly," said Patrice. "She will not change. She, like Gavin, has a choice to develop her gifts further or not."

"We don't have a choice whether these people come to us," said Gavin.

"That I cannot help you with. They will always come. It is up to you to respond." Patrice looked over at Noah. "I believe you have had a glimpse of this gift, but you are unreceptive. Don't worry, it is not a bad thing. It means you are much harder to reach so spirits pass you by."

"That is just fine with me!" said Noah.

Patrice turned to Aspen again. "There is one more thing. Spirits both good and bad can make you see images or experience things that are not really happening, but to you, they seem completely real. You would never die from these experiences, but you can be injured if a particular spirit is able to control the physical surroundings around you, but mostly these experiences are to make you afraid or stop you from being receptive to someone who is trying to get your help."

Aspen again turned to Noah. "The rats," she noticed the puzzled look on Kiryn and Gavin's faces. "And the desk."

"And the old man," said Kiryn.

"Especially the old man," agreed Rocky.

"The lake?" asked Noah.

"When I compare the lake to everything else—it was for sure scary, but it wasn't the same as this other stuff."

"Tell me about it," said Patrice.

Aspen and Noah described the experience at Mystic Lake, as the locals called it. When they finished, Patrice sat back in her chair, saying nothing for several minutes. When she finally spoke, she smiled, "This is, I believe, someone trying to contact for help."

"Help! She dang near drowned," said Noah.

"Ahhh but she didn't."

"Isn't that an odd way for anyone to try and get help?" asked Kiryn.

"Not if it was their only opportunity," said Sara softly.

"Very true. I am not sure why that would be their only opportunity, but maybe that is true," said Patrice.

Aspen sighed. "This is a lot to take in."

"It is, but I hope you can understand—both of you can understand—that these gifts you have are real. They are nothing to be afraid of. You can both do a lot of good and be very valuable to many people."

Everyone was quiet.

A lady appeared in the doorway. "Would anyone like something to drink? I have cookies."

"Thank you, Rebecca." Patrice introduced Rebecca who worked for her.

Rebecca brought a plate of chocolate chip cookies, a pitcher of juice and some paper cups and placed them on a table next to Gavin.

"That was a mistake," said Rocky.

"What?" Patrice asked.

"Putting the food next to him."

"Ah! He is a growing boy. Give him lots of cookies. Rebecca just baked these, especially for all of you."

"Patrice, what about the texts?" asked Gavin.

"Texting?" Patrice looked surprised.

"Yes, Aspen and I have each received a text from Krista."

"Texting. On your phones?"

"Yes, look." Aspen stood, and as she did, she opened her phone to Krista's text. She handed it to Patrice. "See that came from Krista."

Patrice was staring at the phone, slowly shaking her head.

"Mine too." Gavin showed his phone as well.

"I have no idea. I have heard of this—through computers and such—but I do believe this is the first time I have seen a text from beyond."

She smiled at the kids. "You are very lucky—or maybe it is Krista. Maybe she has ways that others don't, or maybe this is a new medium. I'm not sure, but do know that you should both be grateful and take advantage."

Sara leaned over so that she could see the phones. "Have either of you tried to answer her?" Everyone was startled by that question, and both Gavin and Aspen were shocked by it.

Sara stood and started laughing. "I'm just wondering. I mean the phone works both ways."

Gavin and Aspen both looked at Rocky.

"Why are you looking at me? I have no idea!"

"So…try," said Noah.

"Yeah, try it! This is crazy," said Kiryn.

Gavin shrugged, and Aspen just took a deep breath before she typed a text. "Here goes," she said.

"Let's just say, 'Krista are you getting this?' Okay?"

Aspen nodded. "Okay."

"Sent."

"Mine too," said Aspen.

They waited. After a full minute of silence, Aspen sighed. "K, well I guess that didn't work."

"Maybe she's busy," said Kiryn. They all turned to look at her.

"Well, maybe she has things to do. We don't know!" Rocky shook his head. "Maybe."

"Well, let me know if she answers either of you, at any time. I would be curious to know," said Patrice, and they both agreed that they would.

After two more hours, Patrice had not only shared many of her own experiences but also answered a myriad of questions. She also explained how these gifts came down a long genealogy line in her family. She assured them that even if it is not in the immediate close relatives, a search of genealogy would prove that this gift follows family lines.

This left Aspen with two main thoughts when they left. Dad and the place on the stairs.

Rocky took Sara home and the four teenagers piled in the Iroc. Just before Noah started the engine, Kiryn leaned forward and said to Aspen, "Now, about those rats…"

61

First Visit

Aspen and Noah sat quietly in their dad's hospital room while his nurse made sure he was ready for their visit.

This was the first time the doctors had allowed Jackson's children to be in the room when he was awake, and their hope was that it might prove to be a positive experience for him, and them.

Dr. Winslow approached Suzann and the kids before he spoke to Jackson.

"We would like your dad to lead the conversation this morning. Craig and Hannah," he paused to clarify. "They are your dad's counselors. Anyway, we asked them to wait until the four of you have been able to visit, but they, and I, will be close by. We just want to see how this goes."

When the nurse and Dr. Winslow left the room, Noah and Aspen approached their father's bed. He looked up at them, and immediately, his eyes filled with tears.

"Hey, Dad." Noah hurried to his side, sat on the edge of his bed then blurted, "When are you going to get out of this place? We found the coolest lake too—it's not the ocean, but Aspen and I have learned to water ski—not surfing by a long shot, but it's still fun."

Aspen gave Noah a questioning look, but then she plunked on the opposite side of the bed from Noah. "And hard! I never thought it would be that hard, especially holding onto a rope, but it is."

Dad's eyes looked confused as he looked back and forth between his two children. He didn't say anything for several seconds.

"So, you kids like it here?"

Aspen and Noah exchanged a quick glance and then Aspen said, "Well yeah…it's okay…we have some pretty cool friends."

"Actually, Dad, I wouldn't go so far as saying we like it here, but we don't hate it either, right Aspen?"

"Yeah…yeah, we don't hate it!" confirmed Aspen.

Another long silence as Dad studied their faces. He turned to Suzann, and a smirk crossed his lips. "Who are these kids?"

Suzann laughed and looked sideways at her two kids. "So much for letting Dad lead the conversation."

Aspen and Noah exchanged a quick glance and then waited for their father's response.

After several seconds, his face softened, and he reached for both of them. Aspen and Noah leaned down, and Jackson pulled them both close to him. He tried to speak but choked on his words, so he just held them and cried. When he finally released them, everyone was crying, and for several minutes, no one said anything. Mom joined them on the bed, and the nurse had closed the door.

Finally, Jackson wiped his eyes. "I'm sorry, Noah—" but then his voice broke and he started to cry again.

"Hey Dad," Noah hesitated and then blurted. "Love means never having to say you're sorry."

That comment startled his parents and sister, but then Dad said, "You hated that movie."

"I know. It was a stupid movie. I still can't believe you and Mom liked it, but hey—"

She shook her head at Noah's reference to an old love story their parents liked, but one she and Noah found really lame. "Love means never having to say your sorry" was a line from that movie that the family had laughed about since Jackson and Suzann had tortured Aspen and Noah on movie night a couple of years earlier.

"Well, it seemed appropriate." Noah looked at Mom, who smiled but rolled her eyes.

"That's corny, and not true," said Dad. "But I appreciate your effort."

"Can we talk about all of that later, Dad? I'm just happy we can be here while you are awake," said Noah.

Dad put his hand over one of Noah's. "That's a good idea, Son." No one was quite sure where to start or what subject might upset Dad.

Finally, Aspen said, "So how do you feel, Dad? Are you about ready to go home?"

Dad looked past her to Mom. "I don't know. How am I doing, Suzann?"

Mom smiled, "We still have some ground to cover, but we are getting closer."

Aspen looked from Mom to Dad, "And that means?"

"There are some things from my past—"

"And present," added Mom.

Dad continued, "She's right. Some things I need to come to terms with. That's why they are having me meet with counselors."

"Why do they always give you stuff to make you sleep?" asked Noah.

Mom answered, "When Dad sleeps on his own—basically he doesn't—he has constant nightmares. The drugs help him sleep so that he can rest."

"Anything we can help with, Dad?" asked Aspen hopefully.

Again Mom answered only cautiously this time, "Not just yet, honey, but soon."

Dad's eyes became sullen, and he stared past them all. "I just have— some things—that I need to figure out. Things that I left here when I moved to California."

"But now they are back?" Aspen blurted.

Dad looked directly at her. "Yes, Aspen. Now they are back, and this time, I have to face them."

"How long will you be in here?" asked Noah.

"I'm not sure." He turned to Mom. "Do we know?"

"The problem is, when your dad gets upset, his heart starts to go crazy. Dr. Winslow is afraid that if he releases Dad too soon, he could have another heart attack, and this one might be more severe."

Aspen looked quickly to see Dad's reaction to Mom's statement. "It's okay, Aspen. I know." He rubbed his face with one hand.

"Your Dad is a mental case right now."

Aspen smiled and looked at Noah. "Oh, probably not, Dad."

"Yeah, probably not, Dad." Noah laughed.

Dad studied each of his kids and then turned to his wife. "Am I missing something here?"

Suzann raised her eyebrows, "I don't know. Maybe we both are." She smiled and looked directly into Jackson's eyes. "One step at a time."

Mom walked Noah and Aspen to the elevator.

"So what now? Is Dad talking at all about what is bothering him?" said Aspen.

"Not really. I mean, he starts to, but then becomes so agitated." Mom shook her head. "This appears to be a long process."

"Mom—" began Noah, but a sharp glance from Aspen stopped him.

"What?"

"Just— If there is anything we can do, Mom," said Noah.

"Today was the best I have seen your dad. So, I think you have done plenty for now." Mom hugged them both. "What have you got going on today?"

"We are meeting with Hank and those guys from the FBI about the information Dylan brought up," said Aspen.

Mom nodded. "That's right. Hank called me to see if there was any way an investigation could be done at your grandpa's house."

"What did you say?" Noah sounded anxious.

"Well, I called Robin, your dad's attorney in California, and he told me to tell them they can't touch that house until your dad is well and can give the okay."

"What about Aunt Dana, could she?" asked Noah.

Mom shook her head. "They already contacted her. She told them it has been fifty years they can wait a few more weeks or months until Jackson can make the decisions on his own."

Noah laughed. "That's funny. I would like to meet Aunt Dana someday."

"I'm sure you will," said Mom.

"Well, I'm glad. I don't think people should be investigating anything without Dad's permission." Aspen caught Noah's questioning look. "You know…unrelated people….that…you know… don't know Dad…or…"

Mom looked at them both. "I don't even want to know what that was all about." She folded her arms across her chest. "Do I?"

"Uh, no, probably not," said Noah. He looked at Aspen. "We should go."

Mom laughed. "Yes, you should. By the way, I talked to Rocky. He assured me that whatever it is you kids are up to—he is fully aware of it and it's okay. So I am trusting you both. Should I?"

"Have we ever let you down, Mom?" said Aspen. Mom eyed them both suspiciously. "Not yet."

"Well, then no worries." Laughed Noah. He hugged his mother. "We'll check back later and see how the counseling session went."

Mom glanced at her phone. "Oh, they are starting in five minutes. Okay." She gave them each a quick kiss on the cheek. "Bye."

The elevator doors closed and Aspen sighed. "Wow, there is going to be a lot to tell Dad *and* Mom."

"Well, Mom is better now just knowing Drew can't mess with her anymore so let's just leave it at that for now. I'm not sure she is ready to deal with all this spirit stuff."

"You underestimate her, Noah."

"No. That's not true. I just don't want her to go backward. Right there, that mom, the one who kinda sorta scolded us, that is the mom I want back, that's all."

Aspen nodded. "You're right. Me too."

"I'm right? Wow! Put that in the history books," Noah chided.

"Yep, you better." Aspen smacked his shoulder. "'Cause it will probably only happen once."

The meeting with Hank and the two agents, Byron Coulsen and Larry Brimhall, lasted about an hour.

Robin Henderson, Jackson's attorney from California, contacted an attorney in Memphis to put a stay on the investigation until Jackson could okay the release of the journals and give permission to go into the Allen Manor.

"We want you to get to the bottom of this," explained Rocky. "This family has nothing to hide, but we need to do it the right way."

Agent Brimhall warned them, "We could subpoena the journals."

"You could Byron, but is that necessary. As the sister said, it's been fifty years, and besides," added Rocky, "isn't there enough in public records that you could start with?"

Both of the agents agreed. They set up a time to meet with Rocky and the four kids in one month. Hopefully, Jackson would be on the road to recovery, and they could move forward.

When the agents left, Aspen walked out onto Rocky's front porch and collapsed on the chaise lounge. "I'm so tired all of a sudden."

"Mental exhaustion," said Kiryn. "Why don't you take a nap?"

"But I thought we were going over to the house."

"We are, but we are going to have lunch first."

Aspen barely heard Kiryn. The warm sun felt so good on her back. She rolled onto her side and pulled her knees to her chest.

62

DUST TO DUST

NOAH SAT ON A chair next to his sleeping sister and rubbed his eyes with closed fists.

He couldn't help but wonder about his dad and whether or not the doctors would be able to help him get through whatever was haunting him. He had heard of people being hypnotized to help them remember and try to handle things they had buried in their minds. He wondered if this may be needed with Dad.

He looked over at Aspen. *How is she going to get through all of this? She and Gavin were given a lot of information when they met with Patrice. Where do I fit into the picture?*

Noah leaned back and closed his eyes. He found himself wondering if he would be of any help to Aspen since he couldn't see anything she could. He also wondered what Patrice meant when she said he had been passed by or something like that, or that he was not receptive. Rocky had said something like that as well when they told him about someone touching Noah's shoulder that first day in Grandpa's house.

Then there was his mother. She had no idea what had been going on these past few weeks. She was aware that Aspen seemed to see people that no one else could see, but was she prepared to learn all about Aspen's gifts?

Taking a deep breath and slowly letting out, Noah's thoughts drifted to Kiryn. He was startled that his heart skipped a beat when her image appeared in his mind. He smiled and allowed her to dwell there—even though he knew she was just in the kitchen making sandwiches.

Noah liked her. *She's pretty, intelligent and funny, and she has the unusual ability to make everything seem like it's going to be okay.*

"Hey."

Noah practically fell off his chair.

"Well geez! I didn't mean to scare you to death!"

Embarrassed, Noah quickly stood. He felt like he had been caught, although Kiryn had no idea what he was thinking about. "I…I think I must have dozed off to sleep for a second."

Kiryn laughed, "I'd say." She looked at Aspen. "Lunch is ready, should we wake her?"

"No, let her sleep. She's really exhausted."

"Okay, well c'mon if you're hungry."

"Aspen. Aspen…."

The voice was low and gruff. Aspen tried to push it away. She didn't want to wake up.

"ASPEN!"

Aspen jumped up and looked around. "What?"

She was alone on the porch. She yawned and rubbed her eyes and stretched. Where did everybody go?

She stood and walked into Rocky's house. "Hey, where are you guys?"

No answer.

"I thought someone was fixing lunch." Still no answer.

She turned and looked out the window. Rocky's truck and the Iroc were still in the driveway.

"Maybe they're upstairs," she mumbled.

Aspen jogged up the stairs, but there was no one in Rocky or

Gavin's rooms. She walked to the window at the end of the hallway and checked the backyard. No one.

"HEY!" she yelled as she skipped down the stairs.

She went into Kiryn's room and back into the kitchen where she saw no evidence of lunch. She sighed and, pulling out her phone. She decided to send them a group text.

Aspen scrolled the front of her screen and realized she had one unread text. She gasped when she saw who it was from—KRISTA.

Pausing for just a second, she clicked it open—"RUN!"

Still staring at the phone, Aspen froze. What did—

"Aspen." The same gruff voice that woke her up. She whirled around. The old man was standing in the kitchen doorway!

Aspen ran into the den, but he was standing in the doorway leading to the porch! She turned to run back into the kitchen, but he was blocking the entrance!

"Noah!" she screamed.

"Aspen… ASPEN!" the voice was getting louder and louder. She ran toward the porch.

"Noah! Noah!" she screamed again. "Noah help me!"

Just as she reached the open door, the old man seemed to jump right in front of her, but Aspen was going too fast to stop, and she ran right through him—he dissipated into tiny black particles that stuck to her clothes and face. She screamed while trying to brush them off. "*Someone help me!*"

She leaped for the steps, but he was there right in front of her. Sheer panic seized Aspen, and she stopped abruptly, inches from the old man. His steel black eyes seemed to pierce right through her. She froze, not able to speak or breathe.

For several seconds, it seemed as though time stopped. They stood facing each other. The old man's eyes hollow and dark and Aspen's filled with fear.

Suddenly realization flooded through Aspen. Minutes before she ran right through him and he had literally disappeared. In that instant, she lifted her hand and thrust it toward his chest.

The old man dissolved. The same black particles falling at her feet. Relieved and horrified at the same time Aspen covered her face with her hands.

"Noah! Where are you?!"

She felt someone shaking her. "Noah! Noah! Help me!"

"Aspen wake up! I'm right here."

Aspen forced her eyes open to Noah shaking her shoulders. "Noah." She wrapped her arms around his waist and began crying.

Noah didn't say anything, and neither did Kiryn, Gavin or Rocky who were standing behind him.

"Noah the man—he was in the house—I couldn't find any of you. He was everywhere, and I couldn't get away." She pushed Noah to the side. "He was there, on the steps, but then he just dissolved, or something—he was little black things, and he stuck to me…" She began hyperventilating.

Noah yelled, "Aspen!" Still holding her shoulders, he held her at arm's length. "You were dreaming. C'mon, wake up!"

Aspen stopped and looked at Noah. She looked at Kiryn who looked scared and Gavin, who looked confused. Rocky looked concerned.

"Aspen, it's okay. We are all right here." Gavin's soft voice was soothing to her.

Aspen sank back onto the lounge. She wiped her face with her hands. "I…I got a text from Krista."

"What?" they all exchanged quick glances as Aspen reached in her pocket for her phone. She unlocked the screen. "Yeah, she told me to run and then right when I turned around the old man—" She stopped. "There is no text."

"You were dreaming, honey." Rocky's ever sympathetic voice drifted past Noah's anxious breathing.

Aspen looked into the eyes of her brother, her friends, and her teacher. She felt calmer now, although still sniffling, and she scooted herself into a seated position.

"That was one of the scariest dreams I have ever had, but, I think I realize something now."

"What?" Kiryn asked.

"That guy, the old guy, he's not, well he's not real. I mean, he can see me, and I can see him, and I can hear him—at least in my dream I could—but he can't touch me. Not him personally. I, guess, he doesn't seem quite so intimidating."

Noah's eyebrows shot up, "Uh, yeah I could tell—" he began but stopped when Kiryn smacked him on the shoulder. He rubbed his shoulder and pulled a face at her. "Ow," he mumbled, but Kiryn just gave him a warning look.

Aspen turned to Rocky. "What do you think he wants?"

"Well, I think he has been trying to deter you from what he knew was inevitable. That somehow, you would be the one to uncover his deepest secrets. I think his goal was to scare you."

Noah had a faraway look in his eyes. "Noah?" said Aspen. "I was just thinking. If the old guy was concerned that one of us, mainly you, would be able to find out things, maybe it was because, in the past, someone else had that same ability."

"You mean like someone in your family?" asked Gavin.

"Yeah, Patrice said it follows family lines."

"Are you thinking maybe, Dad?" said Aspen.

Noah nodded. "If not Dad, maybe one of his other family members. Maybe Dad knows a lot about the history of the Allen family that he has not wanted to face."

"Allen family secrets." Kiryn's voice took on a mysterious tone. Now it was Noah's turn to return an exasperated look.

"What?" said Kiryn. "It makes total sense."

"Maybe," said Noah. "It's just a thought."

"One that *does* make total sense," said Gavin.

Rocky suggested they finish the lunch Kiryn had prepared while they planned what to do next.

"What's on your mind, Dad? I've seen that look before." Gavin popped a potato chip into his mouth.

"Well, the FBI can't get in the house for a while. Let's take advantage of this time and do a little investigation of our own."

"I like where you're going with this," said Noah.

"You mean about the—boys that disappeared?" asked Kiryn.

Rocky nodded.

"There is something else first."

They all turned their attention to Aspen.

"The other day in the storage room, Ronda spoke to me—at least I think it was Ronda."

"What? How come you didn't say anything?" asked Gavin.

"There was just a lot going on with the painting and all."

"Well?" demanded Kiryn. "What did she say?"

"Find me."

"Find me?" echoed Gavin.

"I don't know, that's all I heard." She paused. "There is something else."

They waited for her to continue.

"I had a dream the other night—after the Dylan stuff—the same dream, over and over. The exact same dream."

They all listened intently as Aspen related her repetitious dream of a few nights before. She described the running and falling onto a surface that gave way when she landed on it and then ending up seeing who she thought was her grandpa, and the box he was holding, "I'm just not sure what it means."

Everyone was silent for several minutes. No one seemed to know what to say to Aspen, but then Noah spoke up.

The shaft. That floor that you bounced on." Noah was talking to Gavin. It was as though a light bulb went off in Gavin's head and his already sparkling eyes nearly glistened with excitement. "We need to go to the house.

63

OVERDUE APOLOGY

THIS WAS THE FIRST time the group had felt they were really onto something, and it didn't take long for the four kids and Rocky to be back down the shaft at Grandpa Allen's house.

They went through the master bedroom and down the stairs, but just as an extra precaution, Rocky made sure the closet doors were closed, hiding any evidence the five were there. Each carried a flashlight, and they brought along some tools.

Gavin was convinced that the floor at the bottom of the ladder held some significant attachment to Aspen's dream and the other's couldn't see any reason not to investigate. Maybe it was that they wanted so badly for something to make sense.

While walking down the stairs, Rocky asked Aspen if she wanted to see if her arm could go through the door again.

"No," Aspen said flatly. "Not today."

"Okay," said Rocky, and didn't press her any further. They climbed the winding staircase to the middle room.

With a black marker, Noah outlined an area on the bottom of the ladder a little bigger than the actual soft spot of the floor. He and Gavin used hammers attempting to loosen the boards within the markings.

"This is what it would be like breaking into Fort Knox." Gavin sighed and turned to Rocky. "Okay, we better go for the sledge-hammer."

The girls and Rocky stood back with the flashlights while Gavin and Noah took turns slamming the heavy hammer into the wood. At last, a swing hit pay dirt, and splinters flew everywhere.

"Finally," said Noah. With the claw end of the hammer, he pried on the center of a slat. It began to pull free, and soon he removed a two-foot square section of wood. He stood and wiped his forehead with the bottom of his tank top.

"It's so hot in here," complained Kiryn and Aspen nodded in agreement.

Rocky had taken over for the two boys. He pulled out another section of slats and then wiped away the dust and wood chips with his hand. "This is solid." He tapped his knuckles on the new surface.

"Metal?" said Gavin. "Yep."

Rocky kept working until he had the entire top of the metal uncovered. It's a little over a foot in diameter, I think.

"Can we get it out?" asked Noah.

"Hand me the crowbar. I'll try."

Rocky wiggled the end of the crowbar down the side of the metal box when he thought he was at the bottom, and then he leaned on the crowbar, attempting to pry the box from its place.

Nothing budged.

The boys dug farther down until Noah put his finger under the edge of the metal. "Hey, it's like a lid or something."

A little more digging and the metal moved. With the help of the crowbar, Rocky lifted the metal lid from the hole in the floor. The lid was about eight inches deep and hollow, but the metal was an inch thick.

They all peered into the gaping hole.

"But...but there is nothing in there." Aspen's voice fell. "Who put a lid on nothing?"

Rocky shook his head. "I have no idea."

Gavin fell to his knees beside the hole. He brushed at the dirt on the bottom. "So we must be at the very bottom. No wait, that's impossible." He pointed to the winding staircase. "What about the ceiling down there?"

Noah's eyebrows shot up. He grabbed a small garden shovel from the pile of tools the five had lugged into the shaft and began digging but only came up with more dirt. Frustrated, he stood. "Why is there dirt here—on a floor that is obviously not sitting directly on the ground?"

The question hung in the air as they all studied the hole.

Rocky looked around the small room, shining his flashlight along the ceiling. "How high would you say this ceiling is?"

"Well, I'm six-four so it can't be more than eight feet," said Gavin. "Maybe seven and a half."

"The ceiling below us isn't that high."

All four kids agreed. "No." answered Kiryn. "Noah and Gavin had to duck a little in that room."

Rocky nodded, "Let's go check that out." He motioned to the boys, and Noah led the way down the winding staircase.

Aspen and Kiryn knelt beside the hole each bringing out shovels of dirt, Aspen with the shovel and Kiryn with her hand.

"What do you think?" said Kiryn quietly.

Aspen's eyes met her friends. "That maybe I'm an idiot."

"Why? It was Gavin's idea to come here."

"I know, but it was my dream that gave him the idea."

"You can't control your dreams, Aspen."

"I know," Aspen sighed. She didn't know what else to say.

Rocky clamored back up the stairs, followed first by Noah and then Gavin. He motioned for the girls to stand up, and then he dropped to his knees. "This hole is easily a foot and a half deep." He took the shovel from Aspen and began digging. Several minutes had passed when the tip of the shovel hit something solid

"Bingo," said Noah, and they all looked at him.

"What?" said Kiryn, "He hit something, right?"

"I did," said Rocky, and he dug even faster. He brushed the dirt away and lifted his find from the hole. In his hands was a square box with rounded edges on the lid.

"Is that what the box looked like?" asked Noah.

"Well, not exactly." Aspen handed her flashlight to Kiryn and took the box from Rocky's outstretched hand. She sank onto the floor and placed the box on her crossed legs. She looked up at Noah and smiled weakly.

Noah smiled back. "Open it."

Aspen's hands trembled as she lifted the lid from the cardboard box. It was the size of a small shoebox.

Noah, Kiryn, Gavin, and Rocky all crammed around her.

The inside was stuffed with yellowed tissue paper. Aspen lifted the paper out and uncovered a small gold metal box. A tiny padlock fastened the lid down. She gasped. "This is it! This was in my dream!"

Slowly turning it over, she searched for the concave space where in her dream, she had seen the little key. It wasn't there. The indent was there, but no key.

Aspen rummaged around the box removing the last of the tissue and there, attached to a piece of very yellow scotch tape, was the small gold key.

Aspen carefully put the key in the tiny lock and turned. The padlock clicked free.

Kiryn gasped. "Oh, this is so exciting," she whispered.

Aspen lifted the lid. The object inside was wrapped in the same yellowed tissue paper. She lifted it out and slowly peeled the layers of tissue away.

They all stared at what they saw.

A small golden angel with her hands clasped together in prayer rested on Aspen's palm. She looked bewildered at Rocky. "What do you suppose this means?" She lifted it to Noah's outstretched hand but then changed her mind when a tiny scrolled paper fell from a hole in the bottom. She placed the statue on her lap and picked up the scroll.

Rocky didn't have time to answer her. A single string tied in a bow held it together. Aspen gently pulled one end, and the string fell to the floor. She unrolled the scroll and read:

My dearest Ronda. I am so sorry. Sorry I didn't protect you. Sorry I lied about your mother. Sorry I pretended you never existed. I was angry and hurt. I thought you deserted your family, and all the while, you lay dead—alone and cold—in an unmarked grave. My heart is broken. My selfishness ruined our family, and now I am alone. Please forgive your foolish father.

I love you, my Mystic Angel. Daddy

The stuffy room was silent but for the sniffles coming from Aspen and Kiryn. Finally, Aspen looked up. "We did it. We did it!" Suddenly elated, she jumped to her feet, clutching the tiny statue in her hand.

Hugs and tears accompanied laughter. They had been successful. They had uncovered and confirmed at least one dark secret from the Allen family's past, Ronda Allen had not run away, she had been murdered.

Kiryn hugged Aspen and Aspen hugged Noah. Noah hugged Kiryn, and she hugged Gavin, and then they all hugged each other.

Aspen turned to Rocky, tears of joy streaming down her face. "It's a start," she said. "I feel like this is a good start, and I feel like we did what Ronda has wanted all along."

Rocky hugged her back and held her a few seconds. "Yes, Aspen, it's a start. A good start."

Excitement and laughter filled the dim room as flashlight beams shone haphazardly around the space.

Aspen felt someone touch her shoulder and turn her around. Grinning, Gavin pulled her to him, wrapping his arms tightly around her waist. Without hesitation, Aspen encircled her arms around his neck and buried her face in his shoulder.

The laughter now seemed far away to Aspen as Gavin traced her cheek with his lips. He paused only to stare briefly into her tear-filled eyes. His lips pressed warmly against the side of her mouth.

Aspen paused only a second, basking in this moment. It wasn't private and romantic. It wasn't accompanied by soft words or tantalizing music.

Nope, it was in a hot, stuffy, dark room where everyone was

sweaty, at the basement of a strange house that had turned her life upside down with her brother who she never, ever visualized sharing this moment with, let alone Gavin's sister and his dad.

No, this was not how she imagined her first kiss with Gavin, but none of this was what she imagined her life to be. Nothing about this was normal.

Aspen gazed back into Gavin's emerald, intoxicating eyes. He slowly inched closer, pressing his lips firmly to hers. Without hesitating, she kissed him back. Unashamed and passionately she drank in his smell, his warmth and she gave in to the magnetic draw she had felt since the first time she saw him. Her head spinning, she pulled him closer.

Aspen heard Kiryn's giggle and realized that all of the flashlights were off. They were standing in pitch blackness with only the sound of chuckles and breathing.

Releasing her, Gavin spoke first, "Okay, you guys."

"We just wanted to give you two a moment," chided Noah.

The lights clicked back on and Aspen shined hers on the small golden figurine. She ran her hand across the delicate features of the face. With his arm still around her shoulders, Gavin twisted a lock of her hair between his fingers.

The others had turned and started back up the stairs. Gavin squeezed Aspen's shoulders as they followed.

A whirring sound and a breeze on their backs stopped all of them, and they slowly turned around. Gavin shined his light back into the dark room where the dust had formed into a small whirlwind.

"What was that?" Kiryn barely breathed the words.

But Aspen knew—she did not only feel the breeze she heard it. When Aspen turned the beam of her flashlight on the golden figurine in her hand, the dust drifted silently to the floor, and the room fell deathly quiet.

Aspen answered Kiryn's question. "Find us."

THE END

Sneak Peek into

Mystic Lake

Mystic Trilogy • Book 2

The intriguing sequel to *Mystic Angel*.

PREFACE

From his hospital window, Jackson could see the lake. People called it Mystic Lake now, but to him, it was just the lake. He would often stare at it through narrow slits in the blinds. Wondering. Watching.

He smiled when he recalled swimming parties, picnics, and fireworks on the Fourth of July. Contests with his friends to see who could jump the farthest from the tire swing and rowboat races that usually ended in purposely capsized boats.

Yet every pleasant memory was clouded with fear, or was it that he did not want to reach that deep into his past? At times, he wanted to remember, but when he tried, he was always stopped by the same images. The same frightening demons that twisted his memory into complicated webs that he could not sort through. So retreating was easier back to the safety of surface memories—the ones that caused no pain.

When Doctor Winslow was made aware that looking outside seemed to cause Jackson anxiety, he suggested moving him to the other side of the hospital, but Jackson resisted.

Staring at the quiet lake, Jackson waited, and at times he was not disappointed. A shimmering mist silently drifted upward dissipating into the air, leaving no trace, no evidence.

1

BONES

BEFORE ROCKY'S TRUCK ROLLED to a stop in front of the little house, Aspen and Noah emerged from the front door and loped down the steps. Orange rays of sunlight visible only through the tops of the trees reminded Aspen that it was barely five am. Still basking in the magic of two days earlier—Gavin's kiss—and finding the statue their great-grandfather had buried in the floorboards of his house, Aspen wasn't sure she was ready to stir everything up again.

But there was no stopping Gavin and Noah. More studying of the hand-drawn maps of Grandpa Allen's house had convinced both there was possibly another hall or tunnel on the other side of the house under the bedrooms. With just three and a half weeks before FBI agents Byron Coulsen and Larry Brimhall would want to meet with them again, Rocky agreed with the boys that they had better step-up their own investigation.

Arriving at the big house, they all bounced out of the truck, but Aspen hung back.

"What?" Kiryn stood beside her.

"I don't know. I feel kind of sad or something."

"Sad? Are you crazy? Why?"

"I don't know. I guess because even though we know what happened to Ronda, it's frustrating to know there are still so many unanswered questions."

"This may be a chance to find more clues," said Kiryn.

"I know, but—" Aspen paused. "Oh, actually, I don't know. Let's go." She grasped Kiryn's arm and pulled her onto the porch.

From the drawings in the notebook Gavin had found, Noah led him and Rocky right to the bedroom where he had felt someone touch his shoulder the first day he and Aspen had been in the house. They had concluded that with its outdated furnishing and yellowing curtains, this was most likely a room that had not been occupied by siblings of their dad.

Kiryn looked around, "Maybe this was Ronda's room."

Aspen nodded, "It would make sense, huh? Maybe they just left it as it was."

The boys had already removed two empty boxes—the only things in the closet—and were now pulling up the floorboards when Aspen and Kiryn walked in.

Kiryn leaned over Rocky, who was crouched in the open closet doorway. "Why are you guys so sure there is a hallway under that floor?"

Rocky held up the small book of drawings Gavin had found in the storage room. "We're not, but the drawings do show some sort of a tunnel under this side of the house and look, this drawing shows it is directly east of the shaft. Right where we are." He pointed to the wall where the baseboard should be. "And besides, all of the other closets have baseboards."

"How do you know that?"

Gavin looked up from his work and rolled his eyes at his sister, "We checked."

"Oh." Kiryn shrugged, and Aspen laughed.

Several boards later, the floor revealed a sunken handle.

"Holy cow!" Noah whistled, and he and Gavin quickly removed the rest of the boards.

Everyone backed out of the closet and Noah yanked on the handle. The hatch lifted.

"Geez, this thing is heavy."

Gavin grabbed the edge. They both lifted the hatch and leaned it against the wall. Gavin shined a flashlight down the opening.

"Another staircase. These guys—whoever that would be—were totally into hidden staircases."

Cold air rushed up at them, and they exchanged looks of apprehension.

Rocky checked the two-way radios to make sure they were on. "You kids be careful. I probably should go with you."

"Who would save us then, Dad?" Gavin grinned and put his hand on Rocky's shoulder. "We'll be fine."

"Famous last words," mumbled Kiryn.

Gavin rolled his eyes. "Seriously, Dad."

"We got this, Rocky. We need you up here. We won't do anything stupid," said Noah.

"Okay, but if you run into anything—you know, dangerous—just get out of there. I'll be right here."

"Okay, let's go." Noah started cautiously down the staircase, the other three following close behind. They each carried high-beam flashlights so they could easily see what was in front of them, and Gavin had the radio handset Rocky insisted they take.

"Okay, this is the weirdest yet," said Noah when he reached the bottom of the stairs. "This is a tunnel." He shined the beam of his light into the darkness, "A very long tunnel."

"Fourteen steps," said Kiryn. "And that was steep. We are down pretty deep."

"Obviously. It's so musty and damp in here," said Gavin. "I'll bet this goes over near the lake." He pushed the button on the handset, "Rocky, we are in a tunnel. It looks pretty long."

Rocky laughed, "You know I can still see you?"

They all looked back up the stairs where Rocky stood at the top. Gavin grinned, "I know, I was just testing."

"Okay. Keep me posted, and be careful."

"Will do," Gavin said into the handset and Noah, and he laughed.

Aspen and Kiryn did not find it so funny and were both grateful Rocky could hear Gavin.

Somehow this adventure scared Aspen. Maybe because now

they knew for sure murder had been committed nearby? Maybe because the one murdered was the girl Aspen could see—Ronda? She couldn't put her thoughts in order. Why did she feel so much apprehension now? She had been trying to shrug the feeling off since this morning, but it still lingered in the pit of her stomach.

"Hey, Gavin, why do you think this tunnel goes near the lake?" Kiryn's voice was quivering.

"Are you afraid?" asked Noah.

"As a matter of fact, I am. This is creepy."

Noah reached back and grasped her hand. "Here, stay by me."

Aspen grinned. She knew Kiryn really liked Noah, and she loved seeing him being so sweet to her.

Gavin stepped up behind Aspen and put one hand on her back, sending tingles down her spine. He hadn't been this close to her since their kiss. She breathed deeply to quiet her heart.

"I'm right here," he said softly. Then louder, he answered Kiryn, "Well, think of where this house is, and the direction the tunnel is going."

"Oh," mumbled Kiryn.

The tunnel was very long, and there were places they had to either duck or walk single file. It was dark, damp, and musty, and no one had much to say. They kept walking.

"This is scary down—" Aspen began, but was interrupted by Noah.

"Look at that!" he yelled and jumped back, almost knocking Kiryn to the ground.

Gavin stopped Kiryn from falling, and they all huddled close around Noah, all their lights pointing to a cave in the side of the tunnel.

"Are those bones?" whispered Noah.

"No! Those are dead people!" Kiryn shrieked. "Ahhh…let's get out of here!" She turned pushed past Gavin and Aspen, but stopped immediately. "It's pitch black!"

"No kidding," said Gavin. He grabbed Kiryn's shoulder and pulled her back, "We have to stay together."

"Who are they?" Aspen felt sick.

"I hate to even imagine," said Noah.

Gavin took a deep breath, "C'mon you guys, we can't have too much farther to go, we've been walking forever." He again clicked a button on the handset. "Rocky?"

"Yeah?" Rocky said something else, but they couldn't hear him for the static. "We found a sort of—I don't know, graveyard."

Kiryn leaned toward the handset. "Actually, it's a pile of bones!" she called.

"What? Maybe you kids had better come back out." Rocky's voice crackled through the speaker, but it sounded like he was yelling now, and they could hear him better.

"We're okay," Noah called. "They can't hurt us now."

"Oh, well, that's comforting," said Kiryn.

Noah winced, "C'mon, let's keep going."

Hugging the wall opposite the cave, the four trudged past the bones, cautiously shining their lights on them as they passed.

Aspen counted skulls but stopped at fifteen. It was just too depressing. "You don't suppose these could be those…those boys from the journal, do you?"

"They could be." Gavin was now in front of the group, as Noah had taken up the rear with Kiryn as they continued to make their way through the blackness.

Aspen shuddered. She kept glancing back and bumped into Gavin when he abruptly stopped.

"Look at this," he said.

The four scanned the area with their lights. They had arrived at a small square room with gray cinderblock walls. The room was empty, and on the opposite side from where they stood was a door.

Gavin crossed the floor and pulled on the door handle. It didn't open at first, but with a second jerk, the door moved.

"Aren't you the least bit concerned about what you might find in there?" asked Kiryn, but when the door opened, a faint beam of light came through and she stopped talking.

"Looks like it may go outside," said Gavin. "There is a breeze.

Can you guys feel that?"

"Good! Let's hurry!" said Kiryn.

Aspen nodded, "I can hear water." Goosebumps pricked her arms and neck.

"Yeah, I can too," said Gavin. "I think I know what we are going to find."

"You do?" Aspen was puzzled.

"Yeah, we have walked a long way and remember my house is two houses from your grandpa's. There is a big cement culvert that comes up near the boat dock. It's old, and the opening is covered with a grate. I'll bet that is where this goes."

"But water would get in here, wouldn't it?"

"Maybe, but the lake is never more than two feet higher than it is right now. You can tell by the shoreline. The culvert sticks out of the ground about four feet."

They stepped into the tunnel that was now concrete instead of dirt. The tunnel began slanting upward, and as they walked, a faint light at the far end came into view.

"Looks like maybe fifty feet." Gavin guessed.

"I just think this is weird," said Kiryn, but no one responded to her comment.

The end of the tunnel was a solid concrete wall, and the light came from a cement pipe about five feet in diameter. It connected to the tunnel above their heads and could be accessed by an iron ladder fastened to the wall. The ladder stretched the entire length of the pipe and went straight up. There was a lot of debris on top, but they could still see the sky.

Gavin was right—a huge grate held in place by four large padlocks covered the entire opening. It was partially covered with debris, but not enough to block out the light completely.

"No one goes near this because there is a big danger sign on the other side," said Gavin.

"Yeah, danger, *bones ahead*," said Noah flatly.

"Do you think that's where Tygert put the bodies of those boys? In that pile?" Aspen's stomach was in knots.

"No." Noah quickly disagreed. "I think those are the ones who weren't lucky enough to make it to the root cellar."

"Lucky?" Aspen narrowed her eyes. "Are you kidding me, Noah?"

"Okay, not lucky, but you know what I mean. The ones in the root cellar are probably at least buried."

"Hopefully," said Kiryn.

"You mean if they are actually there," said Gavin.

"Maybe they just dumped them. Like those back there." Kiryn thrust her thumb over her shoulder.

"Yep, you're probably right—*if* he killed them—we still don't know that." Aspen sighed. "Can we get out of here?"

"Yeah, we better go. Rocky is probably wondering about us," said Noah.

Just then, Rocky's voice squawked through the handset, "Hey!"

Gavin brought it to his mouth. "We're here. We're looking straight up a concrete pipe to the outside. I'm going to climb up the ladder."

"What pipe?"

"It's a culvert, Dad. It was there when Mom and Doug bought the house."

"Stay away from that thing, Gavin. You kids need to get out of there."

"It's okay, Dad, I know where it goes. I'm just going to see if we can get out this way."

"Be careful, Gavin. The ladder may not be very secure." Rocky's voice was surprisingly clear.

"No worries." He handed the handset to Noah and began climbing the iron rungs while the other three watched.

Aspen kept looking back over her shoulder. The uneasiness wouldn't go away.

Gavin was back in minutes. "All I can see through the opening are trees, but I know this is that culvert by the boat dock. I'll show you when we get out."

Kiryn shuddered. "Oh, I hate that we have to walk past those bones again. I wish we could go out this way."

"Me too," Aspen agreed.

"Those are pretty big padlocks," said Noah. He looked at Gavin, "I don't suppose—"

Gavin shook his head. "There is no way. They are not only locked, but they have chains on them too. We're not getting through that."

Kiryn sighed, "Well, then let's go."

As they started back, Aspen said, "I wonder why no one went down in that culvert—you know, the city or something. They would have found the bones."

"That's easy," said Gavin. "The lake is private property."

"That's why no one has seen the mist people are always talking about, no one can use this lake except the people who live here," said Kiryn. "The mist is probably not even real."

They all passed through the cinderblock room, and Noah pushed the door shut. The darkness was dense until their eyes adjusted again, and with the help of their lights, they continued to make their way back through the tunnel.

They stopped again by the bones, and Noah pulled out his cell phone. "At least these are good for something down here." He snapped two pictures of the bones, and they continued. "Just in case they are gone when we come back down."

"What? Are they going to up and walk away?" said Kiryn sarcastically, but the quiver in her voice confirmed she was still nervous.

"Yeah, why would they be gone? The people who put them there are probably dead," said Aspen. "And anyway, who says we are coming back down?"

"I just assumed—" began Noah.

"No, Noah is right. We need to show Rocky and probably the police at some point," said Gavin.

"It is real, by-the-way," said Aspen.

"What is?" Noah kept walking, and Kiryn followed, but Gavin pulled on Aspen's arm and turned her around.

"What's real, Aspen?"

Now Noah and Kiryn had stopped too, and both were listening.

"The—the mist. It's real, Kiryn."

"You've seen it?" Kiryn sounded shocked.

"Yes—" Aspen looked at Noah. "That day—at the lake—when we were leaving, I looked back, and there was a mist—"

Loud shrieking interrupted Aspen, and they all whirled, shining their lights down the dark tunnel.

Kiryn clung to Noah's shirt, "Let's just get out of here!"

"What is that?" said Gavin.

The sound was getting louder, and they all began backing away.

Suddenly a small object flew directly at them, hitting Gavin in the chest, then another and another. They were coming fast; pelting all of them.

Kiryn, Noah, and Gavin turned and ran for the entrance, but Aspen froze as one flew directly into her light. It stopped just in front of her face its tiny black eyes, and sharp teeth seeming to threaten her very existence.

Aspen turned running while she screamed, "They're bats!"

She saw Kiryn and Noah disappear through the hatch. Gavin stood on the middle of the ladder, his arm outstretched, "Hurry, Aspen!"

Aspen ran as hard as she could, but within just a few feet of the ladder, she was suddenly pulled backward, and at the same instance, Gavin was propelled through the open hatch.

"Aspen!" Gavin yelled.

To her horror, the hatch slammed shut, leaving her in total darkness. The piercing shrieking seemed to consume her as she crashed to the dirt floor.

Aspen's pounding heart and anxious breathing were all she could hear as she inched slowly toward the ladder. Frantically groping at the darkness, she found only more dirt. She froze and listened—nothing.

"Noah?" she croaked.

She held her breath so that she could hear any little sound—still nothing. Pulling her knees to her chest, she wrapped her arms around them and shaking uncontrollably, she tried to call out to her brother and her friends.

"Noah! Gavin! Kiryn!" her voice cracked, and the sounds were nothing but whispers.

Blackness. Silence.

She was all alone. Inching backward until she found the corner, she pressed herself against the cool, damp dirt.

Images or experiences of things that are not really happening to you. Patrice's words popped into Aspen's thoughts.

But the others heard the screaming. This is not the same as the rats. The bats hit us.

Exasperated, she covered her face with her hands and whimpered, "Help me. Someone, please help me."

Aspen hadn't moved from the corner. There were no sounds in the tunnel, and she cautiously felt around for one of the flashlights. Her hand bumped something soft, and the image of a lifeless bat made her sick. She pulled away quickly and sank farther into the corner.

Think! What else did Patrice say? Her head was spinning. *Where did everyone go?*

She suddenly thought of the pile of bones not far from her, and she began to panic.

"I have to get out of here! Help! Someone help me!"

Thick blackness only loomed heavier.

How will I ever get out of here? Why is no one coming for me? She buried her face in her knees.

"Please, somebody—if there is a God—please..."

Deathly silence.

She slowly lifted her head. Someone or something was breathing.

Terrified of making any sound, she held her breath. The sound was coming closer.

"Is...is someone there?"